Don't Ask, Don't Tell

To Sharon

Eleanor Hesketh Loxley

Don't Ask, Don't Tell
Post-War France:
Two Families, Two secrets, One Tragedy

Eleanor Harriet Loxley

YOUCAXTON
PUBLICATIONS

ISBN 978-1-913425-52-4
Published by YouCaxton Publications 2020
YCBN: 01

YouCaxton Publications
www.youcaxton.co.uk

For Mike

Contents

France, the present day

I AM REARRANGING lives.

I have always loved the parade of photographs on top of the old *armoire*. Years ago, when they were spaced out, I would trace small paths and bigger roads in the dust settled between them. Mum would snap, "Stop it! I'll make you do the cleaning." Now the frames stand shoulder to shoulder and the dust has trouble getting through.

Here is an array of two linked families. Of linked lies. I keep the French group to the left, the English to the right, out of habit.

"They should be jumbled up," my husband Edward said as he moved a picture or two back and forth. He was right, and the jumbling began before I was born.

Sometimes I sort them into who's here and who's not. Edward tells me off. "Rosemary, really. The quick and the dead - so morbid."

The oldest photograph, on the left, is of Clément and Eva Aubin; a sepia couple posed rigid and unsmiling, waiting forever for the camera in their dark clothes. Their son, Pierre, sits with them in another early picture, a mild young man with a small smile who would leave something fundamental of himself in a German camp. Beside them there is the only picture I have found of his sister, taken at the beginning of the war. I wish I could have met her.

Pierre's wife, Marcelle, is snapped in her twenties. She has dark, shiny hair and a flowered apron just fails to disguise a plump stomach. She looks pleased and not a little smug. In another setting Pierre and Marcelle sit together; she is grimacing with the effort of holding a large baby on her lap. Beside her stands a solemn girl, slim and brown haired. The strong baby is Philippe. Today he's wiry and efficient and runs his parents' farm. The girl is Marthe, Marcelle's second child and my best friend when we were young. I don't have enough photos of her.

Near the front of the cupboard my parents smile out at me from a photo taken when they began their lives in France. Nancy, my Mum, is thin and fair with a wide, generous mouth. She laughs at the camera and leans back against Tom, my Dad. He's not much taller than her and has a hand on her shoulder. His dark hair contrasts with his wife's paleness. I know this was taken before her first baby was born because Mum is so happy. So young.

There's one of a naked boy on a rug, perhaps about to cry. The photo is of Charles, my younger brother. His picture is snug in its frame now but it's crossed with lines where it had been screwed up. I have an enduring memory of my mother when she opened a packet of developed photographs and found this one. I was watching from the kitchen doorway. She bunched the picture up in a fist and threw it across the room. I saw her crawl on her hands and knees to retrieve it. She sat on the floor smoothing it out, over and over, sobbing all the while. Dad came in and collected Mum up. He led her away, saying, "Oh Nan. Come on now." There's one or two of me, fair like Mum and I'm with my older sister Claire, who holds my hand and looks fierce under a mop of dark brown hair. One picture shows almost everyone, squashed up for the camera. A greyer Mum and Dad, Claire beside them. Marthe and I are laughing; I suspect she has just said something rude. We're in sweatshirts and jeans, it must be the summer before I went to university. Marcelle and Pierre are in the second row next to Philippe and his girlfriend Lucette, who will be his wife and is plump for a Frenchwoman but looks as if she doesn't care.

I put a recent picture of myself and Edward at the front. He has short grey hair and grins. We look as we are: newly retired and still content with each other. There's a photo of our twins in graduation gowns: Elizabeth and Harry, both blond like me but more like each other than anyone else.

Next to my parents I moved another one of Charles as a toddler with chocolate around his mouth, never spoken of since my mother's wild crying. I put a recent one of Marcelle beside my parents. She's sitting upright and stern, proud of her wrinkles and crow's feet. She died this spring and I can't bear the gap.

Standing back, I scrutinised my gallery. Not everybody was here.

That afternoon I sat in the courtyard with my back to the stone wall, warm from the day's heat. I was sheltered from the north east wind that always grew stronger in the autumn and I looked across the wide lawns which divided our house from a bigger house on the other side. It had once been a mill; the mill wheel still clung to it, like a round, decaying limpet.

On a slight rise in the middle of the lawn were swings, put up there before I was born. A knotted rope ladder hung against the metal triangle. It was dancing in the wind, jibbering on its old ropes, up and down, side to side. The two wooden seats were better behaved, giving only small, insolent twists as the wind pushed them.

As the afternoon wore on the shadow of the mill house stalked across the lawn. It had been one of the many grain mills built in the eighteenth century just before the French Revolution swept through the countryside. Its proud, private owners had been forced to give it up to a co-operative of men and women who had once been called peasants and who had fought amongst themselves, all equal *citoyens*, to establish a hierarchy of control. Despite, or because of, the disputes, the mill had been a success.

It eventually fell into the hands of one family. In the late 1790s the Aubin family came to own the the farm around it as well and greedily gathered up other parcels of land. The smaller house was built for the mill and farm workers. My stone built cottage, these days substantial thanks to the efforts of my parents, started out with two rooms one up, one down, the privy in the garden. Animals lived in one of the downstairs rooms in the winter and even now I sometimes wonder if I can smell dung in the lounge.

The big mill house still lorded it over the grounds; a great rambling structure with the original stone base and different parts of the walls in odd styles of bricks. Sections of the house had been added over the years as if a dozen different builders had all bickered for the privilege of clamping their own designs onto it. The wheel, long since stopped, stayed stuck to the side of the house either as a curiosity piece or because no one could be bothered to remove it.

The mill house and our house, grand and bright in its own right, with its plumbing safely indoors, were together known as *Les Moulins*.

It never mattered that there was only one mill and one mill race. I never tired of the two houses and the weedy stream that dashed out under the mill and then flowed into the meadows beyond.

When we were children the whole place - the houses, the farm and the surrounding countryside - belonged to all of us. The families, the English Woods and the French Aubins, looked after one another, or so it seemed. I find it hard to remember accurately what we did: the games we played, what we wore, our suppers. Our early freedoms made me feel this is my only real home and I'm glad that Edward and I have agreed to stay. Harry and Elizabeth have their own families and careers and they can do what they want with the house when we're no longer here. The Aubin family will remain, resisting the lemming race to the city and clinging to their land with the bone deep love of it that Gallic farmers have.

My parents, Tom and Nancy Woods, bought our house from Marcelle and Pierre Aubin in 1950. Dad had to come back to central France after the war, tugging his new bride with him and Mum had her first daughter soon after they moved in to what was not far short of a pile of rubble. I was born three years later in England and spent my first three years in Paris with Mum and Dad and my sister Claire. I understand now why they stayed in the city and then returned to the countryside, but the reasons of grown-ups meant nothing to a small child.

I'm rooted in this wide, light country with its big rivers, its forests, its kaleidoscope of colours and puzzling differences. When I had a career in London there was this place in the *Loire* to restore me. I've been given the blessing of two languages; I know what to buy in the markets and what do in a kitchen. When we were children I had the protection of Claire when Mum had her 'vague' episodes. She would stare at us and look from one to the other, as if she wasn't sure who we were. Claire kept me sane. Marthe would arrive and make me laugh. Marcelle gave us cakes and lemonade with not enough sugar.

Other things in my life I don't want to remember: the bad dreams and the feelings of inexplicable melancholy which were unwelcome visitors for a long time. For years I tried to banish them and sometimes that was easy. Away in London at university, meeting Edward there, my work and having the twins kept me busy. We lived there in term time and ran back to France for vacations. Edward became a writer. I think he secretly wanted to emulate my father, who had been a journalist and then a travel writer after the war. I preferred to work at the university and delve into other worlds: the romantic, impossible ones in eighteenth century literature. Reading and teaching Austen, Fielding and Fanny Burney kept my dismal moods at bay. More recently I've taken another role: that of detective; I've examined clues, interviewed suspects, investigated memories.

I went inside for a bottle of white wine. I poured myself a glass and stopped again by the big oak cupboard with its cast of people that stood by the front door. It's been there as long as I can remember and when I was little I was scared that if I climbed inside I'd get lost for ever. I'd imagine wandering around its gloomy depths, negotiating the piles of crockery stored inside.

Standing back, I scrutinised my gallery. Not everybody was here. I'd burnt some recently.

Outside I pulled my cardigan closer around me against the chilly evening. I watched the swings on the lawn dance back and forth. Autumn leaves were restless in the wind. Everything is clear now and I still love this place, and, even though Marcelle has gone, we can live here. Edward wants to retire; write some more, tend the garden, help out on the farm occasionally. I want that too. But I want something to change first.

We're fortunate to have this house passed on to us. My father talked about good fortune and luck. The luck that brought him and Mum had to be here was made in the war, so he said. That never sat easily with me. Not much luck to be shot down from the skies.

He'd spoken sparingly about the war. When he did talk it would be about how they had arrived in this part of central France and about the Aubin family. "Clément and Eva saved my life, and Marcelle was there too, before she was an Aubin."

"It's a very common story," he said. "Some of us got shot down, some of us got rescued, some of us made it home. With the help of the Aubins I managed all three, plus the luck."

This was all he would say. And always in a flat tone that forced emotion aside and presented the facts as he chose. I wondered if he really believed that version of events. How much mental energy must it have taken to keep up such appearances?

I knew that Marcelle, a teenager during the war, together with Clément and Eva Aubin, had risked their lives in sheltering my father when he baled out and landed close to the mill. They were in the *zone libre,* the non-occupied zone, but the Germans were only a few kilometres away.

Dad wasn't always the stern ex-RAF officer. He used to play silly games with Claire and me and Mum would laugh and say, "you're all children together. I want a grown up husband occasionally." Those were rosy days when I didn't hear his sharp critiques of my mother nor her back biting if she thought she could get away with it.

One thing I remember, not his actual words and perhaps after his evening whisky, was that he let slip he was the only one to bale out of that wartime plane. The others with him were shot and burnt beyond hope.

My father never got drunk enough to talk about the other time he came to France in the war. When I found out about his second visit I was shocked and upset and not understanding but by then it was too late to ask him, even if I'd had the courage. While I was growing up I didn't like hearing much. I thought that things like that should be private for my father who spoke so sparingly of it with his face taut and closed. I was happier when he talked of Paris and travelling: little funny anecdotes to amuse me.

How much does anyone really, truly, want to know the gruesome details of their parents' lives? Wouldn't we all be more content if we were untroubled by others' nightmares? But I have been the reluctant investigator of detail, the examiner of hidden memories and of bad dreams, the assembler of those jigsaw lives.

I hadn't wanted to be alone this autumn. Edward was to go to London to talk about a book with his agent. He stood on the gravel path, his bags already in the car.

"A writer ought to be working at home, not gadding about the city." I laughed. But I thought, just stay with me.

Edward lifted his hands, palms up in supplication. "I've got to go. To get the last draft sorted out. This book's part of our pension. Robert reckons it'll sell well. I'll be back quick enough. You know where I'll be."

"I don't see how you'll ever stop working." I tried to keep the resentful whine out of my voice. His work was part of him; you couldn't try to tug it away, even with a gossamer touch, without damaging him.

"I don't want to." He took my hands and looked steadily at me, the serious Edward for once. "I won't be long. I know it's not the right time for you to be alone."

I stared past him at the big house, the long sun coming up over the giant mill wheel, monstrous in the morning light. "It's just that - without Marcelle what will happen to Jeanne? Now that ... I mean, will she be looked after?"

"Philippe and Lucette will keep her busy and they have Camille in the house to help. She's very good with her."

"I know. But the space Marcelle used to fill ... " I wasn't sure what I wanted to say; I was weary of it all. "And I miss her, she was Mum's best friend. I have to miss them both now."

Edward hugged me. "I'll not get the ferry unless I'm away right now. Shall I stay?"

I knew he would if I said so. It was enough. "No. Go! Phone lots."

I waved as he drove off. At the end of the drive I saw the car swerve to avoid the pothole which was never filled in properly.

I wondered whether to go over to the mill house. Although Philippe and Lucette were there it felt empty without Marcelle. Even in her nineties she had been a vibrant presence. She had declined visibly in the previous year, becoming very frail and in February, as winter was just ending, she died quietly of her great old age. She talked to me before she left but I had neither the courage nor the time to ask all my questions.

Contemplating *Les Moulins* without her was hard. As she got older we would visit in the late afternoon and find her pottering in the garden after her nap. She'd lean on her stick and sometimes prod the plants with it, as if they annoyed her. "I don't mind, *mes amis,* being so very old. Just as long as I am able to look after the garden a little.

Look at these weeds - they defy me! And I want to see to my chickens. To make my own coffee. Even the very ancient must have some small independence." She laughed with us about how crumpled she was getting as she led us into the big kitchen for coffee or a tisane and to talk about the tomatoes or a hen that wasn't laying.

We enjoyed the fiction that Marcelle worked in the garden as she had always done and cared for her poultry as if she were the only one who could do so. Philippe took his mother's instructions and told her how well the farm was doing; how the new fence she'd suggested kept the fox out. When something new and different was to be tried, he and Lucette and the farm workers omitted, by an unspoken consensus, to tell her the details because Marcelle knew the old ways were best. We all wanted her to still feel responsible. As she always had been.

I thought back to Marcelle's final Christmas last year. It had been quieter than usual and, for the first time, she had not had the energy to exercise her occasional Catholicism and go to Midnight Mass. She took an early meal and retired to her bedroom and we shared the Christmas Eve feast without her. We knew all was not right with her, but we chose not to look; not to see her skin stretched against her bones nor to comment on how much we had to help her out of her chair.

Edward and I visited Christmas Day afternoon. Everyone had other arrangements: Elizabeth and Harry with their respective partners' families, Lucette and Philippe were with Lucette's parents and my sister Claire remained in the South that year with her husband Jean-Paul. It felt pared down, just the three of us. And Jeanne.

Marcelle, Edward and I sat in the big lounge by the window watching a winter sun fade and steal the last of the colours. Jeanne was in front of the television in a corner, her little button eyes unwavering. It seemed to me that she was becoming less and less communicative. She sneered and scowled more these days, even allowing for her scarred face.

Marcelle had begun more often to ask Jeanne to do small things to save her rising from her chair. A privilege she felt due to her. Often there were little snappy scenes as if Marcelle was asking Jeanne to move mountains.

That afternoon Marcelle said, "pass my glasses over to me, please, Jeanne."

Jeanne stared at Marcelle. "Why should I?"

"Just my glasses, please. I don't want to get up," Marcelle sighed.

"I am old myself, *Maman.*" Jeanne said. "I cannot do everything round here."

"You do little enough. You do not have to cook or clean. We have help. I have only asked for my glasses, not for you to sweep the floor."

"Get them yourself!" Jeanne snapped and limped upstairs, swinging her fat hips to balance her unstable walk.

Marcelle stared after her, red spots of anger on her cheeks. "She should go into a home. That girl. Yes, that great *old* girl. She should no longer be here. Put her away when I die." She banged her walking stick on the floor in a fury and turned away from us to pick up a photo of her long dead Pierre.

Edward and I exchanged glances, eyebrows raised.

Marcelle turned back. "I mean it. Get rid of her." She looked hard at both of us in turn.

When it became too chilly to sit outside mulling over everything and everyone, I went inside and looked over the paint pots and folded lengths of new curtaining. I was going to change the lounge tomorrow - at least refresh the paintwork and put up new, heavier, linen curtains ready for the winter. I'd always heard that after a death it's important to change things around somehow. It's supposed to minimise the gap that's left, but I don't believe that's possible. Change doesn't fill anything, it merely soothes.

We'd talked of moving south to be near Claire but Edward had said, "I don't need any more sun and I don't need that bloody *mistral.* Home's here. And we're nearer to the twins."

I didn't say so, but we could be nearer the twins almost anywhere in France now, with cheap flights and the motorway system. The children - adult children, a different species - had both decided to stay in England to work and use us for family holidays.

As for me, there was nowhere else I wanted to call home, even though the mysteries of my bad dreams are explained. For years they'd been locked up in my head, in a cell of their own. But lifers do get out. If they'd made a getaway earlier, I might have rearranged the photos on the *armoire* differently.

I made an omelette, put on some music for company and drank more wine than I should. I thought I would go over and talk to Philippe in the morning and try again to persuade him about the changes I wanted.

I'd always liked Philippe; he'd been like a younger brother to me. He'd grown up easily, missing the teenage storms and the mantle of farmer fitted him well. He and Lucette took over the farm first in small ways, then doing more and more as Pierre faltered, eventually moving in to the big house and letting their own small house in the village. They'd looked after Jeanne; they were kind and firm with her and she took note of them. But she was becoming increasingly cranky, her 'little difficulties' as they were called, were more frequent of late. Philippe knew what Marcelle had said at Christmas but the talk was still of caring for her at home, not of sending her away. 'Families don't do that' was what I always heard.

I collected my reading glasses and book and went to bed. I could hear the wind roaming around the house, crooning in corners and bringing rain against the windows, brittle and sudden. It would rush at the trees behind the mill house and turn the mill stream crazy with foam.

That night I dreamt without Edward's comforting presence. I couldn't wake and snuggle into his back. Instead the dreams continued seamlessly. The people of the past ran around me. Children laughed and cried, grown ups prepared meals and smiled round dinner tables. I watched couples who fought, made up, made love, made babies. I stood aside, observing myself, my mother, Marcelle and Pierre. I saw hospital wards with all the curtains pulled around the beds and I didn't know who was behind them. I had a glimpse of Marthe, taking my hand and running, saying 'no one will find us' but I don't know where she took me. And then, in the early hours, I could hear my mother screaming at me, 'You must never have children! Do you hear!' When I awoke about seven, I had to peel away the edges of the dreams from the reality of a bright, blowy autumn morning.

I made coffee and mapped my day out. I'd talk to Edward and talk or message Claire. Prepare the room for painting. Go over later and see Philippe and Lucette. The morning was still windy and the swings heaved to and fro. Leaves had gathered in the courtyard and the rooks were departing for their morning's foraging in the fields, battling the wind as they flew south.

As I was getting breakfast, pottering about, there was a small knock at the door. The young woman who Philippe and Lucette employed to help in the house, and especially with Jeanne, stood there, tugging her coat around her against the morning chill. Camille was small and pretty with sharp eyes.

"*Bonjour, Madame Bellingham.*" She held out a folded piece of paper to me. "I have a note for you from *Madame Jeanne.*" She nodded briefly, "*Merci Madame,*" and disappeared back across the lawns to the big mill house.

The page was torn from an exercise book and was creased and slightly grubby, as if someone had struggled with it. The writing roamed across the small squares of the paper.

Bonjour Madame Bellingham
Veux-tu bien me recontrer au grand moulin ce matin à dix heures. J'ai quelque chose de Maman pour toi.
Jeanne

I felt cold reading the laboured writing. Why did Jeanne want me at the house at ten o'clock? What could she have of Marcelle's to give to me? Had Jeanne been ferreting around and found something she thought I might want? Jeanne usually lacked any vital spark of generosity to want to give away anything. Although the others wouldn't say so; they had always been more ready to excuse her than I was. Until recently I'd been on my own with that.

I re-read the note and cast uselessly around for some reason to put her off. I couldn't think of a suitable lie. Unsettling as the idea was, I'd see her if that was what she wanted, after all her mother was dead. I didn't want to think about her and my body felt leaden at the thought of meeting her. If only I could read people the way I could read books. Or write about them? How do you punctuate for unease?

England, March 1950

"HOW CERTAIN ARE you?" Tom asked when Nancy shyly told him she hadn't had her 'visitor' for two months. She pulled her hair round her face to hide the blush that crept up. She didn't tell him she'd been feeling sick for weeks and that her breasts hurt her all day, every day. She felt taken over in some way she couldn't explain.

"It's hopeful," she said. "I'm going to the doctor's tomorrow."

"I'll come with you."

"No. No. It's too - well - personal. Wait for me and we'll have tea somewhere."

"OK. But babies get made in a personal way, you know - very personal." Tom smiled, his eyes crinkling in delight, and her embarrassment melted. The blush stayed as she remembered their wedding on a mild, damp December day and the night in the hotel by the sea where her body betrayed her into pleasures and needs she hadn't known existed and thereafter would blackmail her whenever Tom wanted.

They were staying with Nancy's parents in a quiet corner of Essex that was pulling itself together after the war. The family doctor was two streets away, his surgery a grimy white, pebble-dashed annex to a bungalow. She pulled her shoulders back as she walked up the path. If this was what married women had to do, then she would be dignified about it. Grown up.

The doctor was short and podgy and Nancy felt he was more rough than was necessary. He smelt strongly of tobacco and had fat hands. "You're nearly three months," he said, pulling off his gloves and staring at her while she tidied her clothes. The waistband of her flared skirt was already tight and she wriggled to adjust it, aware of his eyes on her. He didn't indulge in any of the niceties of 'congratulations' or 'how are you feeling?'

He was rude as well. "Starry eyed, aren't you? You don't see what

I see, miss. Sorry, Mrs Woods. I see men who fought in the war, not sheltered young women."

Nancy thought better of sitting down by his desk. She picked up her bag and coat. "I'd like a letter from you, please. About my pregnancy. To give to a doctor where we are going to live." She hoped this was the right thing to do.

"What for? Where are you going?"

"France. We've bought a house to restore and we have friends there now. It's where my husband ..."

Dr Tindale's pale jowls wobbled and red blotches appeared on his face. "France! Wouldn't trust the frogs with anything. You want this baby in safety? Why then, stay here. All that garlic ..."

"Thank you, Dr Tindale." Nancy pulled on her gloves. "I'll collect your letter in the morning. If you can't see your way to writing, I'll manage without it. It is, after all, up to my husband and I where we live. Good day."

She held her head high as she wound her way through the dingy waiting room, muggy with condensation and crowded with people she didn't dare look at. She walked out into a thin March wind and felt she had done rather well in what she thought was 'standing up' to Dr Tindale. She smiled, invoking 'my husband' gave her a certain power. Marriage to Tom gave her courage. Later she might think that this courage was trumped up, a prop that folded up when leant on.

In the teashop, Nancy listened to Tom's excited plans for all three of them. Especially for his son. She frowned at him. "It might be a girl."

"Of course. I wouldn't mind a little girl, Nan. Healthy, that's the main thing." He took her hand and looked intently at her. "We're going to be so fine, Nan. The cottage will be lovely when it's done, there'll be plenty of room. You can have a garden and chairs in the shade in the summer. Marcelle will help, she can speak English and we'll soon pick up enough French to get by really well. I can speak some already."

Nancy hadn't realised that. "When did you learn your French?" It added another layer of glamour, of interest.

"Oh just ... But look Nan, our baby can be bilingual," he said.

"That's going to be wonderful, what an advantage!" Nancy laughed, carried along, believing him, forgetting she'd asked a question. She reached out across the table and brushed her fingers across Tom's hand. She'd support him at home so he would have peace and quiet to write. His book was bound to be accepted. He was getting freelance articles published already, he hoped for a permanent post with a journal. Perhaps they could travel between France and England, even around Europe.

All these plans kept Tom happy and busy. Why not? They might heal anything that still hurt him from his war in the air. Had Tom been hurt much in himself, as it were? Upset still? He appeared completely confident. Never worried about anything and if she asked him how he slept he always snapped 'fine.'

She had heard that men continued to be troubled after the war when the actual, real wounds had healed. This bemused h**er;** the few men she knew always looked alright even though she heard whispers about them, implying all was not well, that they were not quite the ticket in some way. She knew Tom shouted in dreams sometimes, occasionally he made huge sobbing noises. Failing to know the right thing to do, she blocked her ears with the pillow and the racket he made always stopped.

She hadn't been part of Tom's war; she'd been the girl he met afterwards. Someone with whom to carve a future and to stop him looking back. He'd always been insistent that he'd not had a sweetheart during the war, not like some of the other chaps. He'd said it would not have been fair on any girl when it wasn't likely he'd get home. Meeting her was his luck, his reward for surviving. Nancy sometimes thought there must have been some female company. Another blush rose up from her neck. Tom was handsome and charming and many other good things. But not a saint.

Nancy drifted in the warmth of the tearoom. The misted windows conveyed a sense of privacy. She picked at a cake and grimaced at the familiar and peculiar taste of egg powder, stale and dry. She felt a small start of nausea. The tea tasted terrible as well. I don't want to give up cups of tea, she told herself. She'd already given up an earlier life and was drafted into being a wife and mother. It's Nancy Woods now, not Nancy Trowe. And Tom was right, of course, about France and starting a family. Her wishes and feelings weren't such a strong current as his were. She hadn't actually considered wanting a baby, it was something one ought to do after marriage, one was supposed to have children after the war.

When she met Tom he was talking about returning to France, as if it was a given that any girlfriend had to accept. As she did. As she had accepted everything about him from that very first meeting. Sally, an old school friend, had persuaded her to go to the Young Conservatives' dance, a local affair offering chances to meet potential husbands without bothering overmuch about the politics. Tom had been leaning against the wall, cigarette in his hand, watching her as she walked in. He was clean shaven; he didn't have the RAF moustache so many of them had kept as personal mementoes of their flying. Once one of the moustaches had slyly tried to kiss her and she had shuddered away from the horrid bristles.

"Tom Woods," he'd said smiling, walking up to her and offering a hand. He didn't dance, he said. But he'd try to with her, if she could put up with him. Afterwards he'd said he'd remembered a few steps here and there. And no, he hadn't lied as such; absolutely it was only Nancy who helped him, he couldn't have danced so well without her.

She'd read about coach holidays to the South of France and thought of the rich allure hinted at in the newspaper reports. She would have to look again at the map of the Loire region. Even though Tom had spread it out for her on her parents' kitchen table, traced the roads and rivers with his finger, showed her towns whose names she forgot. She wasn't sure how far they were from the south, where the tourists went.

Nancy realised Tom was talking about the woman named Marcelle again. She had looked after him in the war and whose husband was selling them the cottage. These people she didn't know. "I'll wire her this afternoon about the baby," he said. "We'll work out some dates. Get settled there in good time." He pulled his fingers through his brown hair, rubbing his hand over the back of his head as he always did when excited or worried.

"I would like to write to Marcelle myself," Nancy said gently. "I suppose … " She hesitated. Was it her place to write to a stranger like that? She wanted to be the one to reach her with the news of her pregnancy, to begin to forge an alliance with this French woman who seemed so important. She would have to be very polite to someone who knew Tom before. "Tell me how I should put everything."

"That's fine. Let's get home, we'll catch the last post." Tom stood up, fishing in his pockets for money for the teas.

France, March 1950

THEIR JOURNEY TO France was both arduous and exciting. The Morris Minor was loaded with luggage and they hired a van for a few pieces of furniture, the wedding gifts and the boxes from Nancy's bottom drawer. Enough, Nancy hoped, to set up house while Tom worked on the restoration of the cottage. Marcelle had posted a grainy photo of it, showing a broken down wall and a roof that canted to one side. Nothing that promised comfort.

The van was hired with a driver: a short, muscular man called Mark who eased his belly behind the steering wheel with a grunt. He complained, whenever they stopped, about the van's lack of speed, its hard seat and the suspect suspension. His constant carping grated on them both.

Eventually Tom said, "You're paid to drive, not to say anything. Now shut up!" Mark looked sullenly away, not bothering to reply.

At Portsmouth the air smelt of the sea and diesel fumes. They abandoned their car and the van to huge, shouting men who operated the gigantic cranes that lifted the vehicles into the hold of the ferry. On the quayside Nancy hid her face in Tom's shoulder, not wanting to watch the cranes, like giant birds of prey, swaying their captives up in the air. But all Tom said was, "Silly thing. They know what they're doing."

The cabin was hot and stuffy and Nancy was sick throughout the entire crossing. They didn't sleep and the fresh, morning air on deck was welcome. Mark had obviously had enough sleep somewhere on the boat to have the energy to renew his moaning.

After collecting the car and the van from the dock they drove out across flat plains that stretched endlessly to the horizon. Nancy could see heaps of metal that seemed to have been tipped carelessly in the fields. Several thin men in overalls were poking about, as if they were picking over rusty bones. One man was trundling a brown tyre half as big as himself towards the road. The men called to each other as they made iron castles of their finds on the grass.

"Guns, equipment." Tom was short when she asked him what they were. "Left behind."

Nancy wanted to enjoy her first drive through France, despite Tom's abruptness. She thought she liked the rolling countryside that appeared and the small hills dotted with brown and white timbered buildings which looked like they'd been made for children to play in.

"This part's called the *Suisse Normande*," Tom said. "But it's not as pretty as it looks, there was heavy fighting here, it hides a lot of misery. You don't want to know." He changed down the gears and looked in the mirror to check Mark's slow progress behind them.

They had frequent stops, getting out of the too-warm car into a cold wind that bit through their clothes. Nancy hadn't thought of the embarrassment of needing a toilet so often in pregnancy. Tom wasn't as solicitous as she felt he might be; it wasn't her fault. "Again?" he said. But when Mark also began to complain about her, it was Tom who held up a warning hand to stop him saying anything more.

Tom was kind to remind her frequently that the door might fly open and allow her to fall out. He didn't tease her about never having been in a motor car before. She wanted to pretend, even at the age of twenty, that she was used to such sophisticated transport, but her clasped hands and white knuckles gave her away her nerves as they began to speed up on the open roads.

They spent one night in a tiny hotel, its floors uneven and the bed linen threadbare. The receptionist had scowled when she heard Tom's English-accented French and inspected their passports with unnecessary thoroughness. The food in the hotel restaurant was greasy and the wine rough. They bolted their breakfast, chivvied a complaining Mark and fled early.

They crossed the Loire at Blois the next day. The river was wide and brown, bigger than any river Nancy had ever seen. The wind dropped and the spring sun spun out a trace of warmth. The stone bridge took wide strides over the water, its old arches golden in the light. It let them down to a long, straight road that tore through dense woodlands on each side. On this last leg of their journey Tom became less distant. He began to talk more about the countryside as they drove past cultivated fields, through green-dark forests and dusty villages that stared from blank windows. He reached over frequently to take her hand. "Almost there." Or, "Won't be long, Nan. You're going to love the place, I know it."

They arrived at *Les Moulins* in the afternoon. The sky was dotted with clouds and the sun had disappeared. Tom stopped the Morris on the gravelled drive with a last grind of gears. There was no one in sight as they got out of the car. Tom stretched, both arms over his head. "This is the big mill house. We'll give Marcelle and Pierre a few minutes; they'll have seen us drive up." He walked back to the van and bent down to talk to Mark. Nancy saw the driver glance towards her and heard some grumbling replies, muttered so she didn't catch the substance. At least he'll be gone soon, she thought, and we can get on by ourselves.

She gazed at the three storey stone and brick house with its blue shutters folded back. Boastful red geraniums stood guard on the steps leading up to the front door. How unlike an English house. Too gaudy. She walked a little way back on the drive and gazed up at the huge mill wheel clamped to the side of the house. The mill stream ran under it, green weeds horizontal in the current. The March air had lost its warmth and felt crisp and hard. Even in the late afternoon the light was bright and bold; she suddenly missed the softer light at home. She stood still, unsure of herself, slowing her breathing. She wanted this meeting to go well, wanted this Marcelle to like her.

A woman opened the front door and trotted down the steps. She was shorter than Nancy with dark hair in a pudding basin cut. Nancy felt Marcelle's bright, dark eyes assessing her. She thought the French woman had a wise, canny look about her, the air of someone much older.

She held out a hand to Nancy. "*Enchantée, Madame Woods.*" Her hand was firm and dry. She turned to Tom, her face softening as she held his shoulders to push him away and stare at him for a moment, before kissing him on both cheeks. She tilted her head and raised her eyebrows. "Well, you're back again."

As they moved into the house a slight man appeared, walking

awkwardly along the hall. He stood for a moment, staring at Tom and then he looked Nancy up and down, inspecting her. Unsmiling, he shook hands with Tom, "*Bonjour,* Tom."

Tom turned to Nancy. "This is Pierre. Pierre, meet my wife, Nancy."

Nancy shook hands with him, he was still judging her as he kept her hand a moment too long.

They had tea and cakes in a large lounge with bay windows that looked out over an expanse of lawn. The cakes were *nonnettes* - spiced honey cakes, Nancy was told. She tried out her school girl French and at least understood when Marcelle leapt up to fetch a jug of milk, saying she'd forgotten the English take milk with tea. Tom talked, nervously for him, trying too hard with his French. It seemed a relief to the four of them to get this first meeting over and done with when Marcelle put down her cup and said, "Tom, you have the blue bedroom, do you remember where it is? We thought that your first night should be here, the cottage will be very cold. You can make a start over there tomorrow. Take your charming wife and show her round. Tell her your *histoire* - your story - here and show where her new home in France is to be. Dinner with us at seven. We will catch up with you later."

Nancy thought she heard Pierre mutter, *mais pas toute l'histoire, hein?* She pretended not to hear. What's that in English? Not all the story, eh?

Tom carried their luggage up to a large bedroom with dark blue curtains and patterned wallpaper. "We'll unpack later." Impatient, he towed Nancy round the house, opening and shutting doors until she didn't know which way the front door was. He showed her the tiny attic room where he'd been hidden until he could move about properly. He told her a little of what he had to put up with, how stoic he had to be. "You wouldn't believe it, Nan."

Downstairs it was, "Here's the kitchen, the scullery through there, you've been in the lounge, there's another lavatory if you need it." She could hardly stop to get breath. He took her outside, round the back of the house where the farm began. He led her into an old barn that smelt of tom cat and pointed up to a shaky ladder that disappeared into a hay loft. "When I could move about more I used to go up there if there were visitors. It was safer. Someone would nip up to the attic and bang on the door. Then I'd know I had five minutes to get myself out of the house and into the hay."

Outside they walked to one side of the yard. Tom held a gate open for her and pointed across the lawns. "Look over here." He took her hand and strode across the grass. "Here's our house!" Nancy forced a smile as she looked at a long building with an outside metal staircase that ran up to a gaping hole in the side of the second storey. The walls were a patchwork of brick and stone and dingy whitewash. The holes in the roof turned it into a colander. A tarpaulin covered a smelly outhouse, a skirt of waist high weeds around three sides.

"Some of it's sound. The floors are alright and the old tiles round the back we can reuse for the roof. There's a copper we can install. Plenty of firewood." Tom waved a sheaf of papers at her. "I've drawn up plans."

"I can see what it'll become," Nancy said. She took one of the drawings from him and studied it for a moment. "I know it won't be ramshackle forever." She walked away from the house up the small rise on the lawn and looked down. Yes, perhaps a garden there. A paved area there with those trees for shade. She would write tomorrow and ask her mother for advice. The plans showed a big bathroom upstairs and she smiled at the thought. The sun appeared again and her feelings of foreboding left. By the time Tom had finished demonstrating how their home would rise phoenix-like from the rubble Pierre was there, silently watching them. The Frenchman squared his shoulders as if to do something difficult.

Nancy felt her husband tense and take a deep breath. "*Bonjour Pierre.*" Tom called.

"*Tom.* Would you care for a tour of the farm? We're getting going with it. We've time now so I can show you the old mill machinery if you like. It sleeps of course, but it is still interesting." He blinked as if in strong sunlight. "You didn't have time to see it before." He didn't bother to look at Nancy. "Marcelle will come for your wife."

As they moved away Tom was chattering and waving his arms, Pierre limping beside him, not so animated. Why have I never noticed how bandy Tom is, Nancy thought. I hope the children we have won't have such bowed legs.

Marcelle was already standing there, watching the two men walk away and wiping her hands on a flowered apron. Nancy saw her keen eyes dart from Pierre to Tom and back again. She wondered what Marcelle's concern was, tried to dismiss yet another worry.

"I have come to take charge of you and give you a woman's tour of the house," Marcelle said. Nancy warmed to her and her nerves about the impression she would make slowly began to recede; she was too tired for them. It was easier not to talk, only to listen. Tom and Marcelle had shared memories from the war; pain and danger, some happiness perhaps. She wasn't sure she wanted to know.

Marcelle chattered as they toured the outside of the house with its vegetable beds and the bare lawns close cut. The women eventually fell into an exchange of language, a tennis match of half French and half English. At least I've managed so far, Nancy thought. But I must put lipstick on like Marcelle does, even around a farmyard, be more like a French woman.

The back yard was full of scratching hens and Marcelle sang a snatch of song. She beamed at Nancy. "They lay better if one sings." As they walked back to the mill house she frowned and said in her accented English, "'ave you thirst?"

"Do you mean, am I thirsty?"

"*Oui*. Yes."

"*Oui, j'ai soif*. I am thirsty."

Marcelle put out cups and saucers and fiddled with a blue enamel coffee pot. Numerous sleek cats were asleep in shady corners. A row of old bowls, with grubby traces of food, were lined up. Marcelle caught Nancy's glance at them. "*Les chats,* she explained, "must be *en bonne forme.* So, we feed them well and they hunt the rats better. *Oui, les rats.* It is the same in English."

"Rats?" Nancy tensed her shoulders but thought better of saying any more. This is a farm, the country. Hide your fears. Marcelle had taken no notice anyway.

There was an old, grey-muzzled dog, lying on a pile of blankets by the range. Nancy wrinkled her nose at the pungent smell but Marcelle bent to pat him and hand feed him some tidbits. "He has worked well for us and now he must have a few nice things in his old age."

She took Nancy briefly around the house and they ended back in the kitchen where she poured coffee, putting the pot back on the range. "I have your letter." She smiled. "*Félicitations*. We will talk later on the subject of babies."

Nancy thought she would enjoy talking with another woman about pregnancy and babies. Her own mother, rather vague, or perhaps embarrassed, had just said 'well done, dear' and asked her about her packing.

Marcelle wore a grey skirt and a loose blue blouse that skimmed a tight waist band. As she moved round the kitchen she noticed Nancy watching her. Her eyes met Nancy's. "*Oui,*" she said softly. "I am four months now. A little ahead of you, I think, according to your letter. We're both well, *n'est pas?*"

"I'm very well, thank you. *Tres bien, merci,*" Nancy said. They were interrupted by a knocking on the back door. Half a dozen children were standing around in the yard, shifting about and whispering to each other. They fidgeted in ill-fitting clothes that were either too big or too tight and watched Marcelle closely as she brought out a tray of food. They looked thin and nervy and stood stuffing bread and cake into their mouths, staring at Nancy as they ate.

"They're from the town," Marcelle explained. "These two," she pointed at two scrawny, dark haired girls, "are orphans. They board with the ironmonger who doesn't feed them enough. The other four, those three boys and their sister, live with their mother but she has no money, no husband now and I do not think ..." Here Marcelle leaned closer to Nancy and lowered her voice. "I do not think that the little girl has the same *Papa*. She is always left out and neglected. So they come here for some snacks and to play a little. We've rigged up some swings for them, you will have seen them on the lawn. They have to be coaxed into playing. They are all older than they look. They are too short and thin because there was not enough food. They are - how does one say? - stunted. The war stole their childhood. They cannot be war veterans so soon."

Nancy watched the children eating and then looked away, ashamed for them with their dirty fingers and gobbling mouths.

The tallest of the three boys searched the tray for more food. Bony wrists poked out of short sleeves. "Pierre has his eye on him," Marcelle said, nodding towards the boy. "He seems strong so he might make a worker for us later."

Like a donkey or a horse, thought Nancy, with distaste. She briefly remembered the English suburbia she'd left behind. Although there was always the war, the talk of it, the news bulletins; she'd been sheltered from grubby children and farm work and rats.

For dinner Nancy had changed out of her traveling clothes into grey slacks and a blue twin set. She hoped she looked clean enough after a wash in the cold and cavernous bathroom upstairs. She would have liked to have asked for a bath but didn't have the courage. Tiredness made her feel as if she was walking on cotton wool.

Pierre muttered as they came downstairs. "*Bonsoir,* Tom. *Bonsoir,* Nancy." Pierre shook their hands abruptly. Nancy watched his thin, rigid back as he led them into the dining room. He hadn't looked at them beyond a brief glance. At least he didn't inspect her from top to toe this time but there was an edgy air about him, something not welcoming.

A huge dresser, stacked with china and glass, dominated the room. "Marcelle is still preparing the dinner." He poured wine for them both and topped up his own quarter-full glass. His slightly lop-sided smile told them nothing and his hand shook slightly as he stubbed a cigarette out.

They ate a meat casserole of some kind, heavy with garlic. There was fresh bread and goat's cheese, brilliant white, to follow. Nancy rediscovered her appetite and her tiredness lifted. She was eager to try the cheese. She had heard it said that goat's cheese was all the French ever ate, along with frog's legs. It was eaten during the war at home, although her parents shuddered at the idea and said they wouldn't have it in the house.

Tom was saying how well he remembered the cheese, helping himself to more and saying how he had pined for it in England. *Really?* Nancy had never heard him pine for any food. She thought her husband liked the best Cheddar from the Co-Op. The goat's cheese had a smell and taste that filled her mouth with an animal tang, acid and sour. She passed her portion over to Tom when Marcelle had turned briefly to say something to Pierre.

"I've never heard you talk about cheese like that," Nancy said quietly.

"Wonderful," Tom said, his mouth full. He looked away from her as he took more bread and leaned over the table to talk to Marcelle.

Pierre ate little and said less. The last course was a fruit tart, the apples rubbery from storage. As soon as they had finished Pierre was eager to light up. He closed the packet. Then, as if it was an afterthought, passed it to Tom. "Would you care to have *une eau-de-vie?*" He didn't wait for an answer, stood slowly and moved with his awkward shuffle, scuffing his shoes as if each step was a problem to solve.

It seemed to Nancy that when they heard the door to the cellar open the three at the table could relax. There was a strange ebb and flow of tension around Pierre that puzzled her. She wondered how she might dare to ask Tom about it later.

"He will be some time now," Marcelle said. "He insists on going to the cellar, as he always did. As it was his father's place to do so before him. These days, now he is returned from the war, he is damaged and very slow. But stubborn, you see. I could go in half the time." There was a touch of hard impatience in her voice, that Tom and Nancy, in the years to come, were to get to know well.

Marcelle picked up Pierre's cigarette packet and shrugged her shoulders as she took one out and lit it. "One won't hurt," she said, glancing at Nancy as if challenging her to say something. "It's fruit brandy he is fetching," she added as if Nancy had asked.

Before she could stop herself, Nancy said, "What happened to Pierre?" She felt rather than saw Tom's frown of disapproval and resented the idea that she shouldn't want to know.

Marcelle dragged on her cigarette. "Pierre has some toes missing. He went to work in the German factories in 1942 and lost his toes through frostbite." She looked away from them. "He, himself, should have gone missing. Taken to the countryside, done something - any little thing at least - like others who were brave enough to avoid the S.T.O."

Nancy wasn't sure how to interpret Marcelle's tone; one of disgust, contempt, anger? Was there pity as well in the mix? "The Sss tay

O?" She was uncertain how to say it and looked to Tom, wanting to understand; at the same time beginning to feel out of her depth.

"It was the *Service Travail Obligatoire,*" Tom's annoyed look said, why do you have to ask? "It was compulsory work service - Pierre was made to work in Germany. French men had to go to help with Germany's labour shortage. It was believed that prisoners of war would be sent home if they volunteered."

She shouldn't have asked. Her questions always brought up the war, the French war. Or if not ... She'd heard someone say with a derisory laugh the French didn't have a war, just their occupation. Tom's comments about his own part in it all, like short notes off a list, told her little. Her own experience was largely limited to her mother's complaints; endless moans about shortages and queues. Her father cycling stoically to work every day; always worn out. She'd been ten in 1939. Her quiet parents had tried to protect her from the details, avoiding her questions or interpreting the news for her in optimistic lights. If it was bad they said it would all get better soon and she preferred to believe the false notes in their voices. When it ended she was nearly fifteen and what she should do after school interested her more. And, in a dreamy sort of way, whom she would one day marry. The boys in the street had played with wooden guns, shooting imaginary planes in the sky and making ack - ack noises that sent her back to her books and toys. The men in their street who returned home never said much about the war, if indeed they spoke to her at all. Once she tried to talk to her father about a neighbour's husband who had returned after some years' absence. "It doesn't do to ask, dear," he said. As a consequence of all this, Nancy had thought very little about the war years. Until now, in France, with its occupation a ghost in the atmosphere.

Marcelle stubbed out her cigarette with sharp jabs. "We must not talk about the war; not in front of you who are guests, after all. We must not be rude." She paused and lit another cigarette; looking through the smoke at Nancy, weighing up the English woman. "I'll tell you anyway. It was all cruel nonsense, this propaganda Pétain and the Vichy government put out. Pierre pretended to think everything through, to be the thoughtful man, to be the intellectual in the countryside." Her voice was scornful. "But Pierre believed what Pétain said. He should have been like others who stayed away from their homes and maybe made some sabotage. Any small obstruction made them proud. Pierre didn't have that sort of pride, he had this idiotic patriotism that thought work in Germany would help France. He didn't even believe the rumours about Catherine."

Nancy drank some water; the food was salty. Catherine? Tom'd never mentioned that name. She nearly asked but the sudden fierce look from Tom stopped her. Marcelle got up and banged the plates into a stack. "He is too proud to admit he was wrong and too proud also to admit how much his legs hurt." She marched off to the back kitchen and they could hear the sounds of furious washing.

Nancy made to rise. "I'll go and help."

Tom put a hand on her arm, pressing hard. "No, leave her a bit, Nan."

The door from the cellar made a scraping noise and Pierre hobbled back to them carrying a green bottle. He went to the dresser and set out four tiny glasses, his hands unsteady.

"*Santé, ça aide la langue.*" He squared his slim shoulders. "This helps my English tongue."

They dutifully raised their glasses. Pierre drank quickly and refilled his glass. The one he had poured for Marcelle remained untouched. She had returned from the kitchen and sat silent, her elbows on the table and her chin on her hands. Her eyes darted around the table and then fixed Pierre with a stare.

Nancy took the the smallest sip possible and hid a gasp as the warmth from the liqueur hit her chest. She covered her glass when Pierre offered more. Tom refused a third offering. Marcelle suddenly drank hers and then returned to her unmoving gaze at Pierre, as if waiting.

Pierre became loquacious. He spoke of the rebuilding of France after the defeat of Germany, of his sense of betrayal. "We believed in Pétain at first. In his values of family and fatherland. That the Vichy plan and to labour for Germany would be good for France. But over there we were slaves, starved and kept worse than animals. You English ..." He waved his glass to and fro in front of Nancy and Tom, tiny drops of the shiny liquid escaping. "You English helped his treachery. We believed Vichy even more when your Navy blew up the ships at Mers-el-Kébir. We hated you then. You destroyed our ships and murdered our men to stop us giving them to the Germans - or so you thought. But you might have been wrong, you were stupid. No chance our sailors had - burnt or drowned. But later we could no longer think Pétain was right, holding hands with Hitler whose other hand held Laval's. We couldn't believe in the Vichy ideals anymore because we had nothing for France from them. It was all a fucking con to take the best from us, to take the life blood from us. We could trust no one. Just to survive had to be good enough." He turned to Marcelle. "I shall tell them about the camps... shall I tell them about the camp for Catherine?"

Marcelle shook her head, a slow, pleading movement. "*Pierre, non. Pas maintenant, s'il te plait.* Not now, please."

"Very well, I shall tell them about the factories. About the guards who shot men too tired to work ... " He faltered and blinked at tears. He drank off another glass and reached for the bottle. Marcelle took it from him and put her arm across his shoulder.

Tom and Nancy were silent as they went up to bed. The dark, heavy furniture sucked the meagre light from a bedside lamp. Nancy pushed back the curtains, opened the sash window and breathed the chill air. The night had been still but now a thin breeze pushed into the room and she closed the window.

She slipped into bed beside Tom and lay on her back, eyes wide. She thought she should at least say something, venture an opinion about their hosts and his friends. Her friends?

"I like Marcelle. She's kind, and interesting as well," she said, leaving aside the malodorous dog which she had thought better off out of its misery and the skinny children meant for farm work. "And what about Pierre? He's very sad." She inserted another question. "What happened to this Catherine?"

Tom turned away, preparing for sleep. She thought she heard 'don't.'

Nancy tried once more. "And the rebuilding - when will the cottage be ready?"

Tom was asleep and she had no answers.

The following morning Nancy and Marcelle went to the town's small market. They stopped for coffee and sat out on the pavement under a striped awning. They kept their coats on; the vivid blue sky was deceptive and held little warmth. Nancy had suggested, with shy hesitation, that they went to a café the other side of the road; she'd liked the look of its green and red tables and chairs on the pavement.

Marcelle had tugged her past. "Not that one!"

Nancy worried about negotiating the French woman's rapid turns of mood. Was this a rebuke or merely a sharp instruction?

Then Marcelle changed tack and called an exuberant *Bonjour!* to a tall man going into the café encumbered by half a dozen baguettes clasped to his chest. Nancy tried a small wave at him and he bobbed up and down in a greeting, nodding to both women in turn.

After a glance to ensure Marcelle really had lost her fierce frown Nancy looked round, prepared to be delighted with everything, with all this newness.

Marcelle pulled her mouth down in disapproval of the coffee. "I am sorry for it. It doesn't get much better, but at least it doesn't make the stomach bad like the ground up acorns did." She took a deep breath. "You mustn't mind Pierre too much. There is some good in him. He did come home and marry me, after all. The only one ... He is trying to rebuild the farm, make a living and work for his own family. He's made mistakes. Perhaps ..." She looked down at the table, "perhaps I have criticised too much. I don't want to do that in front of you. Now, with the baby, things will be better."

Nancy wondered if Marcelle actually believed this or if it was all a jolly pretence. She changed the subject. There was safety in talking about food with this new woman. "What vegetables should I buy, Marcelle?"

The other woman pondered. "You'll need some leeks and some spinach, if you like it. We have plenty of potatoes to share, turnips, cabbages, carrots, there's apples left. Don't buy too much for yourself, Pierre has made a huge vegetable garden. I'm told the grocery shop on the corner has sugar. Think Nancy, real sugar. We had only a little honey in the war, we were so fed up. Not that there was much of anything."

Nancy went along with Marcelle's easy chatter, even though the backward flashes to the war years always inserted themselves. Marcelle moved from the realm of produce and food to talk of the midwife who would attend them both.

"There is a very good midwife here in the town, who will come out when the time comes," she said, sounding smug at being able to instruct the English woman in the French ways. "She is maybe a little old now, but very experienced. And there is a local nurse who could come and stay after we have these babies." She laughed. "I will try them out first, then you. I shall tell you their little foibles to warn you. My friend, Marie, when she had André, found the nurse helping herself to the soap. But she never said anything because Madame Privat was very good in other ways. But when Marie had Paulette the next year, she said to Madame Privat, 'you may ask for the key to the store room when the soap runs out' and nothing more was ever said. All was understood."

And on and on. Soap, nappies, nurses, how many days to be in bed. To feed bottle or breast. Breastfeeding was for other women; not us, we're better than that. Where to get the best milk powder. Nancy squirmed at the closeness of it all. Sharing not only vegetables but midwives and details of their pregnancies as if they were a bag of toffees. Her mother would never have been so open or intimate; she would not have mentioned such things but discreetly alluded to one's body in a maze of euphemisms, some of which Nancy was only just beginning to understand.

Marcelle was saying, "And the doctor will come out if he's needed. He's old too, but I think still quite useful."

"What about the hospital?" Nancy discretely rubbed her back to ease the tension gathering there.

"The hospital at La Roche has a maternity ward but it's too far, perhaps. A drive of an hour? But we'll see." Marcelle beamed and patted her stomach. "All will be well."

Nancy would have liked some of Marcelle's optimism; less of her embarrassing directness, her bossiness.

As her pregnancy progressed she became worried about the birth, sometimes finding herself suddenly short of breath with a fear that threatened to overwhelm her. She became more tired, more uncomfortable, more irritable. She snatched sleep at night in small parcels, often lying awake imagining undignified horrors of childbirth, based only on disgusted whispers she'd half heard at home. She scratched at itchy skin, disagreed with Tom about names for the baby and had to force herself to tolerate, with some awkward good grace, Marcelle's offers of help and overtures of friendship. She could say nothing about this. She knew, by an instinct she couldn't name, that she should not say anything. Even if her mother had been nearby she would not have complained, her mother being an expert in the silent suffering of bodily discomfort. One had to feel terrified and miserable alone. When Tom asked occasionally how she was, she wanted to say "I'm exhausted. I'm very scared! I don't know how I will get it out!" But she would only say, "Oh, just a little tired," which was what he wanted to hear.

She had tried to tell him once about her fears, blushing at her forwardness. "I'm worried about the birth. What if ...?"

"You'll be fine. You'll cope with everything, Nan." He patted her stomach with pride in his eyes. An invasion and a propriety she disliked. "Grow us a nice family."

With her pregnancy a month ahead of Nancy's, Marcelle grew big and beautiful and made real the cliché of a pregnant woman blossoming. Her skin glowed and she had about her an air of repose. She glided around the house and farm with the elegance of a ship of the line. If she felt any qualms about her baby or her labour, she too was silent.

Although once, when they were sitting in the shade one afternoon, Marcelle fidgeted to get comfortable and laughed, "the men shouldn't see us like this, moving around like cows in calf. And they won't hear us mooing in labour." Nancy smiled a tight-lipped agreement, resenting being considered more bovine than human in order to have a baby.

Tom had thrown himself into changing the crumbling cottage into a home. Undefinable animal smells still clung to it. The huge lounge was a repository for building materials; dust and pieces of mouldy straw wafted about in corners. There was already a rudimentary kitchen area and a pantry cupboard that had windows lined with zinc, pierced prettily with tiny holes. Her mother had had only a small version, like a safe. A fuss was made to get one of the workman to fit the pantry door properly otherwise the ever present mob of flies would get in to spoil the food. The insects made Nancy homesick for a gentler climate. Central France had an occupying army of flying and crawling things unfamiliar to her; the hot days were battle grounds fighting them.

Three bedrooms were being furbished out of the loft area, for them, the baby and the spare room for the nurse who would stay after the birth. The bath had a large space of its own, surrounded by a confusion of pipes and blue and white tiles. The blue tiles were of different shades, dark and light, not matching well. Workmen came and went, yelling at each other in incomprehensible French, so that Tom had to ask Marcelle or Pierre, if they were anywhere near, what was said.

Nancy thought that Tom was becoming as irascible as the French workmen. She watched them from a distance, fearing to intrude. When the men shouted at Tom he forgot his French and came back at them in very loud, slow English, exasperation in his dark eyes. Then the workmen would throw their tools on the floor and walk away, hands waving above their heads in anger. Tom would bellow something after them, as if he were again an officer. Then he would collect himself, breath deeply, follow the men into the garden, offer cigarettes and speak carefully in his upper class English accented French. The men would shake hands, everything now half understood and work would resume. All this punctuating every day as the heat of the summer increased.

Money came in dribs and drabs from Tom's work. He'd started writing articles about his war experiences and found they sold well back in England. Nancy was never allowed to see them. When he wasn't in the workmen's way or attacking a building project of his own, he shut himself away in a small room off the lounge and bashed at an old Remington. He'd then disappear off to the town's post office, behaving, thought Nancy, like a spy conveying secrets to an enemy.

Other writing she could see. There was a series of glamourised pieces about making their new life in France. These went off to Paris together with translations for the English press. They were not recognisable from her point of view; what she thought and did barely shifted from food and washing; enduring the smells and the insects. With the baby coming there was no money for the dresses she saw in the magazines that carried Tom's articles. While Tom bedded himself into the new country she fought a sense of alienation, wanting pale skies and breezes, not the fierce blue overhead and the bullying heat.

Tom tried to explain one or two pieces he was sending abroad about France rebuilding itself after the war; the complications of presidency and prime ministers. He told her a lot about the need for increased production and the problems with communism. Nancy would drift off when he talked about these things, thinking about the state of the house and what to get for dinner. There were some hefty sausages left, the over-seasoned ones Tom liked, and half an apple tart, Marcelle might have some cream ...

She asked once about one of Tom's articles he had secreted in an envelope for posting, he'd said, "They're just sketches, nothing important."

"I don't really understand, dear. Tell me." She patted his arm.

"You know, Nan, a wife might not be interested anyway. Don't worry yourself. What's for dinner?"

At least Tom's writing brought in an income, eked out by her small allowance from her parents, which paid for what the baby would need. How Marcelle and Pierre managed for money she was never sure. The farm was becoming more productive, more energetic to her eyes. But that didn't mean, from what Nancy heard, that there was much cash around, although Marcelle would say *elle était prudente avec l'argent.* Very - how would her mother put it? - careful with money.

Marcelle brought over a closely woven Moses basket, with new, white wool blankets fitted snugly into it. "*Un petit cadeau,*" she told Nancy. A small gift.

"I must pay you for this." Nancy stroked the clean, fine wool. "It's beautiful, but ... the cost ..."

"No. *Absolument.* It is my present for you."

"Where did you find such a lovely thing?"

"Ah, just somewhere. *Ce n'est pas important.*"

Nancy was unsure how to repay French woman who was both

prudent with money and so generous. "Take some coffee with me, then," she said, moving clothes off the sofa so Marcelle could sit down.

"*Non, merci. Je dois me dépêcher.* I must hurry this time." Marcelle flushed and was gone, leaving Nancy with the tiny cot.

There were other presents as well, some terry nappies, a new woollen shawl, expensive items. Nancy wondered if sometimes an aura of shame hovered around Marcelle as she rushed in with her gifts and brooked any discussion about them, red-faced as if embarrassed by the giving and the thanks. The mention of money was not allowed. She was as secretive about these things and the cost of them as Tom was about his articles and stories about the war. There were threads running between Tom and Marcelle shown in the occasional glance, a shared smile. It occurred to her that Tom would know how Marcelle could afford new blankets. Stronger than that was some sort of connection running between Tom and Pierre, not a kind one. A turning away, a straight mouth, eyes not meeting and other small movements set the men apart from each other; a tight hostility woven into the warp and weft of these gestures.

France, August - September 1950

THE COTTAGE SEEMED to sit in a builder's yard. Its old stones, dressed with new pointing, gleamed honey in the strong light. The stones didn't match and the walls were a patchwork of bright browns and greys. Piles of rubble and tools surrounded it and a cement mixer stood silent to one side. A new path crept round the building, fenced off from unwary feet by string hung with bits of material; scraps of dishcloth and torn nylons limp with warmth. A trampled track led across the lawn to the big mill house and the grass had turned beige in the August heat.

Tom paid the last of the workmen as they left. "*Merci. C'est tout.* That's enough for today." He turned towards the two women watching him from a table set in the shade of a tree. "One more day. Then the electrician and then the plasterer." He pulled his arm across his face to wipe away the sweat and lifted his chin towards the blonde woman. "It'll be done in time, don't you worry Nan."

Nancy shifted in her chair so that she could discretely spread her legs apart and straightened her back in a jerky, shuffling movement to ease the burden of her pregnancy. She looked at her dark haired companion, also hugely swollen. "Let's hope so," she said.

The two women smiled at each other, conspirators in their bodies' heaviness.

Marcelle looked at Tom. "Shall I talk to the plasterers for you?" she asked. "So your funny French doesn't get muddled."

"I can manage, you know," Tom grinned. "But thanks. Yes, please."

He reached for the glass of beer Nancy held out, but looked at the other woman. "I don't know how you've done it, Marcelle. The best workmen at good rates. The materials you've found. You know everyone and everything." He lifted his glass. "Cheers."

"This *cheers.*" Marcelle turned her eyes towards the sky. "You must find now the French idioms. *Santé.* Good health. And you know,

Tom, even I have to be careful here." She glanced away. "I might know everybody but I cannot always talk to everyone in the village."

Nancy frowned at that, not understanding; she wanted to change the subject. She smiled, "*Santé*. We're impatient, Marcelle. We want to learn quickly. And we really appreciate all your help." She hoped she didn't sound too eager. Maybe that would sound false. Or desperate.

She started to say something more but Marcelle turned away to wave at a man coming across the grass towards them . "Pierre!"

The man leant on a stick and shuffled himself into a chair, nodding at Tom and Nancy without offering any handshake. They failed to follow the rapid french he directed towards them. He looked pleased, satisfied at not being understood by les anglais.

Marcelle translated for her husband. "Pierre thinks the cottage is going well. He says you have made remarkable progress for English people."

Pierre gave them a lop-sided grin to soften this comment that may have been a joke or a sneer. Tom laughed and Nancy smiled, but looked down as she did so; she didn't want to look at the men. These half-amused prods about the English, these little rudenesses, appeared every now and then and made her feel uncertain. She needed a steady world and had looked to Tom for that; in France she wanted stability from the Aubins as well. She dismissed a fleeting fear of them turning against her. She patted Tom's arm gently, little quick dabs to make her feel better and which he ignored.

Later, in the makeshift living room Nancy and Tom lit candles and ate off a camping table.

Nancy frowned. "Pierre's never very friendly. Does he not like us much?"

"Oh, he's a bit off sometimes, the war and all that." He didn't meet her eyes. He reached over the table for his sheaf of papers. "Look at this. We're on schedule. Plugs here and here, then the bathroom upstairs, and the bidet, of course. And the copper will be fitted in four days' time. We'll get the furniture out of Marcelle's garage by the end of next week."

Nancy felt fobbed off by the abrupt change. But she couldn't ask more about Pierre, she felt slack, used up by the baby and this place.

She peered at the lists and the drawings Tom had spread out. "It's like a military operation with no leave until it's done."

"Look, Nan…" Tom began, taking a deep breath, "I know you're fed up, but the place will be ready." He reached out to take her hand. Nancy stood up to clear the plates as if she hadn't noticed.

"I think this baby's going to be here before the hot water at this rate, never mind what your schedules say. Nothing feels right." She moved away before Tom could see the tears coming.

She walked ponderously out to the kitchen where the sink was propped up on a box. The water container was nearly too heavy to lift and she staggered slightly. She could taste brick dust and almost tripped over a bucket of soaking washing. She wanted to sob with exhaustion; to shout at everybody to go away and leave her alone. Even Tom. Especially Tom, with his endless enthusiasm for the cottage, the baby, the French. To return to where he had been rescued had been a fine idea. To settle where the weather was bright and there was room to spread themselves in this new home and where a baby would make life full and content. These were all fine ideas.

Being eight months pregnant did not feel fine and she hadn't anticipated how nasty the whole process was with the questioning and the poking about of the doctor and the midwife. The embarrassment. The problems of finding materials to rebuild the cottage and equipment for the baby in a country that had not long ceased rationing and was still reeling from the war, seemed to her overwhelming. All was make do and mend. Although in the letters from her mother, England sounded no better. At least, Nancy supposed grudgingly, the French fed well on what they did have and the fresh food was better than her mother's tinned spam and mock cream made with margarine.

It was unexpected and shocking that she should feel so different from Tom. She had assumed they would breeze along, both excited by the baby and the new country. Tom did: his world appeared light and hopeful. As if he'd been carrying a heavy suitcase and put it down for good at the English coast. Nancy's life became drab, a dull place through which she had to drag herself, heavy and swelling, day by day, just to get through endless chores.

She covered the remains of the meat tightly to keep out the flies.

There was the clink of a bottle on a glass as Tom poured himself another drink and she thought of home.

❧

September came as hot as undisturbed summer. A faint smell of autumn confined itself to early morning. Tomatoes rioted red in the vegetable garden, *haricots vertes* bushes were plump with beans. Trees bent under their heft of apples. Kilner jars made an extra wall in the kitchen of the Mill House, stacked ready for the glut of fruit and vegetables to be bottled for the winter.

Marcelle cruised about, directing harvest from behind her belly. She acquired a sickly, flea-ridden nanny goat kid, something that had been half-starved in a back yard. She washed it with carbolic soap and tossed buckets of water over it to rinse off the suds, so it looked hairless and made only of shivering bones. She spent hours with it, nursing it back to health with milk she could ill spare from her other goats.

Pierre grumbled about the kid. Marcelle was adamant they keep her. "When she is well and grown up we will have extra milk and cheese. She's worth my time as an investment here." The children from the village came and watched Marcelle bottle feed it and when, for the first time, Mattie took down a whole bottle of milk, a cheer went up, only to be shushed, lest they frighten the little thing.

The women harvested and preserved fruit and vegetables and tended the poultry, jobs Nancy was reluctantly drawn into, despite saying quietly that she was too tired, she knew nothing about hens and was worried she'd drop the eggs. Pierre limped about preparing for the late autumn and winter, yelling at the lads helping him. A pig was noisily slaughtered and the log stack in the yard grew up to the roof.

Tom had more commissions coming in. He rushed out for the newspapers every morning and took trips to Chatellerault and Tours for fresh ideas. He drafted and redrafted, typed and posted. He gloated with his successes and raged when something was turned down. When money came in he was full of ideas for the house and garden and would charge around interfering with the French workmen and renewing the most recent shouting match. He had an article published in an American magazine and when he received his copy he was enthusiastic about a new piece of kitchen equipment. "Everyone - but everyone - has a refrigerator over there. It's to replace the ice box." he waved the magazine in Nancy's face, so keen he didn't notice her take a step back.

"We'll have one. It'll make things easier for you. You won't have to shop so often. We won't have to share Pierre's cellar."

Nancy supposed she ought to join the others and shout with amazement at the magic of a cupboard that kept its insides cold by electricity. But to enquire about or applaud such a device was too much effort and her lack of interest slid past the others unseen.

The next innovation Nancy should have been pleased about was the huge, square, concrete box being manoeuvred into a large hole at the back of the house. There had been an argument about the trees that had to be chopped down to make way for this heavy, grey monster. Nancy had become fond of sitting under them, looking at a book, resting when she could.

"It's the only place with proper shade in the afternoons," she said. "Otherwise there's shaded places at the Mill House and I don't always want ..." She watched Tom and a burly Frenchman heave and push and pull each side of a saw. She had a short burst of temper. "They're not near the outhouse. Don't take them down, please."

The Frenchman raised his eyes skyward and shook his head. Tom mopped sweat from his brow with a grubby handkerchief. "Look Nan, I explained. You didn't understand, darling. The roots spread a long way; they'll get into the concrete. We'll just have grass here."

"But ..."

"I told you. It's the end of the lav. in the shed, dear. Be pleased. We're going to be modern now, it's our very own septic tank. Everything will be indoors now."

Nancy hated the stench of the chemical toilet in the tiny shed next to the house, hated going out to it with the possibility of everyone being able to see her as she crept round the outside of the house, getting out in the night with a torch. But she wanted the trees and her shady seat in the big, hot afternoons. Tears pricked and tickled. A child's disappointment over losing her tall ash trees. She took a deep breath and tried to be the grown up woman she didn't feel. She pretended enthusiasm, as if she'd been a little bit silly, so stupid to be cross. She smiled. "Tom, I'll tear that horrid little hut down myself."

She made lunch for Tom and the workmen and lay down upstairs while they ate, refusing to join them by shaking her head and patting her tummy. "I'll rest for a bit now."

Marcelle had gone for the day to visit some friends in a village ten kilometres away and had persuaded Pierre to drive her over in their rackety, shabby Citroen. When Nancy heard the work on the installation of the wondrous septic tank start again, she slipped across the lawns to the path that led to the town. She left a note for Tom to say she had gone to fetch some shopping, but doubted, with a shrug of her shoulders, that he'd see it.

She walked slowly, leaning a little on a walking stick that Marcelle had given her.

"You're too thin for all this ... " Marcelle had waved a hand at Nancy's eight months' pregnancy. "I have seen you stumble. And it will help with *les toilettes.*"

She hadn't wanted the solid wooden stick only a grandmother would use, but she hadn't been able to brook Marcelle's insistence. It wasn't elegant although she found walked with more confidence. She paused often. When had she become so breathless? She had not imagined the amount of energy that had to go into producing another life. Pregnancy was never mentioned at home in England. Girlfriends hadn't talked of it nor had her sweetly vague mother. As a girl Nancy had assumed, that after winning a husband, having babies was a duty to be taken up by a wife, as naturally as she assumed the work of the office job when she left school would last until she married.

Tom was the husband of any girl's wildest dreams: good looking, an ex RAF officer, a writer, a man who could be tender as well. Her friends had been savage with jealousy, not only of Tom but of this adventure in France. The wedding and the preparations to move had swept her along; she'd dreamt of this idyll, this new life, new French clothes, even excited about learning more of the French she'd hated at school, without the slightest doubt spoiling her reveries. She had never thought about how it would really be: a wife in a foreign country, struggling with understanding, married to someone she barely knew.

The town house had a small front garden fenced with low iron railings. It had a pink rose bush planted exactly in the centre. Blue shutters were folded back. A brass plaque shone by the side of the door and the bell she pushed sounded muted, as if a corridor away.

A slim, middle-aged woman opened the door. She had shiny hair in a French pleat and perfect make up, her lips fashionably scarlet. "*Bonjour, Madame.* How may I help you?"

Nancy couldn't speak for a moment; she had to swallow first. "*Bonjour Madame.* I wonder if I may see the doctor please? Or make an appointment?"

"He is in today and he may be able to see you. You are lucky, he does not have a patient at this time. May I ask your name?"

"Madame Woods."

"Of course," she smiled, revealing perfect, small teeth. "You are of the English couple at *Les Moulins.* I am Madame Jauffret. Please come in."

She showed Nancy into a long, tiled corridor that smelt of polish and flowers and gestured to a row of cane chairs. "Take a seat and wait a moment, please" After a minute she held open a door. "Doctor Jauffret will see you now, Madame."

Doctor Jauffret stood up behind his desk as Nancy entered. He was very tall with a big head, heavy grey eyebrows and a grey moustache that drooped round his full mouth to frame a smile. He offered his hand. "*Enchanté, Madame.*" To Nancy's relief he then spoke in heavily accented English. "Sit down, please. How may I help you?"

The child's tears were there again and she bit her lip to keep control. "I am eight month's pregnant, the baby moves but I ..." She was cornered by this man's complete attention, trapped by his alert face. How different from that awful English old boy who hadn't cared less.

"Continue."

"I don't feel quite ... I don't feel as I should about the baby. I can't look forward to it as I should. My pregnant friend is always wanting her child, planning for it. She names it every day. But I can't find any names to give this baby, to give this pregnancy meaning. I can't find anything good to think about, there's nothing to look forward to. I'm very scared of the delivery."

She took a deep breath and she twisted a small handkerchief around in her fingers. Her complaints rushed out. "All around me are kind, I have help and I am able to rest, yet I feel exhausted all the time. I am so utterly tired. I can't eat. I don't want to be bothered with anything. I feel it's my fault but I don't know how. I don't know what's the matter with me."

She carried on, detailing her misery. She was able, suddenly, to talk without putting on a front. This is what doctors do: like priests they listen to confessions. She looked past Doctor Jauffret to the window behind his desk. She saw tidy lawns bordered by walks and pots of bright, red geraniums. The light was gentle in the consulting room, soothing. She could have sat there for a long time, staring out and smelling beeswax polish.

"Tell me," he said, "how much do you actually eat. You look thin."

"Some soup, some fruit. I try to eat properly but I'm still sick at times."

"Excuse me." Doctor Jauffret leant forward and took her hand. He pressed a finger nail between two fingers and released it. Again, "Excuse me, please." He gently pulled down the lower lid of her left eye.

She sat very still. How nice he smelt, of soap and cologne. How must she smell to him, when she couldn't be bothered to wash half the time, too big to bend over a sink or to fill that bath Tom was so proud of?

"And you use a walking stick?" Doctor Jauffret nodded to where she'd propped her stick discretely in the corner.

Nancy's blush rose from her neck to cover her face. "It helps walking because I am so heavy and it is useful when I go out and - ah - when I must use the - *les toilettes*. My legs aren't strong enough now." She hated all this in France. The smelly holes in the ground hidden behind rank bushes in the corners of the French towns. They disgusted her.

Doctor Jauffret inclined his head in approval. "But how sensible and intelligent of you, Madame. Of course you need a stick to help you. It preserves your dignity. And now …"

He stood up and opened the door an inch. "Céline?"

Madame Jauffret appeared immediately. Nancy realised she'd been listening.

"Help Madame with her dress and onto the couch, please."

Doctor Jauffret turned his back and studied the view of the garden while his wife settled Nancy onto the leather couch and arranged, with much discretion, her skirt and underwear, placing a clean but threadbare blanket over her belly and thighs. Nancy focussed hard on the thin blanket while she was examined. Nothing new, even in a doctor's house. The war again. She was tired of its past privations intruding on her and always reminding her of itself. How had these two managed? How had they got on? Now they still had threadbare cloth, foul coffee; the maimed men and new widows they had to see.

When she was seated in front of his desk again, Doctor Jauffret gently inclined his head. Madame Jauffret had faded away into the house. "You will be due, I think, in three weeks time. The baby feels in the correct position and all seems normal. But you, yourself …" He paused and his moustache rose a little with his smile. "I think you are a little anaemic. You know, anaemia causes tiredness and despondency. And you are too thin. I will give you some pills. You must eat well and stop worrying. You must eat green vegetables and red meat. Take a glass of red wine. It is necessary to rest."

She frowned. So many musts. She resented them already. But then, she must have this baby. Somehow. "Thank you," she said. "I do have one other concern."

Doctor Jauffret raised his woolly eyebrows and tilted his head. "Yes?"

"I live out at *Les Moulins*. It is assumed - there - that I'll have the baby at home. I'm frightened of that, so far from a hospital. Apparently the midwife will come, but …"

Doctor Jauffret rested his long chin on his hand and looked thoughtful. Nancy was weary and felt huge and awkward, scruffy and grubby. She wanted to walk away at that minute and sit in the shade.

He picked up his fountain pen. He had evidently made up his mind. "I have a colleague who is also a friend at the hospital at La Roche. He will take care of you when your time comes if you wish to have a hospital delivery. It might be wise given your anaemia. I will write to him and also give you a letter to take in with you when labour begins. If you would be so kind as to wait a moment I will have the letter for you. My wife will arrange your payment." He stood up and offered his hand. "It has been a pleasure, Madame Woods."

As she left his office she glanced through the window. Madame Jauffret was seated on a bench, half in and half out of the sun. She was smoking and sat with her long, elegant legs crossed, nylons silky in the sun. Her knees were just covered by her green dress and her small waist neatly encircled by a belt.

At home Tom was leafing through advertisements in a Parisian magazine. There was an envelope on the table, addressed to *L'Humanité, Saint Denis, Paris*, ready for the post. Another had *Paris Herald Tribune* on it. Nancy told him what the doctor had said. He glanced briefly at her, "I would have come with you and waited outside."

She knew he would have inhibited her if he'd been there, made light of what she'd said. She sat down heavily. "No, Tom. I needed to go on my own. At least there's a reason why I'm so tired." She thought she'd been brave going by herself and resented Tom not mentioning her courage.

He straightened up the papers on the table into a neat pile and dragged his attention towards her. "Go and lie down. I'll bring you some tea. Take your pills for that baby." He smiled. "I'll be back from the Post Office as quick as I can."

Nancy went upstairs without saying anything. So that's alright then. Just take my pills for the baby. Perhaps she was ungenerous. Tom cared, she supposed, behind his offhand manner, his energetic enthusiasms.

She drank the lukewarm tea Tom had made and took the iron pills, nasty little green pellets. She dozed and woke up to the sounds of hammering from the lounge. Downstairs she found Tom putting together a set of shelves, some of them already painted a pale blue. The air was full of sawdust and glue fumes.

"Hey," he said. "Take care. There's stuff everywhere - can't have you tripping. Take care of him inside and all that."

Nancy stared around at the room she tried to keep tidy, at the dust and wood shavings, which she knew she would have to clear up. She pushed sweaty hair away from her face.

"It's me, Tom, under this bump. I'm not just a baby growing machine. Have you noticed recently? Have you looked at me lately? It's a wonder you miss me I'm so big. And I might look worn out and horrid, but I'm here." She wanted to spit out her rancour, stamp a child's foot at being ignored.

Her breath was short and her voice rose. "And what if we have a girl? You never get away from 'him.' Have you ever considered things might not go your selfish way for once? Who do you think will clear up this lot? Do you ever stop to think?" She kicked out at the set of shelves, sending them crashing to the floor. She picked up a hammer from the top of a stack of sawn timber and brought it down on the shelves, smashing at them until the wood began to splinter. Shards of wood flew up. "All this - all the time. Build this." She crashed the hammer down again and again. "Build that. Get this ready."

She wanted to destroy the room, the things that Tom had made and in the violence to lose herself. The floor came up at her and she staggered. Tom caught her and held her. "Oh Nan, stop it, dear. What's wrong? Please, I can't bear all this."

She slept again. Through the bedroom window the sky was darkening. She could see a flight of birds streaming across the navy background to roost. She didn't remember Tom putting her to bed.

He was sitting beside the bed, staring at her. His eyes were puffy and red. As she shifted to sit up the baby kicked and she had to squirm around. It might have disappeared, running from her rage. Of course not.

There was a bottle of red wine and two glasses on the bedside table. Tom handed her a glass. "I thought this might help."

"Thanks. I don't know what to say."

He might once have replied, 'sorry would be a good start' but instead he looked at her and said, "Tell me, Nan. This isn't like you. I don't know what to say either or what to understand."

"I'm frightened. I'm scared of the delivery. I don't like myself much any more. I want this baby but I can't ... I can't think about it as a person. There's no connection with it. I'm sure there ought to be."

"There's something else." She took a gulp of wine and flushed at the memory she'd suppressed all afternoon. "When I went into the town I - um - had to use that awful lavatory in the ground and when I came out Pierre was walking past. He saw me with my stick. He had his walking stick as well. He shook it at me. 'Hey,' he said. 'A cripple like me, are you now?' And he sneered with that half grin he puts on sometimes. 'Can't get off the pot, can you?' he said. 'Too big, like a fat sow. Now you can join all of us who need sticks - *le club*.' He made me feel dirty. Not wanted. Or like some creature he could torment. He just walked off laughing to himself."

She shook her head. "He made me feel so cross, Tom. And ashamed. I took it all out on you. I wanted to break things, I don't know why, it's not because of you."

"Oh God. You poor thing." Tom took her hand, he felt warm and solid. "He wouldn't have said that if Marcelle had been there. Look, Nan, don't take any notice. He's been bad with everyone for days now. He just gets these spells and he wants to be nasty to everyone, it's not just you. He's damaged by the war; the men who went to Germany came back with crippled minds as well as bodies. They were starved and tormented and at times they forget to be human again. He thinks back to it all and gets angry. God knows how Marcelle puts up with him but it's not his fault. And there was ..." Tom broke off. "Look dear, there's always other things - about Pierre and here - things you don't need to know, nothing to upset you. And he's been good to us, selling the house. He and Marcelle understand ... "

"Understand what, Tom?"

"Don't listen to him Nan, you mustn't. It's all finished." He stood up abruptly. "Look Nan, have some more wine and get some rest."

Nancy sensed a distance in the change of subject and frowned. "What is it?"

"Nothing, Nan. I'll go down and find us something to eat. There's stuff in the cold store."

Was this supposed to make her feel better? Mixed with Tom's

concern for her was this siding with Pierre and his war damage as well as something else. Unfinished, despite what he'd said. To do with the bloody war again; to do with whatever it was Pierre and Marcelle understood. Clearly, she wasn't to be told. Pique came as quickly as self pity. No-one understood how she felt; for sympathy she'd have to stand in the queue behind the French.

Rosemary

I REMEMBER MY mother telling me about how she wrecked a room and trashed - she drawled this in the fake American accent she liked to use - the bookcase Dad was building. She turned it into a funny anecdote when I complained how cross I was with a boyfriend. I must have been about seventeen and had fallen out with a lad called Gerard who didn't, in my mind, pay me enough attention.

"It was because he wasn't noticing me," she said. "That and always defending other people over me. Don't tell your father I told you." She turned towards Dad's study in cartoon mock fearfulness. But her amusement, years after her efforts with a hammer, wasn't genuine, just defensively put on. Maybe no longer shocked by her own behaviour she was still hurt by my father's attitude towards Pierre. I couldn't envisage her being so violent nor Dad putting up with it.

I can understand her being thrown off balance: pregnant at twenty and with little sense of what to expect from marriage and a baby, let alone dealing with being bounced into a world miles away from English suburbia. Dad was ten years older and seemingly certain, assured and experienced. He could be kind but he wasn't a tolerant man. Not of his wife, anyway.

Brought up in another way, in a different time or place, Mum might have coped better. But her home was in a foreign village, full of stares and gossip and undercurrents she didn't understand. At least Marcelle took her hand.

France, September 1959

AUTUMN CONTINUED. AT daybreak there was a flat blanket of mist across the fields.

The year turned cooler; the mornings and evenings made Nancy more comfortable. Tom seemed solicitous, or maybe he was just careful about what he said. She no longer cared. Her focus was the child that shifted inside her, her own sense of being so big consumed her. She was removed, by her bodily concerns, from this idea of settling in France, of renovating the cottage, of their new life. The big idea split into bits which floated away into the atmosphere.

Marcelle began to bore Nancy with her continual commentary on how everything in the country was changing. She wasn't interested. I've nothing to compare it with, Marcelle. Don't go on so.

She didn't care about the local buses. Transport, in the form of a few wheezing coaches that stopped dozens of times on their journeys by request, seemed the height of luxury for Marcelle whose pregnancy hindered her driving and whose husband was too busy to take her anywhere. She would explain the privations of the war to Nancy, taking delight in this, especially when she gathered Nancy had been so sheltered at home in England.

"Distance was measured by our feet, how far we could walk." Marcelle put a confiding hand on Nancy's arm. "Old Pascal Debarge had to walk eight kilometres and back each day to look after his fields and he was nearly eighty." She repeated this often, altering the names and distances. If she could see no change in Nancy's expression she would push her face closer and added, in a deep, gloomy voice, "the war killed him, you know. As sure as if he had pointed a gun at a German in defiance and got shot first."

Nancy didn't want to use buses, to hear all this information. The more she heard about the shortages in the war, the lack of food, the hardships, the less she wanted to eat. Marcelle's pregnancy had given her a lustre and an obsession with food. She would talk about the next chicken they could kill, how to preserve the duck for the winter. Nancy disliked the idea of cooking duck in vast pots of grease and making the bloody offal into a rich paté she couldn't stomach.

"You're too thin, you must feed yourself and this baby. All this picking and pecking will do you no good," Marcelle said.

Tom nagged her as well. "Are you ready to come over, Nan? Marcelle's cooking some rabbit and she said to tell you there's a *tarte au citron.*"

"You go over to dinner on your own, I don't feel well enough. Make an excuse for me, Tom."

"But they've asked us, Nan," he said. "Come and eat with them. Marcelle likes to tempt you with her cooking. I'd like to see you with more flesh on your bones, not just that huge bump."

Nancy shook her head.

"I don't understand. You should be happy. Enjoy the baby coming like Marcelle does. What's wrong with you?" His voice rose in a temper he checked, as if he'd stubbed his toe and had to press his lips tightly together until the pain faded.

"You go. I'll have some soup here."

"You must have more than soup. Remember what the doctor said. You know, Nan, you don't understand - not at all. These people had nothing in the war, they were all too thin. They gave me food while they went without. Now they have something they want to share it and you're too stupid to even try to be friendly, to be grateful."

So it was out. Nancy was a stupid stranger among people who were clearly better than she was. She dashed tears away. She wanted to say something, anything, to ameliorate Tom's rage but stood dumb. She had to wait, always, on his moods.

"Look Nan, you're not bright but you have to grow up out here. Don't play the poor little hard done by girl with me. You've always been looked after, Daddy's pet, Mummy's little darling. Not like Marcelle and Pierre who've had it rough. And while I'm about it - don't moan to me about him."

Nancy reached a hand out to him but he wasn't there any more. He was striding through the garden, smoking. An old flower pot split into chunks when he kicked it out of his way. He marched off to the big house without looking back.

Nancy might have tried to plead again that she didn't want to spend time in Pierre's company. Tom knew that if she saw Pierre from a distance as he made his way across the farmyard, smacking his stick at the weeds near the hedge as if he hated them, she would turn to go another way. Now, with Tom's defence of the farmer, his excuses for Pierre's rude attitude, she realised she had to be mute.

A still afternoon saw Nancy and Marcelle very slowly picking fruit together. The sun dripped gold on the trees and the air was thick with heat and scent. Swallows and house martins swirled and swooped high up, chasing food to rear their last broods before the long flight south. Both women used sticks to help them move, to support their bodies heavy with pregnancy as they climbed cautiously onto stools to detach the ripe apples from the trees. The apples were laid in big baskets, the wickerwork dark with age, as carefully as new born babies, so they wouldn't spoil in winter storage.

Nancy thought of Pierre, of his silent inspection of *les anglais* at the dinner table, his lop sided smile that held no humour. Her relief when he left his unfinished plate, drain his drained his glass and hauled his way out of the room. Yet she was curious. She could ask Marcelle when she couldn't ask Tom. "How is Pierre? We see little of him."

Marcelle rearranged a row of apples. "That's better. "She straightened up and folded her arms across her huge stomach. "He has a lot of pain in his back. His toes are gone - this throws his spine and everything else out, and he aches. His temper, too, is thrown out. And he has always been an uncertain man with that. But he doesn't hit me, like some men hit their women."

Nancy was slow to reply. She let her gaze drift across the orchard, over the scuffed and scrubby grass under the trees. She mused on men who hit women, or who didn't. Her father's worse chastisement was to shake his grey head slowly and look disappointed. Even now, in spite of her upsets and vague ways which she knew irritated him, and with his own short temper, Tom didn't raise his hand. Usually, when he was angry, he went into the garden or over the fields to walk and smoke. Or he wrote out his rough ill-humour on the old typewriter.

She saw him sometimes, crouched over it, a cigarette in his mouth, hitting the keys before they dared to hurt him back.

Marcelle laid one more apple gently with the others. "Aah." She sighed and arched her back. "What Pierre is really thinking," she said, "is that he may not live long enough to see his child grow up. He came back from the labour camp with a few other men from around here. The poor fools went together. And they stayed together - just about alive - to come home. One has already died, an infection in his stomach nothing could help. Another, old Georges, from the farm over that hill ..." she waved her stick upwards, "and who, I'll tell you, Nancy, was a very bad influence on Pierre because he thought it was a good idea to help the Germans, he now has such trouble breathing he won't last much longer."

"That must be ..." Nancy began, but stopped. 'Difficult' wasn't enough, nor adequate. The baby kicked and screwed its head down, deep into her pelvis.

Marcelle pushed at the basket of apples with her toe. "The lads can fetch these. They're too heavy for us." She put her arm through Nancy's and together they moved over to an old, rough bench in the shade of the hedge.

They sat in silence for a while. Without any breeze the air trapped the sweet smell of the apples: candy and cider. A wasp lazily explored a windfall already broken into by a previous adventurer.

"What was Pierre like, before the war?" Nancy asked.

"Oh, nice looking. He smiled and laughed more. He always wanted the farm. He loves this place and it was his parents' intention that he carried on after them. He worked the farm when he was very young because Clément, his father, couldn't do much - he was gassed in the first war. Three steps and he had to gasp for air. Four steps and he would cough for hours."

Marcelle shifted, easing her back against the wooden slats of the bench. "Pierre was always intense and serious. He thought things through and through and would take his time doing that. Not always correctly, of course. Going off to Germany wasn't right. But Clément had been at Verdun and thought Pétain was a good man - the way he organised the soldiers at the front. So Pierre's father believed in the

Vichy government and Pétain for a while and that influenced him. Then Clément and Eva saw quite soon what was happening to France and they began to hate Vichy." She moved to sit upright, putting her hands in the small of her back. "They were extraordinary, Nancy. I was proud to be part of it all, even though I was young. They were just ordinary farmers who lurched into bravery, taking in these airmen and sending them on. They were terrified all the time. They wanted their steady, safe lives back. But they carried on - always frightened of being taken and shot. And there was what happened to Catherine ..." She stopped abruptly and glanced away.

Nancy glanced quickly at Marcelle. "Who is Catherine? Was she another girlfriend?"

Marcelle fidgeted and looked away, towards the Mill House. "Oh, no. No. I will tell you another time. You were asking about Pierre?"

Nancy knew she was being fobbed off and went along with it. It was too hot to challenge Marcelle about her mysteries. "Go on."

"Pierre can be compassionate as well, you know, as well as having *un sale caractère*. He is bad tempered and unhappy because he can't forget all that's happened. He wanted me, after all, when he came back. Which was good, for I had no choice, unless I went away to the city to work and find a husband there, and I didn't want to do that."

"Marcelle, you must have had lots of choice!"

"Ah, no, Nancy. Here, in the village and across these few farms that spread across the valley into the next commune, everyone knew my family. I don't know how it is with you in England, but in communities like ours there are very few secrets." She moved again, making the bench creak. "People take sides, it's natural of course. What happened in my family set everyone against us. Except Clément and Eva and Pierre. They knew I was different from my mother." She looked straight ahead. "I might tell you sometime, not now."

"That's fine, Marcelle." Nancy put her hand on the other woman's arm. They sat quietly for a moment. The wasp had been joined by noisy companions, marching slowly around the brown rim of the crater that led to the apple's interior. Nancy pushed at the apple with her stick but the wasps didn't budge from their sweet feast.

Marcelle straightened up, pushing her hands down on her thighs.

"I think, Nancy ..." She broke off, pulling a face and taking a deep breath. "I think, perhaps, the best thing to do, if you are able, is to help me back to the house. If you can see Pierre or one of the hands near the farm, give them a shout for me." She caught her breath again, her face pale. "This is hurting now."

Nancy sat with Marcelle for as long as she could, upstairs in the big bedroom with the curtains pulled against the late afternoon sun. The heavy furniture and the dark oak bedstead made the room claustrophobic. When evening came she parted the curtains and lifted the sash window to let in some fresh air. She dozed when Marcelle snatched some sleep, then she would wake and hold her hand through the contractions, not knowing what else to do, fearful for Marcelle and for herself. Tom knocked on the door and put his head round. "The midwife is here now, she says she'll take over. Come on home, Nan, get some rest. She'll send someone across if anything more happens."

Nancy walked very slowly back to their cottage, leaning on Tom's arm. They were linked, she and Marcelle. The distance between them had diminished as their pregnancies progressed and this commonality at once reassured and terrified Nancy. If Marcelle came through this, then she would too. If Marcelle's baby was fine, then the kicking presence inside her would be as well.

Two days later, Nancy sat in the back of Tom's car holding a bulging, groaning Marcelle. Their clothes were damp with sweat. When the contractions were not getting stronger or closer together the midwife had called Doctor Jauffret who ordered Marcelle to the hospital. She had wanted Pierre to take her and they had lodged her somehow onto the back seat of his old car, which had whined and stopped several yards up the drive. Marcelle hadn't seemed aware of being helped from one car to another and Tom set off with the two women in the back and Pierre in the front. Tom drove slowly, tense with caution.

Nancy kept up a monotone of soothing sounds set against the gasps and grunts Marcelle made. Pierre stared at the road ahead, his mouth pressed into a thin line. When Tom tried to speak to him, the Frenchman just shook his head.

They were met at the hospital entrance by two nurses starched into long, white aprons. Marcelle was extricated from the back of the car and put in a wheelchair. The professional nurses' smiles were for her but not for Nancy, Tom or Pierre. The gentlemen are not allowed to stay with Madame now, she is in good hands. There's a waiting room. We'll let you know.

As Marcelle was wheeled away away down a long corridor one of the nurses gave a disapproving glance at Nancy, up and down. "Given your condition, *Madame*, ought you not to go home?"

The waiting room was painted a dull brown with chairs in mock leather that matched the walls. Pierre sat upright and silent, hands folded tightly in his lap. Tom walked a circuit of the room, then back in the opposite direction. Nancy propped herself up in a chair as best she could, trying to ease the ache in her back that had grown worse throughout the journey.

"Are you alright?" Tom frowned at her.

"Fine." She grimaced. "I've strained my back holding Marcelle, that's all."

Another nurse, young and prim, brought them coffee and biscuits. "The gentlemen could go home," she suggested, gazing at them; not wanting them there.

"I can wait," said Nancy. "I'll telephone as soon as anything happens."

There was a rapid exchange in French between the nurse and Pierre, rude because he continued sitting, looking up as he was harangued. Tom stood aside, staring and twisting his mouth with his effort to follow. Pierre got to his feet. He looked relieved that a nurse was telling him what to do.

Pierre made to leave. "I have two cows to milk, some things to do. The nurse says they will call and Nancy may wait here." He almost smiled, pulling a face that told of a moment of reconciliation. "They don't want men around; let's leave the women to it, Tom."

Tom looked at Nancy, who shook her head. "Go back with Pierre if you want," she said. "I ought to stay here."

Tom watched Nancy stand up, stretching her bulk and walking heavily round the small room. "Pierre, you have the farm to run. Take the car and go back," he said. "I'll stay with Nancy while you do what you have to do. Make sure someone will hear the 'phone. Come back in a couple of hours."

"As ever, Tom; you have the good suggestions. We do what we must. But thank you."

Time dragged in the dingy room. The one grimy window let in a thin light. There was no fire and the air was chill. Smoke from Tom's cigarettes hung blue in the air. Nancy was half asleep, the ache in her back keeping her awake. Eventually, she heaved herself off the hard chair. She put her hand on Tom's arm. "I must find the lavatory, I won't be long."

The toilets were at the far end of the corridor down which Marcelle had been wheeled. Next to them was a brown, varnished door left ajar. A white enamel sign said *Salle d'accouchement*. Delivery room. Nancy could hear voices. She checked that no hospital staff were in the corridor and peered in. Marcelle was at the centre of a gathering of doctors and nurses. Her bottom was at the edge of a big couch, her legs strung up and held apart by leather stirrups on poles. There was blood on the floor and a sharp smell in the air. One of the doctors advanced to look closely between Marcelle's legs. Nancy saw instruments in his hands, then her view was blocked.

She heard Marcelle shout, "What are you doing?" Then a series of grunts which ended in a shriek.

A moment passed; there was a small cry, another. A nurse wrapped a white cloth around something and carried it over to a table at the side of the room, a doctor close behind her.

The young nurse who had brought them coffee came out, nearly tripping over Nancy who was leaning against the door jamb. "Ah, Madame," she said. "Your friend has a fine girl, *elle va très bien. Madame Aubin* will be recovering now. She has had a long and difficult time, but, hopefully, all will be well." The nurse looked less prim now and her face was sweaty; strands of dark hair escaped from her white cap. "I am going to telephone *Monsieur Aubin.*"

She put out a hand to Nancy. "Go home now, Madame. You must care for yourself, you look very tired. Return to visit when you have rested."

Nancy continued to slump against the door. The nurse hesitated.

"When are you due, Madame?"

"I have another two weeks," Nancy said. "I have a letter for the hospital. Doctor Jauffret wanted me to come here."

The nurse frowned and looked hard at Nancy. "Do you have the letter with you?"

"Would you like to see it? It's in my bag. In the waiting room. My husband is there."

Nancy suddenly needed to get back to Tom. She tried to stand straight, pushing against the wall. Down the corridor the walls seemed to sway in and out. The nurse darted back into the delivery room and brought out a chair in time to help Nancy drop onto it. She leant forward, her hands on her thighs, a huge ache like a girdle around her. The floor flooded as her waters broke.

The walls of the delivery room were tiled in white, she could only see them if she moved her head from side to side. She stared at the ceiling as pains washed through her back and belly; they would reach an unbearable peak and then recede. Too fast to give her much respite, the tide surged back. A bag of fluid swung above her on a metal pole and she felt a needle prick in her thigh. Tom had watched her being wheeled in. He had stood back from the trolley, his eyes wide with astonishment, his face pale and slick with sweat. A midwife bustled up to him in the corridor. "You must leave now, *Monsieur* Woods. I will examine your wife and the doctor will come soon. Please go and wait."

Nancy tried to say, no, I need him nearby, even in the corridor will do. The pains became cross tides, meeting one another. Maybe she screamed out loud with them; she didn't know. The voices around her were strange, she had lost her grip on the French and understood nothing. The clear fluid in the bag above her had been changed, she tried to focus on a red bag, it moved slightly as she wriggled on the hard bed. She remembered something about anaemia and bleeding that Doctor Jauffret had told her but she couldn't think back that far. Time wasn't stable, it didn't tick second by second as it should.

Someone was shouting at her. "*Poussez!*" And then, "*Non, en anglais*. POOsh! with the next pain, POOOsh!." They'd found the word. Push, they meant, but she wasn't sure how. When the pains came she didn't know what to do.

In her mind's eye she could see Marcelle with her feet in the air and realised she was in the same position; she had no recollection of anyone lifting her legs. Her back was slippery and wet and she swallowed bile. She felt a great tugging and wrenching. Then it stopped. She looked sideways and saw a huddle of white coats, away from her with backs bent over a table and she heard a high, thin wail.

As if coming back from a long way away, she remembered. "How is my baby. What have we got?"

The midwife's eyes searched her face. "You have a girl, Madame,"

"Can I see her? Where is she?"

"Not just now, Madame."

"Why? Is she alright?" Nancy wanted to hear *très bien,* fine, like Marcelle's baby.

"We are going to have a little look at her and she will go to the nursery for a while. You must wait for a doctor to come and see you. There is some stitching to be done, nothing much."

Nancy pulled at the thin scrap of towelling that covered her stomach, she wasn't decent. Tom mustn't see her like this. "Where's my husband?"

Another nurse came up, smelling of soap. "You'll see him when we take you up to the ward, after we've helped you wash." She laid a hand on Nancy's shoulder. "Be calm, Madame Woods. *Doucement.*" Gently. Only the continued pressure of the nurse's hand against her told Nancy that she was agitated. She tried to sit up and found her legs still high in the stirrups.

❧

They could have been two dolls a child imagined in a toy hospital. Nancy and Marcelle were side by side, propped up on pillows and held firmly in their beds by white linen. They nodded at each other, acknowledging their joint ordeals.

Two rows of iron bedsteads ran down either side of the ward. Each bed had a wooden cupboard next to it, bearing a carafe of water and a glass covered by a square of white cloth. Some of the beds had cradles next to them: woven contraptions like little shopping baskets on wheels. High windows, cords dangling from sashes, allowed a meagre evening light into the ward. The last streaks of sunlight lit up dust motes near the ceiling.

At intervals up and down the ward a nurse would arrive at a bedside and bid the mother to say goodnight to the tiny occupant of the basket. The nurse would wheel the basket importantly away, arms stiff and straight in front as if to keep basket and baby the furthest possible distance from her.

The centre of the ward was a parade ground for the nurses, their starched aprons matching the bedlinen. In preparation for the night a trolley was stacked insecurely high with porcelain bedpans. Another trolley at the other end of the ward held the evening hot drinks and snacks.

Tom had appeared briefly, to hold Nancy's hand and cautiously stroke her hair, still dark with sweat, back from her face. "Well done, Nan," he said. "The nurse told me we've got a little girl. That's wonderful." He sat stiffly on the edge of a chair but he kept her hand in his and smiled. He might have been acknowledging his mistake in wanting a boy. "Is she here?" He glanced around, uncertain of what to look for. There was no basket beside Nancy's bed. "They say she must stay in the nursery because she's a bit early and a bit small."

"But she's alright?"

"Oh, yes." Nancy had to be sure, for Tom and for herself. She was too tired to think otherwise and closed her eyes for a moment.

He looked across at Marcelle. "Well done, Marcelle. How are you?'

Marcelle smiled, her bright, dark eyes shone with achievement. "Very well now, thank you, Tom."

"And you have a girl as well?" There was no need to ask. A nurse had discovered him in the waiting room. "*Monsieur* Woods? Yes? *Monsieur* Aubin has been telephoned to tell him he has a fine girl. He has asked me to find you here and tell you this."

"What are you calling her?"

"We're not decided. Maybe Claire. For a middle name, perhaps Catherine." Her eyes held Tom's for a fleeting moment. Tom turned back to Nancy. "What are we going to call her?"

They hadn't talked much about names for a girl. Nancy had had so many little tempers about the subject and Tom had always listed boys' names, so that in the last month neither of them called the baby anything at all.

"Jean," Nancy said. "My mother's middle name, what do you think?"

Tom raised an eyebrow. "That's nice."

As Tom left, Nancy heard him saying, "Jean. Jean." She allowed herself to be settled down for the night by the stern French nurses and imagined dressing a baby called Jean in pink.

The first day after the births a nurse wheeled in Marcelle's baby basket and gathered up a bundle of cotton wrappings. The nurse held the baby lengthways on her arm, its head in her hand and guided the quiet creature into Marcelle's arms. She looked at the bracelet around the baby's wrist. "So this is little Claire Catherine for you." She gently passed her hand over the baby's red and pointed head. "This is because she was a long time in the tunnel. The bones are soft and were moulded, you see, on the way out. It will all disappear and she will be quite normal, you will be very pleased with her."

This nurse was older than the others. Tall, with a long neck above her stiff white collar and curly brown hair that escaped in wisps from her cap. When she smiled at Marcelle with her baby a network of fine lines emphasised her large brown eyes giving her a gentle, bovine air.

The nurse turned to Nancy. "Madame Woods, I am Nurse Favier. I am sorry but your baby must remain in the nursery for - well - at least a day or two. We want to know if you have a name for her, please?"

"It's Jean."

The nurse tilted her head on one side. "Jean? *Non, Madame, c'est Jeanne?*"

Nancy summoned some French. "*C'est l'anglais. On pronounce le prénom* 'Jean.'"

The nurse still looked puzzled. Marcelle sat up in bed, carefully cradling her baby and spoke quickly in French.

"*Ah, je comprends.*" The nurse took a little book from her pocket and made a note. "Now Madame, we will help your baby feed in the nursery, that's the best place for little - Jean - so early and small. You must remain in bed to regain your strength. Madame must not worry herself." The nurse slipped quietly away to disappear through the double doors at the end of the ward.

The days on the ward kept rigid time, routine dictated washes, meals, babies to be fetched for the mothers, babies to be returned to the nursery. Visiting times were brief and patrolled by nurses who looked sternly at watches pinned upside down on their aprons. Nancy and Marcelle were allowed to shuffle to the toilets and then to the bathroom for salt baths in the huge cast iron bath which was fed by a boiler that hammered and groaned like a beast in pain.

Marcelle became impatient and began to complain about the behaviour of the nurses, her confinement on the ward, her stitches, her lack of contact with her child. "I will hold her a moment longer, if you please," she said when it was time for Claire to be returned to the nursery. "I don't need this much rest." Marcelle's dark eyes glittered with irritation and the regular tussle to keep Claire with her was a pantomime that amused the other women and annoyed the staff.

Nancy watched this go on with something akin to boredom. Marcelle was always so pushy. Why bother? If the nurses will feed and change the baby, why do it yourself? She dozed away the days; tidying herself before Tom's visits was a chore. She ought to worry about who was cooking for him, but she supposed he wasn't starving. She resented Marcelle, who, after only three days, was smiling and feeding her baby as if she hadn't spent days in labour, given birth strung up like an animal, and now was stitched so tight she could only hobble like a lame donkey.

Sometimes she had to remember to ask about Jean. The memory of the delivery was hazy, as if it had happened to someone else and the sense of having a baby belonging to her was vague. She slept all night and on and off during the day. When she did ask the answer was "We will let you know, madame. She is not ready to leave the nursery yet." She would arrange with herself to worry later about the baby, missing the over-bright looks on the nurses' faces when they said anything about Jean.

Tom came to visit, bringing flowers and fruit from the garden and an article he'd written for dispatch to the States. "That'll give you something to interest you," he said. "It's about French farmers building up their stock again after the war." Nancy let the papers lay on the bedcover, out of reach. Tom handed her a magazine. "It's *Life* from the States; lots of pictures in this one." She saw a photo of a thatched cottage, incongruously English in an American magazine and felt a tiny nudge of homesickness. She had carefully folded her parents' congratulatory telegram into her handbag for safe keeping, she would reread it after Tom left.

"When can I see Jean?" Tom asked.

"Not yet. They want to keep her in the nursery for a while. They say there's nothing to worry about." Which wasn't exactly what anyone had said but it was better for Tom to hear and for Nancy to believe.

Tom was silent and watched his wife lying there as pale as the starched sheets. "There's time enough, Nan. Get yourself better." As if recovery was something she alone could hasten. She disliked the idea of such responsibility and closed her eyes. Tom sat for a while longer, holding her hand, saying nothing.

Marcelle wrapped her candlewick gown around her and slowly walked down the ward, leaving Tom and Nancy alone. The stairs to the nursery on the lower floor were at the end of the ward near the bathrooms.

A nurse came up to the top of the stairs. She was carrying a stack of bed linen in her arms and stopped, panting slightly. "Where are you going, Madame?"

"I have come to visit Claire Aubin. My husband isn't able to come to the hospital so I would like my visiting time with my child. If you are not going to bring my baby to the ward as often as I think right, then I myself will make the journey to the nursery."

The nurse stood for a moment, then walked on, shaking her head. Madame Aubin's outspoken attitude was well known. Let someone else deal with her.

The double doors in the basement were cream painted metal and shut. A printed notice in large black letters was pinned up: *Accès interdit au public*. Marcelle paused, frowning. Well, one would see about that.

The nursery was a large, square room, brightly lit with cream coloured walls. There was a pot bellied, cast iron stove in the centre, pushing out waves of warmth. The cots were in a row down the right hand wall, with a chair and a small table by each one. Arranged along the opposite wall were cupboards and sinks. The wall facing her had a long, thin window letting in a view of a footpath running alongside the basement. Weeds pushed through the paving stones.

A nurse sat feeding a baby, crooning a small tune to it. She didn't notice Marcelle. Another baby was crying. Such a lusty cry must mean a boy.

Marcelle found Claire, her tiny face calm in sleep. She marvelled at the light brown fuzz of hair on the head that was already losing its helmet shape. Not as dark as me, Marcelle thought, more like Pierre's colouring. She hadn't missed him. There was an understanding between them that he would not visit much, but stay at home to get the farm work done and make preparations for their return.

There was another cry: a series of thin, high notes. Marcelle looked towards a nurse sitting at the end of the row of cots, a tiny baby held upright on her lap. Marcelle went over, sniffing with distaste the sour smell at this end of the overheated room.

The nurse watched her with hostile eyes and adjusted a muslin wrapper around the baby. "You must not be in here, Madame."

"Well, I am here. I've come to see baby Claire." Marcelle remained where she was.

"I saw you look at her. Now, *Madame*, please leave."

Marcelle recognised her as Nurse Favier who wheeled the babies onto the ward. She no longer had such a kindly look; she was pale, as if kept underground in the nursery too long.

"Whose baby is that?" asked Marcelle, folding her arms and ignoring the command.

The nurse's glance flickered over her and then down to the bundle on her lap. Her expression softened. "This is baby Woods. Baby Jean." She tried to pronounce it the English way. "Jean," she repeated, inclining her head with the effort.

"*Jeanne,*" said Marcelle. The French way sounded better. "She's sweet, may I see her?" She bent down towards the baby and made to pull the wrappings away from the child's face. The nurse moved quickly so that the baby was out of reach, her long body between the baby and Marcelle.

Marcelle's sharp eyes scanned the table. Thin tubes like worms, an unnatural bent teat attached to a bottle, a syringe, a jug of milk, muslin squares, cotton wipes. So much equipment.

Marcelle looked at the nurse then down at the crowded table. "Is she taking her milk?"

The nurse stared at Marcelle; their eyes met in a silent acknowledgement.

"Some," the nurse said.

"Will she live?"

The nurse inhaled sharply. "What a question, *Madame* Aubin!"

"Yes, what a question. Will she live?"

"Perhaps." Reluctant.

"Madame Woods will have to know sooner or later."

The nurse pursed her lips, the sharing of information stopped. "That is our business, *Madame* Aubin." Her voice was cold and her large eyes hard. "You must attend to your own child, your own affairs, and let us get on with ours." She dismissed Marcelle by turning completely away, her back rigid.

At visiting time Tom found Nancy with more colour in her cheeks. She'd put on lipstick and offered a smile. He took this as a sign she was better. "I have the nursery ready now," he said in his 'I'm in charge' voice.' "And we have someone to come and help. The sister to Marie who works for Marcelle. Marie's a bit of a handful, so we'll have Jacquie. She's the quiet one." He turned to Marcelle in the next bed. "That's right, isn't it?"

Marcelle looked up from her knitting. "Jacquie will be fine for you." Her face was carefully neutral and she returned her gaze to her wool and needles.

Tom leaned forward and took Nancy's hand. "And - I've written to everybody. They've all had telegrams but they'll have letters as well now. I've sent your love and said we have a splendid girl." He never dreamed of mentioning anything about the labour or Nancy's health. "When can I see her, Nan?"

"They haven't let me see her yet, Tom. I've asked, but always they say she has to be kept in the nursery for a few more days." She had asked only once or twice, then slipped back to not minding and lying quietly in bed. Nor had she seen the relief in the nurses' eyes when she didn't ask further.

"Can't they take you down to the nursery to see her?"

"They say it's not allowed." Nancy shrugged.

A nurse stood at the end of the ward and tinkled a brass hand bell.

Tom got up. "That's calling time." He kissed Nancy's forehead. "Get some rest."

Nancy closed her eyes. It was all she ever did.

"Tom. Wait." Marcelle spoke softly, glancing across to Nancy. "Go and talk to the sister in charge. Ask about Jean."

Tom looked from Marcelle to Nancy, who hadn't appeared to have heard.

Marcelle stared steadily at him, "talk to the sister," she repeated.

The consultant's office is smart and clean and warm. It smells of polish and after shave. An expanse of oak desk separates the paediatrician, Doctor Jean-Pierre Bourdet, a large, hairy man, from Tom Woods. Tom has arrived early and waits for Nancy to be fetched from the ward by a nurse. Tom doesn't know where to look; he studies his hands.

Pleasantries have been exchanged and Doctor Bourdet toys with a fountain pen and makes notes on a pad, looking up every now and again to acknowledge Tom with a twitch of his lips from under his abundant, fair moustaches.

Nancy is brought in by a nurse who helps her sit down. Surprisingly, Doctor Jauffret, their doctor from the village, also comes in. He shakes everyone's hand and takes a seat by the window at the side of the big desk. There is a knock at the door and another nurse enters, pushing a wicker basket cradle. She sits in a corner with the cradle next to her by the wall and a faint smell of vomit slides into the room.

Doctor Bourdet clears his throat. He is about to make a speech in very slow French so they understand. He is good at speeches. "*Bonjour*. Mr Woods, we have already been introduced. Mrs Woods, I am Doctor Bourdet. This is Doctor Jauffret, whom of course you know. Our nursery nurse today is Madame du Pont." They all nod and smile and shake hands. He looks round the crowded office and then directly at Tom and Nancy.

"We are here to introduce you to little Jean, but before you see her it is best that you understand something about her. There is a problem with her mouth and face. She has a condition called *le bec-de-lièvre*. We are trying our best with her, but you will understand that feeding is very difficult for her. We have kept this from you for a few days in order that Madame Woods recovers somewhat from her delivery and begins to regain her strength. For some couples this may be a shock. We will keep her in hospital for a while longer, but Madame Woods may now return home." He looks steadily at Tom and Nancy, although mainly at Tom, and then regards his manicured hands which are flat on the desk before him.

This is his set piece. He has no more to say to the parents. As a paediatrician his only concern is the baby and this unpleasant duty to adults is finished. At least the child is still alive. Telling parents the very bad news is worse.

Tom and Nancy stare blankly at Doctor Bourdet. Tom reaches for Nancy's hand. "Yes, but ... wait," he says. "You will have to explain further. What is this - this *bec-de-lièvre*?" He frowns. "I'm afraid my French doesn't have many medical terms."

Doctor Bourdet confers with Doctor Jauffret in a soft voice designed to exclude parents. They must wait. Doctor Jauffret takes over in his accented English. "It is what you call a 'hare lip' in English. The baby is born with a split through the middle of her lip. It is a fissure that makes sucking difficult. It extends back into her mouth."

Tom licks dry lips, "What do you ..."

Doctor Jauffret commands silence with a hand raised, fingers spread.

"We are able to correct this with surgery. Doctor Bourdet himself will operate," continues Doctor Jauffret. "She will stay here for some time. You may visit. As we've said, feeding is difficult, she needs expert hands. And there may be other problems which we discover in the course of her treatments. I'm sorry to tell you she will be scarred."

Doctor Bourdet scowls at all this. He would not have said so much, so soon. He prefers to say as little as possible to the parents, sparing them, and himself, from too much emotion all at once.

There is a silence that loads the air with anxiety. Doctor Jauffret studies Nancy intently. "Perhaps." he says carefully, "it is time to look at - to meet - little Jean." Doctor Bourdet nods a curt agreement. "*D'accord.*"

The nurse scoops a bundle out of the basket and places it in Nancy's arms. Nancy is sitting upright and her arms round the baby are stiff. There is no give in her body. She licks dry lips. She doesn't know what she should feel and tries not to feel anything at all. Tom stands close behind her, looking over her shoulder.

The nurse folds down muslin wrappings from the baby's face. The baby's eyes are unfocused and she begins to whimper at the two strangers gazing at her.

Her top lip falls away and the inside of her mouth bulges pink from the split. Her button nose is distorted sideways; her lower face is without its proper top. It is a gargoyle face.

"Dear God." Tom says. He reaches out for Jean then brings his arms back down. Recollections from the war pile in. The shot and the burned men he helped from planes, men without mouths or eyes or cheeks, flesh bubbled. The men who are now the hidden away faces. He had thought himself inured to these mutilations, able to leave them to the medics. Jean doesn't fit into any sense he has of damage, she isn't part of a war. He has never doubted his child would not be whole and beautiful.

Tom takes a deep breath and reaches forward to take Jean from Nancy's unresisting arms. The nurse says 'excuse me' and helps him hold the baby upright. He tries to rock her, ever so slightly. There is a thin, milky dribble down Jean's chin and she makes tiny, snuffling noises. He stares and stares at her, then looks at the two doctors. The doctors are trying not to look at him.

"Can you really do something about this ... this ...?" Tom doesn't know what to do with the baby in his arms, he just hangs onto her. He wants to ask 'will she live?' but can't. He doesn't know Marcelle has been braver than him.

"Of course, we will try our best," Doctor Jauffret says, still watching Nancy.

Tom gives the baby back to Nancy, who is sitting still as stone. She holds the baby away from her on tense arms, then swings round to the nurse, thrusting the child at her. "Take it. That thing cannot be my baby."

Tom says, "Come on, Nan, we'll get through this. They say they can help." He goes to put his arm around her, but Nancy is already getting up. She walks unsteadily to the door, her eyes dull.

France, October 1950

MARCELLE WAS HOME from hospital long before Nancy. The doctors suggested Nancy stay a few more days to recover from the shock. At *Les Moulins* Marcelle began a seamless routine of housework, care for her poultry and looking after Claire, pausing only to chivvy Marie and to visit the hospital.

She had had a long conversation with Dr Jauffret, almost a dispute, to persuade him to talk to his colleagues about Nancy. "My friend," she said. "My good English friend is in difficulties. She has a problem with love for her child. Can I not just take my baby to her in visiting hours? To see my Claire will help her, I'm sure. After all, the ward is full of babies, one more would not be noticed."

"You want to break the rules, Madame Aubin?"

"But of course. "

She took Claire with her on her visits, asked Nancy to hold the baby. Nancy showed little pleasure in her visitors. Tom and Marcelle alternated. He would sit and hold Nancy's hand, talking trivia about his writing, how the house was progressing. "I'm not sure she's interested in anything," he said to Marcelle when he got back to have supper with Marcelle and Pierre who insisted he didn't eat alone.

Marcelle put on a bright face. "I'm sure she will be, Tom. Everything is strange now, but she will come round. You have to give her time." Pierre produced his thin smile and his glance slipped away as he lit a cigarette.

When Marcelle visited she fired a salvo of questions at Nancy: how is Jeanne? Have you tried to feed her? Do you sit with the nurses to learn how to feed her?

Nancy always began with her tired correction of Marcelle's pronunciation. "It's Jean, Marcelle." Then, "the nurses look after her, she is better with them. She cries with me, not with them. They don't mind her ... her face."

Marcelle lifted Claire towards Nancy. "Here, have a little cuddle."

The baby blew small bubbles of saliva.

Nancy shook her head and put her hands up, palms outwards, fending the baby off. "No, you keep her, I might not hold her properly."

She bowed her head, as if in a confessional although without the safety of a black, lattice curtain between them. "I'm sorry. I'm not a good woman, you know. There must be something wrong with me to have produced that ... that child. You shouldn't bother with me." And she turned her face to the wall, settling her body away from Marcelle as if preparing to sleep. Marcelle laid a hand on her shoulder and looked down at her odd, English friend, eyes filling with tears.

Doctor Jauffret and Tom sat either side of Nancy's bed. Tom held her hand and glanced expectantly between his wife and the doctor who had driven over from the village, offering to talk to Nancy.

"Madame Woods," Doctor Jauffret began. "Listen to me. It is time for you to be discharged. They have to keep *Jeanne* - Jean - a while longer but you must leave the hospital now and prepare for her to come home to you. You will feel better ... " he paused and looked down for a moment, thinking. "This lethargy and this sadness will be cured when you are back with your husband and friends. It is a phase that will pass and once you have your own household around you, not a regimented hospital, *comme ça ...*" He twirled a hand around to encompass the ordered ward, "your spirits will lift."

Nancy could not identify this particular phase she was supposed to be going through. It sounded temporary but, whatever it was, she did not know quite when it might have started nor could she imagine an end to it.

"That's right!" Tom reached down for Nancy's bag and stood up. "I'll help you pack your things, darling."

He shook the doctor's dry hand with vigour. "Thank you Doctor Jauffret."

Nancy watched her husband, aware she had to be bright and energetic too. To stop being passive: get dressed, go home, go out. She had not contemplated the details of such a brisk future. The ward had protected her from any outside busyness and the intrusive realities of Jean or *Jeanne*. She didn't want to give up the hospital and return to the cottage; to making meals and looking after a baby. Nor to Marcelle and Pierre; their farm, their Frence ways.

"Come on, Nancy! We'll miss visiting time." Marcelle called up the stairs. "Tom's got the car outside. Are you ready?" The car's horn peeped, backing up Marcelle.

Nancy came slowly down the stairs.

"You're still in your dressing gown," Marcelle sighed. "Have you forgotten it's visiting day?"

"Yes, I must have done." Nancy pushed limp hair back from a sleepy face. Her eyes were patched purple in a waxy skin. "I've a headache. You go with Tom to see her."

"Nancy! She's your baby! Come on, put some clothes on quickly, your headache will go."

"No, honestly - I don't think I can."

"They only allow so many days in the week. You know this."

Nancy shook her head. "Really, the headache's bad ... "

"Next time then, Nancy." Marcelle walked away, stiff with temper.

"She'll run out of excuses sooner or later," Tom said when Marcelle got into the car.

"We'll have to visit for Jeanne's sake." To Tom's surprise Marcelle had a catch in her voice. "These children like Jeanne ... " She took a long, hicupping breath and fished for a handkerchief.

"What's the matter, Marcelle?"

She held the handkerchief over her face, tight fingers pinning it to her forehead while she pulled in noisy breath. She pulled the cotton veil down, wiping nose and mouth. "These children - like Jeanne and worse - they didn't have lives. They were taken, killed." She leant forward and beat closed fists against the dashboard.

"Marcelle ..." Tom stopped the car and put his arm across her back. "Tell me. This storm from you - what's this all about?"

"The locking away, the hatred for anything not perfect - the evilness of it all."

"Oh God, you mean the orphanages in the war? I'd heard something ... We only knew later about ... "

"No, Tom! They weren't all orphanages! Those children - the ones who had things wrong, who had twisted limbs and backs and mouths

- they were taken from their families and put there. Their mothers thought they would be made better, that there were new treatments. Then they were collected ... there was only one treatment, a final one. So now we must care for the maimed." She sat back and wiped her face again. "Just drive, Tom."

The first time Marcelle and Tom arrived without Nancy, the nurse on the babies' ward said she could not allow Marcelle to learn how to feed Jeanne. "If that is what you are here for, *Madame*. It must be the mother's task, *Madame*. You may be her friend but this is not your baby." She did not consider Tom at all. He stood at the side of the room, Marcelle sat by the cot watching Jeanne sleep. When the baby began to whimper the nurse appeared and picked Jeanne up. Marcelle put a hand on her arm forcing her to put the baby down and launched into a long speech.

The nurse was tall and fierce, with a ferrety face and a country accent. Tom stared at her with a puzzled frown. He tried to follow the altercation in loud and rapid French that rose and fell as the women argued and threw their hands into the air. They ignored the tiny cries from the cot over which they stood and the wailing from a new baby nearby abruptly woken by the row. Tom looked towards the door in embarrassment, prepared to move away. Then, as suddenly as the storm had started, the women were calm. Marcelle and the nurse were sitting side by side, shoulders touching, with Jeanne on Marcelle's lap. The nurse was guiding Marcelle's hands round the feeding bottle, adjusting the baby's position. "A little more upright, *Madame. Voila*!" When all the feed was taken, the spilt milk mopped up, Jeanne massaged into a belch and the possetting wiped away, both women crooned and smiled.

When Jeanne fed well or grimaced at them with either wind or an early smile which distorted her broken mouth, the nurse and Marcelle would beam and exclaim, "*Là*! What a good girl she is!" And Tom would smile, uncertain of how to respond further, wondering at how this ferocious nurse could become so tender and at how these women could bear to gaze at this smelly, deformed creature he ought to love. That his wife ought to love.

Nancy did visit when she was harried by Marcelle. She took so long getting ready their hour was reduced to twenty minutes. A nurse looked pointedly at Nancy and Tom walking into the ward, staring her disapproval at them. She checked her watch. "There is not enough time now, *Madame,* to show you how to feed your baby. I will feed her." Tom pulled a resigned face and lit a cigarette as if he didn't care. Sometimes the nurse would only make a half hearted attempt to help Nancy feed Jeanne, taking her back from Nancy's fumbling hands with a look to Tom, who would nod as if to say, you do it, it's fine by me. If Marcelle visited with him she took over, chattering with the nurse while Tom watched. Neither the nurse nor Marcelle ever offered the baby to Tom who sat back staring away from the women. His place was not by a cot and he planned, although barely recognising he did so, to leave it to Marcelle and stay away.

Marcelle

SOMETIMES IN THE big, dark bedroom that overlooked the lawns, Marcelle would wake alone. The heavy, wine-red curtains, hung every winter since the end of the first world war, cut out all the light and Marcelle peered at her clock in the grudging light from the bedside lamp. She would always try to guess what the day would be like before pulling a dressing gown around her and opening the curtains to see if she was right. There was little to see in January except frost on the grass and a belligerent red sky, streaked with dark rain clouds.

If the other side of the bed was empty, she would search for Pierre. Sometimes in the night he went to sleep in another room or, too restless to lie down, he went to sit by the range in the kitchen, wrapped in an old blanket with one of the dogs by his feet. Occasionally, she found him still beside her, lying awake, wide-eyed and motionless, as if waiting for something to happen.

Marcelle would take him some coffee to revive him from the waking dreams he had. She would bank up the range, remind him of the time and fetch him bread and soup in the kitchen before he started work outside.

She had hoped for more of him when he returned, thin, bewildered and lamed, from the German camp to the farm at the end of the war. Then his support for her and his capacity for work were unreliable, inconstant. At first the happiness that he was still alive had been enough. It was sufficient for he and Marcelle to marry. And useful; the marriage solved problems. She had to stay away from the village. The farm needed her, Clément and Eva Aubin wanted her with them and Pierre would be better with a wife to care for him.

There were many months of adjustment. She had been running the household and doing a lot of the farm work during the last war years. After Catherine was taken there were no more airmen to hide and the fear of discovery that ground into their bones stopped. Elderly

Monsieur and Madame Aubin stayed alive waiting for their son, and perhaps their daughter, to return. This *attentisme* - this patient waiting - consumed all their energy. With Pierre at home and Marcelle continuing to do the work, they did nothing else for the house and the farm ever again. They were pleased to be at the wedding, when Marcelle wore Eva's own wedding dress, adjusted to her smaller figure and Pierre was in his old, dark suit altered three sizes down to fit his gaunt frame. Catherine's letter had reached them two days before the wedding via an American network which was helping prisoners released from the camps to contact their families. It had said only that she was alive, recovering, would come home soon. "If she were here she would wish you well," Eva said to Marcelle. "Just the letter is enough. Even if she doesn't know you are marrying her brother, it's a blessing for you both."

It didn't matter to Eva and Clément that the wedding was a small affair, with only the curé and two friends of Madame Aubin there. They didn't mind what the village thought, as long as they had their son back and they could see his health being regained with a new wife's care. And Catherine alive as well. If some of the village did not approve when the gossip spread, well, *tant pis!* After the marriage they faded quickly, too tired at the end of a long war, to hang on for Catherine. They died peacefully, one after the other, in the big, gloomy bedroom with its heavy curtains.

At first Marcelle concentrated on Pierre's health, trying to feed him up. He slept a lot in the beginning and she would watch and wonder what had changed within this silent man. With her new found authority as a wife, she made him go to the dentist for false teeth, giving him tincture of cloves after the painful extraction of a remaining, rotten tooth. Eventually he began to talk about the farm and she began to ask him to do things for her: the coal was very heavy to fetch in, there were logs to be chopped, would he look for a lad to help with the cows? Even though she had more right to ask him things as his wife, she hesitated when he didn't help and left her to do a man's work as well as hers. Sometimes she thought he wasn't a proper husband after all, but a rescuer, the only man who would have her after she had fled to the farm, and shamefully stayed there. She felt he was a proper husband when he was well enough to make love to her but then she doubted herself; he had been a long time without sex, perhaps any woman would do?

France, January 1951

WHEN CLAIRE WAS asleep, Marcelle would drink her coffee and dunk some bread in it, taking a little *confiture* from the pot on the dresser. She gazed at the baby's pale face, watch the pouting lips push in and out with contentment and took her thumb gently to the side of Claire's mouth to wipe away a dribble. She thought about the other one, having to be repaired, stitched. How she would grow up.

Marie was chivvied at the start of the day. The shiny-haired girl with her sullen mouth and full figure was always late for work.

"*Bonjour,* Marie," Marcelle glanced at her clock on the wall. "Can you never be on time?"

"I have work to do at home before I come here."

"You're very rude this morning, Marie."

Marie shrugged "Oh, well then, *Bonjour Madame.*" The girl's mouth was turned down. She had suspicious eyes: she might be asked to do too much.

"There is the copper to heat, the rest of the laundry, there are scraps for the hens. Please put the baby's bottles to soak. Get on." Marcelle's expression softened. She supposed sooner or later Marie would marry and leave, to become just as resentful of her own unceasing domestic work in a husband's home.

Marcelle turned to her chores, tidying, preparing vegetables, organising meals. Claire slept in her basket in a corner of the kitchen and Marcelle watched her every few minutes; she enjoyed the perfect form of her. Pierre took his breakfast in the kitchen, lit a cigarette and pushed himself up from the table. He shuffled his way out to the farm, unlatching a shed door as he went. Two dogs joined him: skinny, scruffy, barking things that dashed to and fro. He stumbled and fended them off with his stick.

"Hey, Pierre!" Marcelle called and handed him a bowl. "You've forgotten - feed your dogs for once. They're too thin."

Pierre turned his lop sided smile to her and and tilted his head at the jumping dogs, "come on, then."

Two hours later Jacquie arrived, breathless and eager. She was shorter and slimmer than Marie and didn't paint her mouth like her older sister. She had a toothy smile and a quickness about her that made Marcelle wish Jacquie could work for her. But Nancy needed Jacquie more and sulky Marie would not have acquiesced easily in Marcelle's plans. When she had first thought of asking Jacquie to tell her about what went on in the Woods household she was disturbed by such ideas. She was disturbed with the way the English couple had sidled back into France, although she had gone along with it and welcomed them. Now, here they were and here *Jeanne* was, home after her first surgery in December. Nancy not coping, Tom not knowing what to do. Marcelle determined to do what had to be done, to help the child live.

"*Madame* Woods is up, but not yet dressed. She has taken breakfast." Jacquie behaved as if a soldier in Marcelle's special domestic army, reporting from a front line in her concise sentences.

"*Monsieur* Woods is in his study writing. I have fed and changed baby Jeanne. She took three quarters of her bottle. She didn't cry much."

Jacquie had learnt from the visiting nurse how to care for Jeanne when she came home and how to manage the special feeding bottles. She could calm the fretful, restless infant as well as Marcelle and the nurse. Her other duty: to report on the Woods household. "Not to spy," Marcelle had said. "It is so I am able to know how little Jeanne is doing, so we both know how to help *Madame* Woods if she needs anything."

"*Madame* Woods was running her bath when I was with Jeanne," Jacquie said, anticipating Marcelle's next question. "She didn't reply when I called through the door that Jeanne was fine."

"Very well. I'll call over later. You must go back now."

Jacquie hesitated. "*Madame* Woods lives in her own world that does not include others. She drifts about. She tidies. She avoids *Jeanne* and me. *Monsieur* Woods also avoids - always typing, typing, typing, with his pipe in his mouth. Sometimes he shouts in English; I don't follow that so well." Jacquie took a deep breath. "*Madame,* I don't understand *Madame* Woods. Little Jeanne is nice to look after and I don't notice ... her face. And I don't believe what people say, that's it's a mother's sin coming out. Do you believe that, *Madame*? If she were mine I would love her despite her face. I wouldn't think of sin!"

"Jacquie! Go back now! It is your place to tell me what goes on so that we may both care for *Madame* Woods and *Jeanne.* It is not your place to have opinions. It is not your place to discuss sin - leave that to the priests."

Marcelle ordered her day. Claire slept while she put stock and vegetables to simmer, broke eggs into a bowl ready for omelettes for lunch and prepared dinner: a scrawny hen, sprawled in death where Pierre had dumped it on a small marble slab on the work surface.

She shouted for Marie. "Don't forget to take the nappies out of soak and put them to boil!"

A distant, grudging voice came from upstairs. "*Oui, Madame.*"

"I am going to visit Madame Woods. Remember to stoke the range."

"*Oui, Madame.*"

Marcelle packed the baby into the big carriage pram, tucking pink wool blankets around her. A light frost was clearing from the grass as she pushed the pram over to the other house; her breath billowed white in the winter air. She stopped for a moment in the small dip where she could not be seen from either house and lit a cigarette. She didn't allow herself many moments alone to think, even briefly, about why she had wrapped herself round the English couple's lives but having Claire had reawakened images of Henri more often; they came sad and unbidden. She had held her brother as he died, small for his two years and burning with a fever the doctor had refused to treat. She saw hectic spots in a white face and heard his breathing fade. She saw baby Jeanne's bad face and looked at perfect Claire. She prayed that Claire would have more time and Jeanne might ... what? ...manage to survive with that face in a cruel world when others did not?

She ground the cigarette butt under her heel and forced her attention to how she might persuade Nancy to give up her dull stare and her inertia, so that Jeanne could have a proper mother, not this shadow figure. The English woman hadn't wanted to come here really, to France, not for herself. She had just followed her husband with a stupid dream of love. Her youth and her cotton wool English background did her no favours. Marcelle wondered if Nancy ever guessed Tom had deeper reasons for living out of England. Certainly, she knew that Nancy hadn't understood, when she married Tom, that one has to be careful what one wishes for.

"*Bonjour,* Nancy!" Marcelle shoved the door open with her hip, her arms cradling Claire. "*J'arrive!*"

Nancy greeted Marcelle with the kiss on each cheek. "*Bonjour. Café?*"

"*Oui, avec plaisir.*" Marcelle propped Claire up into a nest of cushions in an armchair, so she could blink at the world. Nancy walked past Jeanne's cradle to the kitchen without a glance. She made coffee very slowly - taking her time - to delay talk of babies, of motherhood. Marcelle bent over Jeanne's cot to soothe the beginning of a whimper. As she picked her up, the tiny face screwed itself up against a slash of stitches on her top lip and there was a cry of pain. Pity hadn't been at the top of Marcelle's work lists. But there it is, not love - it would have to do. She stared into the child's eyes, fancying she saw the beginnings of self pity there.

Nancy brought a tray through to the lounge. "Put her down, Marcelle. Jacquie will deal with her if she needs changing." She poured two cups, added milk to her own. "No, I won't take her." She shifted away as Marcelle offered her the bundle.

Marcelle gazed into Jeanne's face "I do believe she's starting to recognise me."

"She knows Jacquie as well." Nancy turned towards Marcelle, her voice flat. "That's more than she does with me." She took a sip of coffee. Her smile didn't reach her eyes. "I don't mind, you know. I don't deal very well with her when she screams." She briefly stared at Jeanne. Ugly thing, was what she didn't say.

Jeanne twined her hand round Marcelle's finger and blew bubbles of saliva. Marcelle bounced her gently. You're not wanted, she thought. I'll have you. Make up for Henri. Make up for a lot of things. She might say this to Nancy perhaps, when the time was right. But the English woman was staring out of the window, disinterested in her friend or her baby.

Rosemary, the present day

MY MOTHER LEFT no convenient diaries and there are only the few photographs carefully hoarded on the big cupboard. I've tried to make sense of her life for a long time: sheltered in her English suburb by my grandparents from the rubble and blood of the war, then towed in Dad's wake to France. He was ten years older and very persuasive. Easy to love.

There was always this air of vulnerability drifting around Mum, with her big blue eyes and alabaster skin. She never tanned; she liked sitting in the shade, wearing long sleeved white blouses and a sunhat. I remember the abundance of face creams on her dressing table.

My sister and I learnt early on to avoid her when she had one of her 'turns', when she didn't speak and became distant and neglectful of us. It was as if she drew silence around her like a cloak that kept us from even the edges of her.

When he noticed, Dad would raise his eyebrows, wink at us and take us into the kitchen to concoct something to eat. He wasn't clever with food and sometimes he would take hours to notice Mum's state. By then we'd be so hungry it didn't matter what he put in front of us.

Dad had called all the shots; what they did and where they lived. Perhaps he didn't brainwash her - that would be too strong - but he never brooked an argument. He must have realised she was foundering, especially after Charles' death. In my younger days I disliked both of them: this dominant and passive pairing. Understanding and compassion only arrive later, sort of delayed in the post.

How would Mum have managed without Marcelle? I always saw them as best friends even though they were so different. Marcelle was the bigger partner; the more vigorous woman. My mother didn't smoke, didn't drink much, didn't laugh easily. Was she ever jealous of Marcelle? Who smoked, drank, be amused as quick as a flash. She gained a figure while my mother stayed stick thin.

Did they ever exchange any stories of their past? Ask: how did you grow up? Tell each other: it was like this for me. Perhaps my mother had very little to tell. Marcelle had a thicker history but would never say much to my mother beyond what they had - or rather what they didn't have - during the occupation. These details were simple to relate: the Germans took the food and the horses, we drank acorn coffee. It would have been all about Marcelle's surface, not how she arrived at the farm or how she knew Dad before.

I doubt there were many questions. Mum was too worried about herself to ask and Marcelle had too large a story. I discovered that later. Something must have glued them together.

I wanted to go back in time and put my hands on my mother's hard shoulders and shake her - just a little - and say 'talk to me, Mum.' I wanted to look into her eyes and understand. I wanted her vague eyes to meet mine.

I can only think back and imagine fitting parts of the jigsaw in place. I can remember visiting briefly one summer not long after we had the twins and overhearing two very old women talking about *Les Moulins.* They were in a dark corner of a dusty hardware shop, looking over tired china ornaments and fingering ashtrays engraved with *Souvenir de la Loire.* I'd gone in to buy furniture polish, too lazy to drive out to the supermarket.

I heard the words, "*C'est une erreur...* that weird creature à Les Moulins... her mother's done something wrong there ... *c'est une méchanceté*"

This *méchanceté,* this badness. Whatever I know about it I still want to stay here in France. Those elders won't be here for ever and France changes, moves on in its erratic way. I hope no longer the sins of the parents will be seen or discovered in the children.

France, 1951

MARCELLE CALLED AT the house one afternoon, dashing away tears with the back of her hand and her face fierce, distraught. She had Jeanne in a pram heaped up with baby things. Claire was propped up at the other end, squashed in a brown woollen cardigan next to a pile of nappies.

"Nancy, you must help. Pierre is very sick, it is necessary that I am with him. The doctor will be here soon. You have to take Jeanne back, I can't mind her for you now. And keep Claire for me as well, please. There's everything you need in the pram. I can't do it all at this moment."

Nancy frowned. Being asked to care for the babies was quite out of order. She didn't want to understand what was being asked of her. Jacquie had her half-day off and she had been content to leave Jeanne at the big house while she took an afternoon rest. Marcelle never minded.

Pierre had been found in a bedroom never usually used, a stinking, full chamber pot by the bed. He was not properly conscious, his cheeks sunken and his eyes hollow. The dysentery he had caught in the camps cramped his stomach so that he winced and writhed in a half-sleep. "It's happened before," Marcelle said. "He wasn't eating yesterday and he was taking himself off to be apart from everybody. The lads told me they had to do the milking without him. But if I say anything too soon all he does is shout at me to get away from him. I have to bide my time, then get the doctor." Fear wound her voice high.

This insistence wasn't to be avoided, nor was an ill husband. "What do you want me to do with them?" Nancy asked. Perhaps Marcelle was cross with her; she didn't like that. She tried to keep the resentment out of her voice, at six months' old the babies were a handful.

"Push them out for a walk. They'll need feeding in an hour or so. And stay away from the farm for a while." Marcelle turned and ran back across the lawns.

Nancy saw the doctor's old jeep pull up by the big house. Marcelle was at the door, talking rapidly, hands outstretched, shaking her head.

An ambulance had quickly followed the doctor and Nancy watched it clatter away down the drive. Early daffodils were shooting green sticks out of the ground and the lawns brightened under a fitful spring sun. She thought while the children slept she'd pick some new buds for the dining table. She shoved the loaded pram inside the house, bumping it over the step.

Tom appeared from his study, pipe in his mouth. "What's going on, Nan?' The babies started to cry, tasting the worry in the air.

"We have to have Jeanne back and keep Claire as well. Pierre is ill, the ambulance has just fetched him. Marcelle went with him."

Tom saw Nancy's bewildered look as she unloaded the pram and then tried to lift Jeanne out. The air was suddenly pungent. He wrinkled his nose. "You'll have to change her."

He stood by as Nancy struggled with the baby. "I'll drop her, Tom!"

"No you won't. You've done this before - just be firm with her."

Nancy put Jeanne down on the dining table she hadn't thought to cover up and started to tug at the baby's clothes. The cries became screams and Nancy stepped back, shaking her head.

Tom put his pipe down carefully and picked up a nappy. "Here, for Christ's sake, Nan! Get her changed. Why can't you do this? This isn't my department, you know. Just tell me what to do and I'll help. Let's get it done, Nan."

Telling her husband what to do with the babies was almost more than she could bear, but she let him take over. Jeanne smelt of shit and stale milk; she dribbled down Tom's shirt and then pulled away, throwing her head back and arching her body, making her high pitched, gargoyle noise.

Together they dealt with Jeanne who cried throughout the changing and the feeding, resistant to soothing. She tired quickly sucking at a bottle and between them they managed to spoon soaked rusk into her, taking it in turns to hold her and push the wet mess into her mouth. Nancy changed and fed Claire on her own. Tom went back to his study without a word.

He didn't settle. He straightened a pile of papers, lined up pens and pencils. Nancy's voice came through the closed door. "Please, please don't cry. Don't cry any more; it's alright, it's alright."

He went back into the lounge. The soiled nappies were in a bucket and feeding cups and bottles were strewn across the sideboard. "It's a rum do, all this with *Jeanne,*" he said. He turned his mouth down. "It smells a bit in here, Nan. Can't you clean up a bit?"

The two babies were back in the pram, one at either end, and Nancy was rocking it with short bursts of energy that served only to prevent them sleeping. Her eyes were huge and pale in the dim light of the room, her face tight with panic. She began to breathe rapidly, pulling in snatches of air. Both babies were crying, their voices rising and falling in a jagged disharmony.

"Tom, they won't stop. I can't make them stop!"

Tom looked for a moment and put his hands over Nancy's. He began an easy movement. "Like this, Nan. Slower. Slower. That's it, steady now."

Claire was the first to reach a hiccuping stop. Jeanne, as if not wanting to cry unaccompanied, drew long, sobbing breaths and began to close her eyes.

"We can't have this," Tom said. "I'm going to drive to the village and find Jacquie's house. I'll ask her to come back tonight and stay for a while." He patted the wallet in his jacket pocket. "I'll settle it with her parents. Don't do anything, Nan. I'll be back as soon as I can."

Tom pushed open the front door and held it for Jacquie to go through. He put her bag down and looked around the big, empty room. The pram had been pushed into the far corner near the archway into the kitchen. Nancy was no longer there and the house was silent. The whole space was as littered as it had been before; there was a cold cup of tea on the floor, the smell of nappies and sour milk hung in the air.

"Nancy!" Tom called. "We're back."

He thought he heard something and turned towards the staircase.

"I will go, if I may, *Monsieur* Woods," Jacquie said. Quicker than Tom, she ran up the stairs. In the lounge Tom picked up things, looked around and put them down again. He heard Jacquie talking and Nancy reply. As he went to go up, safe from the chaos now Jacquie was there, there was a sound from the pram. They hadn't noticed it; he assumed Nancy was upstairs with the babies, although what state she might be in he didn't want to guess. He went over to the pram and found Jeanne lying on her back with a cloth tucked tightly round the lower part of her face.

Gently he pulled the material away, damp with saliva. Jeanne's lips and her scar were red from the pressure and her eyes were wide, staring at him. She wasn't crying, only whimpering. He picked her up and cradled her, staring at the wall, not his daughter.

Jacquie bounced down the stairs. "*Monsieur* Woods, I have found *Madame* and Claire. They are comfortable but baby Jeanne is not with them ... Oh!" She came into the room and stopped when she saw Jeanne. "Her face ...?"

"There was something tied round it. She was in the pram."

Jacquie met Tom's eyes for a moment. She held her hands out. "Shall I take her?"

At arm's length Tom gave Jeanne over to Jacquie. He avoided looking at her and thinking the child was his. Why was she flawed? Because of his seed? More likely, something from Nancy's side? Because Nancy hadn't cared for herself in the pregnancy? He glanced at a small photograph of their wedding, neat in its silver frame. Nancy perfect in her plain, white dress, innocent. He had dismissed the old wive's tale about a mother's sin staining the child. How could you tell?

He watched Jacquie stroke Jeanne's face, coo and smile at her. He couldn't imagine doing that and busied himself trying to pick up odds and ends again. Anything to avoid an idea that Jeanne mocked him with her twisted mouth and that this was retribution.

Pierre was in hospital for five days. Marcelle would rise before dawn to get her chores done and start the farm work, chivvying the farm hands in Pierre's absence. She left work lists for Marie, sternly reminded Jacquie to tell her if anything was amiss in the Woods household and then drove the rickety Renault to La Roche to visit Pierre for the precise hour she was allowed. She didn't look over the lawns to the Woods' house.

Pierre came home in a sullen afternoon dark with black clouds driven by the March winds. Tom had driven to the hospital with Marcelle to fetch him home. She had asked him to go with her; her direct gaze telling him that anything he could do to help Pierre was welcome. A small reparation implied.

They got out of the car and as Tom turned to hold out a hand to steady Pierre the rain came in torrents, bouncing off the gravel drive and hissing into the drains.

Pierre winced as he started to walk. "I can't hurry, Tom. Run on ahead."

"That's alright, lean on me, we'll both get wet. Marcelle - you run indoors, I'll help Pierre."

The men made a slow march to the house, arm in arm, their heads bowed against the rain. An old blanket from the car Tom had thrown over both of them clung sodden to their backs.

Inside, their clothes steamed in the warmth of the big kitchen. Pierre flopped into a chair by the range. "Don't fuss," he said, as Marcelle peeled his coat off and served some soup. "I'm alright," he snapped. "All I need is to get my strength back. And don't ask me about the hospital." Marcelle began to say something, then changed her mind; Pierre needed to pretend nothing had happened to him.

He spooned his soup in quickly, wiping his mouth with the back his hand. "Thank God I'm out of that place. The nurses are even stricter than you, Marcelle. And the food ... This is good. Chicken." Then, suspiciously, "which one did you kill?"

"Never mind," said Marcelle, "just eat."

"Someone's fed the dogs?"

"Of course."

Pierre put his empty bowl down and cocked his head. "It's quiet. Where's Claire? Have you got Jeanne today?"

Marcelle's back was turned as she brought out a pie from the bottom of the range. Tom cleared a place on the table for the dish. He could see that she'd heard but she didn't reply. She'd run the house and the farm without pause and her face was pulled down with tiredness. She'd had no time to fuss over Nancy and he realised both women were exhausted. Marcelle, clearly - too much work for one. Nancy? Well, almost on her own with Jeanne and Claire, only coping with Jacquie there. The things women do.

Tom remembered what his father would say: leave it to your mother; don't get involved. Or, my wife will do that. To the young Tom: don't cry, don't be soppy; chin up - that's the ticket. He and Pierre didn't talk about the children or the wives or anything else. "The babies are with Nancy," he said.

Pierre glanced up, a quick look of alarm. *"Vraiment?"* Really? *"Ils vont bien?"*

"Yes. they're okay, don't worry, Pierre."

Marcelle turned round. "It's fine. Jacquie stays with them."

"Certain?"

"Yes, Pierre. Jacquie's a marvel," Tom said. He stood up awkwardly. "I'll get out of your way now." He fetched his coat from the clothes horse by the range. His heavy duffle coat smelled of wet dog. "I'll look in tomorrow," he said. "Get well, *mon ami.*"

Pierre lifted his head in acknowledgement. He began to close his eyes and Marcelle was fussing with plates and cutlery. Tom stopped by the door. "Shall I have Claire brought over to you?"

Marcelle paused, stretching to straighten her back. "Will Jacquie cope for one more day? That would give me time to get him settled." She looked towards Pierre, who was dozing, his head nodding.

"Of course, just let us know."

The rain had stopped as suddenly as it had begun and Tom made his way across the wet grass to his house. The lawn squelched under his feet. He felt sweaty and unbuttoned his coat. Will Jacquie cope? Not will Nancy cope? Not his wife.

He paused before his front door, stealing himself against the mess. Jacquie's here, he thought, it won't be so bad. Everything was tidy and he could hear Nancy and Jacquie upstairs with the babies. "I'm home," he called as he peeled off his tight coat, looking for somewhere to dry it out. He fished in the inside pocket for his cigarettes and found instead an old tobacco tin of Pierre's. He'd taken the wrong coat; he'd go over tomorrow with it. Something else was there as well. A photo of a young woman.

It was dim inside the front door and the lounge was lit only by two table lamps. He put his coat on the rack by the fire and stepped back outside to stand under the porch light to look at the photograph.

If he thought anything, it was that some men carried photos of girls in their pockets, a normal habit from the war years, although he had never done so. He held the photo up, expecting to see Marcelle's face and idly imagined it had been a comfort to Pierre while he was in hospital. The woman was not Marcelle.

She had dark hair in a bob, a black beret set at an angle, a short black jacket and a knee-length checked dress. She looked boldly at the camera, and stood beside a wire fence with one hand resting on the top strand. He knew that set of her strong jaw, that straight back. He'd seen her once the first time he was in France; a glimpse when he looked down the stairs from his attic and saw her embracing Eva Aubin. It was enough for him to want to go on looking; to want her to return. He stared at the photo. He found he couldn't remember what her voice sounded like. He couldn't bear it if he did.

He turned it over. No date, only two lines in a sloping script. *Voici ma dernière photo. Gardez-la avec les autres en souvenir de moi. Catherine.*

Here is my last photo. Keep it with the others in remembrance of me.

Oh, Catherine! He read it again. It might have been the most recent to add to a collection, of course. Or had she thought it would be the very last photograph?

He stayed in the porch, staring out over the dark lawn to the Mill House. He remembered lights flickering on the ground, heard the pilot screaming 'too low! 'Felt the heavy impact as the plane hit the ground and remembered climbing out, rolling into a ditch, thinking that if he could do that he wasn't badly hurt. He remembered gunfire and shouting and betrayal; the cold, damp earth against his face.

They were all dead now - they had to be.

Catherine? He hadn't known she was there that second time. Was she the reason he'd come back here? Not because the whispers about him in England were growing louder, dragging with them rumours of threats of investigations. Not for the country, nor in thanks for the help he'd had after the first crash. For expiation after what happened when the last drop went wrong? Did he think people wouldn't remember or talk? There was that tacit agreement between himself and Pierre never to look back. Had he got it wrong? Had he dreamed up Pierre's invitation to come and buy the house when it was clear he couldn't stay in England? And the Frenchman's comments - barely spoken, little drifts in the conversations that slid meaning between the words - about how he knew why Tom had had to leave.

He pushed the front door open, went in and tucked the photo back in Pierre's coat. Nancy mustn't know. He owed her that much; he owed her for helping him forget.

She was coming down the stairs. She looked less worn, her hair newly brushed. He caught a hint of perfume, warm and spicy after the cold rain. "Hello, Nan. How's things?"

"They're asleep. Perfect. Jacquie's an angel, she has the hang of Jeanne alright. Claire's been lovely, of course. How's Pierre?"

"He seems OK. Tired, but you know … What about a drink?"

Tom took the coat back the next day. "It's Pierre's - I took it by mistake. Do you need any help with him while he's still a bit - not quite right - or anything?"

"It's you who look pale today," Marcelle said.

"Worry about Pierre, not me."

13th May 1951

MARCELLE HAD ASKED her to go and buy extra bread. "I haven't the time," she'd said. "I must spend all morning preparing the lunch. Both Marie and Jacquie have to help me. Pierre is not here, he's gone over to *Loches. Donner un coup de main à quelqu'un*."

Marcelle's voice was hard and angry and Nancy took a step back. Had the Aubins fallen out? "What's that, Marcelle?" she asked.

"To help someone. No one you're likely to meet." Marcelle held the same obdurate tone. "It's Jean-Serge Legros. He would say he's an old friend of ours if you were to bump into him. He expects Pierre to invite him today, but I said no. He's not welcome and Pierre doesn't see the sort of man he is: a mischief maker and a liar. The whole family behaves above its station when they're really all scum. They're all trouble, worse than that in the war."

Marcelle's lips were a thin, cross line as she hunched over the table to write down names of shopkeepers. She handed the list to Nancy. "If you could manage a short walk with the babies to the *boulangerie*? The one at the top of the street, please. His bread is better than that stupid *Lagrange* baker at the other end."

Nancy took the list; getting away from Marcelle in this mood would be a relief although she felt weak at the prospect of wheeling the babies out in the pram along the busy High Street - on her own, all those stares again. She looked round the kitchen as if seeking a way out of her chore, then picked up the shopping bags and nodded at Marcelle.

Red and white bunting hung limp across the street. There were queues outside the two bakers' shops, and a florist had taken a prominent position in the square. A small market, mainly vegetable stalls and one poultry seller, was set up in the *Place de Henri IV* even though Sunday wasn't the right day and the market had been there the day before.

It was the second Sunday in May, decreed by law to be *le jour de la libération*. Victory Day. More people than usual would attend Mass to celebrate the end of the war. There would be a military march through *la grande rue* after Mass. Afterwards there would be families and friends lunching together, everything special.

Shops and houses sported the big French *Tricolore,* some with the twice banded, red cross of Lorraine on the white middle section, showing who had fought with the Free French. Not all, though, and she knew enough now to realise that the village was stuffed with old tensions: between those who'd fought, those who'd resisted at home, those who'd collaborated and pretended they hadn't.

Nancy would have preferred to spend such a fine day in her garden, enjoying the balmy air before the afternoon thickened with heat. She wanted to sit in the shade with a cold lemon drink and do nothing for a while. She resented the cloying warmth of the French spring without an English breeze to lighten it. She missed the possibility of a small shower, the slight comfort of a flimsy cardigan.

Claire was sitting up at her end of the pram. She smiled back at Nancy and chewed happily on a wooden monkey that Pierre had fashioned to help her teeth through. At the other end, Jeanne was propped up by two small pillows; her efforts to remain sitting not always successful, sometimes she flopped down and cried. When she did sit up she would look round with bright, dark eyes and try to smile, her scarred mouth twisting with the effort.

Nancy reached down every now and then to tuck a scrap of muslin around Jeanne's mouth. A good game for Jeanne, to drag it down again, like the peek-a-boo games Marcelle and Jacquie had taught her. Nancy hadn't wanted them to do that, always guilty she wasn't the playful one.

She queued outside the shop and rehearsed her careful French, nervous buying bread on her own. She liked to go with Marcelle when they left the babies with Marie and Jacquie. Marcelle would laugh and gossip with her friends and repeat choice tidbits in slow French to make the village amusing, a play for her to watch. Now alone, she felt curious, hostile eyes on her. Guarded faces noted her foreignness and wondered about her: how she dressed, her manners. She knew what they whispered about; what did the child look like? They wanted a close up view, the detail.

Nancy remembered that when she was little she would wait in queues with her mother enjoying the anticipation of a treat from the shop keeper. An apple or a twist of paper with a sweet in it, handed to her with a wink. Mum chatted to her all the time and made her feel important.

When the war came the queues were very long and there were no treats. Her mother began to talk with women she normally never noticed. Nancy had to stand by, waiting, while her mother chatted with the other women as if they had never passed silently in the street before. Nancy was uncomfortable, watching these borders broken down.

As an afterthought, Nancy was introduced. "This is Vera, Nancy. Say hello. Vera's husband's away and she helps in the garage now. This is Mrs Ellis, her daughter's working in the factory." Nancy nodded politely and then stepped back, thinking of sweets and dreaming of small freedoms she might have as she was growing older.

Here, standing in the shade of the shop's awning, she wished for the reassurance of her parents' ordered household. She wanted her mother with her, not just the brief letters of gossip, the garden and best wishes; hope you're keeping well and your lovely baby is blooming. Home today was the place from where she wrote lies to England. Tom saying, don't tell them. Home was Marcelle's instructions and this endless, fluid chatter, this struggle to understand. The hot streets, the stone house she had to keep, the husband to cook for.

Were she to return to England to live, would she like it better? Did she think that was what she wanted? She didn't know. Anyway, a married woman with a child didn't go back to her parents. Certainly not with ... this child, nor with her shame about it.

Her frowning, distant father, who never spoke about his war which had left him slow and tired, had only said, "Are you sure?" when Tom had asked her to marry him. In reply to her wide smile he'd said, "well, you have yourself a hero. Be careful; you'll be stuck with what you get." She hadn't understood and ignored him.

She wanted to be away with the bread before anyone noticed the babies. She found the French inconsistent. Their social mores escaped her. Sometimes they would be friendly and smiling, yet another time they would almost snub her if she greeted them with any enthusiasm, or worse, forgot to say *Bonjour* before anything else. She felt that even six years after the war, they were suspicious of the English, sometimes questioning her, probing her about her English ways and gossiping behind her back.

"The English," Nancy said when she and Marcelle had discussed their differences, "are more reserved about children. We look from a distance and then ask first to see a baby closer. You French, " she laughed so Marcelle would take this as a jest, "just barge straight in. *O l*à là! Un b*ébé!* You are more ... " she searched for the right phrase. "You are more open with your delight. " She'd seen the women in the street with Marcelle, clustering round, stroking Claire's sleeping face, while she had lurked behind with Jeanne, keeping her eyes down, trying not to be noticed.

"We are all brainwashed into having babies." Marcelle. said. "France is short of children and now especially after the war it is very important to replace the lost. We are always told have more babies, have more babies. It's in the air around us. The government hands us extra money to give birth and thinks it is the true nature of women to deliver these babies and work in the home. Pick up any newspaper - they all bleat about it." She put her arm round Nancy's shoulders. "Maybe it is built into woman's nature, maybe not. I don't know. It is the men who tell us what to do - but these men, they don't push, they don't bleed, they don't wipe bottoms."

"I think in England it is much the same. But we dislike talking so much about such things." Nancy frowned. Babies are supposed to be perfect; but she didn't say it.

Nancy jiggled the pram outside the baker's. It would have been fine with just Claire. She charmed people with her pale skin and fine dark hair. She could hold toys, gurgle and smile, showing off two white teeth at the front, and throw down a toy for any willing slave to pick it up. Jeanne's smiles were ugly, her mouth stitched as if the tailor had been drunk and if anyone was tactful enough to ignore her mouth there was the odour of rancid milk to make them stand back. Nancy tapped her foot in irritation, silently urging the shopkeeper to hurry up, to stop her stupid chattering.

She left the pram outside when her turn in the queue came closer with only two women in front of her. She'd seen others leave their prams outside so it must be alright. Inside the shop the air was fuggy and warm, aromatic with new bread. The girl helping *Madame* had bright lipstick and a thin, sharp look. She glanced at Nancy and started a conversation with the two women in front of her. A rapid fire of anecdotes and laughter between them went on and on. The girl took quick looks at Nancy as if to say, I know you're waiting; I'll take my time.

When at last she came out of the shop, her arms full of long, fat baguettes, the queue after her had formed a circle around the pram. One woman, older than the rest, with grey hair poking out from under a headscarf and with an apron over a faded blue dress, was gazing down at Jeanne. Her fingers were hooked round the muslin she had tweaked from Jeanne's face. Her nails were rimmed with black and her thumb and forefinger were nicotine yellow. She peered up into Nancy's face and then, scowling, looked towards Jeanne again, as if searching for something. A resemblance? A fault in the breeding?

Nancy took a deep breath. "*Bonjour Madame.*" She laid the bread across the pram, released the brake and, nodding at the woman, swung the pram round, ready to go back up the street.

The woman stood close to her and put a restraining hand on her arm. She spoke quietly and very clearly. Her breath smelt of cigarettes. "In my day, *Madame* Woods," she said, "we left children like that out in a draught. It is better that way."

Nancy didn't reply. The pram was heavy and unwieldy as she pushed it away from the small crowd. She kept her back straight and her head up to get through the shame and embarrassment that clogged her feet. Jeanne, then Claire, began to grizzle, their faces puckered and miserable. Behind her someone sniggered.

When Nancy returned with the baguettes she was thirsty and tired. The big skies were a solid, cloudless blue, there had been no shade as she walked back. She put the bread on the kitchen table, took a glass of water from the tap and gazed out to the field that sloped up from the house. It was bounded by hedges at the back and down the left side where an oak tree broke the line of bushes and provided shade. Beyond the hedges cows grazed, overseen by Pierre's old white bull, huge and gentle. To the right was the concrete yard, fenced off but with the gate swung wide open. Hills rose in the distance, tumbling over one another in a blue-grey haze.

On the far left side of the field there were chairs and small tables that would take advantage of the shade from the hedge and the oak tree in the afternoon. Nearer the house, where the ground was level, were four trestle tables, set with white cloths, shining glasses and cutlery. Yellow place mats and vases with white *muguet,* lilies of the valley, made a pretty show. They smelt sweet and sickly in the midday warmth. Bottles of water stood on the tables, wet with condensation.

A small group of men, dressed in dark Sunday best, glasses in their hands, stood talking, their faces close. One looked across at the window where she was standing, then quickly dropped his gaze as if caught prying.

Marcelle was slicing baguettes, turning to tend a pot on the range, calling for someone to take the bread out to the tables.

"How many are coming?" Nancy asked.

"Not too many. There are people I won't invite. They look back to the war and remember my mother. They like to think I'm the same as her; they will make comments, pick up a plate or finger the curtains and ask how my family paid for everything. Then I will speak my mind and the day will be spoiled. So, no, those people won't be here. There are some who were like my mother, of course. They won't be here either."

Marcelle pulled a chair from the kitchen table and sat down, reaching for a small glass of wine. "There would be a whisper of an old story about me; just enough said so they make sure I don't forget the rumours." She shook her head. "All this prejudice and dislike and malice - it sneaks around with the old gossips, clinging to them like a bad smell." She looked up with a mocking smile that finished the subject. "The rest are alright."

Nancy had not heard Marcelle say so much about herself before. She wanted to ask her about these whispers and allusions that seemed to poison the air and to tell her about the woman at the bakery. She wanted Marcelle to make her feel better about the sneering laughter but the babies were restless, rubbing hands across red faces. Saucepans of boiling water were ready on the range, turning the kitchen into a steam bath. Marcelle was picking over greens. She wiped her forehead with the back of her hand and looked up at Nancy, "will you take them, please?"

Nancy didn't reply. She scanned the yard and the field for Jacquie or Marie. She could see neither of them. Near the gate there was the woman from outside the bakery - familiar in her worn blue dress but without her apron, a cigarette in her hand. She was looking around as if searching for someone. She walked to the gate and met another, younger woman, talking close to her face as they both looked out across the field.

Nancy's eyes were wide with panic; she didn't want to be seen by that awful woman. She was safe here in the kitchen and her sudden fear was overtaken by surprise - these women weren't the class Marcelle had as friends. She couldn't mention what had been said now; not with the woman herself here. As she watched the farm truck came in and pulled up abruptly against the fence, its engine stalling. Pierre got out and walked unsteadily over to the two women. The grey haired woman turned to him with her hands on her hips. Well, look at you, her posture said. Pierre shuffled and both women laughed. The second woman put a hand on Pierre's arm and nodded towards Marcelle who was coming out of the kitchen with plates in her hands. You're in trouble.

Jeanne began to howl, that particular, unstoppable wail. Nancy couldn't ask Marcelle anything. And if Pierre had come home drunk there would be a row; she'd be better off out of the way. Sighing, she turned back to the kitchen and began to assemble clean nappies, baby food, rusks, warm milk.

After the lunch the afternoon heat lapped round the field like a viscous tide. The visitors settled into small groups, some over by the hedge, some still in the sun at the lunch tables. More wine was set out and Marcelle wandered around the knots of people, topping up glasses as she went.

Nancy had found the meal tedious and it was a strain to pretend to enjoy so much food. Having charge of the babies put her off eating and both Jacquie and Marie were helping at the tables, serving and clearing. Tom made it easier, quietly eating half her share of the greasy chicken, with its thick sauce of wine and tomatoes, then he had gone to talk with some of the men. She felt as if she had been parked in the shade, like a vehicle not required for the moment. A short distance away three women, whose names she had forgotten, chattered and giggled and upturned empty wine bottles in mock disappointment. Further over, Pierre sat alone in the shade.

"I'll be back for Claire in a moment," Marcelle had said as she headed towards the house. "Just keep an eye on them." Nancy watched her return and begin her rounds again at the furthest side of the field.

The oak tree shaded the play pen beside her. Jeanne was quiet for once, propped up on cushions with a rattle she could wave or put to her mouth. Claire lay on her stomach over a cushion, gurgling and trying to roll off it. When she had rolled and wriggled to her satisfaction she lay calmly, clutching the shabby brown bear she liked to suck for comfort.

Nancy sat in a chair beside the babies. The big house was indistinct on the far side of the field and the heat altered her vision so the long hedge to her right became blurred. She saw Marie walking in her direction, collecting plates and glasses on a tray.

"Marie!" Nancy called. "Can you come over here for a moment."

Marie ambled over, her head to one side. "*Oui, Madame?*"

"Will you watch the babies for me, please. I am going to the house."

Marie set her tray on the grass and peered down at Claire and Jeanne. She shrugged, her mouth turned down. "*Oui, Madame.*" She raised her eyebrows but said nothing more. Nancy walked across the field without a backward glance.

There was a queue for the toilet and the women in front of her were talking too fast for her to follow. The heat seeped into the dark hall, dingy with its brown paint. Nancy leaned against the wall, her flower print dress sticking to her back. She would find Marcelle first, hand over Claire and then seek out Jacquie to take Jeanne. She wanted to get away from everyone here, to go home and take a bath..

She closed her eyes and breathed deeply to allay the dizzy feeling and the buzzing noise in her head.

When she came out the sunlight stopped her seeing anything. As her eyes adjusted to the bright afternoon light, she scanned the field for the tree and the play pen in the patch of shade. People were beginning to leave in small groups, some kissing each other on both cheeks, some waving, others linking arms as they walked away. She saw Tom standing in a group of men by one of the tables near the house, the cigarette smoke vertical in the still air. He was laughing and making wide, open-handed gestures, placing his hand on another man's shoulder to steady himself.

The wine Nancy had drunk made her mouth dry and her concentration foggy. She had only a vague idea of the direction she should take. She tried to remember what someone had said, where she had wanted to be or if Marcelle had told her to do something. She would have liked to sleep. Not the false sleep she had at night, when she lay with open-eyed dreams of England and her mother, but a proper, deep sleep, on her own in her own bed, the soft one from her childhood.

She looked over to the left, away from where Tom was, to the oak tree and wandered slowly in that direction. No one noticed her or called *au revoir!* The friends of the Aubins detached themselves easily from the English couple, or at least from her. Tom seemed to be always in the middle of a group, working his French, handing out cigarettes or pipe tobacco, laughing at jokes the points of which she missed. She supposed she could go over to Tom and ask him to walk her home.

Then Marcelle was running, heading towards the house. She stopped in front of Nancy. "Have you got her?" she shouted. The people leaving on the driveway turned to look at them, the sunlight bleaching the colours from the women's dresses.

"Who?" It was unclear what Marcelle meant. The heat and this odd hissing noise in her head stopped her attending to anything.

"Where's Jeanne?' Marcelle bawled. "Jeanne!"

"Jeanne?"

"She's not in the playpen. We have Claire. But when I came to find you, Claire was alone. Jeanne wasn't there. I've looked round - no one has her."

"I left Marie watching them for ..." How long had she been away? She'd waited in the house for a while. "For a moment. Only a moment. I said I'd be back quickly." She hadn't been quick. She stared out over Marcelle's shoulder to the field, trying to think. They were a long way from the oak tree.

Marcelle held her hands up as if to shake the other woman. "Nancy! Look at me! Jeanne is not in her play pen."

"But she can't - she can't get out by herself."

"No. Of course not." Marcelle's voice rose, shouting at a deaf person. "Where were you? Marie said she saw you walking back and you waved, so she understood she could leave the babies safely. But it wasn't you? Someone must have picked Jeanne up or taken her. Maybe she was crying. We've started searching. Get Tom over here. I haven't told him yet. And the man with him. Claude's from the next village, he'll help.

Marcelle turned back to the field and spoke to one of the farm hands, pointing him in the direction of the far hedge, where a few men were already walking slowly, shoulders hunched, stooping and looking. She fixed her gaze on Pierre who had found a shaded seat and was still sitting with a glass and a bottle. She went up to him and took the glass out of his hand, sloshing the contents on the ground. She slapped her hand on the table and Nancy could hear her shouting, but not the words. On and on. Louder, "I don't care who hears me!"

Pierre stood up. "*Merde! Merde!*"

Marcelle turned away and Pierre made to follow her. She waved a hand at him. "Sober up first. Then come and help - if you can!"

Tom was still talking, telling some tale and laughing. "Darling - meet Claude," he gestured grandly at a tall, wide-shouldered man with brown hair over his collar, who looked Nancy up and down and grinned broadly.

"*Enchanté, Madame Woods,*" he said. Then he stood back, aware of Nancy's distraught state, looking between her and Tom, his face quickly changing.

"Tom, Jeanne's missing."

"Give over, Nan!" Tom shook his head in disbelief, perhaps to clear it. "You're joking, Jeanne can't go anywhere. Someone's got her somewhere."

"Marcelle can't find her and she thinks perhaps someone's taken her."

Tom swayed slightly. "Why"

"I left Claire and Jeanne with Marie for a minute. Marcelle found Claire alone. Jeanne had gone."

"No - surely not. Who would want - oh God."

He stopped. Nancy thought that he might have said, who would want her anyway? No, not you, Tom. Nor me, if we were honest. But we're not.

Claude spoke rapidly in a dialect she couldn't follow. He repeated himself slowly, talking to simpletons. "We will find out how far Marcelle and the others have got and spread out beyond where they are. Is Pierre back yet?"

Nancy pointed, "He's over there."

Pierre was staring after Marcelle who was striding away from him.

"He's not up to much," Claude said. "*Eh bien*. Let's go."

The men moved across the field calling, "*Jeanne! Ma petite Jeanne!*" They walked slowly, stopping to listen and to peer into the hedgerows. Nancy half walked, half ran after them, until she caught up, breathless. Everyone was strung out, looking down, sometimes shouting at each other. Every few minutes Marcelle would hold her hand up for silence, then they all stopped, rigid, listening. Everyone looking for her child. She remembered the grey haired woman at the baker's and later at the gate. What she said: we left them out in a draught.

They had gathered back outside the house. A *gendarme* stood drinking coffee and listening to tales of possible disappearance. He looked tired and as if he wanted to go home. Nancy went into the kitchen to fetch a glass of water. She let the tap run for a moment, holding her fingers under as it became cooler. She felt her heart race and began to catch her breath. She watched the water run from the tap then splashed some on her face and let it trickle cold down her dress, between her sweaty breasts.

She slipped out of the door, avoiding the others who stood in a circle, talking all at once, not noticing her absence. Claude's big, farmer's hand rested on Tom's shoulder.

She walked round to the north side of the house, where the old mill wheel was fixed. It had been enclosed at one time, but all that was left were heaps of brick rubble, damp and weedy. It looked monstrous close up, its rust stained blades still. A disturbed blackbird cracked alarm notes. Water flowed fast underneath the wheel, a dark green artery that went on to pump white over a small weir and then meander out to a larger pool. The stream had been deepened and cleared of vegetation. Mud was piled up on the banks and sprouted rank weeds and ferns. Nancy had heard talk of making a feature of this side of the house, with the ancient wheel and the watercourse, although it was always damp here and, except in high summer, had cold air syphoning along it.

Near the wheel, almost underneath it, rubbish had been moved aside, leaving a narrow path, moist and green, between the water and the pile of debris from the stream; the mud was cracking on top as it dried out. From the space between the stream and the mound of mud and weeds came a tiny cry, a high pitched whimper. Nancy stood shivering in her thin dress as the chill from the water reached her.

She thought she heard shouting in the distance, but it might have been the rush of the stream.

❧

"Call me if they wake," Marcelle said. Marie stood watching Marcelle tuck Jeanne into a cot. Claire was already asleep.

"*Oui, Madame.*" Marie had lost her sullen looks, frightened by ideas about how someone could steal a child and grateful not to be blamed for what might have been seen as her neglect.

Marie had had rare tears in her eyes. "I was sure *Madame* Woods lifted her arm as if to say 'I'm coming back.' *Je suis certaine, Madame.*"

Marcelle nodded. "*Tu te fais des soucis pour rien*" Don't worry.

Marcelle found Tom and Nancy in the kitchen. The heat of the day had not yet dispersed and big room was stifling with the range still warm. Nancy was sitting close to it, shivering, hunched up over folded arms. She looked bewildered, as if she was searching for something and had forgotten what it was. Tom, pale and gaunt in the evening light, stood by her. He had a glass of brandy in one hand and patted her shoulder with the other.

Nancy was saying over and over, "I'm sorry, I'm sorry."

"It's alright, Nan," Tom said, his fingers moving his hair away from his face.

Marcelle gently found Nancy's hand and put a glass in it. "Drink this, Nan."

Nancy coughed at the warmth of the spirit and wiped her mouth with a bunched handkerchief.

Marcelle turned to Tom. "Get her home to bed. Let her have some rest and I'll bring Jeanne over in the morning."

When they reached their house, Nancy began her litany of "sorry" again, until Tom put both hands on her shoulders and looked hard at her. "Stop it, Nan! It's alright now. Jeanne will be fine." He turned away from her and said softly, "and you knew where to look."

"I saw that dirty old woman wandering round. She'd said ..." Nancy wiped tears away with the heel of her hand. "She said something this morning when I went into the village. That it was better for babies like Jeanne to be left ... left out in a draught. She was hateful. She must have taken her to the mill stream. Why did Marcelle have her here?"

"Who knows about the people Marcelle knows. It's not to do with us."

"She shouldn't have let her come here. Marcelle told the gendarme she didn't know who might have taken Jeanne; she's let that old cow off scot free. She must have known."

Later, when Nancy was finally asleep, Tom kindled a small fire for company and sat for a long time with another brandy. He watched the bottom layer of ash glow and piled two thin logs on top, the crackle and spit the only sound in the room.

He tried to reconstruct what had happened but too much wine with Claude fogged his memory. He hadn't seen Nancy after lunch until she told him about Jeanne. Just now she had blamed some woman who had said something dreadful and then blamed Marcelle for having the woman at the lunch. Snatches of conversation from the afternoon came back to him. He'd heard it was Marie who had left the babies unattended when Nancy went into the house. Someone else had said Nancy had left them alone. No one had mentioned the grey haired old woman Nancy had seen.

He'd also heard Nancy had been seen walking around with Jeanne in her arms. Unlikely, he thought. She didn't pick Jeanne up if she could help it. It had been Claude's wife, Yvette, who had apparently seen Nancy with Jeanne. Yvette was as small as her husband was large. She was friendly and funny, with a heart shaped face and large dark eyes. Pierre had told him a while ago, in an unguarded, drunken moment, that if you want to know what really goes on in the village, ask Yvette.

At the Mill House Pierre also lit a fire. He was chilled with the shock of the English woman losing Jeanne and by sobering up. He had ordered the farm hands to do the late work with the animals, laid the fire and fetched a bottle from the cellar. He poured careful glasses for himself and Marcelle who sat beside him. The shadows thrown by the flames made the oak dresser loom like a cliff behind them and the old sofa, covered in tired, blue chenille looked stretched in the dim light as if it could seat a dozen. They sat silently for a while, swamped by the furniture from a different age. They stared at the fire or at the picture above the mantelpiece. The portrait showed a plump, dimpled, blond girl in a pale blue dress. She held a white dove in two hands and simpered at her onlookers, as if mocking them.

"It was the only place we hadn't looked," Marcelle said. "I asked Claude if he'd been round the mill side, but he hadn't. I heard something. Perhaps a cat ... Nancy was there. Just standing there, like stone, staring at the mill race. Jeanne was behind her on the path by the bank. And when I called out, 'Nancy! Pick her up!' she looked as if she didn't know who I was or what to do. I had to push past her to get at Jeanne.

"It wasn't Renée Drouin. She's been a good friend over the years, whatever she said to Nancy. I know she's got a nasty tongue and she hates the English, but she wouldn't touch a child - even one like that."

"What do you think Nancy would have done?" Pierre lit two cigarettes and passed one to Marcelle.

Marcelle inhaled slowly, sighed the smoke out. "I think she might have left her there, pretended not to have found her."

"Just walked away? That path's dangerous; it's dirty and cold, there are rats. It floods when it rains. I wish they had never come back. Tom should have stayed away. Taken his useless bride somewhere else."

"You arranged the sale of the cottage, Pierre. You made some sort of pact with him, set it all *en route*. Why then, if you don't want him here?"

"I pretend, Marcelle. All the time. What he did before ... when I was away. And he couldn't stay in England."

"So?"

"I knew he had to move so he paid. We've started the farm well. I didn't want to live off what your mother left - you know that, especially if I could get a lot out of Tom. I've made a mistake; we could have managed." He stood up and limped over to the dresser and picked up a photo of a dark haired woman in a silver frame. "I'll put this away, somewhere they won't see it. I want to shout at him. 'remember her!' and smash it in his gob."

"He didn't know who it was until after," Marcelle said.

"So he told others. I think he did. I'll tell him who she was anyway, make him look at the coward in the mirror every morning."

"All this bitterness, Pierre. Is this why you disappear over to Jean-Serge? Does he stoke you up with hatred? He's said enough about the English couple, mocks them to anybody who will listen. I hear about it in the village."

Pierre poured another glass of wine. "He says enough about a lot of things. You, for instance. Uppity bitch, he calls you. I'll shoot him one day, miss the fucking rabbit."

Marcelle finished her wine. "Not that again. First you regret Tom coming here. Now the old story of myself and Jean-Serge, that you choose to believe. He never had me and he torments you with doubt because he's cruel. He puts too much wine in your stomach and maggots in your brain. Do you really think Claire is his?"

Pierre looked away from the fire, turning towards his wife who still stared into the flames, her profile etched against orange light. He reached out, a rough hand covering hers. "No."

Marcelle looked at their hands. "What about Jeanne? Who left her there?"

Pierre peered at his wife's face. "You think ... ?"

Marcelle only nodded.

"It's a good job we have Jeanne here tonight," Pierre said. "But what about tomorrow? And the day after? You can't do it all." He shook his head. "Easier if they went but they won't, it's too difficult."

Marcelle poked the fire until a lick of flame burst from the last log. "Nancy can't look after herself, let alone Jeanne. Jacquie and I do more for that child."

They stayed talking long after the fire died and the air grew stale.

"Go to bed," Marcelle told Pierre. "You're done in. I'll check on the babies."

Pierre shuffled stiffly to the stairs and turned back to Marcelle who was picking up glasses and ashtrays. "I'll wait for you."

France, April 1953

IT IS AN early spring afternoon, clear and scented, the sun getting warmer towards evening. A lithe, brown haired child runs across the lawn with a daffodil in her hand. "For you. Mama!" She skids to such a sudden halt she nearly topples over and the pale, blond woman scoops her up and swings the giggling girl into the air.

"I won't be able to do much of this soon," the woman says, putting the child down. "Come on, we'll put this pretty flower in some water." She ruffles the girl's hair. "And we'll put this pretty flower in the bath."

Across the lawn, past some swings that tip in the breeze, in front of a large house, a dark haired woman lifts a child out of a push chair. She finds this difficult as she is growing plump. "It's time to wash and have some tea, then a story," she says. The little girl never takes her eyes from the woman's face and smiles a crooked smile. "Ma-ma, ma-ma," she babbles.

The next day the two women go to the market, shop, take some coffee. It is their twice weekly ritual. Help at home, good girls who can keep secrets, sets them free for this. The sun appears shyly from behind some clouds; it is not so warm today.

"Nearly four months now," says the blond woman. She stirs sugar into her coffee, sips and grimaces. There is fear in her eyes, her mouth is tense. She takes a deep breath. "I mustn't look back. Tom says I must look forward all the time."

"And you are well, not like last time. The arrangement works for us. As for me, I am fine, no hospital for this one!"

"Tom is enormously pleased," Nancy says. "And Pierre?"

"*Bien sûr.*" Indeed.

"Tom says ..." Nancy pauses and blushes and hides her mouth with her hand. "Tom says that it is a good job that the frostbite took only Pierre's toes."

They laugh together like schoolgirls, then return to their

responsibilities. What food to prepare for dinner, which bottled fruit to use for dessert, the quality of a neighbour's goat's cheese. What to arrange for the coming babies, how to tell their daughters about a new brother or sister.

At the big house, Marcelle opens the door and calls, "I'm back!"

Marie comes into the hall with a frowning little girl who tries to tug her hand away.

Marcelle produces a box tied with ribbon. Inside is a small cake with pink sprinkles on top. "Look what I've bought you. Say thank you."

The girl grabs the cake and plonks herself down on the front doorstep. She pushes the cake sideways into her mouth, avoiding her skewed top lip. She doesn't say anything. The crumbs fall into her lap and onto the ground.

At the other house across the lawn Nancy calls, "Hello! I've something for you!" She has a small, coloured box from the baker's in her hand.

Jacquie looks over from the garden where she is pegging out washing. "Mama's home."

The little girl puts a toy down on the grass and runs up to Nancy - really, that girl never walks anywhere. "Thank you, Mama."

"Eat it nicely."

"Yes, Mama."

France, May 1953

THE EVENINGS STRETCHED out. Tomorrow, if it stays fine, Nancy thought, I'll set the table on the patio for dinner. She gave one last brush stroke to her hair, clipped on pearl earrings and got up from the dressing table. Tom had gone down to *La Poste* for the second time today to check if there was anything for him. He'd been agitated recently, and secretive. He was that way sometimes. She knew it was the right thing to do: to put up with these closed off moods, but she failed to get used to them or to the bruised atmosphere in the house which made her breathe carefully.

"Are you alright, darling?" she had said yesterday, feigning carelessness. "You're a bit - well - worried?"

Tom rolled his eyes upwards. "For God's sake! I'm fine. I just hope you are, Nan. You're the one who's worried. Don't go imagining things. You know ..." he waved a hand vaguely towards her. "With the baby and everything."

She hadn't said any more and now she was smoothing down a new, roomy dress as she walked downstairs. She was pleased with her figure, the swelling bump made her feel womanly and she had fuller breasts this time. There was a *daube* in the oven, already smelling deliciously savoury. The house was tidy and some wine opened. This, she thought, is how it is supposed to be. A young wife waiting for a husband to come home. A child upstairs asleep and another to arrive in four months.

She smiled to herself, remembering Christmas Eve. Waiting for Tom to come home before they went over to the Mill House to have dinner with Marcelle and Pierre. He'd arrived and opened some champagne. "A drink before we go, Nan." He stood in front of Nancy. "Close your eyes and hold out your hands."

Obedient, she blindly held her palms up.

"Now look."

She was holding a small box snug in its nest of blue and white ribbons.

"Open it, then,"

"It's beautiful."

Tom draped the three strands of pearls around her neck. They glinted pink and were interspersed with tiny glass beads and rhinestones, which shimmered in the small light of the lounge. Two pearls hung from the clasp and tickled her neck as Tom fastened it. He pulled her back into him, his hands round her shoulders, his face in her hair. "A small celebration of our own now. We're going to be a little late for dinner."

He had been more considerate than ever before, had waited for her. Afterwards, as she lay curled into him, relishing the close afterglow, his confession astonished her. She patted her stomach once more as she thought back. "I had a talk with Dr Jauffret," he'd said. She'd kept completely still, too surprised to say anything.

"You were still not yourself and I went to ask if there was anything that could be done. You know what he told me?" Tom didn't wait for an answer. "The good doctor just said, 'give her another baby.' " He slipped his hand between her thighs; a lingering intimacy. "Now I might have done just that."

She wanted this second pregnancy to be different. She wanted Dr Jauffret to be right and her mind slid away from the shadow memories of three years ago. She had found a way to blank them out. To breathe deeply and empty her mind; with each breath the hurts and the shame from that time would swivel away from her. As if nothing had happened, as if the child upstairs, so pretty and biddable, had always been in this house. Sometimes, when she played this mind trick, as she called it, it didn't work perfectly. An irritation would overcome her. She knew she ought to think and feel and worry about the other daughter. But she would breathe and count each slow inhalation and forget.

Only going out was difficult, almost impossible. She couldn't take her child through the village. Very occasionally she did but then she had to make sure she saw someone to speak to. She would look slyly around, scanning for a familiar face. She would say, "I'm taking

Madame Aubin's little Claire out for her. Madame Aubin is so very busy today."

One whisper of what they had done would bring angry people - who should mind their own business - to the doorstep, shouting names. They would ostentatiously avoid her in the village. This wasn't England, bitterness and ill meaning curiosity didn't ripple through the streets there as they did in France. Disapproval kept to itself in England; it was discrete, passed on quietly behind hands that shielded mouths and with knowing glances. French society was loud with its discontent and disapprobation; it had long memories and had practised calling them out. Old resentments were nurtured and fed, new ones tended carefully.

✨

Tom banged his way through the front door, letting in the fresh evening air. "Nancy! Are you there? Nan!"

"Coming." She opened her arms to him.

He squeezed her waist, kissed her cheek, then her mouth and stood back, grinning. "I've something to tell you." He brought out a long brown envelope from his jacket pocket.

"What? Tell me." Nancy handed him a glass of wine and waited.

He opened the envelope and handed her a letter. She frowned at the fancy lettering of the header across the top of the page. "It's from England. There's a correspondent's position going for one of the Sundays. Based in Paris. They wanted someone in Europe, to interpret European events for the British press. I wrote for it months ago - they want me. We can go now, Nan, while you're still able to travel and set up home." He took a big gulp of wine and snatched the letter back. "Here, Nan. Here's the job description and the salary and they say they'll help with accommodation."

"Move to Paris?" Had she heard him correctly?

"That's right, Nan."

"What about Claire?" She put a hand over her stomach. "What about this baby?"

She saw a sneer cross his face, as if she was stupid. He pointed a finger at her. "You're well, aren't you? Claire can come with us, why not? We'll make such a handsome family - good for my job, a piece of cake with you two pretties by my side. What do we want to do, Nan? Give up our chances? We can give Claire better schooling than ever she'll get in these back woods. Better than Marcelle and Pierre can afford."

Tom stared hard at her. His mind was made up regardless and she felt her new found safety and sanity slipping away. Her new looks, her new child. Take Claire? Suddenly she was forced to think: was she still a pretend child? Not now, surely? Leave Jeanne? But Marcelle wouldn't let Claire out of her sight. Even though it was *Tante* Marcelle now, Claire was watched very carefully from the big house and Marcelle ensured that the child spent a lot of time there. They couldn't go. She got up from the table. "I must put the vegetables on."

Tom slammed both hands down on the table. Glasses rattled. "For God's sake!" Then, "We're going. Or I am."

In the kitchen Nancy stumbled and dropped a glass. She felt as shattered as the shiny fragments sprayed over the floor. She took another bottle of wine from the clay cooler and drank half a glass straight down. There was no decision for her to make, she would have to go. There was nothing else Tom's wife could do. Her mother always followed her father's decisions without question. The way of it.

An advantage stole into her mind: she would never have to be reminded of her great fault in her child; never have to look at Jeanne. She and Tom could make a new life, one from which they needn't come back. Paris, a pretty daughter, Tom's status, the modern apartment, the maids of course. After all, she wouldn't mind running away from here. Marcelle would be alright. She could visit.

She served dinner and touched Tom's hand. "It's a great opportunity. I'm pleased. It was just a shock at first ..." She smiled and hoped to look genuine.

The next evening as Nancy cleared the plates away there was knock on the door. "Stay there, I'll go," Tom said, patting her on the shoulder.

Pierre stood on the doorstep in his blue overalls, silent and fidgeting a little. There was a broken shot gun over his arm and a long, thin dog at his heel.

"Pierre, what's the matter?" Tom frowned at this intrusion. He raised his eyebrows at the look on Pierre's face: the arrogance there, and something else. Even so, it was a cold night and he couldn't forget his manners. He held the door open. "Do you want to come in for a drink?"

Pierre glanced down at the gun. "Don't worry - this isn't for you." He stared at Tom and produced his lop-sided smile, without humour. "I need a piss, where's the bathroom?"

"Up the stairs - you know where it is."

Pierre turned to the dog and held up a finger. "Stay there." He pushed past Tom, leaving a smell of wine and sweat behind him.

Nancy looked at Tom and wrinkled her nose. "He's drunk. And vulgar."

Tom didn't meet her gaze. His mouth was set in a tight, straight line and he started to move some papers away from the table, the details of the promised job and accommodation with a map of Paris included. "It's good thing we're going," he said, more to himself than to Nancy.

When he came back downstairs Pierre edged his feet along the floor and flopped onto a chair at the table.

"What will you have?" Tom asked sharply.

Pierre ignored the question. "Catherine's coming back. She's visiting next week." He leant back and his small smile became a smirk.

Tom carried on picking up papers and tapping them on the table to make them neat and straight. "Who's Catherine then?"

"Pierre's older sister." Nancy sidled up behind him and put her hand on his elbow. "Didn't you know, darling?"

Tom turned to her. "How do you know?"

Then to Pierre, "What's this about?"

Nancy took a step back. "I saw a photo in Marcelle's lounge. She told me it was Catherine. Tom, I thought you knew all about the Aubin family? Wasn't she here in the war?"

"What did she say?"

"She said...she said you wouldn't have mentioned Catherine much."

In the sticky silence that followed Nancy gabbled, "I don't know why, Tom. It was ages ago. We were just looking at photos. You know

- the ones of Eva and Clément. And I just found - and I said, 'who's this?' Marcelle's my friend, I can ask her things."

Pierre stared at her. "What else did she tell you?"

"Nothing. Just that you had a sister."

Pierre turned sly eyes towards Tom. "I'll have that drink, Tom. And I'll tell you both. What Nancy ought to know and what you ought to be reminded of." His voice was cold. "And what we hadn't thought of in the agreement. The past was to stay buried, eh Tom? But it won't stay away, will it?"

Tom pulled out another chair opposite the Frenchman. He leant back, with his legs spread out and an arm hooked over the back of the chair. "You're drunk, Pierre. One glass with us, then go home."

Nancy fetched clean glasses from the dresser and poured wine for them. She fussed about, tidying the table, going back to the kitchen. What agreement? Tom never said ... to do with the sale of the cottage, perhaps. She didn't want to know, she felt this horrid scene was too much. "I'll leave you two men to get on, then," she said. "I don't think this is for ladies' ears."

Pierre stared at her, unblinking. "No. Stay!" He'd commanded the dog like that.

"But I'm tired ..." She couldn't move away from Pierre's eyes. She sat down abruptly and pulled her fingers through her hair.

Pierre settled himself at the table and carefully moved a place mat to one side. He lit a cigarette and tossed the packet over to Tom. "No?"

Tom filled a pipe, not taking his eyes from Pierre.

Pierre took a sip of wine, extending the silence. "You'll remember a night in August, 1943, Tom? You were helping out with S.O.E drops by then, weren't you? Picked because you knew the area from the year before." He nodded. "Specially selected."

He turned to Nancy, dislike on his face. Now he was at the table there was a farmyard smell on him under the wine: cows and dung and dogs. "Imagine, Nancy. The weather forecast was good and the moon was right, then the wind got up, there were more clouds than there should have been - the visibility they'd expected didn't happen - and the rain came horizontal across the fields." He moved his hand sideways with a cutting gesture. "The pilot brought the plane in too low, much, much too low. The group was deafened by the noise. They were waiting in the hedges, ready to pick up the packages. They ran out to light torches to guide the drop even though the plane was nearly sitting on top of them." He took a long drink. His eyes flicked from Nancy to Tom. He stubbed his cigarette out, drank again. "Everything turned to bad then. Either the Boches got lucky or the group was betrayed - I don't know. But they were there and they opened fire. Do you think the airmen knew they were going to die? Seeing the lights, hearing the guns, realising things were going wrong. The pilot tried to take the plane up again but he couldn't do it."

Nancy shook her head and held up her hands. "Wait, Pierre. What's this to do with Tom? He was shot down in 1942 and got away to England. And what you're saying - men died? Well, he's here. And the S.O.E.? What's that?"

"Special Operations Executive." Tom said. "They organised drops of arms and equipment to resistance groups." He stared straight ahead, Nancy and Pierre might not have been in the room.

Pierre poured more wine for himself. "Your hero husband came back for a second visit. You knew about that, didn't you, Nancy? This time only one man survived. The plane dropped and careered across the field into the hedge. It came to standstill on its side, the wing buckled. The pilot was killed instantly, his neck broken. I was told the other man was trapped inside and bled to death. No one stayed to try to help him."

He reached forward suddenly and grasped Nancy's wrist, his fingers like iron bands, his breath on her face. Just as quickly he let go. "They were fortunate, perhaps? They didn't burn. Just crushed and broken and bled out. Not too painful, eh? Not like some."

He lit another cigarette, looking at Tom as he drew on it. "This man I was talking about. The third one in the plane. He managed to climb out and crawl away into a ditch. Oh, Nancy, but your husband is *so* good at getting out of planes. Dropping in from the air, so to speak. While the others in the plane didn't make it, Tom here ... " He raised his glass, "Tom here wasn't hurt, not this time. The plane didn't catch fire so there was no light. The resistance group ran for their lives in the dark, tripping over bushes, slipping in the mud, trying to scatter.

The Germans started running towards Tom's ditch, hunting the others. Tom shone his torch to where he thought the French were running." Pierre waved a hand expansively. "I imagine he took a deep breath and he shouted, *'Da drüben!' Schnell!* Over there!'"

Nancy stood up from the table, not wanting to hear any more. She felt dizzy and had to sit down abruptly. "That can't be true, Pierre. Tom can't speak German. How do you know?"

Pierre stared at her. "He's got enough German to get by, just in case - they all had. Part of the English preparation." Disgust and contempt thickened his voice. "The Germans caught all but one of the eight résistants. Young Leon Labrousse had got confused in the dark; they'd separated and spread out; he was furthest away from everyone. He got behind a tree to hide. He heard these German words called out and saw a torch beam from the ditch light up the other running figures. He crouched and watched, horrified. He couldn't work out why one of the Germans was in the ditch. He didn't dare move. He waited and waited, for everything to be over, for the Germans to come back for their man and find him as well. The silence went on and on and he thought perhaps they weren't coming back. He could hear nothing and planned to move quietly away when the man in the ditch began to drag himself out. Leon heard an oath in English. Leon was sure of it. Then he did move. He slipped away from the tree, crawled under a fence and ran to the nearest farm. He came back with old Georges Patin. Together they got this man to safety at Georges' farm and then over to Marcelle.

"You never asked, did you Tom? You never wanted to know who the men were who helped you then. To say thanks. Who knows what they might have heard or seen?"

Tom's face was grey, his mouth in a thin line. "I don't remember, Pierre. I banged my head when the plane crashed."

"You were not so concussed, *mon ami,* that with Leon's help you were away within the week, as soon as Marcelle could arrange safe transport. You pretended to be perhaps, not very talkative when you stayed on the farm that time. I heard you were quiet after your bang on the head."

The fire was dying and a down draught from the chimney filled the air with smoke. Pierre's dog scratched at the door from outside.

Nancy got up. "I'll let him in, he'll be alright in here." Anything to make a crack in the atmosphere.

Pierre shrugged. The dog stalked in and settled his rough coated body at his feet.

Tom got up and put a log on the fire, poking at it until sparks crackled and spat. He kept his back to Pierre and Nancy.

"I'm grateful. Is that what you want me to say? We've agreed not to look back."

"But it's more than that now, Tom. We didn't know about Catherine then." Pierre lit another cigarette and raised his glass in a small salute. "*Santé*. There's more to come. The Germans took everyone except Leon. They shot all they took except one. They kept Catherine. My sister. They'd been after her for a long time. She'd been part of a communist cell in Paris and then she'd come back to the Loire. The resistance was in chaos down here so she was sent to organise drops and arrange rescue paths. What luck for the Germans! She was interrogated and tortured, then sent to the camps. She managed to hold on until the liberation.

She lives near Chartres these days. Now she's coming back to see the Englishman who betrayed her with his flashlight and his clever German."

Pierre turned to Nancy. His eyes travelled insolently over her body, up and down, pausing on her breasts and her stomach. "My sister may tell you about the camps, maybe not. Maybe she'll tell you how she survived. Women had something to sell there, Nancy, in order to live. The young and pretty ones, anyway. How do you think that makes me feel - eh? Maybe she'll tell you how her health was broken, woman to woman. Too many men, you see. Then you can tell Tom all the fucking details. All the intimate details." He swayed in his chair, the alcohol hitting him suddenly.. "So you'll meet my sister Catherine. My wild, determined, brave, gorgeous sister. Who joined the resistance at the very beginning, who never came home to the house for fear of betraying us - except only once, or perhaps twice - I was told different things - who was always somewhere else, who organised the return of the airmen." He rested his gaze on Tom, as if assessing stock at market. "One airman she shouldn't have bothered with."

Pierre drained his glass and stood up to leave. "I'll bring her round." He snapped his fingers at the dog.

Tom stood up and thrust clenched hands into his pockets. "Don't bother, Pierre. We're leaving."

Nancy took a long time walking over to the Mill House the next morning. She'd lingered over her bath then slowly wandered around her cottage, noting everything: the old faience pottery that Marcelle had given her, with its bright blues and yellows; the sofa from a junk shop, the new cane chairs that didn't match the oak table. She'd instructed Jacquie to begin packing some clothes instead of bathing Claire. She had dressed Claire herself, putting her in a new frock and polishing her little strappy shoes.

Tom had gone out early. She hadn't seen him since he had banged the door shut on Pierre and then gone into his study, slamming that door as well. Nancy had cleared away the dirty glasses and had called through to Tom but received no answer. He didn't come up to bed and when she got up after a restless sleep there was only a note on the table. "Gone to the post office. T."

Marcelle was standing at the front door of the Mill House watching her walk across the lawn. Her eyes rested on Claire who bounced and skipped at Nancy's side.

"*Bonjour,* Nancy. *Bonjour* Claire." Her voice was strained, formal. She raised her eyebrows at Nancy but said nothing more. She led the way into the kitchen and bent down to stroke Claire's head. "Marie is playing with Jeanne in the lounge. They have a new toy to show you. Will you go and find them?"

"*Oui, tante Marcelle.*" Claire ran off calling for Marie and Jeanne.

Nancy followed her. "I'll see what Jeanne's up to."

Marcelle stayed in the kitchen and prepared coffee. "Three years it's taken for that woman to go to Jeanne. Now she's leaving," she told the walls. She knew what had been said, that the Woods can't stay. That Tom should not meet Catherine. She knew they'd take Claire. Give her a better life? Like the children in the war who were moved, hidden, taken to freedom and who kept their lives? No, not like that. It's not the war. She felt her chest tighten: the panic of having to confront a loss, then the short wait for the hurt to start.

Nancy went into the lounge. Jeanne was sat on the floor pushing a toy swing to and fro, with Marie beside her holding a doll on the swing's seat. Jeanne rocked forward to push the little swing and rocked back as it fell towards her. She was laughing, her mouth open and her eyes shining. The sunlight on her face made her skin glow and hid the stitch line under her nose. Her hair was put up into two bunches tied with yellow ribbons that matched her canary yellow smock.

We're doing Marcelle a favour really, Nancy thought. Claire will be better with us, there's more for her in the city. What Tom said: schools, culture, educated friends. Jeanne will always be looked after here. And Paris isn't that far. We can write, swap the children's stories. I don't have to give anything up.

She swallowed and called across the room, "*Bonjour Jeanne!*"

Marie looked up. "*Bonjour* Madame Woods."

"*Bonjour*. Marie."

Jeanne continued to rock, ignoring Marie and Nancy.

"Jeanne, say *bonjour* to *tante* Nancy," Marie said, taking the doll off the swing for a moment.

Jeanne didn't look up but snatched the doll back and shoved it onto the swing, pushing and pulling with insistent energy.

Marie flushed and looked up at Nancy. "I am sorry, Madame. I am sure she will say hello in a moment. She really loves her new toy, like the big ones outside. I think she cannot play with this and be saying hello at the same time."

Claire appeared from searching the toy box in the corner. She'd found a large china doll with only one eye. She offered this to Jeanne and tried to put it on the swing's seat but Jeanne continued to shove and tug as if the other child wasn't there. Marie put one hand on the swing to steady it and tactfully block Claire. She held her other hand out. "We'll find your doll some clothes in a minute, Claire."

Nancy stood and watched the girls. She jumped when she felt Marcelle's hand on her shoulder. "Come into the kitchen, Nan. Marie's fine with both of them. Jeanne is often like that, a bit obsessive with things and toys. A bit fussy. Those swings we put up for the village children years ago, she really loves to go on them when it's fine."

Nancy silently followed Marcelle to the kitchen and thought of those village children; the boys who would be good workers, like beasts; girls who would marry and have children and their lifetimes of housework. Claire would have a different, better life. She hated feeling fearful of Marcelle. Once they were away from *Les Moulins* she would not be so upset nor be worried all the time abut Tom. She accepted a cup of coffee, hunching up and wrapping her hands round it; she was cold from the shock of it all. Everything she had wanted to say to Marcelle disappeared from her mind.

Marcelle went over to a corner cupboard. "This will make you feel better," she said as she tipped a small trickle of brandy into Nancy's coffee. She sat down opposite Nancy and sipped her own coffee. "Pierre told me you are going. He told me what he'd said. Tom has never said anything at all?"

Nancy shook her head. "I thought Catherine might have been a girlfriend once. He's entitled to his secrets of course but not about something like this ... " She drank some coffee and coughed at the sudden warmth of the spirit. "I can't believe he'd betray anyone."

"It would have come out sooner or later. Now that Catherine has written ... "

"Pierre mentioned an agreement? About the cottage?"

"Tom paid for the cottage. That was straightforward. Your husband had other reasons for coming France. You know he did."

Nancy frowned. "No, I didn't, Marcelle. What could he have ... ? It was because he wanted to be here in France with you." She shook her head at the other woman. "I really can't imagine ... "

"Ah. *Eh bien.*" Had Nancy been more acute she might have sensed Marcelle's caution, how the Frenchwoman picked her words. "Also there was ... *un accord entre eux.* It was a gentlemen's agreement between them, as you say in English. Tom and Pierre would put aside the past. There was a visit - Tom came over just after he left the RAF - to make amends, I think. Perhaps, to see this place after the war -although he knew well enough what it would be like. Pierre can be very deep; maybe it was some sort of act of forgiveness on Pierre's part, or some other reason." Marcelle stretched across the table to reach for a cigarette. She fiddled with a battered lighter. "Pierre made mistakes. As did Tom. Your husband was likely to get killed in the flying operations; possibly - no one says this, of course - he wanted to come here to be sorry because he lived. Survivors are always guilty of being alive. And how do any of us make amends?" Her gaze was inward, she wasn't seeing her kitchen and the steam drifting from a pot on the range.

Nancy stared down at the kitchen table. It was scrubbed every day; Marcelle insisted on this. Nancy wanted some of Marcelle's determination, some of her strength to shore up her own when she didn't understand the men here, the place, the past that always nudged itself into the present.

"I'm to be uprooted miles from here, when I've only just settled," she said. She looked briefly at Marcelle. "It's taken me three years to get used to being here. I want to stay, even with ... " She glanced towards the lounge where Jeanne pushed her swings.

Marcelle slowly shook her head. "Oh, Nancy. That is not the truth. Don't we both know? My heart has a weight on it. The weight says anger, with you - you dream of a Paris apartment and a pretty family, do you think I don't realise? This weight has anger written on it for other things too and regret also. For my history, my life before and for what happened to children like Jeanne in the war. I'll take Jeanne for you."

Nancy held her face in her hands, looking down at the scoured table. "It's not my fault," she whispered. "Someone else or some thing must be to blame. The bloody war. Perhaps Tom should have stayed in that ditch like Pierre said."

Marcelle stood up. She collected her cigarettes and lighter and turned to leave. "There's no point, Nancy." The door to the yard crashed shut behind her.

Nancy went back in the lounge and watched Marie play with Jeanne and Claire. She thought she ought to do this. Her baby wasn't what she had wanted, she might love Marcelle's child more. Tom wasn't what he seemed. Nor Pierre. Now the sister. She couldn't bear any more of this - what happened in the war; the misery people endured. Their memories sticking out like half-buried bones through tilled soil. Like Catherine's bones must have stuck out in the camp. She didn't want the images of blood and rape that occurred to her; she should have been protected from them.

The door opened and Marcelle came back in bringing the faint smell of the farm with her; her cheeks fresh air red. "Marie, get Claire's coat," she said. Then, "Nancy, it's time you should go. Just go. But don't forget Paris isn't far."

Rosemary

I KNOW MUM and Dad left St Jacques in a hurry in the small hours, driving out when the village had its eyes closed. Someone was awake and told on them so I found out later this was to avoid Catherine's arrival. My parents said it was Dad's new job that needed him to start very early in Paris. They didn't say I was to be born in anonymous Paris away from the history of Jeanne.

Dad would have been in his element; a specialist correspondent for an English Sunday. A prize for him; prestige, more money, his press card an entry to fascinating circles and the Channel still between him and the men in England who wanted him to ask him questions.

My charming father with his good looks, in his English tweeds and flannels, pleased everyone. Except his parents, apparently. They had thought Mum not classy enough, too provincial to merit their approval. Another burden for her to bear. Did he tell Mum not to concern herself about them? I hope so. Arthur and Marian Woods had decided during the war all the French were cowards so his move to France was frowned upon. I never met my paternal grandparents. Dad didn't bother with them or their opinions except for duty at the occasional Christmas. No one else's feelings mattered very much either; his charisma and manners were just for show. He probably enchanted my mother with a golden promise of a glamorous city, shops and luxurious apartments with lifts and refrigerators, with, of course, the unspoken caveat that the domestic side of life was hers alone. As far as Dad was concerned her main job in Paris was to raise children and to look good when she was expected to.

"There was all this activity," she told me a lot later. "We went to parties, out for drinks, to the theatre. It was so much fun! I had an extra allowance for dresses. Baby sitting was a problem, of course. The maid…" She peered at me, her memory working hard. "Have I told you about the maid?"

"I'm not sure, Mum."

"Anyway, out all the time. And I had to entertain. I wrote to Marcelle for recipes." She rushed on regardless. "Such fun! I noted down the names of everyone who came to dinner, all the dishes I served. What hard work! Do you realise how exhausting it is- this being a hostess?"

"Yes, Mum," I said. What I thought was, oh God, how could she? What about Marcelle? What did she feel about letters from my mother in Paris requesting recipes? My mother with Claire and having fun while Jeanne had to be cared for at St Jacques.

Her tone changed again, the fun lost: sad now, that sudden shift I became familiar with as she grew old. "So wonderful but so tiring. These people! Once they've met you a few times they think you're this discreet English women and they talk to you about all sorts. And I'll tell you, Rosemary, when you get to know people it's like the village all over again. All these whispers: who did what and when, who told on whom. Gossip, gossip. I didn't like it." She laughed abruptly. "Not quite the village though. At St Jacques there were some things not repeated to me, I was still too innocent then. But in Paris - the most important gossip is who is sleeping with whom!"

As I sifted through her moods, her sorrows and her giggling laughter, it was clear that Paris was not the happy place my mother had wanted it to be. It may have been the city of lights but it was also, less than a decade after the war, a city of dark corners and lurking prejudice; of bad actions not forgotten and *soirées* of back biters. For all its similarities, the city, frenetic in its recovery after the liberation, was a very different France from the countryside she had grown used to.

She was by herself most of the time with Claire in the apartment. Dealing with a maid of whom she was almost frightened increased her feelings of isolation during the day. Evenings were better: the social engagements and sometimes quiet evenings in the apartment just with Dad occupied her, even relaxed her. But she was alone always with her fears about this new pregnancy; her terrors of the birth itself and what the baby would be like.

She talked of the small things that upset her. "That lift," she said. "it did so worry me: it was never fixed properly. We were told how lucky we were to have a lift at all but this horrible contraption would creak and groan and stop half way. I had to shout and yell for help and Claire would cry. The *concierge* took her time to get it going, I can tell you. And I had to get past her to get in at all; she'd never help with the shopping. She took far too much money for what she did - most of the time she just sat in her nasty little cubby hole, smoking and staring at me.

And the maid! Did I tell you about the maid?

"Well. She would rearrange my things and she would tell me what to wear. Lay my clothes out and look arch. She'd say how her previous employer had such class and had worn this or that to go out, as if I wasn't good enough for her. A mere maid! Sometimes I was wicked; I hoped she'd be ill and not come."

"You're not wicked, Mum," I soothed. "What about the shops, weren't they exciting?"

"I suppose so. But the women in them - they were only shop assistants after all. You'd have thought they owned the buildings - so stuck up. Just like the maid - they handed you clothes as if you were too stupid to know what you wanted. Horrid, superior little creatures.

"Oh, Rosemary, and let me tell you, the alleyways in Paris. Useful shortcuts I was told. Everyone told me: take this turning or the next one; it would be half the time to get home and avoid all the traffic. They smelt of ... well, they smelt. I didn't dare use them and I always had to walk the long way round." She sounded indignant and although she'd laugh about it these little details pinched her. Her memory shied away from any larger picture. I saw my mother intimidated in the big city, overwhelmed by everyone. Did she ever make the time to wonder about what Marcelle told people in St Jacques? Were there other letters apart from those asking for recipes?

In fact I was born in England, not Paris. Mum travelled with Claire to England to see her parents; a visit long overdue. Mum wanted to see them before she had the baby. Then she became ill. It might have been the return of her anaemia or just her state of mind, always fragile. Apparently the English doctor wanted her to stay put. No one ever said. I've had to guess a lot.

It can't have been easy for my mother, again uprooted. Was getting ill in England and having to live in her parents' home again a time of miserable disappointment, of claustrophobia and resentment? Or did she feel safe there, back with her mother, without the demands of Paris and the great weight of shame that she'd left with Marcelle at *Les Moulins*?

Claire told me something she remembered. We were in a café in *La Roche* before Claire left for university in Aix en Provence. Against Dad's wishes she'd opted for the south and a degree in languages. "Why not Paris?' I asked. "Weren't they planning to stay there?"

"That's what Mum told me but then Dad has this thing; not Paris but London. Definitely not Paris."

"I'm fine with London when my turn comes," I said. "Mum won't be bothered wherever we are, she just goes along with Dad anyway. So are you going to Provence just to defy Dad?"

Claire pushed her dark fringe off her forehead. "Maybe. But Aix does the languages I want. Dad - oh God! - he wasn't pleased. He found out I'd got Pierre to teach me some German. You know Pierre picked up some German during the war? He said he didn't mind my asking because it was a long time ago and he'd teach me what he knew. Apart from the swearing. But Dad minded. He shouted at me. 'I will never hear German spoken in this house!' So I'm going to Aix. I suppose I'm a bit different, I'll go my own way whatever."

"You should have told me," I said. "I could have buttered him up a bit. My pay back. You've always been good to me, helped me out when the parents were being off, looked after me when Mum had her funny turns and forgot about us. You helped with the nightmares as well, you know." I didn't often say anything so soft to my sister but she was going away and I'd miss her. She used to shake her head in mock sorrow at the antics Marthe and I got up to, calling us *enfants terrible* but then baling us out from trouble if she could. Now we would have to try to behave ourselves and keep out of mischief without her.

She looked sophisticated with her hair in a new, angular shape and a tight skirt above her knees. I knew a different Claire of course: I'd spied on her as she was packing and saw she taken Brumas, the toy polar bear she'd had since she was little. She'd rolled him up in her favourite jeans, the ones she'd practically lived in at home, with the patched patches on them.

She laughed and tilted her head in that way she had. "I haven't always been good. I must have been bad when we went to Granny's in England because Mum hit me."

"Never! Mum didn't hit us, Claire. She might have been vague and strange but she wouldn't raise a hand. What happened in England?"

"I'll tell you."

Perversely, for all my curiosity, I wasn't happy to hear things people remembered. It might mean I had to try to work out if I remembered anything and then I might find something horrible. I drank my coffee and wished I'd not asked.

England, 1953

NANCY WAS EXHAUSTED: living with her parents, being pregnant and the constant edginess of keeping three year old Claire from bothering the orderly household wore her down. They were kind. "We love having you both to stay," they said.

It was their house, though. They insisted all meals had to be on time and got testy when their quiet routine slipped away from its timetable. If Nancy didn't make her bed her mother crept in to do it for her, tightening the sheets into straight jackets. Claire's toys were picked up with a 'tut.' She could see her father wanting to get away by himself. When Claire didn't settle upstairs and had to be brought down again, he would yawn and offer his excuses. "I'm for an early night, dear," he said as he kissed his wife and pecked Nancy on the cheek. He smelt of tobacco and tweed jacket.

Once, when he slowly climbed the stairs, pausing every few steps, her mother pursed her mouth crossly. "What he really means, dear, is that he wants to lie in bed reading. He can't read down here now, can he?"

She had not wanted to become such a burden; her child stopping him picking up his book. Her mother was more diligent in taking an interest in Claire but said too often, "Sweetie, you are *so* energetic. Shall we have a little rest now?"

Nancy's guilt and her parents' obvious, sighing efforts to accommodate her made the atmosphere in the house dense and claustrophobic. She fell into the habit of taking long walks with Claire, only to find she became more tired and more breathless as the pregnancy wore on. She'd hoped to retrace some of her childhood paths but the scrub land and the tracks through the fields that she remembered were gone, eaten up by building sites. The old windmill on the hill had gone too. The weather-boarded column topped by its wooden sails had been a delight for her. She thought back to the picnics in a nearby meadow where she lay on the grass dreamily giving each sail a name as it slid through the wind.

Now, she walked the dusty pavements past half built houses and bungalows, with piles of rubble in front where gardens would be made. Her mother always ostentatiously swept away any dust that crept into the house and Nancy brought in even more, together with a fretful child that needed yet another bath.

Her mother would occasionally offer to help. "I'll bathe her and put her to bed this time," Mrs Trowe said one evening when Nancy had flopped into a chair after tea. "You look done in. Come on, Claire, Granny will give you a bath. We might have a story if you're good."

Despite her mother's martyred look Nancy could hear giggles with the splashing from up stairs. Her father looked up from his paper and smiled. They're sweet even to try, she thought. They had raised her in their careful way, trying to keep her apart from the horrors of the war, always consoling her when there was news of battles and bombs, retreats and dead men. She had been enough for them; they had both said that she was their perfect jewel and no other children would come along to disturb their threesome. Now it was disrupted again.

When she left home to marry Tom they got on with their lives. They wrote, or rather, her mother wrote and sent father's best wishes. To begin with, she missed them a lot in France. After three years, the missing was merely weak nostalgia and a gulf grew, not least because she kept a secret from them left behind across the Channel. The gulf was still there; she wanted to have the baby and get away.

She had still been vomiting when she and Claire were due to return to Paris. She'd seen her parents' doctor. Old Doctor Tindale had retired and this Doctor Smythe was better tempered. He pronounced that all was well with the baby but he advised her not to travel. He didn't have any medical notes from France and accepted Nancy's mild statement that her first child had been a normal birth. He could see there was nothing wrong with Claire.

"She's asleep," said her mother from the kitchen, filling the kettle and rattling cups. "What a good child she is - no trouble, just like you were. I hope this one will be just as good, but you never know, do you?"

Nancy didn't reply. No, you never know.

"Claire said something strange when she was falling asleep," Her mother continued.

"What?" Nancy frowned.

"She said - it sounded like - 'I think I have two Mamas. In France there are two of them.' "

"I can't think what she means, Mum. I'll go and ask her." Nancy stood up, placing her mother's *Woman's Own* carefully on the table.

"Oh, don't bother her now, she's only little and probably just got muddled. You live quite near the ... what's their name? In France. Next door to you. Don't worry, dear."

Nancy was already walking up the stairs.

Claire had fallen asleep clutching the white polar bear Granny had given her. "It's all the rage for children over here," she'd said.

Nancy sat on the bed and shook Claire. "Claire wake up. What did you say to Granny?"

Claire peered sleepily at her. "Nothing, Mama, nothing." Saying 'nothing' often enough meant Mama would go away after a while.

"No. You told her you had two Mamas."

"I don't know. Nothing, Mama."

"Never, ever, ever say that again. Do you hear?"

What Mrs Trowe heard, listening at the foot of the stairs, was her daughter hissing loud words, the sharp sound of a slap and a child sobbing in shock.

The next morning Mrs Trowe didn't speak to her daughter. Claire was a buffer zone. Nancy avoided looking at her parents, fussing over Claire until the child irritably pushed her away.

Lunch was an endurance test. "Claire, sit up straight at the table, please."

"Claire, do what your Mummy tells you."

"Claire, eat nicely please."

"Claire, best manners for Granny."

When Nancy took Claire out for another walk Mr Trowe took his wife a cup of tea and said, "this has got to stop. What's going on - why can't you talk to each other? Both of you have to get on together. She didn't mean it, I'm sure. Don't let it all worry you, dear."

It stopped when Nancy went into labour a few days later and her mother was too busy to keep up her disapproving airs. The new baby arrived safely, if messily, in the spare room.

"You have a beautiful granddaughter," the midwife said to Mrs Trowe. She bent down to smile at Claire. "Mummy says you can see your little sister now."

Claire thought Mummies with new babies ought to be pleased but her Mum had tears like rivers running down her face.

"Look, darling, your baby sister. Isn't she perfect? "

Tom arrived a week later bearing flowers and instructions to start packing. Nancy was sitting in the living room, holding the baby asleep in her arms.

"Hello, Nan. Couldn't get away before - you got my telegram?" He bent down and kissed her cheek. He handed her a fat envelope. "Tickets. We're flying back to Paris this time. The job can't spare me for long and I'm on tomorrow's flight. You're to come over a week later. Oh, and by the way, there's a new apartment. The details are in there. You'll find it easy enough." His eyes lingered on the small bundle Nancy nursed. "Everything's fine?"

Nancy took the papers without a word. "We're just fine, Tom. You can see how well we are." She turned Rosemary slightly towards him.

He shook hands with her father, accepted a cup of tea and stood awkwardly with Nancy's parents. Yes, the baby was lovely. The weather not bad for the time of year. Pleased Claire has been good. He said a few words about the new job; better opportunities, wonderful over in Paris for the children, we'll be able to come back often.

Nancy's parents looked suspiciously at the set of tickets and the important looking papers she held. Then Mr Trowe found something to do in the garden and Mrs Trowe went to prepare lunch.

Rosemary

MY MOTHER HAS been dead six months and I sit in her particular chair in the lounge; a high backed one that puts your feet up for you at touch of a remote control. I used to sit opposite and try so hard to find out about her life. A tiring enterprise which only lasts forty minutes or so until she is sleepy and I am restless. I don't want to think of Mum as an old lady and I need to walk in the garden instead.

She tells me about her flight from London Airport to Paris. "The stewardess, well! Such a short skirt - all the rage then I suppose. These high heels, she could barely move about with drinks and little meals. Lots of make up ... "

"Mum, didn't you wear short skirts then? Lipstick, heels?"

"Well, yes." Mum looks straight at me, not laughing any more. "She was just so glamorous; I wasn't up to her standard. I felt really insignificant. I wanted to ask her about the colour of her lipstick, where she bought her shoes, but I didn't dare. She was so lovely and made such a fuss of Claire, asked her name, found her a cake with icing. You, Rosemary - they looked at you and said what a beautiful baby! You were - really - just such a pretty baby."

It is implied I'm not so pretty now; middle age isn't quite the same. Mum changes again, begins to look a bit vague. "Passport control was alright as well. Your father said it would be."

"What's that about, Mum?"

I get only a sideways glance at this and I get up to make tea..

Now, in her chair, with her voice in my head, I have a small leather writing case on my lap. In one side are tucked theatre ticket stubs, cards for restaurants and hairdressers, a faded flyer for an exhibition, a thank you card for something. The half written letters are in the other flap of the case. The all have her parents' English address and begin with *Bonjour Marcelle* in her small slanted hand.

These are fragments, pieces of ancient, unfinished manuscripts.

I hope all is well with everyone at Les Moulins and I have something to tell you ...

We will soon be back in Paris and Tom says we are going to stay ...

We are to live now in Paris all the time and we are going to have a new apartment. Tom won't tell me why we've had to move. I will send you the address. Please don't be angry...

I have never been able to lead Mum to a point where she would talk about Marcelle and this strange arrangement they have. How do you write a letter saying you're going to live four hundred kilometres away with someone else's child and stay there.

And Marcelle? Had she been led to believe my parents weren't intending to stay in Paris? That Claire would be returned to *Les Moulins?* Mum - or Dad, for that matter - might have said, 'Look, there's an electric railway now. You could visit.' Even, 'We'll come back and see you.'

Marcelle or Pierre might have written, 'We'll come up to Paris.' Although that would have been the more difficult undertaking, leaving the farm and the heartbreak of returning without Claire.

I don't think any letter was sent; Claire's stay in Paris was uncontested.

Paris, 1953

WHEN TOM GAVE her the documents to fly to Paris he said, "It's a piece of cake, Nan. Like it was on the ferry coming over, it'll be the same at the airports. No, don't ask me again where they came from. Don't stare at them when you hand them over. And for God's sake, Nancy, smile!" It was easy: she managed her prettiest smile, she remembered her French well and the men at the passport controls for London Airport and Orly Airport barely glanced at her name and and that of her daughter Claire Woods.

The new apartment appealed to her; it had taller, lighter rooms; there were no dark corners where her fears could lurk and she knew the address was better than the one before. A huge refrigerator muttered to itself in the kitchen and the chairs and tables were modern with stick thin legs posed like starlets. A television in the lounge flickered to invite Claire and Rosemary to stare open- mouthed.

She set about erasing the masculinity of the place. Tom had found the apartment a few weeks before and had arranged everything with a stark, military neatness. He ordered the furniture and the new, terrifying electrical appliances, and perfused the atmosphere with pipe smoke. The rooms had a woody scent from tobacco, with notes of aftershave and cleaning fluids. There was an unopened packet of *Dux* waiting for her on top of a bulky and intimidating washing machine. Tom had sent his laundry out; now it was hers.

The new maid was Sophie. "I asked around," Tom said. "Someone in the newsroom had used her before and she's supposed to be very good." As if she was a new kitchen gadget.

But Sophie was as superior as the last one, eager to help by telling Nancy what to do. There was yet another concierge sitting still as stone in her little kiosk, smoking and looking and costing too much.

Nancy had no one to complain to. If she had, she might have said she found her husband unreasonable and irritable and the Parisians overbearing and dictatorial. The neighbours in the apartment block were seldom seen or heard. Those that she did see occasionally were, like good children, always polite. They each had their own particular distance from her, never very close, across which they would nod or reach to shake hands.

Madame DuPlessis was next door. Nancy planned a small campaign of approach. She noticed the time *Madame* always returned from her morning walk with her dog and was on the stairs ready to ask *Madame* if she would take a coffee with her.

"*Avec plaisir.*" Madame DuPlessis was short and stout and held her chin high as if always stretching her plump neck. She tucked her small dog under her arm and sailed into the apartment with a curious and obvious gaze.

"I am delighted to *pratiquer* my English," she said, sitting down promptly, reminding Nancy of a new cushion on the sofa.

Nancy had thought it would go down well with her neighbour if she offered something English. It would be of interest and, besides, she wasn't up to the fancy French *patisseries* which she always left to Marcelle or the clever village bakers.

"*Madame Duplessis*, please try the Victoria sandwich." Nancy held out a plate of neatly cut sponge. She got up - too quickly for good manners she realised. "Excuse me, I've forgotten the napkins."

Her visitor ate quickly. As Nancy returned *Madame DuPlessis* licked a finger theatrically. "Madame Woods, your cake was absolutely delicious." Her dog, settled like another cushion at her feet, had a smug expression on its squashed little face. Nancy saw a minute crumb on its whiskers.

Tom had been cross, nearly shouting, when she related the visit from the neighbour. "I wanted to get to know her," Nancy said. "It just didn't work."

"Did you tell her anything about me?"

"No. She did ask but I wasn't sure what to say - only that you wrote for a paper."

"That's enough and no more. Look Nan, stick to your own kind. Talk to the English wives you meet about pastries and dresses and so on - not about my work."

Nancy rarely met any other 'English wives' to talk to. There were a few who went with their husbands to jazz clubs where the music precluded any conversation. The Parisienne women were more sympathetic to her and made efforts in slow French or hesitant English to engage her on preferences for clothes and make up and food. She made an extra effort with red lipstick for them. Tom's colleagues whom they met at dinners were formal and appeared kindly. Or patronising and evasive if she ventured any question about the newspaper.

She was surprised to find so many Americans in Paris. She made fleeting acquaintances with some of the wives; meetings for coffee or walks in the park. They called her 'honey'; her girls were 'so cute.' But she was shy with them and they were always leaving the week after next; any proper friendship didn't have a chance to put down even one root.

There were parties: birthdays, engagements, leavings and arrivals, impromptu get-togethers. Men and women remarked on the theatre or the weather and how to enjoy the best of Paris in each season. Nancy would stand at these gatherings, almost at attention, glass in hand and wearing her most recent best dress. By some osmotic process she was barely aware of, she knew who to talk to and who to tactfully avoid. Tom dropped little instructions in her ear every now and then. "Don't bother with him darling, he's such a bore." Or, "Go and see Patrick over there. You'll like him, he's good fun and he doesn't understand much about politics." Nor did Nancy. She had tried to read the newspapers to glean some idea about the French government but found Tom didn't approve. She preferred her magazines anyway. From the little Tom said, Nancy knew that these were fluid times, many opinions washing to and fro like tides; how to even paddle was beyond her.

As Paris flowed around her she found thought more often about rural France and *Les Moulins*. The countryside and the air. Marcelle her solid bridge into French life. She'd almost forgotten Pierre's cruel tongue and began to miss him with his strange ways and his sudden flashes of compassion. Once she found him in tears, his breathing ragged, a gun in his hand. The old dog whose back legs had gone was dead at his feet. And he loved Jeanne, she knew that without ever being told.

They spent their first two Christmases back in England. Tom's parents issued royal commands and called them back two years running: chances for Tom to ingratiate himself with his disapproving family. They'd seen Nancy's parents as well but then Tom decided that they'd done enough duty in England and he wanted to be at home in France for the season. Nancy agreed of course, no matter that she was confused about exactly where home might be.

Christmas in Paris glittered and sang and ate and drank its way through the dark December days. The restaurants courted their customers with patés and game; opera cakes, macarons displayed like rainbows, proud, glossy chocolates. Nancy longed for something fresh and simple like Marcelle's spring vegetable soup or a light, aromatic *bouillabaise.* She wanted some space, away from the dirty heat of the city.

The day after Christmas the kitchen sink was piled high with dirty dishes, greasy wine glasses lined up beside it. Both the oven and the refrigerator were full of left overs to be made into a Boxing Day meal.

Nancy looked bleakly at the mess, supposing she'd have to get down to it. Sophie had taken herself off for the holiday, saying she would be back the day after Christmas. Nancy had woken with a terrible thirst. She drank a glass of water and her throat felt as if it had been peeled raw. Breathless, she could barely swallow.

Claire wandered into the kitchen, rubbing her eyes and smiling. "You said something special for breakfast, Mummy."

"Did I?" Nancy whispered.

"Yes, you did. It's holiday, you said."

"In a minute darling, go and play for a while." Nancy pulled her robe tightly around her and shivered. When she went into the bathroom she saw an unhealthy flushed face shiny with sweat.

She heard the girls arguing, then a scream of temper from Rosemary. "Mummy, Claire's taken my banjo!" Good, thought Nancy, maybe Claire will break it. I hate the awful twanging. It never stops. The child size banjo had been a present from Rose, one of the American wives, now in the States, safely away from its ear-bursting assaults. Rosemary loved it and yesterday had produced an endless, tuneless cacophony until Tom shouted and the child had to be distracted with *bonbons.*

There was a shout of outrage from Claire. "She's got Brumas!"

The usual contested object: the much-mauled and grubby bear her mother had bought. Nancy tried to drink some more water and put the kettle on. Tom emerged looking frowzy, tying his dressing gown around him. "What's going on, Nan?" Dark stubble made him look fierce and unkempt. "Can't you keep the girls quiet?"

"I've got a sore throat," she croaked. Her voice didn't seem to belong to her. "Tea or coffee?"

"Coffee, please. God, you look awful."

Tom watched her fill the cafetière with hot water and find cups to wash from the Christmas Day wreckage. "I'll get dressed," he said.

He came back into the kitchen freshly shaven and smelling faintly of sandalwood; looking smart and English in a new tweed jacket. He stood to drink his coffee, sipping quickly. Nancy sat at the kitchen table with trembling hands around a cup of tea, a packet of Aspirin in front of her.

Tom cast a stern glance towards the sink. "Where's Sophie?"

"I don't know."

"The girls are wrecking their room, you'd better do something about it. I've got to go out for a bit. Have some tea, you'll feel better soon."

"Where are you going?"

"Someone wants me to cover a meeting at ten o'clock;"

"On Boxing Day?" She was answered by the front door closing.

The girls had quietened down, playing with a large wooden jigsaw of the Eiffel Tower. She started to pick things up in their room and told Claire to help Rosemary wash and dress. The banjo was tucked under Rosemary's arm and Claire had regained Brumas.

"Come on, bring your very favourite toys and that box of chocolates from the sideboard. It's new game for Boxing Day: we'll all stay in Mummy and Daddy's room for the morning." She crawled under the bedclothes, folded her candlewick gown tightly about her and waited for the aspirins to stop her shivering.

She opened gluey eyes to find Tom shaking her. "What's the matter, Nan? Why aren't you up?" He fetched her some water, walking unsteadily across the room.

"What time is it?"

"Four o'clock? Something like that?" He leant with his hand on the wall. His mood had softened; he helped her take more aspirin and began to clear up. She heard him talk to the girls and ask Claire to run a bath for them.

After the holiday Tom found a Doctor Bodin, a tall, thin man with a hesitant manner who frowned intently down Nancy's throat, took her temperature and left her with some white tablets of penicillin.

The next few days seemed anonymous. Claire and Rosemary were restless and Tom was absent for long hours. The first day of the New Year Sophie returned without apology and took over the apartment. "You are able to go out now, *Madame*," she said. "You look pale, if I may say so. The fresh air will be good for your health." She helped Nancy bundle the girls up in winter coats. There was a sprinkling of frost in the park. "Like icing," Claire said. Snow came the day after, painting the grimy pavements white and and this time Sophie took the girls out to catch snowflakes in their open mouths and complain there wasn't enough snow for a snowman like the one they'd seen on the television.

Nancy decided to tackle the drifts of papers that had washed up on the bureau over Christmas. A pile for Tom and two for her. A short letter from her mother hoping all was well. Her parents now had a Mrs Granger coming in every day to help. For a long time Nancy had wanted her shrinking parents to bring in someone to help; to keep an eye on them as well as give a hand with the housework. She hoped Mrs Granger was honest and kind; at least the bathroom might be cleaner; her father was getting less and less particular. She felt a twinge of guilt at not wishing to return there for a while. The last stay with them had made her want to run and stretch and push the walls down.

The second letter came with a New Year's card from Marcelle. Few letters had come from the Loire. Before opening it, Nancy took out her leather writing case where she stored the small history of Marcelle's letters.

The very first one had arrived shortly after they settled in the new apartment. Nancy set it aside for a week, not daring to open it. Central France seemed a thousand miles away from the city, yet Marcelle's condemnation and fury could travel easily across half the country. She had waited until Tom had banged his way out to another newsmen's meeting and poured herself a glass of whiskey before slitting the thin envelope.

It was brief. "*Bonjour Nancy. I understand. I do not judge you. Just look after Claire. I also know you will return to us. A matter of time, Nancy. Cest tout.*"

There had been a few other, friendlier letters, saying little, as if they were acquaintances keeping lightly in touch. Nancy was always worried about much she should write back about Claire. She included small pieces of news: an outing, a special lunch with the children present; that the girls grew bigger and did well at school. She related what she had learnt about Sophie's family - how she felt sorry for the girl after all. She wrote about *Madame DuPlessis* and her dog. She said she had given up English baking.

Now she slit the envelope open with the anticipation of a child at Christmas. The card showed a tipsy cherub reclining in a champagne glass, her plump legs dangling over its rim. The letter with it was longer than the others had been. Marcella's thin, dense, looping writing was dense told about events on the farm and how it ran: more cows, a better market for the poultry, they had bought some land from the son of Pascal Debarge because the family was moving to the town. The Aubins weren't going that way; they were staying on their land.

Pierre was well at the moment. Marie was getting married - not a moment too soon, everybody knew why. The new baby, Marthe, was three years old -imagine Nancy! The same age as Rosemary and it is certain they are both charming, sweet and advanced for their age.

A tiny photograph was enclosed, not mentioned in the letter. It showed Marcelle sitting outside on the patio with Jeanne in a chair beside her. The sun streaked across Jeanne's face, making a white band that hid the scars on her mouth. The child had grown, she looked bigger than Claire. Marcelle smiled at the camera and was plumper than Nancy remembered. She sat down and stared at the photo. Picture and writing blurred and there was a tug inside her, as if she'd mislaid something precious and knew - absolutely knew - she wouldn't be able to find it. Her breathing trick to shut down her rising anxiety didn't work. She didn't like these unsettled feelings: her body tense and her pulse fast. She sometimes thought she was managing here, learning to enjoy the city; the panic told her otherwise. She imagined Marcelle's new child, Marthe. What were they doing? What was happening to Jeanne? Surely Marcelle would have mentioned any more operations? The surprise that she wanted to know made her cry.

She reread part of the letter. *Things are changing here, the movements from Paris reach down even to our little village and the small towns around us. There are so many goods in the shops that we haven't seen for many years, we are able to have a new tractor. It is called* Le Percheron. *It is a big horse! The Germans gave our government the model and told us how to manufacture it. The huge wheels are bright red so they remind me of all the blood of the war. How does one get over it?*

Then again, Nancy, you should see my new best dress! I'm sure you will know all about the latest dresses in Paris - you can tell me!

So we can sell more and buy more. But France has been baled out financially by America. Do you ever talk about that with the Americans in Paris? I feel sometimes that France has been bought with American money. Do you see any Americans? Or talk about politics with anyone in Paris? What do you hear?

Don't forget your country friends.

Nancy folded the letter away and roused herself as the children rushed in, breathless and laughing with Sophie. Tom followed close on their heels. "Hi everyone, I'm home."

Claire and Rosemary ran up to him, dropping their coats for a scowling Sophie to pick up. "Daddy! Daddy!"

"Lift me up!"

"What have you got for me!"

Nancy winced. We've all been bought.

He pecked Nancy on the cheek. "I'm home to change, then out again. I'm starving, what about a snack?"

Tom emerged from the bedroom in his tweed jacket and flannels. He said when he dressed like that he appeared more honest than when he wore grey suits like all the other newspaper men. This Englishness encouraged people to talk to him. "It's my English look, Nan," he said. "The way my accent smoothes the way is just wonderful. They laugh at what they call the 'British manners.'" He squared his shoulders and made her a little bow. "Then they'll tell me everything and forget I'm the press man."

Nancy walked into the kitchen where Sophie was slicing a baguette. "There's post for you," she called, nodding at the metal table that was Tom's desk in the corner of the room. Marcelle's letter was in her pocket for later.

Tom thumbed through the pile of envelopes, his pipe in his mouth. He opened one and looked up, waving a cheque at her. "Freelance money, darling. There's a new coat for you on this."

He went through the rest carefully, putting some aside and some in the waste paper basket. One letter held his sudden attention. He placed his pipe carefully in the ashtray. Nancy saw the rigidity in his neck and shoulders.

Sophie walked in with a tray as Tom stood up and pushed past her, tucking the letter into his jacket and grabbing his hat. "Back later." Nancy and Sophie stood still and the front door slammed.

Nancy looked at Sophie and rolled her eyes. "Is he going to come back for dinner?"

"I don't know, Madam."

"We'll expect him anyway, perhaps about eight o'clock." She talked to Sophie about food: chicken basque, a favourite, some brie, chocolate tart to follow.

She saw the children to bed without a story, merely *bonne nuit*.

"*Vous êtes distraite, Madame?*" Sophie asked.

"*Non, non. Ca va.*" All well. "*Vous pouvez rentrer chez vous maintenant.*"

After Sophie had left she put on a full skirt and a flimsy top that Tom liked and choose Dior perfume. She found the envelope he'd left behind; there was no address, merely typed TOM WOODS.

He came home at half past seven and went straight to the sideboard to pour a whiskey. "Want one?" He raised another glass.

"OK. A small one." She was working out the best way to ask him about the letter and how to navigate his fluid changes of mood.

He was mostly silent during dinner, ignoring her hesitant start to any questions by saying the chicken was good. Nancy tried a direct approach. "That letter, Tom. What was in it that worried you so?"

In answer, he tossed a single sheet of paper over the table to her. The closely typed spaced lines made it look mean.

"Who's sent this?" she asked. "You're English for God's sake - you flew with the RAF! You were never a collaborator! How could you be?"

"No. Never. But that's the latest fashion." There was a sneer in his voice. "I don't know who wrote that. I can guess. Maybe. It ought to be signed a well wisher." He pushed his plate aside and leant back. "Twelve years since the Germans surrendered Paris and still it goes on. Someone's got me in their sights, they want the communists out now, but they all feel too guilty to do that; the commies were most of the resisters. So it's not done like that. Quickest way isn't it? They can't get you out because of the party so suddenly you're not a commie but a *collabos.* Then you're a game bird for the collaborators' hunters guns. The officials aren't involved; plenty of others do it for them. Whoever wrote it knows about two articles I've written. They're not published yet, I've been waiting for the right time, the right climate if you like. I was going to wait for things to shift a little, to make some money out of them."

"What climate? They can't accuse you ..." She stopped, stayed very still.

"Look Nan. The newspapers aren't interested in facts. It's all say-so and slant since the bloody war."

"You mean, Tom, you were just going to make money out of all these ... what? Articles? They're not proper news?"

"Opinions, not hard facts. Someone told me the British had no philosophy - well the French don't do anything else but their fucking philosophy - so why not make a bit out of it while we can. They've got to hate the commies because America does - it's American money that pays here. The Yanks tell us it's a cold war with the Russians now. My ideas are showing that up for the rubbish it is - just bloody paranoia - and my the pieces will sell well to the right people.

Yes, I suppose I'm a fellow traveller. A sympathiser, if you must know. You wouldn't understand." He lit his pipe, drew on it, pointed it at Nancy. "I don't know how they were found. I might have been stupid - left carbon copies in my desk, someone could have picked the lock." He picked up the letter and waved it at her. "Someone's got hold of something, anyway. I've been to meetings to find out things, there's a snitch from there, perhaps."

"You're like a spy!"

"No, Nan. We all just weave and duck a bit here and there."

"What will happen now?"

"We'll go back to *Les Moulins*. I'll resign from the paper, go free lance."

She fingered the letter in her pocket. "Are you sure?"

"What are you worried about, Nan? The money? For all your complaints about Paris, you like that well enough!"

"No, Tom. It's not that … "

"Start to pack up. We're going."

She thought of *Les Moulins,* where she could be, if they hadn't made their home in Paris with its glamour and its conspiracies. Marcelle would be there to help her again. She had asked if they talked about politics, mentioned American money. She knows, Nancy realised.

Tom was pouring himself another whiskey. She held her glass out, "Top up, please. I'll tell Claire's school tomorrow that she's leaving."

She went into the girls' bedroom to decide where to start with their things. Tom was on the telephone. She wouldn't tell him about Marcelle's letter. It didn't matter; they were going back.

Rosemary.

I WONDER NOW if either of them ever gave a thought about Claire and me. Or about Marcelle, whose child they had spirited away. What had Marcelle told people about how she came to have the English woman's daughter with the split lip? Perhaps, after Paris, my mother thought it was alright as long as she returned to *Les Moulins* with what did not belong to her. And Marcelle would look after her again. The move was all about where Dad decided he had to go; then Mum got to live back in rural France without doing anything. I have never had any sense that they worried about the disruption to a six year old and a three year old who were always hushed and only half-glimpsed and half-heard the dramas.

I plundered Claire's memory from that time to work out how they came back. Claire remembered folding clothes with Mum, the suitcases gaping open on the floor. She heard a furious thumping at the door and peeked out of the bedroom to see Dad open it to two men who filled the narrow entrance with their heavy shoulders. There was shouting. Dad saying, 'No. Now look … Give me an hour." He slammed the door hard on them.

Claire told me Dad pushed her out of the way and put his hands on Mum's shoulders. "Not a word, Nan," he said. "Keep out of it" Dad dragged his jacket on and banged through the apartment to go out.

Claire snooped and pryed as much as she could. She saw the big, bulky men come back, their raincoats belted tightly and their faces hidden by trilby hats. She watched Dad give one of them a fat envelope and the man's huge hands shuffling francs like a pack of cards. She remembered the smell of papers burning in the crystal ashtray and black bits floating up to the ceiling.

When I helped Mum sort out Dad's things in that short interval after his death and before she herself slipped away, I found his party card kept in his desk all these years. A tatty little thing in a tired, red cover. My frail mother didn't need such a reminder of the painful parts of the past, so I palmed it it and took it away with me, treading in my father's footsteps like a second rate spy myself.

Mum was bound to Marcelle as well. Did she feel safe in France with Marcelle to help run her life? What were they all like together when my parents returned from Paris to *Les Moulins?* Mum and Marcelle were always unlikely best friends.

Jeanne was the glue between them. Marcelle was proud of her care of Jeanne and wasn't infected by the shame Mum carried. While Dad mostly ignored his daughter's 'little conditions' as they were called, for some of us humiliation was like a chronic, familial disease we tried to hide.

If I try to remember anything from when I was three the answer is: not much. Paris was busy, like a crowded house having a party. The pavements whirled with all sorts of people and bright colours promised excitements. A big river rushed scarily through the middle of everything.

A procession of baby sitters spoiled us. Sophie blamed us for the mess left by them. We were irritable and tired and Sophie would grumble, "*On a dû vous coucher très tard.*" So late to bed.

Leaving Paris meant a long, long drive in a car. No pavements for ages, only the countryside: trees, dark forests, huge fields. Sleeping and waking, asking when we'd get there, squirming with boredom. Being told to go to the toilet, having my face and hands rubbed with a wet flannel. Wanting to cough and choke on fumes that found their way into the car from clogged streets of small towns. Horns blaring and then no one about again.

Claire tried not to cry. She was told to hold my hand and not get upset because I would too. When I cried Dad shouted, "tell her to shut up! We'll be there soon enough." At last we went down a little track and the car bumped and rocked over the ground. Dad said, "God, I'd forgotten the potholes."

There was something else, something very special, to remember. On the first day I met Marthe, who gravely held out a hand to me. Later, she gave me a yellow plastic duck in our shared bathtub, after the shock. It was the reason I was in a bath with Marthe. It had something to do with being pulled about and getting very wet and dirty. Everyone was really, really nice to me and I think I loved Marthe then because we'd been through this important something called *le choc* together.

France, 1956

THEY CLAMBERED OUT of the car, stiff and tired. Nancy lifted Rosemary out. "There, no more asking when we'll get here. We've arrived!"

Claire looked puzzled. "Will I remember them, Mummy?"

"You might do - oh, probably - no, come back!" Claire ran up to the front door, ready to test her memory.

"Wait!" Nancy called. "*Tante* Marcelle will come soon." She held herself back, at once relieved to be there and apprehensive of Marcelle's reaction. The early summer air was soft, a blanket of warmth. Jays screeched from the trees at the back of the house, shouting their territory like bad tempered children.

Marcelle came down the steps from the front door holding the hand of a little girl who had short, dark hair and a solemn expression. Pierre was behind her and then Jacquie in her flowery apron, who grinned with delight at the Woods family. "*Ma famille anglaise est arrivée,*" she said softly to herself. There was another child in the doorway, hanging back in the shadows. Bright eyes followed the movements of the adults.

Marcelle came forward and kissed Nancy on both cheeks and shook her very gently. "So long away. You're back - that's all that matters."

She turned to look at Tom and hesitated for a moment, her back stiff as she put her arms out to him. "Tom," was a whisper.

She bent towards Claire and Rosemary. They stood very straight and quiet. Nancy had lectured them on their manners throughout the journey.

"*Bonjour,* Claire and Rosemary," Marcelle said. She kissed both girls but her gaze rested on Claire.

She brought the little dark-haired girl forward. "This is Marthe."

"*Bonjour,* Marcelle. *Bonjour,* Marthe," the girls managed, not quite in unison.

Serious dark eyes stared at them. "*Bonjour,* Claire and Rosemary."

Marcelle turned and tugged the hand of the child in the dim hall, pulling her round to her side. "Claire, Rosemary, this is Jeanne."

"*Bonjour,* Jeanne," they said.

Jeanne said something back, a harsh sound. Claire and Rosemary held hands quickly and would have stepped back if Nancy had not been immediately behind them, her hands on their shoulders. No one spoke. A cow lowing somewhere carved the silence.

Nancy and Marcelle exchanged quick smiles. Tom looked towards the French man who stood to one side smoking. They shook hands, a swift contact. "We'll talk later," he said.

Marcelle held the door open for them. "Well done, Jeanne," she said, bending down, still holding the child's hand tightly.

Rosemary and Marthe regarded each other. Rosemary smiled, liking Marthe's face. Marthe produced a sudden, toothy grin.

They took tea in the big lounge, with its views over the lawn. Pierre talked of the farm, Tom the details of the journey. The children sat still, careful of their plates and glasses of milk, the three girls shy. One was missing.

"Where is the other little girl?" asked Claire.

"Jeanne likes to take her milk and cake in her room," Marcelle said. "She'll be down soon. Come and see her later, when it's quieter," she added, leaning towards Nancy.

Marthe was sat next to Rosemary. They had twin small chairs. She piped up, "we have some *poussins.* Would you like to see them?"

Rosemary frowned, not understanding. She had a few French words now, greetings and words to go with manners but not *poussins.* She looked up at her mother.

"Some baby chicks," Marcelle explained in English. "They hatched two days ago, they're sweet." She switched to French. "Marthe, are you able to take Rosemary and Claire and show them? Then there are the swings on the lawn. They might amuse you. Don't worry, Nancy, Marthe's only small but she can find her way around. They're safe in the yard and the farm lads will watch them. I think these children need to run round after a long journey and Marthe has spent the whole day sitting at the window waiting for you."

When the children left Pierre produced a bottle of the local *cremante de Loire*. He raised his glass. "Welcome back, Tom and Nancy." His face showed no emotion; Nancy found it impossible to tell whether he meant it.

Tom raised his glass and held the French man's eyes. "*Santé*, Pierre." Nancy saw her husband relax slightly; maybe it really would be alright, running back here. She forced aside a recollection of the men calling at the Paris apartment: their bulk in the doorway, the bulges of guns under their coats and the fat envelopes exchanged for the papers Tom burnt in the cut glass ashtray.

Pierre topped up their glasses and stood back, smiling at his wife. Marcelle toasted everyone with a sweeping gesture. "Our news," she said. "We have had the cottage redecorated for you - a bit of a rush that, after your call. I hope it is to your liking. And we have decorated another room here." She beamed, smug with her cheeks glowing. "Maintenant, *je suis resplendissant de santé*." Blooming with health, showing how well she was before telling them her secret.

"Marthe now has the larger bedroom and the small one next to our room will be the nursery. Once again, one must rearrange things."

Tom stood up to shake Pierre's hand again, more warmth now. "Congratulations, both of you. When?"

Marcelle sat back and took a cigarette from Pierre's packet when he turned to Tom. "It will be ... " she began.

Then they heard the shriek. "Mumeee!"

Claire thought the chicks were pretty but she wasn't so taken with them as Rosemary and Marthe. She wandered off to find the swings Marcelle had told them about. The lawn was really big; she liked all this warm, quiet space around her. She found the swings: two wooden seats and a rope ladder. They looked inviting. She swung idly on one of the wood seats.

Claire decided she didn't like the other girl called Jeanne because she didn't smile and her voice was funny, she didn't know what she said. She felt she should have understood. When they lived in the apartment in Paris Mum and Dad had spoken to her in both French and English so she didn't think much about which language came out of her mouth or which one she heard. It just depended who she was with.

Jeanne came up and sat heavily on the swing next to her. She began rocking to and fro very fast. Claire slid off her swing and walked back towards the yard where Rosemary and Marthe had been. She could see them; they were by a pond with ducks on it. Behind her she heard shouting. Turning, she saw Jeanne following her, shouting "*Attends-moi!*" Wait for me! in her odd voice.

To avoid her Claire slipped behind a big hedge just before the yard. She watched Jeanne go past her and sat down behind the hedge. A bright green grasshopper jumped away from her. She spotted others sitting in the long grass and she tried to get her hand round one before it leapt away. She even caught one and closed her fingers over it. It tickled her and she let it go quickly. Tired with the grasshoppers Claire got up to go and find Rosemary and Mum and Dad when she heard screams coming from where she'd seen the duck pond.

She ran towards the noise. If they were playing a game she'd like to join in. She saw Jeanne holding Rosemary and Marthe either side of her at the edge of the duck pond, swinging the girls towards the dull green water. It wasn't a game. Rosemary was crying and Marthe had a furious look as she she tried to pull away from Jeanne's hand.

Claire ran as fast as she could towards them, yelling, "Mumee! Mumee!" She wasn't in time to stop Jeanne twisting sideways and letting go of her sister's hand. Rosemary fell onto the muddy edge of the pond and slid into the water. Jeanne tried to do the same with Marthe who was turning and shouting. Then she was let go as well and slid backwards into the mud on her stomach, her feet reaching the brown water.

Claire stood at the edge, crying and shouting together, wanting to help but frightened of Jeanne who was laughing. Tom reached the girls first and waded in to pluck Rosemary out. The slimy water had only reached her waist but even her face was covered in brown mud. Mum and Marcelle reached down for Marthe. There was a rotten weed stink in the close air.

Pierre hobbled up behind, the farm dogs following him, barking with excitement and disapproval. He grabbed Jeanne's arm and shook her. "What were you doing?"

"It was a game. We were playing." She looked round at everyone's faces, pleased and then pulled away from Pierre who struggled to keep his footing in the mud. "Get into the house," he shouted.

Marcelle handed Marthe and Rosemary to Nancy. "Will you take them in for me? " She snatched at Jeanne's arm and dragged her roughly along with Pierre limping close behind. Claire followed, her face puckered as she tried not to cry. Pierre reached down and took her hand. He looked into her face. "It's alright; you mustn't worry," he said.

Tom and Nancy wound their way through the house, upstairs to a cavernous bathroom. Nancy ran the bath and stripped the girls. "Look," she said, "it's deep enough to swim in."

Rosemary was unhurt, only shocked and cold, puzzled about what had happened. "We wanted to see the ducks. Jeanne said she'd help us, " she said.

Marthe looked solemnly at Rosemary and handed her a yellow plastic duck then floated another one across the surface of the bath water.

"What's this?" Nancy asked Marthe, looking at the child's hands. "Have you hurt yourself in the pond?" Marthe babbled at her so fast Nancy missed what she was saying. "We'll ask *Maman*, shall we?" She wrapped them both in big white towels she'd found in the airing cupboard in the bathroom. Our first day back and already something is wrong, she thought. I'll take them down to Marcelle, she'll know what to do.

In the lounge there was no sign of Jeanne. Marcelle produced hot chocolate for the three girls, calling Claire 'her heroine' and Rosemary and Marthe her 'brave babies.'

"Have you seen Marthe's hands?" Nancy asked.

Marcelle shook her head and turned Marthe's hands over and over in her own. She put her head down next to Marthe's, cheek to cheek, looking in front where the child looked and whispered questions.

"What?" asked Nancy.

"We have some small problems here," Marcelle said. "It's Jeanne, of course. I'm sure we can sort them out - she's needs some help sometimes and she must learn not do things like this."

"Help Jeanne - yes, naturally, but it didn't look a nice game. do

153

you mean she was playing out there and it got out of hand? Do you chastise her?"

"Yes, we do - but always for her own good, you understand. She thinks it's just a game. And the rash on Marthe's hands ...there are red ants in the garden. They bite. Marthe said Jeanne told her to put her hand in the nest."

"Why?" Nancy frowned and shook her head. "No, that can't be true."

"Nancy, listen to me - Jeanne doesn't mean these things, she's really a very nice child. She told her to do that but ... *ce n'est pas sa faute.* It's not her fault, Nancy."

Nancy kept her eyes on Marcelle's face, not looking at a little girl rubbing a towel across red spotted hands. It was my child caused that rash but it's not her fault? It was not her fault by the duck pond - just a game? Dear God! I hope Marcelle's right.

"Marcelle, do you tell her off? What do you do?"

"No, she is not told off. *Ce n'est pas sa faute.* The doctor helps with some medicines. We look after her; she can't help these little things. Come up and see her - wouldn't you like to?"

"I can't ... Not just now, later perhaps." Nancy swallowed bile; the journey, nothing to eat yet, all the upset. She tucked Rosemary's towel closer around her, stroked Marthe's hair. "In a little while, Marcelle. I'm so sorry."

"*D'accord.*" Of course.

Rosemary. London, Summer 1972

LONDON WAS SUFFOCATING, gasping in petrol fumes and dust. The college grounds wore a patchwork of bright clothes: students lay on the faded brown grass, dozing or reading or getting close to each other, laughing face to face. The sun turned the circular lake to a dull silver and shabby mallards sheltered, bad-tempered, in the reeds.

My book lay open unread in front of me and my back was burning through my thin blouse. Underneath the book was Mum's letter, a prompt in her small, sloping hand for me to make up my mind about coming to see them in the summer vacation. I'd already taken more than a week to reply, the longer I left it the guiltier I felt. I didn't want to upset Mum but there were so many things I hadn't written to her about. If I went home and let her know some of them - only some, mind - she'd be offended. She'd say, "Why haven't you told us this before?" There would be that look of hurt because her daughter had been neglectful of her parents. I was quite good at writing about the details of my studies, how the exams went, the college societies I'd joined, the plays I'd seen in London. Sometimes I wrote pleasing little lies to protect her. Always a thank you for the extra money and love to everyone.

They didn't know about Edward. The very idea of discussing him and portraying us as a couple filled me with stomach churning embarrassment. What would I say? That he was a year ahead of me and also reading English? That he wanted to be a writer, that he was tall with shoulder length dark blond hair. That I was on the pill? Should I say he made me laugh and live in the present and that looking into his kind eyes stopped my gloomy turns. That he put up with my moods and woke me from bad dreams? That would give it away.

Would Dad like him? Or would he find fault if he thought Edward was taking his darling daughter away? If he did, then would my father's especially selected sarcastic quips and hard stares send Edward running?

What would my protective big sister Claire would make of him? She'd bite the base of her thumb and look him up and down, assessing him, study on her face, ask her questions.

I hadn't heard from Claire for weeks and when she did contact me she confined her writing to sharp notes on postcards. I'd expected more from her. I knew she'd always be on my side however far away we were but when we next met I would ask her for more than a postcard.

I was fifteen when she'd gone a long way south to study, to the overheated university town of Aix-en-Provence. That had left me and my parents at home. Mum had more and more of her 'vague' turns and I have never learnt what to say when I found her crying again over Charles' photograph.

I knew I shouldn't accuse Dad of neglecting Mum, but I did, if only to myself. Travel and tourism in France was proving popular and Dad was an energetic travel writer. Always too busy. I gathered that when they came back to the Loire from Paris he'd taken a part time job writing for a small, local French paper but raged against what he called its petty minded bureaucracy; he'd manage on his own, thank you very much. I imagine my mother sighed and thought about her housekeeping. Dad then began to arrange trips away to research travel books; he was only cheerful when packing, barely hiding his eagerness to get away. "Look after your mother," was his goodbye to me. I loved my parents but I think between them they made my application to a university in London feel like a bid for escape.

I missed Marthe. I'd spent more time with her than anyone else. As we grew up we traded on our wet and slimy adventure; the *choc* of the duckpond which, in truth, we barely remembered. The sparse memories had been reshaped and rewritten to suit our teenage sense of drama. Even so, we never mentioned ... why it happened. The two families had an unspoken understanding that it was not the right thing to do to talk about Jeanne. *Ce n'est pas sa faute.* Not her fault. Always whispered: poor thing. I never said anything. I knew she could be kind and funny and endearing in her own way; I was sorry for her too. I just kept out of her way.

Before leaving for London, I used to eat more often with Marthe, Marcelle and Pierre and little Philippe in the big farmhouse kitchen than at home with Mum and Dad. I suppose that hadn't been very kind to my parents. I ought to go back for the summer. And I'd see my best friend.

Marthe had opted to stay at home and train as a nurse. I always knew she wouldn't wander far and that I would go, at least for a while. It didn't matter. When we met we just picked up where we left off and our letters crossed the Channel once a week. She knew very little about Edward - I was saving him as a surprise for her.

I sat up and rubbed my eyes. Was I brave enough to ask Edward to come with me? We could visit Mum and Dad and the Aubins and then travel south to see Claire. Would that be too much? Not if they were short, flying visits. I'd write to Mum and I would make another effort and write to Claire.

I stretched and shifted my sticky blouse away from my skin. The heat was cloying and close. Thinking about Claire reminded me of something I'd put to the back of my mind. She'd written to Marcelle. I don't think Mum knew; she'd never mentioned anything.

When I was getting ready to leave for London, to my horror my mother jerked herself out of her dreams and scuttled around to organise a party for me. I wasn't sure I wanted such a rite of passage but there was no stopping Mum, her thin frame suddenly energised. She'd run out of eggs and asked me to dash up to Marcelle's to get some.

I knocked at the back door and went straight into the kitchen. No one was there and I went across the room to shout into the hall. Half tucked under the fruit bowl on the kitchen table was an envelope addressed to *Mme Aubin, Les Moulins, St Jacques, 37462*. The familiar writing was Claire's generous hand. I edged the fat envelope out and felt its weight: a long letter. I was about to open it - God, how stupid that would have been - when I heard the downstairs lavatory flush and I put the letter back. I'd forgotten about it in all the newness of the last nine months. But why had Claire written to Marcelle when everyone else merited only a post card?

Was it worth asking Marcelle? Would I be seen as prying. Ask my sister? Both families, the Aubins and the Woods, had ways of making you feel too nosey, although Marcelle asked questions enough for everyone. Sometimes at home, when I asked a question, it was as if I'd touched an unseen switch by accident and then smiles got brighter, eyes glanced sideways and conversations swung away to another topic. Such clever, subtle operations always rendered me mute or desperate to talk only about what was for dinner.

It was Charles of course; no twist in a conversation that held the possibility of turning down a path towards him was allowed. There were other roads down which one didn't travel: another child who couldn't be blamed for anything. The war, of course - for any of them - never ask.

I missed my brother. In my nine year old memory I hated the gap left when he died. One day he was there, pestering us, laughing, playing games. Then he wasn't. All I could remember was Mum screaming when he was found; a terrifying, keening sound that made me hide away from its piercing racket. That first evening without him was silent, the house in shock. Everyone was struck dumb and I didn't dare speak. I ate some of my tea and went up to my room. I can't recollect the days after.

My bright, boisterous brother was always running, his curly brown hair bouncing about in the wind. I have quick looks at home at a photo tucked away. The one of Charles running with his arms outstretched towards Dad, who is reaching down to catch him. Next to that, in my mind's eye there's Dad with his hand over his mouth, shaking his head, tears on his cheeks. And I hear Mum screaming.

A shadow above me stopped my thoughts. "Penny for them?" asked Edward, dropping his long frame down on the grass beside me.

I put a hand out to touch his face. "What to do in the summer." I started to pick up papers and my book and picked through words I might use.

"I'd like to get out of London," he said. "And out of England?" He raised his eyebrows in a question and smiled. I liked that smile: so easy and quick to light up his face. He'd dropped hints about visiting France before. I'd found fuzzy replies, unsure how I was to introduce him my family, and the French one …

Panic nipped at me. How much do I tell him? And then, why should I worry? I'll just say my family is a little peculiar. If he wants me he'll put up with them and there are good things at home as well.

"I'll have to do a duty visit to Nan and Grandad, Mum will nag me otherwise but then we could go over to France - home - that's if you want to." I got a kiss as a yes.

We celebrated our plans later with some *Rosé d'Anjou* Edward had bought. He grimaced in mock horror as he poured. "This is the colour of the pink rock we had as kids, the stuff that made our teeth ache." He took a sip. "No change there, it tastes the same."

"You're such a wine snob already," I laughed. "We'll do better when we get to France, I promise."

"Who's going to be there?" He asked.

I told him about the Mill House and the farm and my parents' house the other side of the grounds. "There's this big sweep of lawn between the houses and we all just trot to and fro. There are swings in the middle ... "

"So you can go back to your younger days and play when you're there?" Edward teased, drinking some wine and pulling a face.

"I never go on them. They make me feel sick."

He looked sharply at me. "Alright - what did I say?"

I shook myself silently. That came out wrong. "Oh, I just don't like swings much - never have, don't know why.

"OK. Who'll be there? Big sister Claire's away in the south. She's the clever one at languages and does things in the tourist trade. She's a really good sister. There's Mum and Dad, of course. Dad might be away, probably not this time of year. You can talk to him about his travel writing and what you want to write. Mum can be a bit - well, she sometimes gets absent minded, but she's nice really.

"And then there's Pierre and Marcelle. That's the French family on the other side of lawn. Pierre runs the farm with Marcelle. She looks after the poultry side of things. She's Mum's best friend, and looks out for her." I paused. "Actually Marcelle runs everything! The world wouldn't turn unless Marcelle was doing something about it.

Philippe's their son, he's fifteen now and not bad for a lad. Then there's Marthe, my age. We're like sisters and best friends. She's doing her nurse training and she'll have at least half the doctors after her by now."

Edward nodded, so keen. It must sound very different from his home in Hertfordshire: just him, father a politician, Parliament, posh lunches; mother at home, gardening club and sponge cakes. Not quite the hurly burly of *Les Moulins*.

I didn't want the differences to disappointment him. What shouldn't I say? That Dad might in fact be pushing off somewhere, packing bags and patting his jacket to make sure he's got his passport. That Mum might have a 'dippy' turn, and be silent and tearful; that Pierre would be drunk and Marcelle inevitably too inquisitive? Edward might take one look at Marthe's French smile and bold looks and change his mind about me?

I've left two out. What could I say about Charles, never mentioned? Whose small grave was tended so very carefully: every week fresh flowers laid alongside the ceramic ones in red, pink and blue.

There was Jeanne as well with her uncertain temperament and poor face. I'd already said enough and felt exposed; I'd pick my time for those two. I always worried that if I showed my family to anyone important I would be deserted, left alone in rural France with this ill assorted crowd, I don't really know why. They weren't so bad; people were welcomed, there was laughter and hospitality. And Jeanne? She sometimes joined in happily with all of us. She was cared for, loved. Couldn't help how she was. It was just me, I suppose, always thinking no one would like what - who - I had at home.

Edward pulled me towards him and shook his head as if in regret. "And - if you can bear it - I'd like you to meet my parents." My heart did a silly, teenage acceleration. "Not for long," he said. "Or we'll both be diagnosed with the Hertfordshire disease called terminal stuffiness."

The heat wave had given up by the time I got to Nan and Grandad's. The sky was grey and I was glad of a cardigan. I hoped they didn't mind me in jeans. They were more frail than I expected but the house was tidy and Mrs Granger had left a hot meal in the oven. She had organised her son Clive to keep on top of the garden as well so I could at least reassure Mum they weren't trying to do too much. And selfishly I thought that I wouldn't have to go so often to visit and check on them.

They were embarrassingly pleased to see me and insisted I had cake with my tea, even though it was nearly time for an evening meal. They talked as they always did, a lot about my birth, Nan reminiscing as if I'd been her very own baby for a short while, when Mum stayed with them to have me before joining Dad in Paris, which they called that 'big French city.'

"It was all so exciting, Rosemary! On a plane to go back as well. Your mother was so brave to do it."

Grandad mopped up every detail about Paris I could remember, which wasn't a lot as I was only there for the first three years of my life. I made some stuff up to keep him happy and steered clear of what little I could recollect about maids and baby sitters while Mum and Dad went out.

Nan beamed at me. "You were such a good baby. And little Claire adored you, right from the start." She reached a dry hand out to touch my cheek. "It was such fun, having you born here. Such lovely children, both of you." There were sudden tears in her eyes and she blinked them away into her lined, pale face.

I tried a joke. "Claire didn't pinch me out of jealousy, then?"

But Nan and Grandad drew deep breaths and raised their sparse eyebrows in horror. "No, dear. Of course not!" they cried in unison.

I thanked them for their kindness and the nice food. Mum and Dad would come from France to visit soon. I would write; I would ask Claire to write.

Where was I going now? To visit a boyfriend's parents? How wonderful! Haven't you grown up so quickly. We can remember you as a baby ... "

"My mother is vague and may well forget to feed us," Edward said on the train to Berkhampstead. "And my father is pompous and will talk at you until your ears fall off."

I could manage vague mothers. I'd had a lot of practice. Pompous fathers? Well, all I cared about was making a good impression so that I didn't let Edward down. I planned to be presentable - no jeans. I wore some tailored slacks and a neat blue blouse I'd borrowed from Mum and forgotten to return. It was good for concerts and so on. I'd tied my hair back in a respectable pony tail and left off most of my make up. "Sure it's you?" Edward said, with a quizzical look.

I hugged Edward's arm tightly, enjoying the wiry feel of him. "I don't mind what they're like. Come on, we'll be away in a couple of days." I fished the timetables of trains and ferries out of my bag and sought to distract my increasingly nervous boyfriend with travel arrangements.

"Let's check these over. Think about something else before you explode with worry." Oh, Edward - just wait 'til you meet my lot.

Mr Bellingham was waiting for us at the station. He was tall and rangy like his son but the shoulders of his expensive jacket were tight and a paunch strained against his belt. Too many political dinners. He and Edward had the same blue eyes and the same big smiles but there the resemblance ended. Bellingham *père* had a calculation behind his eyes and took a surreptitious look up and down at me that he didn't quite care to hide. His handshake was predictably too firm. "*Enchanté, Mam'selle,*" he said with such an appalling accent I had to work hard not to wince. Or laugh: it was so phoney and patronising. He held the back passenger door open for me with a big flourish and Edward, tight lipped with embarrassment, was motioned to get in the front.

Edward's mother was short and her long fair hair, streaked with grey, was drawn into a bun, from which generous clumps escaped. She wore a floaty dress which billowed around her when she moved. But she greeted us with genuine happiness and hugged Edward for a long time. She took my hand in both hers. "I'm so pleased to meet you. So pleased that Edward has - um - found you." She turned to Edward as if, for a moment, I wasn't there. "I'm so pleased to meet Rosemary. Would you like tea, dear?"

She put the kettle on and gazed round the kitchen, biting her lip. "There's cake somewhere."

I spotted a tin that looked as if it might contain cake. I caught Edward's eye and pointed.

"Here, Mum," he said, picking up the blue and white tin from the dresser.

We had tea and dry sponge in the lounge with Mrs Bellingham and answered her questions about university and our plans for the summer. Edward's father had taken a cup and plate and disappeared without a word. I wondered, from the way he frowned at her, if he actually approved of his wife, less smart than he was and a bit scatty. Did he worry she might let him down at his council functions?

When a lull came in the conversation and we refused more tea Mrs Bellingham stood up, looking uncertain. "I'll show you to your room, Rosemary, if you'd come with me. Edward, your old room's ready for you."

She led me up two flights of stairs into a tiny corridor which ended in a small, cold room.

"I hope you'll be comfortable here," she said. "The bathroom's down the first stairs and on the right." She hurried off, as if the strain of inviting guests was too much for her.

The room was chilly. It must have been the servant's room years ago, I thought, where they stored her when she wasn't working. It was probably the room furthest from Edward's. Nothing untoward would happen in this household, where Mr Bellingham barely acknowledged his wife.

The room smelt of disinfectant and had a single, narrow bed with a white candlewick cover. A good job I'm thin. There was a bedside table without a lamp and a small wooden chair by the window.

I sat on the bed and unpacked my overnight bag; laid out a nightdress and toiletries bag. This wasn't a comfortable household and maybe, in different ways, it had something in common with my own. In France the rooms would be warmer; although not always the atmosphere.

Our two days went thankfully quickly. Mrs Bellingham did indeed forget mealtimes. Edward would search for his mother in the garden and tactfully ask her what was for lunch and could we help get it? She spent her time gardening with an intense ferocity, doing battle with weeds and pruning savagely, the green spoils piling around her feet.

Lunch was for the three of us. "Your father's working," Edward's mother said, sounding unsure of herself.

The first evening she couldn't 'do' dinner. Mr Bellingham was dining in London and she'd arranged a meeting of the local gardening club. Could we sort ourselves out for food? She didn't want to be inhospitable but ... if we'd let her know earlier we were coming ...

We escaped gratefully to the local pub for chicken and chips and pints of beer and laughed like conspirators about one more day to go.

For the second evening Edward's mother put down her trowel and found the kitchen. There were prawn cocktails, a roast chicken and, for dessert, a gateau with too much cream and sugar, topped with tinned cherries. Mr Bellingham carved and served me first, calling me *Mam'selle* again and smirking at his own wit. He regaled us with stories of the House, as he called the House of Commons. It sounded to me like a club specially for backbiters with their endless lobbying for conflicting causes, all cancelling each other out. Edward composed his face into a polite expression of interest and I hoped the one, sly wink he gave me wasn't noticed. Vague as she was, his mother saw it and got up in cross silence to clear the plates.

We could hear the angry clatter of crockery from the kitchen and I tried to ease the tension by asking Mr Bellingham about his work as a member of Parliament. He looked smug as he poured more wine and carefully turned the label so I could see its gold lettering and admire his taste in wines. "A Bordeaux Supérieur, my dear."

Instead of answering my questions he waved his glass in my direction and addressed Edward. "You know, I approve of your choice. That's a good girl you have there. Asks the right things. Pretty as well. Mind you hang onto her."

I sat as silent and furious as Edward's mother obviously had learned to be in the years she had been married to this bore. I hoped nothing like it had rubbed off on Edward, although he seemed to - so far -be the very opposite of pomposity.

Mrs Bellingham served coffee in the lounge, her mouth straight and angry. Her husband poured brandies and went to pass a glass to her. She shook her head and suddenly, as if some courage had arrived a little late, said, "No thank you. And you've had too much already."

"Oh well dear, I'll just have this small one." He surprised me by sounding so meek and I wondered at the change.

An uncomfortable silence settled in the room. Then Mr Bellingham stood up and fished around on a side table, moving glasses and papers. "Edward, take these." He threw a set of car keys at Edward, who fumbled and just caught them. "Take the Austin to France. I've done the insurance for you. Papers are here somewhere." He rummaged around again and passed a bundle of documents over. "It's sitting doing nothing and I was thinking of selling it. But I'd rather give it to you. I'll put Rosemary on the insurance, now I've met her." He jerked his head towards his wife. "Don't need two cars. She doesn't drive any more. In fact she suggested it. Good idea."

Edward stuttered a thank you and looked at the keys in his hand as if they were miniature aliens who had dropped in. I thanked his father and beamed my gratitude at Mrs Bellingham, bemused by this sudden generosity of spirit from both of them.

Mr Bellingham looked awkward. "Make your trip across much easier. Wonderful to drive through France - don't bother with the trains. Watch the carburettor though - it floods easy." He gazed into his glass, perhaps hoping it would refill itself. He looked at Edward, then me and then lingeringly on his wife who was sitting with her hands folded loosely in her lap.

"Time for bed, dear," he said. "Goodnight children."

Rosemary. France, Summer 1972

I TOOK OVER the driving after Edward had pulled out onto the left hand side of the road too many times for my nerves. I was grateful that Dad had got me behind the wheel as soon as I was old enough, shouting and cajoling in equal measure, as he had done with Claire before me.

We'd been quiet for a long time; I was watching the road and Edward was gazing out at the lush countryside. The warm air carried scents of grass and cattle. We'd been excited by this great adventure and actually being in a car but the atmosphere changed. I was bad tempered and complained about other drivers. Edward's silence seemed morose.

Driving kept my mind away from how to tell him more about my family and in how much detail. After meeting his parents I realised he might understand better than I had hoped; better than someone from a family that had no forbidden places on its map.

We both spoke at once. "Look, there's … " The tension eased. "You first." "No, you."

Edward wanted to know if the country near home was like this: green rolling hills and brown and white timbered houses stuck onto the hillsides like marooned ships with their great gable ends jutting out like prows.

"No, it's more gentle in places and hotter and drier. We're a long way from the sea. And cold in winter. There are big rivers and orchards and vineyards."

I didn't want him to expect too much. "The house isn't as grand as yours and there are one or two things you ought to … " I paused to brake and hoot at a car pulling out ten metres in front of me.

"I'm sorry about Mum and Dad," he was saying as I crashed down the gears and began a winding descent into a valley.

"There's no need," I said, sensing some reassurance wouldn't go amiss. Edward was endearingly not like his father. "I liked your Mum. I suppose I found them - well - she's got a lot to put up with and your father - one minute he ignores her and then he behaves like a little boy. He shows off, all awful bluster and then gives you a car."

"They used to have the most dreadful rows. I think Mum left him for a bit before I was born. She went back to him because he pleaded; he'd change, stop drinking so much and he wouldn't bully her. He said he needed a wife to help his career and that would be good for her too. Then I came along but it seems I wasn't enough for Dad. Mum couldn't have any more, some woman's problem. I used to sit on the stairs and listen to the rows when they thought I was asleep. I heard my mother say, 'if you want any more children, find someone else! If anyone else will put up with you!' They never checked much on me, too busy muddling up their own lives but I think now I've left they've calmed down, come to some sort of agreement about how to live together."

"Did you want brothers and sisters?" I asked.

He shrugged, looked out of the window briefly, then watched me drive. "I suppose … you don't know about what you haven't got, do you? I had plenty of friends. I preferred their houses to mine, their parents didn't leave egg shells around for you to tread on."

I opened the car up as we reached a flat plain, the road disappearing into the distance. "We're not short of egg shells at home," I said.

Later, Edward took over the wheel again. The temperature had gone up and the sun coming through the passenger side window made me irritable. "Look, can't you put your foot down." I heard my voice rising.

"No, it's all I can do to drive. Give me a break, Rosemary."

He wiped his brow with his shirt sleeve and started to slow down. "I'm stopping."

"Not here!" I yelled. "Up there - in that lay-by."

It wasn't a lay-by but a shallow entrance to a field and a truck behind had to swerve as it roared past, its horn deafened us and the driver shook his fist.

I was beginning to think this was going to be our first row but Edward held his hand out to me. "I'm sorry. Truce?" This way he had of calming me; I was so grateful.

The long drive and the heat had got to both of us I suppose. "An overnight stop can't hurt, can it?" Edward said.

We found a small hotel on the edge of Tours. There was a telephone box outside. I tried my parents' number but it seemed to ring forever in an empty house. Then I tried Marcelle who answered as if she'd been standing by the phone. I stood for a long time in the smelly cabin persuading Marcelle that we were very tired and that it would be better if we stopped now and arrived tomorrow when we had rested. I was told in no uncertain terms that they would all be disappointed but eventually she said *à demain, bonne route* and I could put the phone down.

The hotel receptionist had grey hair dragged back by brutal pins and a straight, hard mouth. Her eyes travelled to my hands, searching for a ring; I put my left hand in my pocket and she looked even crosser. Edward asked in halting French for a double room and I could see that she was going to refuse, guessing we weren't married. As she started to say they were full up, Edward put his arm round my shoulders, "Wait just over there." He turned me gently aside and I retreated to look at a bad still life that hung on the wall. When I glanced back from the gaudy bowl of fruit Edward was tucking his wallet back in his jacket. At the desk the receptionist was smiling, showing a gap in her teeth and, I think, offering to send up some wine.

The next morning promised heat. Our surly receptionist put out excellent croissants and bread for us in a dim dining room in which the contrasting aromas of stale cigarettes and fresh coffee fought a battle. We were on the road quickly, more cheerful than yesterday, more friendly. We'd decided I would drive; Edward could practise on the French roads when we didn't need to be anywhere in particular. We were a couple going on holiday and my heart sang.

"Tell me again," Edward said, "who are these people I will meet?" His face was scrunched up with concern. "My French isn't too good; a guide to the introductions might be handy."

I was pleased his father's egotism hadn't rubbed off; that felt good and stopped me dropping into my inexplicable doldrums. In fact, nothing on that shining morning would have upset me. Except for the traffic of course, but that's a game played on the roads. I tooted at a car nosing out into the traffic and it slunk backwards into a side road.

"Right, here's your revision. My parents, Nancy and Tom. I said Dad travels but he's at home now, Marcelle told me yesterday. There's Claire, my big sister in the south. She's bossy so I have to behave around her.

Then the Aubin family: Pierre and Marcelle and their daughter Marthe, my best friend, remember? So keep your eyes off her." I pushed Edwards gently and laughed. "And Philippe's their son, the youngest. He's alright."

I took a deep breath. "They have another daughter at home, Jeanne. She's the same age as Claire and she's had a few problems. She probably can't speak any English where all the others can." She can't speak well in any language, I thought, then berated myself for being mean.

"What was wrong?"

"She was born with a hare lip, it's affected her a bit and I think there're other things as well. She's not very sociable. Everybody helps her out, we all look after her and she can be very sweet. It'll all be fine, you'll like everyone. They'll all like you." I kept an optimistic note in my voice and concentrated on overtaking a rattling, elderly Citroen with its exhaust dangling from a wire.

Edward was still watching me as I drove. "That's a shame for her; does her mother worry?"

"Oh, Marcelle manages very well."

"Is that the lot, then? You and Claire ... " he listed out the names.

"Not quite. Mum had a son at the same time as Marcelle had Philippe. Mine and Claire's little brother. Everyone adored him. But he died when he was four. I was nine then. We were all devastated."

"Oh lord, I'm so sorry. I can't imagine ..." Edward put his hand on my knee. "What happened?"

"There are swings on the lawn. I told you. They've been there since the war. We all played on them and Charles was found dead by them. He tried to get on by himself and got caught up in the ropes. We can't talk about him; Mum still gets too upset." I paused for a minute, assembling careful words. "The awful thing is that no one will take the swings down. I don't know how Mum bears it, seeing them all the time. They have to stay there because they're Jeanne's special thing. She loves to play on them for hours and has tantrums if anyone suggests they have to go. She doesn't have as much fun as every one else, she really loves the swings and they're supposed to be good for her. So it's a bit - well - difficult sometimes; you mustn't mind."

Edward kept his hand on my knee and I drove on, letting the noise of the traffic and the car throbbing on the road drown out the other sounds in my head.

Edward. France, Summer 1972

EDWARD HAD MET Rosemary at the beginning of his second year at university. She had arrived for her first term and he found her in a corridor, staring clear eyed about her and clutching a plan of the building. She wore a bright waistcoat and jeans and a bag of books rested at her feet. She was lost, she said. He showed her where her lecture theatre was and, without thinking about it at all, asked her to go for a drink. He hadn't expected to meet anyone; he'd not bothered much. All his first year he'd worked, gone out drinking occasionally, been glad to be away from his father's disapproval. When he had told him he wanted to read English as well as having the temerity to add that he wanted to write, a storm descended. He was wasting his father's money, he was made for better things, he had to study for something useful, not read namby-pamby books. 'Something useful' meant reading law and going into politics. Challenging his father about this, "useful for who, Dad?" brought another blast whilst his mother watched in disappointed silence, not on his side.

Now he was half way across France going to meet Rosemary's parents and this other family she talked about. He'd got an acquaintance from another department to crash him through some French dialogue for the price of a few beers. It partly made up for the failed French 'A' level he hadn't cared about.

He worried that he didn't have enough French to get by and what about meeting all these people? Despite Rosemary's kindness, he'd be judged. Had he been sympathetic enough about the girl she said wasn't quite right? How much all this mattered surprised him.

There had been teenage liasons, enough to find out what should happen with the opposite sex and enough to show him how little he was attracted to the husband hunters of the home counties set. This, with Rosemary, was entirely different.

They were bumping down a long drive, the little Austin creaking and complaining in second gear. He dried his sweaty hands on his jeans. 'No need to dress up,' Rosemary had said. He hoped she was right.

They pulled up by a big, ivy clad house which had the crumbling remains of an old mill wheel stuck on one side like a disfigurement. On the steps stood a short, dark-haired woman, smiling and waving. Beside her was a willowy girl, brown hair framing a pale face. She had a serious mouth and a look of concentration about her. That'll be Marthe, he thought. Then they were down the steps hugging Rosemary and shaking hands with him. He remembered *enchantés*. Pleased to meet you all.

Marcelle beamed at him "We are very glad to meet you here with Rosemary," she said in heavily accented English. "We 'ope you will enjoy your stay. My husband, Pierre and my son, Philippe, are out at the moment on the farm and you will meet them at dinner."

Running across an expanse of lawn was a tall, fair woman, more gaunt than comfortably slim and unmistakeable as Rosemary's mother. She was followed by a man in his fifties with a taut frame, dark hair greying at the temples and filling a pipe as he strode up to them. Ex RAF, Rosemary had said. Mr Woods looked the part.

Mrs Woods swept Rosemary up in a hug. "Let's look at you, darling." She held her daughter away from her. "You're well?"

She turned to Edward and held out her hand. "You must be Edward. How nice of you to come."

Mr Woods greeted Rosemary with kisses in the French way and shook hands with Edward. "Good drive down?"

"Yes, sir. Very easy."

Tom Woods gestured with his pipe as they talked for a time about the sorry state of the roads in France. He was freshly shaven and had, Edward thought at first, an open face with frank, hazel eyes and none of the old officer arrogance he'd expected. Although as they talked he noticed the older man hesitate occasionally, a discomfort about him as if he was uncertain or watching for something or other.

"I've hogged you enough," Tom said. "Let's join the others. You'll want to settle in."

He steered Edward to where Rosemary and her mother, Marcelle and Marthe were talking. Rosemary and Marthe had their arms round each other like young children. He'd give them time together, he thought, and wander around by himself a bit. So different, he thought, from my lot.

Nancy broke free from the little group and smiled at Edward. "I'll show you to your room while these girls chatter and Marcelle grills Rosemary. I don't suppose they'll miss you for a while."

She took him across a wide lawn which rose slightly to the centre where a set of swings dangled in the still, hot air. Edward tried not to stare at them and not to think of what Rosemary had told him. Mrs Woods speeded up her walk and looked straight ahead towards a stone house, smaller than the Mill House but certainly not a cottage. The patio was bright with geraniums and to the side was a terrace with chairs and a table set out under a yellow parasol.

Nancy showed him up to a small bedroom at the top of the stairs overlooking part of the lawn. He couldn't see the swings from here. Fields stretched out beyond the garden, fading into grey haze at the horizon and there was a rise of hills in the distance, their colours leached by the heat. The room had a double bed with a patchwork quilt of blues and greens and a wardrobe in dark oak that met the ceiling and gave the room an old fashioned, heavy feel.

"The bathroom's down the corridor on the left and Rosemary's room is next to that." She didn't quite look at him. "Tom and I have discussed it; you two can make your own decisions about rooms. Times change."

Rosemary's mother had clearly made a leap into the modern world. He managed, "thank you, Mrs Woods," and hoped she didn't notice the blush he could feel.

"We're to join Marcelle and Pierre for dinner. We'll meet on their terrace for an aperitif at six o'clock." She turned to go, then stopped as if to say something, but changed her mind and walked quickly out of the room.

Edward washed and changed into a clean shirt. The mirror in the bathroom showed a face pale again and blue eyes with shadows of tiredness under them. His worries about the visit began to lose their intensity; the family seemed welcoming and not at all stuffy.

Rosemary's father appeared decent. There had been those sudden glances away, brief shadows across faces but perhaps he was making that up. And what he'd heard about Charles; he couldn't imagine a grief like that with no brothers or sisters to lose. One blessing from his parents, he supposed.

He combed his hair and hoped no one disapproved that it fell over his collar. He winced at the recollection of his father shouting, "Get your hair cut! Coming home looking like some yob!" He didn't think that would go on here. Mr Woods had short hair and smart looks but he hadn't cast any frowning eye over Edward's appearance. Rosemary had exchanged the slacks and blouse she had worn to his parents' house for jeans and a loose top; Marthe was dressed in the same way, her tee shirt saying *Je ne regrette rien*.

He set out to walk across the lawn and saw that the swings were occupied. There was a figure of a woman, legs sticking out from a skirt, silhouetted against the chalky blue sky. Curious, he walked forward a few steps. She was sitting on the nearest wooden seat, her hands grasping the ropes at shoulder height, rocking to and fro rather than swinging, pushing with her heels on the ground, her feet at a sharp angle. This would be Jeanne, the one Rosemary had said he 'mustn't mind.' She didn't seem to know he was there; he looked away to avoid staring at her.

He could hear an off key song, the tune endlessly repeated. A shimmer of heat eroded the boundaries of the garden and from where he stood he couldn't see the other house. He felt for an instant cut off from everyone apart from this stranger singing to herself. Marooned. He could either move away quickly before she saw him or go up and introduce himself, the most polite option; she must know about visitors coming today. Uncertain, he continued to stand there, almost rocking in time, until he heard faint sounds from the direction of the big house as if the laughter pushed through the air to find him.

Rosemary. France, Summer 1972

I HAD BEEN about to go and search for Edward when he appeared, panting and frowning, at the top of the steps that led up from the back of Marcelle's patio. He looked at me and pulled an embarrassed face, mouthing "sorry" and pulling his fingers through his hair.

Everyone turned to stare at him but Marcelle got up immediately. "*Bonsoir.* What may I offer you, Edward?" She poured him a glass of white wine and looked amused at his dishevelment.. "I think you came over the long way round."

I patted the seat beside me and Edward sat down. "Sorry," he said again. "I found a path that went alongside a field of cows and then through the vegetable garden."

"Why did you come that way?"

"Ah, I was ... I set out across the lawn but there was someone ... I didn't want to walk past and disturb her."

"That'll be Jeanne," I said.

"I'm looking forward to meeting her," he said. He looked eager and sympathetic at the same time. I hoped they would get on; that she would have good day tomorrow and enjoy his kindness.

Marcelle was passing around a plate of *rillons,* the tiny roasted pieces of pork, my favourite. "She'll come over later. We leave her be when she's on the swings. Pierre and Philippe will be here soon too."

"Where are they?" I asked.

"They've gone to move some cattle to another farm. *Monsieur* Cotin wanted to do it this afternoon and wouldn't wait. He's more grumpy than Pierre these days."

I wondered what Edward would make of us all. He'd recovered from his embarrassment by the time we sat down for dinner. He whispered to me that he had been unnerved by the cows, who had wandered over to the fence to inspect him, their breath heating his face and the air whining with flies. "Bit scared, actually. Big beasts."

Marcelle had placed him between Mum and Pierre and he was getting on well with Pierre. I'd told him earlier that speaking in English was fine with everyone but Pierre wasn't quite so good at it, although I knew he understood very well. Edward had switched to his slow and deliberate French in order to talk to Pierre, asking him about the farm and the weather. I heard Pierre say, "Your French is very good, Edward." I watched Edward fitting in, becoming comfortable with himself and with the company, smiling at Mum and listening carefully to her. With her help, a whisper in his ear to translate, he was also managing to understand and laugh at the Frenchman's more obscure sentences and ironic jokes. Pierre reached to top up Edward's glass, his left hand holding his right wrist to stop a tremor. That had got worse since I'd last seen him.

Philippe had changed. I'd been away just less than a year and he was taller, looking gangly in the way teenage boys do in their fast-growing years. He laughed a lot, showing good teeth. His eyes were a fraction too small like his father's and he had Marthe's serious, straight mouth. Eager to talk to Edward he spoke across Mum to ask him questions. Would Edward help him with his English, what was university like, which bands did he listen to? Before each question he always excused himself first to Mum, who nodded and raised her eyes skywards at Marcelle across the table.

I was sitting next to Marcelle with Marthe on my other side. They talked to me individually, or to each other across me and sometimes both at once to me. I'd catch up with Mum and Dad later. I loved my parents but I basked in these French friendships, their chatter and their ways; Marthe putting her hand on my arm and leaning into me, "I must tell you …"

Marcelle was encouraging me to eat: apparently I looked thinner. Did I eat properly in London, how could I manage the awful English food? She'd made *agneau farci,* the stuffed leg of lamb she excelled at. "Your favourite," she said. "It will put some weight back on." The last thing I wanted but never mind. She told me about the new wine growers, complained about the help at the farm in the same sentence and stole a cigarette from Pierre's packet between courses.

I looked round the table for Jeanne The space between Dad and

Pierre was laid for her and I wanted to see how she was doing, if she was well. I turned to Marcelle and gestured towards the empty chair. "What about ... ?"

Marcelle looked cross. "I have told her - insisted - but she doesn't listen. You know what she's like." She sighed, "*ce n'est pas sa faute.* Rosemary, if you don't mind, would you be very kind and see if Jeanne's in her room. She's been waiting for you and I don't know why she's not down. She'll be so pleased to see you and then she'll come down without a fuss."

I didn't mind. I was happy to be home and to have Edward here, and it would be nice to go to Jeanne's room and say *bonjour Jeanne* on my own. But Marthe stopped me with a hand on my arm. "No, stay here Rosemary. No one's seen enough of you yet. I'll fetch her."

Marthe got up quickly and slipped away, avoiding Marcelle's glare.

"Make sure she washes her hands," Marcelle called after her. "I wouldn't have asked her to go," she said to me. "Those two haven't been getting on lately ... ah well."

Jeanne ate quickly, staring at Edward, the stranger. She chewed loudly. She couldn't help eating with her mouth open; we always ignored it but this time I felt disconcerted because Edward was there. I soon forgot to worry; Edward didn't appear to take any notice and I was distracted by Marthe and Marcelle. When Pierre turned to find her napkin and remind her to wipe her mouth, Edward turned away and asked Mum something who laughed and lent forward round Pierre and Jeanne to call over to Dad, smiling like a trick of the light. I felt silly with pleasure, with fondness for Edward and my two families.

Marcelle brought coffee in, putting cups on the table and helping herself to Pierre's cigarettes in one seamless movement. Jeanne stood up. "May I leave the table, Mama?"

Marcelle glanced down at Pierre, who nodded. "Off you go."

As Jeanne left, Pierre got up and shuffled away. "Just a moment." He returned, slowly and carefully, with two bottles of wine that trembled gently as his hands shook. "Now we relax a little more." He paused and spread his arms wide towards the table. "Even more!" He pretended to count his cigarettes with a big, mock frown and Marcelle turned away theatrically, puffing smoke high into the air and grinning.

The sky was July white and the road a restless glitter. I was trapped inside the Austin, sweating in the metallic tasting heat. The huge, gentle centre of France gave way to big rolling hills and long avenues of plane trees that ushered us into silent, red roofed towns, shuttered against the afternoon sun.

"What's she like, your sister?" Edward asked, raising his voice above the rushing air from the open windows.

"She works all the time. All we hear from her is busy, busy, busy." I was driving and took one hand off the wheel to wipe my forehead with a handkerchief. I thought of the letter to Marcelle I nearly opened. Not as busy as all that ... "She studied really hard at school and after she got her university place we didn't hear much from her. Now she has this job we only get postcards." Marcelle gets letters.

"But I'm the baby sister, she wants to see us. She's nosey about you, - she'll check you out."

"Oh God, I hope not." Edward draped a hot arm over my shoulder and I shook it off. "No, That's not fair," he said. "Your family - they're all lovely."

I was pleased with myself. The visit had gone well, even Jeanne had been amicable and happy. Mum and Dad had taken to Edward, Marcelle said she and Pierre approved and Marthe had given me a cheeky thumbs up behind his back on the first day.

Although I'd thought about it, we hadn't actually planned a visit south. A short letter - surprise! not a postcard - arrived at *Les Moulins* in our first week there.

Dear Mum and Dad, Bonjour Marcelle and Pierre, Marthe and Philippe and Jeanne.

All is well here. How are you all? Dad, how is the writing? Don't work too hard! I hope Mum is in good spirits. How does the farm go? And Philippe's studies and Marthe's nursing course? I hope Jeanne is well.

Aix is as hot as ever this summer but the mistral will come soon enough to give us all good health.

Work is always too busy. We are setting up more tourist offices here and also now in Germany. I must brush up on my German and work out a schedule of business. The Germans are very keen on schedules.

I haven't heard from Rosemary for ages. Her last letter said she might visit you with a New Boyfriend.

If she's with you, Hello Rosemary. Sorry I haven't replied to your letter; you know how it is. But come and see me and stay for a few days. Bring the N B with you and let's have a look at him! There's a map enclosed to my apartment and the phone numbers of home and office. Don't get lost!

Love, Claire.

As much as I enjoyed home it was good to get away to have time with Edward alone. I'd had one or two of my weird dreams which left me hot and fretful. I'd turned to Edward for comfort, but when he wanted to know more about what was wrong I said "*Ça ne fait rien.* It doesn't matter."

I slowed the car, pulled into a lay-by and pointed to a stall selling *pêches.* "Quick stop?"

We sat under what shade a hedge provided and bit into the peaches. Edward wiped the juice from his face and peeled off his shirt. "I'm too hot."

"You'll burn, have the sun cream."

"You put it on for me." He grinned. "You can admire my body at the same time."

I slapped him gently. "Turn round then. Have you knocked yourself on something?" There was an irregular purple mark on his arm just above his elbow. "Or did you get bitten by the old horse when we went over to *Monsieur* Cotin's farm - that mare of his is getting senile." I peered closer. Oh, damn, that's not a horse bite.

"Ah, no." Edward looked at me, apology on his face. "I - um- wasn't going to say anything."

I raised my eyebrows. "What?" But I knew.

"Yesterday, while you were packing I went for a walk and met up with Jeanne by the swings. I felt I couldn't ignore her so I just said '*Bonjour*, Jeanne,' and held out my hand. She seemed nice and shook my hand and managed to say '*Bonjour*, Edward.' Then she gave me such a pinch. She ran off to the swings then, laughing as if it was a huge joke. I didn't know what to do, so I just walked away."

"How near was she to the swings?"

"Oh, just a few feet away."

I stroked his arm. "I'm so sorry. You weren't to know. She gets a bit strange by the swings; the doctor wanted them left there because he thought her rocking on them might sooth her. He told Marcelle to let her have them, even though ... even though Charles died ... they're supposed to be good for her." For her, not for my sad, grieving mother.

"I don't know how Mum stood it, having them left there after Charles. Dad didn't help very much - he agreed with the doctor even though Jeanne really isn't his business and Mum simply doesn't mention anything now. I don't know how Dad feels either, to be honest; he seems to bear it all better than Mum does."

"Forget it," Edward said. "It's only a bruise. It's not important. And even if the swings are - well - difficult for other people, Jeanne's a poor thing with that face, you can't tell her off or anything."

"Well, yes, you can, actually. For her own good a telling-off doesn't hurt. She has a good life with Marcelle and Pierre. She gets these funny turns and Marcelle has to keep her indoors or give her something to calm her down."

"Surely she's harmless enough? She's just a bit ..." Edward tailed off.

"A bit unstable, you mean." I ignored his concerned gaze. "Sometimes she can be a real worry. Pierre used to beat her when she was younger, probably still does. And she never does anything to him; some sort of respect for the punishment, I suppose."

"I thought she needed help, not a beating."

"That's the way of it here; it's the way Pierre and Marcelle cope." I stood up. I didn't want to think about Jeanne anymore. "Come on, let's get going. We're on holiday."

He put a bare arm round my shoulders as we walked back to the car. He's kind, I thought. I want someone kind. I won't let him be pinched any more.

Edward drove through Aix, cursing the chaotic traffic, managing not to hit anything, although not by much. "Where's the turn?"

I looked at the rough map Claire had drawn. "Next left and her apartment block's a white building - look, there she is!" I could see a figure in a short, lime green dress standing in the street, shading her eyes from the sunlight.

We parked on the pavement and got out; the air in the street even thicker with heat than in the car. I hugged Claire. "You look amazing. This is Edward. Claire, Edward Bellingham. Edward. My sister, Claire."

Claire spoke rapidly in French to Edward - testing him. She hadn't checked with me how good his French was.

Edward held out his hand. He smiled at her, understanding, not phased at all. "*Enchanté,* Claire. *Comment allez vous?*"

We squashed into an elderly lift that wheezed its way up to the fourth floor. Claire showed us round: the tiny, yellow kitchen, dominated by a refrigerator humming to itself in a corner; the lounge with the windows opening onto a small balcony, bright with geraniums, and our guest bedroom, painted blue with gaudy yellow abstracts on the walls. A vase on an old oak *armoire* held a forest of blue irises and there was a box of chocolates, festooned with blue ribbons, next to it.

"This is lovely," I said.

"Yes, well - you're welcome." Claire handed me a kir. "Your favourite. *Avec peche, pas cassis.*" I sipped my wine. I had seen so little of her for nearly four years that I worried a gap might have pushed itself between us; she felt more distant than I expected.

"I've booked a table at *La Brasserie Café Le Verdun.*" Claire said. "My treat. It's the best Provençal cuisine here. We can eat outside and watch all of Aix on parade for us."

We talked of trivia throughout the meal. Edward praised the food: the vegetable terrine, the *Coquille St. Jacques*, the steak. Claire looked smug and played the perfect hostess. She talked of the university, one of the most prestigious in France although Dad hadn't thought so, and her work. "The company's expanding - tourism's the thing to do - it's how to get on. And the Germans love us! Coach loads turn up, all fussing about accommodation, diets, trips running on time. I think they have forgotten they were the invaders, *l'occupation.*" She pulled her mouth down in distaste. "It upsets some of the older people here; I don't like that." She held my gaze, wide eyed, "what would Pierre and Marcelle make of it? Of me working with Germans?"

She refilled our glasses, not giving me time to reply. "But I make a lot of francs and the company expands all the time. What are you two doing tomorrow? I'm going to have to work."

Later, I said, "That's typical of Claire. Ask us down, dinner, this room, no expense spared, then working tomorrow." I was lying next to Edward in the big, spare bed, just touching him. The windows were open and the curtains fidgeted in a hot, night breeze.

"I want her time as well - is that selfish of me?"

"I suppose sisters would want to spend time together." He sounded awkward. "Is it me?" he asked. "Should I wander off by myself?"

"It's not you." I turned towards him. "It's just Claire - she only gives to people in her own way. She likes you, I can tell that."

He looked at me, seeking my approval. He put a hand on my shoulder, the wan glow from street light making both of us look intriguing to each other.

At breakfast Claire put out coffee, orange juice, croissants, bread, jam and some fruit. She was dressed in a powder blue suit, her brown hair short and slick. She produced tourist leaflets and chartered us through the details, selecting itineraries.

"Cézanne's last studio is open. His equipment's been left. There's the Bibemus Quarries where he drew and the view across to Monte Saint-Victoire is superb."

Edward's eyes sparkled with interest and he nearly snatched the brochure.

"You're the perfect person for tourist work." I said.

❧

The room was replete with light and smelled of last century's dust. We'd come through a door twice the normal height of a man, leaving the official in charge outside in his little hut in the sun.

I glanced at the leaflet. "This door is tall so that Cézanne could take extra large canvasses out into the light." I pointed at a shelf running along one wall. "Look, he's forgotten his hat. And he hasn't washed up his wine beaker." I turned in a circle, pretending to stare and gasp. "He might come back any minute!"

Edward peered over my shoulder. " *'Personne n'entre ici que moi.'* Nobody comes in here but me," he read on a door. "His very own bolt hole. Now there's no one here but us."

I picked up some wooden rosary beads, ticked them through my fingers. "Everything as he left it. I wonder what he really thought about painting here. A job or a passion? Something inside him he couldn't help?"

Edward sat down on a low bench painted blue. "I don't know - I think he just had to do it, to give way to whatever was in his head. To show the world what he had. Isn't that what we all want?" He stood up and wandered over to the long shelf and fingered an empty wine bottle.

I put the beads back, guiding them into the same position I had found them. Marcelle had rosary beads; occasionally I would see her running them though her fingers, murmuring gently. I envied the comfort others got from their rehearsal of that gentle tap-tap.

On a shelf there was a white plaster cherub that had ragged bumps where its arms had once been. I stretched out one finger to touch it. What funny things we keep as precious. Like Claire's bear, Brumas. Still on her bed when I'd peeked into her room.

I headed for a rickety staircase. "Let's see what's upstairs."

The room was cluttered with easels, paints, brushes and canvasses. An old sweater was draped over a chair. I picked it up and put it down quickly. "Authentic twentieth century sweat - the watchman's. And this beer bottle is vintage yesterday."

Edward wasn't listening. He stared at a poster of one of Cézanne's paintings. "The curves and the colours could take you over if you let them, stop the world for you, make you crazy - I'd like to try to do something like that."

I put my hand in his. "A writer to be and now an artist, Mr Bellingham? And you want to be crazy?"

He grinned. "Why not?"

"No, you have to stay sane for me."

We went back into Aix to shop for some artists' materials and ate lunch, squashed and sweating side by side in what shade the café parasol on the street offered. Edward ordered a carafe of wine and drank most of it. "Careful with that," I said. "The afternoon's going to get hotter. Heat and wine aren't good friends." But Edward was flushed and laughing and planning art classes back in London.

The view from the quarries across to Mont Saint-Victoire unrolled across pantile roofs, over cypress trees and rounded hills, to the peaks of mountains which surrendered their colour to the distance. I dreamed away an hour or so in the shade while Edward sketched. I thought of coming back here when our degrees were finished, how we'd tour France, write, paint, perhaps make a life near the families at *Les Moulins*. Away from Edward's constricting home - not much freedom or room to breathe in Hertfordshire - he could be himself. There was space and light enough here to banish my stalking shadows.

I looked across at Edward. He was sitting bending his head between his knees and wiping a pale face with a handkerchief. Brushes and paper were strewn like rubbish on the ground. I found the flask of water, made him drink some and poured the rest over him. We got slowly down the dirt track with Edward stopping to be sick and found a taxi whose driver I had to tip outrageously to get us back to Claire's apartment.

"I told you so," I said as I helped Edward into bed and offered another glass of water. It's mild sunstroke plus the wine." I called Claire at her office and said I would make dinner rather than go out. I said Edward was too fair and too English to cope with the dangers of the Provençal sunshine and had gone to bed with a cold compress.

I stuffed tomatoes - bigger than my fists - with sausage meat and herbs, whipped egg yolks and cream for a crème brûlée, laid out a cheese board. I'd nearly come unstuck buying food. The corner shop Claire directed me to was dark and cool, full of southern produce and I was served by a tiny, bent man with blue tinted spectacles. His French was different from mine and I had to point at what I wanted and hold out a palm full of change for him to help himself. I realised belatedly that he was speaking Occitan. I wondered if this was Claire's joke or her attempt to wrong foot me.

I set the table with blue and white china and lit a lamp. Claire's flat was dark, even on a summer's evening; the narrow alley next to it forbade much light. I burrowed in the dresser for napkins and cutlery and noticed a small, silver framed photo of a laughing boy, running towards the camera, mouth wide in a laugh. Charles.

Claire came home with fresh bread and a box dressed up with lavender ribbons. "Gateau," she said, putting it on the table and taking two bottles of red wine from her bag. "How is he? Sure he doesn't need a doctor? There's a super one here who'll come out if we need him."

"He's alright now, just sleeping. Thanks." I took the glass of white wine Claire poured for me, chilled and stone dry.

"Tomorrow," Claire said, gulping greedily, "I have a day off so I can indulge tonight."

We ate and chatted and the talk fell to *Les Moulins*. I braved the topic I had promised myself I would bring up. "Mum and Dad would like to see you there more often, you know."

Claire cast a watchful glance at me. "Too busy. It's a long drive." She refilled our glasses and took some of the goats' cheese, moving aside its casing of brown foliage. "What do you think of the *Banon*? They have to count the chestnut leaves when they wrap it."

I babbled about the families. "Mum and Dad are fine but Dad still works too hard. He says his books are their pension, but really he just likes hitting the typewriter keys. I don't think he goes on so many trips; now we've left they seem to get on better. Mum hasn't had many of her funny spells lately, she stays with us more."

"That's good," Claire touched my hand. "Put some flowers on the grave for me." She didn't need to say 'Charles.' The photos: here and at home, the absence we all felt even now, the hole gaping in Mum's heart.

"Marcelle's the same as ever," I went on. "Running the farm with Pierre, running everyone's lives. Pierre hasn't been well again, but you know what he's like. Then he'll have another good patch. Marcelle's like a broody hen with him and he just grumbles at her." I took a sip of wine and wondered why Claire was attentive but at the same time distracted by something. "Marthe's still nursing at La Roche. There's yet another boyfriend on the scene. This one's different, a trainee doctor - Didier. *Très* beau. He's smitten - they both are from the sound of it."

"Well done, Marthe. And what about Jeanne?"

"Jeanne ... well, she's OK, although she's putting on weight these days. Too much of Marcelle's cooking but no one minds and everybody takes care of her, calms her down when she has her usual moods. Marcelle carries on: teaches her things, plays games with her. They still won't take the swings down; Jeanne is so odd without them - what can they do?"

"I don't know. I worry for Mum ... she doesn't have the energy to shout about the swings, to find a voice to demand they're pulled down...I wish...Rosemary, isn't she more important than Jeanne? " Claire rested her chin in cupped hands as if head was too heavy.

I hadn't seen it quite that way before; it was naive of me. When I thought about my mother I was sad, pleased when she was happy, concerned when she wasn't. But my anxieties for her hadn't stretched into trying to help her find ways to ask for what she wanted. I couldn't see how to make her speak up for herself. She was so passive in the face of the others; I wanted to shout for her. Everyone pretended that ten years ago they hadn't seen a dead boy underneath those swings.

Claire was abrupt. "And Philippe? What's he up to?'

"He's fine, a bit lazy. School, rugby, hanging out with his friends, loud music. But he helps Pierre and Marcelle willingly enough."

"Well, that sounds good."

There was another silence, longer this time. I noticed Claire had drunk most of the second bottle of red wine. She nursed her glass and looked across to the window, at herself reflected back from the dark.

I stood up. "I'll see if Edward needs anything, then I'm for bed."

"No, Rosemary. Check on him and come back here."

"Well, you're drunk, my bossy sister." I went back anyway.

"I'm going to tell you a story," Claire said, pouring coffee into tiny cups and offering brandy that had appeared on the table in my brief absence.

"Once upon a time there were two families living next door to each other. And the eldest girl used to help the other family out with their children. And one day she saw something she couldn't explain."

I sipped my coffee and pursed my lips with impatience.

"Do you remember," Claire asked, "that I used to look after Philippe sometimes? If Marcelle was extra busy or if Jeanne was ill. When Philippe was about six and Marcelle was with Jeanne, and, I don't know, trying to run the farm, doing everything, I was playing with Philippe. There was no one else around. I don't know where you or Marthe were. We had a silly game of chase and he ran into the farmyard and went sprawling in the muck heap. He was covered in straw and dung. Completely! God, he stank!

"I was terrified Pierre would appear and shout at us. I didn't dare tell Marcelle, that would have been worse, so I dragged him upstairs, got him into a bath and some clean clothes. I gave him a good telling off as well but all he could do was giggle."

I sighed. "Oh, come on Claire - get on with it. This is a not very funny story about a little boy years ago."

I stood up to take the cups out and go to bed. I was tired from a long day and fuzzy from the wine and brandy.

Claire stood up with me and took her blouse off.

"Now, sister. I'm sure you're drunk."

"Do you remember this?" She pointed to the top of her right arm. Just below her shoulder was a dark brown birthmark about five centimetres long and shaped like a boat with a curved bottom and a straight deck. It could be half a circle but when we were young we'd called it a boat. I'd forgotten it completely until now.

"You tried to scrub it off once," I said. "Mum told you it was there because you were special. I was jealous of that." I tried to joke but the expression on Claire's face stopped me.

"When I bathed Philippe that time, I found exactly the same mark in the same place on his right arm. Rosemary, have you ever seen it?"

I tried to look back, to force my bleary mind to visualise Philippe as a small boy with short sleeves. I saw a fair tanned child forever on the move but I really couldn't recall the top of his arms. Why should I? "I don't think so - I can't remember. If it was there I might have just - I don't know. Perhaps I got so used to it I didn't really see it? No, Claire. I didn't see it."

"I thought like that too. Perhaps we simply stop seeing small things.

I've tried to forget it ever since but for us to have the same mark? It's so odd, Rosemary. I've never mentioned it to anyone before - it's just been on my mind. And what would I say, Rosemary? Ask Mum, 'Are Philippe and I related?' Well, how could that be? Dad and Marcelle? I can't see that! I couldn't ask any of them!"

She waited for me to reply and I waited for something to turn up in my head so I could say it. Silence fell flat between us. I had never looked at Philippe's arms with any attention; I couldn't remember noticing any mark. The candle on the table finally spluttered out. This was all just rubbish when Claire had too much to drink and the wine was making her imagination do silly dances, cavorting around something she might have seen when she was a child. Or had grown only in her imagination.

"It's just chance," I said at last. "It might have been a smudge of dirt. You're not remembering anything properly. Go to bed, Claire."

She looked at me without speaking for a long moment. I fidgeted and got up. "I'm off."

"Sure."

Sure of what she had seen or sure, you go to bed and don't believe me then?

The next morning Claire and I took coffee at a café on the *Cours Mirabeau.* I had to admire the statue of Good King René, she told me, look he's clutching a bunch of Muscat grapes. Did I know there were over a hundred fountains in *Aix?* There were many other things a tourist should know - she kept telling me. I stayed quiet, wondering about my sister; her peculiar upset yesterday evening over a mark on a boy's arm, her incessant chatter this morning about the town that swirled around us. The boulevard streamed with life: tourists ambling, looking, pointing cameras; business men pushing forwards, swinging important briefcases; women walking dogs, delivery men heaving boxes. Plane trees bent to make an arch above the wide boulevade, whispering to each other, trembling in the extraordinary, brilliant light.

Edward, recovered by a long sleep and lots of breakfast, had gone shopping. I wished him back quickly; I wanted some company other than my brittle sister.

Claire fished a photograph out of her handbag. "It's from Mum's birthday a year or so before I left. Everyone's there. I think one of the farm lads took it. It's the only photo I have with me." No, not the only one; she didn't know I'd seen her photo of Charles.

Mum and Dad were central, Mum smiling, wearing a short, pale dress that showed off her long legs. Dad, smart with a neat tie and jacket, wore his get-on-with-it expression. Behind them stood Marcelle, a little to one side because of Mum's height, and Pierre just behind Dad, only his face visible, his lop sided smile clear. Philippe was standing next to Marcelle, an embarrassed lad's grin on his face and on the other side, next to Pierre, was Jeanne, frowning, with her dead straight hair in a pudding basin bob that did nothing for her poor face. In the front row, sitting at Mum and Dad's feet were Claire, Marthe and myself. Marthe and I were giggling conspirators, shoulder to shoulder and Claire, half turning, beamed indulgently at us.

"Who looks like who?" Claire demanded. Her story of the birthmarks was such nonsense. But these families were mine; I loved every one of them and hated anything that might be a slur against them. Whatever Claire thought, whatever she had made up, there was nothing wrong. I would forget the whole episode, as she ought to do. A rift between Claire and I would be unthinkable so I was quiet; I would not give credence to anything she had told me. Weirdly, I had an acute longing for my doll, Cherie. She was safe in my suitcase in Claire's flat. I'd packed her with me, I always did. Edward thought it a sweet eccentricity.

I picked up my coffee and took a sip, ignoring my sister and watching the street's little acts. "Who's like who?" Claire thrust the photo in front of me.

"No one, Claire. We're all a bit different." I pushed my cup away and pointed. "See that man over there - he's got to be fifty. Do you think he dyes his hair? It's much too black."

Claire set the photo aside and waved irritably at a waiter for more coffee. She pushed her hair back from her forehead with a flick of dissatisfaction.

"I like the cut," I said.

"I can never get it to fall like yours." She tilted her head sideways like a bright bird inspecting me.

I didn't look at her. The rangy figure of Edward strolled towards us and I stood up to wave.

Rosemary. London, Autumn 1972

A BLANKET OF cloud had wrapped up London for days. Single, giant drops of rain fell reluctantly and the downpour waited and threatened. I was curled up in an armchair in front of the gas fire, dozing over an open text book; the manners of seventeenth century dissemblers failing to engage me. My LP had finished and I was too lazy to get up and turn it over.

Sheets of notes were spread in a circle at my feet. I felt squashed in this room; the bed, living area and kitchen corner had no separation; books lined the walls and piles of them roamed across the floor. It wasn't as bad as some bedsits in London but I was glad Mum and Dad hadn't seen it.

I thought I heard the rain start in earnest, clattering against the ill-fitting window that let all the heat out. Then I realised it was the telephone ringing two floors down. It stopped abruptly. Occasionally it was so irritating I would haul myself down the dusty, uncarpeted stairs to the hall to answer it, to take messages no one collected.

"Rosemary! Rosemary!" Lois, from a room one floor down had a high, penetrating voice. "A call for you!"

Lois held out the receiver to me. "Someone from your French side." She always talked of my French and English sides, making comedy out of my way of switching languages. She raised heavily outlined eyebrows and pursed her mouth in a pouty kiss. "A man speaking from France, oo la la!"

" 'Allo?" I listened for a minute or two, asking questions in French.

Lois waved at me and wiggled her hips as she ran back up the stairs.

I sat down heavily on the last stair. "Anyone else? Who's there with her? Does Claire know?"

I put the phone down and dialled Edward's number. I waited as it rang on his staircase. Please be in.

"Rosemary? I thought you were writing an essay?" He sounded half asleep.

"I've got to go over. Didier called - Marthe's in hospital. Somehow she's eaten poisonous fungi. I've got to go soon ... " I didn't want to cry; took a deep breath. "Didier says it's very bad -she might not ... it's very bad, I must be quick."

I packed a bag and told Lois, who said, "oh my God," and gave me a hug, the comic looks all gone.

Edward found a booking for a night ferry but there were no cabins. We slept fitfully on a hard couch in a beery lounge.

I took over the driving when we came off the boat. I wanted the distraction. Edward had driven in England like someone demented so we could catch the crossing and now I needed to do something. There was no light in the sky for a long time and the windscreen wipers slapped against heavy rain. I thought of nothing but the slick road, not daring to imagine what might be ahead. Every so often Edward asked, "are you alright?" I would nod and then we'd be silent.

When we reached home the honey-gold of the house had gone; just sombre grey stone greeted us in the gloom. Mum and Dad were waiting in the porch; they'd heard the car crunch on the gravel. The rain stopped but the air was heavy with wet and it was dark again.

Mum hugged me and then Edward. "You both look awful. Some coffee quickly and then we'll go. Marcelle is staying with her all the time. Claire is there too. She got here this morning."

Dad appeared, pipe in hand. He looked drawn, his mouth a thin, tight line. He hugged me and then shook Edward's hand, "Thanks for coming with Rosemary."

The hospital room was too bright: florescent lights ageing faces and deepening shadows of tiredness on everyone. Marthe was asleep, her skin like wax, with her brown hair laying damp on the pillow. A tube ran into her arm and another snaked out from under the bed covers. The room smelt of disinfectant and air freshener. The sickly lilac smell of the aerosol caught in my throat.

I went up to Marthe and reached for her hand. "Hello, Marthe. It's Rosemary. I've come with Edward to see you. How are you?" I could think of nothing apart from stupid banalities. I looked at her and remembered her laugh. I saw her running over the lawns to call for me.

Marthe's eyes opened briefly, showing the whites turned yellow. Her lips parted and she took a little breath, like a sigh. Then she appeared to fall back to sleep. I felt a great weight collecting round the inside of me. I held my eyes wide open so the tears wouldn't spill out.

Marcelle and Pierre were siting side by side opposite me. Marcelle's face was grey and her eyes were circled with fatigue black. She came round the bed and hugged me and Edward then returned to her seat, fixing her look on her daughter. Claire and Philippe were in the room, both of them embraced me and shook hands with Edward.

By the head of the bed was a tall, dark man who had to be Didier. I looked across and he held my gaze in a long stare, telling me. A nurse bustled in, tutting to herself. She was an older woman, with an officious air. "Only two visitors at a time, please," she said. She bent down and spoke softly to Marthe and felt her pulse. As she straightened up her stern expression softened and she shook her head gently, a tiny movement. "You may all stay. Let me know if there's any change." She looked at each one of us and then went over to Marcelle and put a hand on her shoulder. "Please, Madame Aubin. Take a few minutes rest. Just a few. Something to eat perhaps. There's coffee at the nurses' desk in the big ward." But Marcelle hadn't heard and sat unmoving.

Throughout the night we drifted in and out of the room to a visitors' lounge furnished with old armchairs in green leatherette. The lights were softer here, a coffee table was strewn with magazines, greasy with use. A pile of dirty coffee cups were stacked on a shelf under the window. There were flowers here as well, not allowed in the ward. Roses, beautifully expensive, were on the table and next to them was a small bunch of Michaelmas daisies with a note written in a shaky hand, 'From Jeanne, xxx.'

Edward and I fetched coffee for ourselves; Claire took cups into the room for Marcelle and Pierre. Apart from visiting the lavatory, they refused to move away from Marthe's side. Mum and Dad stayed with them.

My sister came into the lounge, sat down and took my hand. "What happened?" It was the first chance I had to ask.

"Apparently Marcelle made a mushroom risotto for dinner and only Marthe ate it. She and Marcelle were to eat together but Marcelle was called out to the farm. Something about a break in the fence and she had to hold a lamp for the lads. When she came back in she didn't feel like eating. Pierre was over at Monsieur Cotin's farm, doing odd jobs and drinking with the old man."

"Not Philippe nor Jeanne?" I wondered where Jeanne was; I hadn't questioned her absence. Had she visited or been left at home to save her any upset?

"Marcelle said that Jeanne had had one of her grumpy moods and taken herself off to her room with some cake. Philippe wasn't there. He'd gone over to a friends' place to study. There was just no one around. Even Didier. He was supposed to come over but he phoned to say he'd miss dinner - the car or a patient or some hold up ... " Claire tailed off. She bunched her fists up to her mouth and started to cry. She wiped her eyes and swallowed. "About three hours later Marthe was terribly sick and had diarrhoea and felt really bad. Didier came over eventually - a good job - and spotted mushroom poisoning straightaway. Apparently it's really obvious. He called an ambulance and it seems that they thought Marthe was going to be alright. Marcelle said she was getting better - then she suddenly deteriorated - now her liver's stopped working. There's nothing ... Marcelle blames herself, but she mustn't. Mum's been wonderful, very practical. She's being strong for Marcelle now."

Philippe came into the lounge. He had grown taller since I last saw him, even though that wasn't so long ago, and his slight frame was taking on a solidity, showing the man he would become. In any other circumstances I would have been pleased to see him; laughed and joked with him. He was the next best thing to a brother for me and I ached for him. He kissed me on both cheeks and then hugged me, stifling a sob. He shook his head when I asked him if anyone knew how poisonous fungi got into the risotto. "*Maman* said Marthe had picked them."

"But the poisonous ones are in the woods at the back," I said. "Aren't they the - *champignons de bouchons* ... no, that's not right. " I struggled with the French. "*En anglais, Philippe* - death caps?"

Philippe nodded. "*Champignons vénéneux.* Poisonous mushrooms.

She must have been in the woods. Didier says it's the yellow death caps - they're the deadly ones and might be confused with chanterelles. The doctors know. The *gendarmes* took everything away to analyse." He bit the base of his thumb and frowned.

"I wish I'd been home," he went on. "If only I'd not been so keen to go over to Bernard's house. We didn't even study much - just hung about and listened to music. God, I'm so selfish."

His voice cracked and Claire put her arm round him. "No you're not - it's not your fault. You weren't to know." Philippe put his hand up to touch Claire's on his shoulder.

I felt I didn't understand anything. What had Marthe done? "Marthe would know not to pick them from the woods," I said. "I used to get the mushrooms with her. We were told time and time again - only the white ones from the lawn. Never the yellow ones in the woods. Never, ever, to go into the woods for them in case we made a mistake. The fungi there were for the grown ups to pick: just the yellow chanterelles. We might get them muddled up with the bad ones - everyone was strict about it." I thought back. "Even when we were older we didn't - we still wouldn't go in the woods. Last year it was just the same; we stayed on the lawn as usual and left the woodland ones for Marcelle." I saw Marthe and I competing over how many we could gather; filling golden willow baskets with white treasure, searching all the big lawns for it. "How did Marcelle know Marthe had picked them anyway? What did Marthe actually say?"

Philippe looked bleakly at me. "Ah, well. Jeanne told *Maman*. She said she'd seen Marthe on the lawn by her swings and then she said she'd seen her later in the woods, under the oak tree, where the death caps are. Everyone asked her: *Maman, Papa,* Tom, Nancy. The *gendarmes* asked her. Jeanne got really flustered. After a while she put her hands over her ears and ran off to the swings. Poor Jeanne - it's not her fault - she doesn't know anything. You know what she's like ... "

"Marthe didn't say?"

"No, there wasn't a chance, Didier just got her to the hospital - really quickly. I suppose we thought we could ask questions later. It was such a panic! She got a little better but after that she went downhill so fast."

I felt cold in that overheated lounge, as if a window had been opened to let in the freezing night air. "What have they done with - er - what have they told Jeanne about Marthe?"

"Just that Marthe's a bit poorly. She's upset enough. And she's been a bit peculiar these last few weeks. She had the ear infections again." Philippe looked away and down at the floor. "To tell you the truth, I'd been staying out a lot. Jeanne and Marthe were rowing, really irritating me. Something about the electricity. Jeanne leaves every light on and Marthe goes round turning them off, shouting about the waste of energy. Marthe hasn't been very patient with her. I mean, Jeanne's not right - the doctor's been out to her quite a few times. So we haven't said much to her and *Papa* gave her some pills to keep her quiet."

"They're sisters growing up, Philippe," I said. "They're bound to not get on sometimes. I'll go and see her when we get back."

"Would you? That's kind - thanks. When we've finished ... " He looked like a little boy again, tears brimming.

We waited, the two families, for another day and night. Marcelle and Pierre never left Marthe's bedside, Didier with them. Philippe and Claire were in and out, restless and tearful. Mum and Dad, Edward and I dozed briefly in the visitors' lounge, only to start awake, feeling guilty, and then go and sit by Marthe's bedside with the others. We watched Marthe's face change colour, from pale yellow to a deep orange as her liver failed. We listened to her breathing: stop ... start; stop ... start; stop ... In the last hours of the night Mum got up to clear the window of the condensation that had collected in the stuffy room. We saw the sky lighten to a cold, clear dawn. Marthe died as a low sun turned the horizon rose gold.

No one spoke as we all made our way back to the separate houses at *Les Moulins*. Philippe stayed close to Marcelle and Pierre. Edward and I went home with Mum and Dad and Claire.

"I must do something," Claire said. She made coffee, tidied the kitchen, fed the cats. Then she left us abruptly, saying she wanted to see the others, running without a coat across the lawn to the Mill House.

You don't think - in your twenties - anyone will die. Your friends are there forever. Marthe and I had always joked about how we glued the families together, in and out of both the houses. Mum and Marcelle together had to agree on how to discipline us when we got into mischief otherwise we'd make sure to be let off by one or the other. If Dad or Pierre got involved it was worse. They never wanted to know what was going on and if they did find out there'd be trouble. It was Marcelle, of course, who decided to forbid us cake for tea or make us do extra chores. We didn't mind the jobs if we did them together and Marthe always managed to steal something sweet from the larder. I didn't want that taken away: I wanted to cling tight to the memories. To stay with all of us at *Les Moulins*. But with Marthe's death the ties slackened.

I went over the next day and found Marcelle and Jeanne cuddled up on the sofa. Jeanne was sobbing and wiping her face with a handkerchief. Marcelle was making soothing sounds and gently rocking them both. I didn't know what to say except to offer to make some coffee or a tisane.

"Thank you," Marcelle said as I put a tray down.

"Where's Pierre?" I asked, relieved he wasn't there. He had looked hollowed out by Marthe's death, so bereft that I couldn't bear to see him.

"He and Philippe are moving some cows to another field." She shrugged. "Something to do."

She moved away from Jeanne to take a cup. "Here, Rosemary - make Jeanne smile again." She put Jeanne's hand in mine.

Jeanne snuffled and sniffed up tears and snot. "Funny English," she said in her heavy accent. She didn't have many foreign words but saying the few she did know made her laugh. It was always our game to teach her more Funny English words.

"Yes, Jeanne. Funny English. Let's try 'not sad.' *Pas triste*. Not. Sad."

"Not. *Pas triste*." Jeanne giggled and reached over to take one of the biscuits I'd found in the kitchen. "Not. Sad. *Pas*. Sad."

The curé turned up the day after, first to the big house and then to us, spreading condolences like jam and drinking coffee with brandy. He was a red-faced, rotund man in a black soutane that didn't quite camouflage the food stain down the front. I found little comfort in his visits. I had prayed after a fashion in the hospital. Dear God, let her be alright. I'd always declined - with permission - to attend church services and I had only a hazy idea of any god. On occasion when there wasn't a service, I'd peered into the great cold church fumy with stale incense. It just seemed to me full of dead people named on plaques. All that Latin.

Marthe's funeral was a week later. Before, I'd thought of the Sunday Mass as full of bored people, there for the gossip and the lunch to follow. Now the church was full of broken hearts; a cavern that gathered up the echoes of the priest's words and the muffled crying. The chill, scented air seemed to contain the tears and a dirty sky wept rain when we went to the grave.

Afterwards a kind of lethargy spread across the houses. Claire visited Marcelle and Pierre before she returned south. I saw her standing by their door, hugging them, drooping over them as if she couldn't stay upright. She said only a brief goodbye to me. She took a handkerchief and wiped Mum's tears for her; put her arms round Dad and then left silently. Philippe came over to us once, raw faced and red eyed. He told us Marcelle was spending a lot of time with Jeanne who had some pills when her distress was too much. Marcelle and Pierre he said, were 'holding up.' They had to concentrate on Jeanne. I didn't see Jeanne again. It was as if she was placed at the epicentre of everyone's grief. I should have done more but I didn't relish the idea of trying to console her, of holding her hand and watching her tears switch to smiles like a weather vane turning.

Edward and I hung about at home trying to help with chores that Mum and Dad could do perfectly well. I put together meals no one wanted and I found Mum with Charles' photo. Dad always seemed to have a whisky glass in his hand.

Back in London Edward was my rock, my timetable, my cook. He kept me to the university routine, such as it was, and we both got through the term. He became my best friend in place of Marthe as well as my lover.

I looked at my books and made notes which I instantly forgot. Marthe arrived in my thoughts all the time. I should have written more to her; stayed home and studied at a French university. Stayed close to her; been a break on some of her wilder ideas. Once, I stopped her swimming nude in the great, gloopy *Loire* a few summers ago. I should have been there to stop her sudden fancy to pick mushrooms in the woods.

I could see her yellow face and hear her not breathe. I saw the fat curé in the rain at an open grave. There was a coil of barbed wire in my stomach that hurt me whenever I looked back; I welcomed and hated the pain. We had endlessly swapped stories as we walked along the river shore, mud oozing though our toes. We'd bothered the fishermen to see what they'd caught. Teased each other and tried to ride *Monsieur* Cotin's old cart horse. She picked me up when I fell off. We'd hung around Marcelle's kitchen like the hens waiting for food. I was always going to go home to her with tales of London. I was going to bring her back with me to see the sights. She would tell me about the hospital, the matron she hated, the handsome doctors and embellish all the gossip.

That year we went back for Christmas and trod gentle footsteps around Marcelle and Pierre. Philippe spent a lot of time with his friends. I cheered up Jeanne with the Funny English game. At home, Mum tried to be bright but gazed at us with vague eyes. Dad drank. There was too much food left over from a Christmas Eve feast that was garnished with small, sad smiles.

Afterwards tensions grew, developing in sharp looks and silences. There was an extraordinary atmosphere between Dad and Pierre; both drinking too much, unusually spending time together, ignored for the most part by their wives. I found them the day after Christmas in Dad's study. They were sat across from each other, arms folded, an empty bottle on a table. There was a flaring bruise on the side of Dad's face and Pierre's stick lay on the floor the other side of the room. I had to call them for a meal. Instead I said, "you two look very cross with each other." I couldn't believe these grown men - my Dad and my friend - had been fighting; I wasn't sure what men looked like after a fight. They stared at me. "Supper's ready," I said and ducked out of the room, wishing I could run straight to Marthe who would understand our fathers for me.

All the next year we stayed away. France was home but I didn't want to return. The families were swaddled in grief and there was too much at *les Moulins* to tug at my heart. Ghosts pulled at me, making me see Marthe again: her serious look, her smile, her face, dying orange in the hospital. Nor had I forgotten the scene between Dad and Pierre. I'd thought of asking Marcelle - not my mother - about it when we went back and, in odd moments, worked out how to put my questions. When I thought about it, there was always this current of tension between the two men, it ebbed and flowed, never disappearing completely. I felt I couldn't say anything to Edward to try to puzzle it out with him; his calmness and kindness wouldn't help me plunder the men's histories.

The second university year was hard; I had to work despite everything. Edward took his finals and there were plenty of normal things to keep us very busy. We studied hard, we had friends and parties; the arguments and the makings up as any couple did. The music was fabulous and I lived in long skirts and optimistic, embroidered tops. But we were anxious in London, bombings and security always in the news; we talked of settling, eventually, in France. Edward got his 2.1 and found himself writing for an advertising agency in the day and for himself in the evenings. I ploughed through my final year and the day the university notice board told me I had a 2.1 honours degree Edward asked me to marry him.

I liked the hermetic world of the university. I stayed on: Jane Austen's measured prose was safe to study, Fielding amused me and a grant for a Master's degree was available for two years. I found my thesis more difficult than I anticipated and I was sick with nerves just before the results came out.

Except it hadn't been nerves making me so queasy. I collected my degree and visited my family doctor who confirmed I was pregnant.

My first appointment at the ante natal clinic was when I was about three months. The midwife who examined me frowned. "I'll ask Mr Summers to come in, if you don't mind."

"Is there anything to worry about?" The gynaecologist shook his head in answer and pushed gently at my already obvious bulge. I was larger than the other pregnant women I'd seen at the doctor's surgery but had thought nothing of it. Slim women showed more, didn't they?

Mr Summers had bushy eyebrows that raised and lowered themselves with remarkable rapidity. They accelerated upwards as he smiled. "I think you've got two babies in there, Mrs Bellingham."

Edward had found *Krug* champagne from somewhere. For the second time we toasted my fertility: twins! How clever of us! I could drink very little and watched Edward get merry on most of the bottle.

"How are we going to tell the parents about twins?" I asked. "It was bad enough when we thought there was just one. My mother's 'little episode.'"

"Ah, yes. Yours, you mean. Mine won't mind any number of babies. She'll do nothing else but knit more baby clothes and give up gardening."

"Your mother will never finish any knitting because she'll forget where she put it down," I said. "My mother may have another turn."

"Oh God - like the last time."

"I don't know what she was on about. Some weird bee in her bonnet. How she could say such things." The painful memory of mother's angry face when I'd told her about the positive pregnancy test was as fresh as yesterday.

When we'd visited France earlier that summer I'd arranged to be alone with Mum in the evening to tell her I was pregnant. Dad was coming in later but I wanted to tell Mum by myself. It was important to do it that way, I'm not sure why. Perhaps because of Charles I was fearful of her reaction. I didn't want to upset her; revive her loss with my good news. And I didn't want others to be around to dilute my news. Now I was to be a mother myself I wanted more closeness with her; I would understand her better. I'd become obsessed with the details of producing a new life and in awe of women who had given birth. I'd know myself how Mum had felt and I wanted another mother at my side, my mother. I wanted a better connection with her to make up for past distances. I imagined her not vague as she had been so often when I was growing up. This time she'd be attentive to me and my child. She'd want to be a grandmother, to share my babies.

The plan had been that Edward would go over to see Marcelle and Pierre and have a game of table tennis with Philippe. He would tell them and crack open a bottle. I would tell Mum and then Dad when he came back. The three of us would go and join them and we could all celebrate. We'd phone Claire from the Mill House.

Mum and I sat on the patio soaking up the evening heat. Pregnancy had made my senses more acute and the luxurious scent of sweet peas drifted across from the borders of the lawn.

I'd produced a decent bottle of wine and some of those tiny *rillons* we liked. "I've some news, Mum."

She didn't turn round. "Yes?' Then she looked at my middle and I wondered if Marcelle had guessed and said something. Mum wasn't so acute but Marcelle could spot a pregnancy even if a woman's stomach was board flat.

"I'm going to have a baby, Mum."

She sat very still. "When?"

"I'm about two months so it'll be in February."

Mum poured herself a glass of wine and tilted the bottle towards me. I held my hand over my half full glass and laughed, "Can't drink so much now."

"Are you well?" Mum sounded as if she was a mile away, somewhere else.

"I'm really well. It's wonderful, Mum!" I watched Mum down her glass of wine and reach for the bottle again, her face set. This wasn't the mother and daughter encounter I'd envisaged. I wished she'd look at me properly.

"You can't have it." She made the baby sound like a toy I'd reached for when I was a greedy child. "What about your career?"

"I can carry on at the university - take maternity leave. People do that now - Edward earns enough for us to have some help."

"Get rid of it."

"Mum!"

"I mean it - there are terminations these days. Go back to London and find someone to do it. A clinic. I'll pay." Anger and fear I couldn't understand chased each other across her face, made her eyes wide.

I didn't get it. I felt as if she's slapped me. This instruction to murder from my own mother. I wanted to scream, grab her and shake her. All I could say was, "What do you mean?"

Mum was drinking like a thirsty man without manners. She became pompous. "Of course you can't have children; you mustn't. It's not for you. No." She paused a moment. "It's not a safe world for them. All those bombs in London - everywhere. The world is awful. And you don't know what you'll get." She looked as if she might spit at me.

She made children sound like a disease one caught in a dangerous place. What I'd get. She stood up and wobbled, straightening her back with a slow, deliberate stretch and placing one hand on the wall. I helped her up to bed, saying, "you've just had a bit too much wine, Mum - you don't mean any of this."

She'd never been like this, she wasn't herself. Something else must be wrong, something not to do with me. She'd come round, hug me tomorrow, be pleased in the morning. She could be tearful and neglectful sometimes, but never so furious and slanderous. It was the wine talking, she hadn't known what she was saying. Perhaps she thought I was someone else although I couldn't imagine who it could be.

When he came in Dad hugged me and kissed me with his whiskey breath. I told him as soon as I could, getting it over with, fearful of another strange reaction. He was pleased but quick about it. "Lovely girl. Well done." He looked around, eyebrows raised. "Where's Nan?"

"Mum had a bit too much, she's gone to bed."

"Ah. Well. We'll go over to the big house now, shall we?"

In the morning Mum formally inquired about my health and busied herself in the far side of the garden. The hoped for apology didn't come. I couldn't believe how spiteful she was and over lunch I watched her tight, unhappy face and resented her. I realised - dimly and reluctantly - that she must be miserable herself in order to say such things. I wanted to say something to make her better but couldn't find any generosity in me to even attempt to do so.

I thought of the warmth at the Mill House yesterday: Marcelle's arms immediately around me, Pierre's kisses on my cheeks, Philippe's handshake and his embarrassed, lightning hug. Jeanne had smiled and put her hand on my tummy. "*Bébé là-dedans*?"

"That's right; in there. It's only tiny at the moment."

"What are you going to call it?"

"I don't know yet, Jeanne. I might ask my Mummy to suggest some names." That was bitchy; I don't know if Marcelle heard and told Mum or not.

I counted the days until we could go back to England and avoided my parents when I could. I wandered around after Marcelle and talked with her about baby clothes and prams. When we drove off to catch the ferry I looked back. Everyone saw us off as usual but Mum and Dad stood a little apart from the others. I watched Dad do something rare: he put his arm round Mum and held out a handkerchief to her.

❧

"We'll have to tell your mother, Rosemary. She might have got over whatever it was by now. We'll just say two are on the way. Have your Dad there this time - it might help. And me." He squeezed my shoulder. "Come on, we'll do this together.

In the end, I wrote to tell them about the twins, like a coward, ducking out of another scene with my mother. I composed what I hoped were kind letters, without any emphasis on either the joys of looking forward to the babies or the trials of a twin pregnancy. As long as they knew about the twins and that I was doing alright, that was enough. These missives felt like the letters I wrote home when I first came to London: written with the utmost banality and as carefully edited as any sensitive press bulletin. The letters back were equally insipid; good news about Dad's writing, comments about Marcelle and Pierre and the farm, a new recipe for chocolate cake. Everyone was 'fine'; poor Jeanne hadn't been very good, but much better now. I was pleased to hear Philippe had become engaged. He and Lucette were to live in the village at first, but there were plans for them to move up to the Mill House when the time was proper. I thought about wedding presents.

It was the autumn term. The university work was a blessing. I didn't have to think about families, unless they wore Regency dresses or tailcoats, alive only on paper, not saying awful things to me personally. Edward was busy and we didn't have much time together to look at diaries to decide when to travel over to France. I couldn't face the usual half term visit; I would be embarrassingly large in front of Dad and be risking another outburst from Mum. I tried hard to forget what was said and I didn't want to jeopardise what peace I had found. My peculiar dreams had stopped, I was cheerful every day; pregnancy seemed a cure.

I was too huge at Christmas to endure the ferry and the long drive across France. Edward and I celebrated quietly, taking the break from work to sleep and rest. I started maternity leave from the English department and then spent the next six weeks in lumbering anticipation.

I loved Mr Summers. He declared, wriggling his eyebrows, that he would prefer to perform a caesarian instead of letting me deliver normally. It would be very difficult for me he said, why not take the easy way out?

Everything hurt afterwards. I'm ashamed to say I behaved like an invalid and Edward had to help a lot. That was frowned upon in his office but already he was thinking of writing full time and declared a complete lack of interest in what others thought of him. When I recovered he went back to work and I drowned in nappies and feeds. When I wasn't too tired to be merely an automaton there was delight in Harry and Elizabeth. I sent photos over and mined the return letters for traces of warmth and interest in the grandchildren.

Rosemary. London and France, 1982

WE GOT THROUGH the next five years with only fleeting visits to France. Mum behaved as if nothing had happened. On the first visit with the babies she was a fraction less than friendly as we pulled up on the drive. "Thank you for the photos," she said, as if I'd sent her a postcard from Margate. She stood back and gazed at my twins as I lifted them out of the car, her expression unreadable. After that a switch was turned on: she delighted in them. She cooed, she played, she produced baby clothes in the right size, brightly coloured toys and garish, zooming mobiles. I was glad, although I still kept a wary barrier between Mum and I, organising our time so that we mixed in with the French 'side' where the twins were taken from me to be adored by everyone.

I taught Jeanne how to hold them, pleased for her that she should enjoy them and learn their names in her Funny English. It's Harry and Beth," I said.

She giggled. "*Arri et Bet. Arri et Bet.*" I wondered how Marthe would have been with them.

A longer summer holiday was suggested when the twins were five. Mum and Dad wanted to have a discussion about their wills. Who wants to see their parents get older and talk of what happens when …? No one does. Dad said they'd get it out of the way, sooner rather than later, then we could all relax and they could enjoy their grandchildren.

We were both working hard: the university made endless demands and gave me too little time for them. Arranging child care and working full time were a fatiguing series of acts in the family play. A long holiday felt deserved.

Edward had taken the plunge and given up the day job after a first, surprisingly successful book. We'd moved to a bigger flat, the process a full time job in itself.

"Let's go, it'll be alright now. Your Mum's lovely with them - she's been fine ever since she clapped eyes on them," Edward said, as ever wanting to brush any lingering trace of unpleasantness under the carpet. "We could do with a break and it's time these two were immersed, they're not getting enough French here. They need to be bilingual." This was his winning card from the pack.

I thought the sun and the space would reach out to me as soon as we got home to *Les Moulins*. The perfect antidote to London, which was always in a fever about something. But that first night, with the same blue and white quilt - my faded favourite - on our bed, I couldn't sleep. I should have done. The exhausting drive with two five year olds, Marcelle's good food at dinner and Pierre's treasured bottles from his cellar were all steps in a recipe to ensure instant sleep. But no. I was hot, chilly, hot again, uncomfortable. I tried to adjust the quilt and avoid waking Edward. I thought of Marthe and suppressed the tears; I worried about Pierre, more scrawny than he used to be. Mum and Dad; too many glasses of wine for both of them. She didn't used to drink so much. When I did sleep the dreams came: Mum had painted huge, sad, clown's tears on her cheeks and my heart squeezed with pity for her. Dad pointed his pipe at her, said, "Look Nan." There were screams and shouts and something just beyond my understanding. I woke in the early hours and any joy of coming home was spoilt because I couldn't remember something important. I fell asleep again and dreamt the curtains were pulled across with the sun outside and the drapes were too tight to budge.

I wanted to get through the next day on auto pilot; to do everything and tell everyone just what I was supposed to. I counted the hours until I could get back to bed and have a proper sleep. I planned to manipulate my parents or Edward - better, all three - to take the twins off my hands for a while so I could nap.

Then there was this bright blue Citroën crawling along the drive like a giant insect negotiating the pot holes. I almost saw the antennae.

Claire got out of the car, stretched her back and held her arms out to us. She scooped Harry and Beth up, nearly dropping them. "Gosh, they're heavy!" She pulled shopping bags and a case out of the car and looked smugly at the pile by her feet. "Presents from the South!"

She handed me bars of nougat and *Les Calissons d'Aix,* "For the children - put them away for later." Beth and Harry saw them and stared wide eyed at the sweets, waiting like baby birds. They'd have to share *Les Calissons,* the almond paste confectionary was my favourite.

Claire looked up towards the Mill House and her face lit up when she saw Jeanne running, in her wobbly way, out of the house. "Here's something for you, Jeanne," she called, holding up a flat, beribboned package. Claire stood back while Jeanne held up the white, embroidered blouse. "Go and change and don't even look at all these sweets." Jeanne's eyes had strayed towards the nougat and the *calissons.* She pushed Jeanne gently. "You're too plump for any more goodies. The blouse will make you look wonderful."

Jeanne laughed, sounding almost adult for her, and went back to the house clutching the blouse and its tissue paper. The poor woman - girl? - won't grow up any more, I thought. She was trapped with her repaired mouth and in her uncertain, heavy body, at the mercy of her uncertain moods. There'd be more help if she were born today. Sadness and guilt vied for my attention. I was sorry for Jeanne but now I had the children, to my shame I didn't always like being with her, amusing her. Marcelle looked after her well enough, Philippe was kind, Claire played with her when she was here. Jeanne was never short of attention.

Marcelle nearly pushed me out of the way to get a hug from Claire, looking at her with eager eyes. She picked up a bag from the ground. "Ah! *Tapenade.*" She inspected the jars, two black, two green.

"Your favourite, Marcelle," Claire said. "From *Monsieur Cassou's* shop.

"He's still there?"

"Oh yes. Just the same. I understand *l'occitan* a little better now. He's delighted with my progress."

Marcelle reached out again to Claire. "Come up to the house, it's nearly lunch time."

I felt a twinge of jealousy; my sister being taken over. Mum and Dad smiling and not minding. I grabbed the children to stop them getting at the sweets and to hide that little thorn-prick of envy. I'd wait and see my Claire alone. I wanted to talk to her about Dad; the row between him and Pierre years ago had nagged at me recently, I didn't know why after all this time. There were one or two other things as well. It's time, I thought, that daughters were grown up enough to ask questions about their parents.

At lunch everyone was there. Except one. I do miss you, Marthe. Jeanne was well behaved and sat proudly showing off her new blouse. It hides your rolls of fat, dear.

Afterwards I had a chance to lie down. Mum was playing some jolly French music and dancing with Beth, twirling her round and round. "Well done, darling! Look, Tom, she's a natural!"

Dad grinned, his eyes following Beth as she spun.

"Clap hands, Harry," Mum called, moving to the music. She and Dad both got more lively for a while after lunch. 'Hypocrite' occurred to me and I was cross with myself - it was ridiculous that her outburst over five years ago still lurked in my memory. But today Mum could enjoy herself, enjoy the children. Something I could gladly give her.

Jeanne wandered off again; she'd tried to talk to the twins but they were shy with her, with eyes that said they wanted to be elsewhere. What Beth and Harry really wanted was this rare person, *Tante* Claire to play with them. They left Mum with her *musique folklorique* and Claire and Marcelle began another game with them. Also, I suspected, to ruin the twins' teeth and appetites with nougat. Dad and Pierre and Edward had gone off to talk about tractors or writing or to sit in the sun and gossip like men did, although they always said they didn't, tittle tattle being only for women.

I could drift away. Our bedroom in my parents' house was cool. I left the windows open and drew the curtains so the light dimmed like evening. Children's laughter and women's voices drifted in. I fell into a deep sleep for a while and awoke feeling irritable and restless; the obscure dreams had been there again. I went downstairs to find Beth and Harry already being given tea and smiled my thanks to Mum and Marcelle who were waiting hand and foot on my children.

Pierre and Dad were arguing in their own particular mixture of French and English about the best way to light a barbecue that evening. Claire said she was worn out by my brood and we sat on the patio with some wine and the gigantic, Provençal olives she'd brought with her, watching the children playing at the edge of the lawn. She was wearing a green, sleeveless top and I noticed the boat-shaped birthmark, tanned darker by the sun.

I didn't want to be reminded of it or of Claire's fantasies. I suppose I might have said something but Claire saw me looking at her arm and stalled me. "Not now, Rosemary, forget it." she said, her voice flat.

"There's something else, Claire," I began, "it's about Dad and Pierre ..."

"I said, not now - leave it for a while, Rosemary."

I didn't pursue it. I was too tired to worry about what the matter was with Claire. I had a headache and would have liked to go back to my room. I changed the subject. "Mum loves those two to bits - you wouldn't have expected it somehow."

"Why not?" There was surprise in her voice, but then she didn't know. "They're lovely, she's great with them. Being a grandmother's easier than being a mum. You've had all the hard work. You're doing a really good job with them."

"Thanks."

Something nagged at me, the pain in my temples was worse. Out of the blue I said, "You didn't let them go near the swings, did you. Did Mum stop them?" The words arrived on their own; I didn't know where they came from, why I said it.

Claire looked straight ahead, her voice exasperated. "What a strange thing to say - of course they had a play on them. Why shouldn't they? I took them over and pushed them - Harry and Beth had a great time.

"Mum made tea when I did that. She doesn't like to see children on them, even now but Beth and Harry just love the swings, they don't know anything. Mum's much better about it, Rosemary. Charles was a long time ago. They can't be taken down, that's for sure, they have to stay there for Jeanne. She needs them. And why can't she have something special? Marcelle told me Pierre dismantled them a while back and Jeanne went off her head. I thought I told you - remember?" She shook her head, as if to dismiss me, the little sister with a poor memory, fretful over nothing and needing reassurance. "It's OK now, Mum's alright and Jeanne's kept happy."

The swings had been the subject of a stilted discussion on one of our very brief visits about a year ago. No one could mention Charles' death but the swings hadn't murdered him. It was a freak accident. Only that. They kept Jeanne quiet and it was tacitly agreed that they should stay and my children - or any other children for that matter - could enjoy them. Yet talking about them had been like dropping stones into a deep pond and we all had to wait for the ripples to subside.

I watched the swings edging about in a small breeze.

Claire peered at me. "You look pale."

"Just a headache; I shouldn't have slept this afternoon.."

"What about a refill then? I'll wait on you." She picked up my glass and headed off to the house.

I don't know what happened. I was irritated by the sound of Beth's laughter that came across the lawn and I closed my eyes against the evening light for a second. When I opened them I watched Beth running over to the swings. She grasped a rope and began to haul herself onto the seat. Then I was over there, pulling her away and slapping her legs. "I said *not* the swings. *Not* the swings!" With each 'not' I brought my open palm down on her thighs. For each second, each slap felt good; as if it was useful and satisfying to smack a child until she screamed with shock and pain and fear of her mother.

Claire was pulling me off her. "Stop it, Rosemary!" Mum ran inside with Beth and Harry followed, howling to match his sister's cries.

Edward led me to our room and put me to bed. For a few minutes I didn't realise why he was doing that or why I was crying. Why he was fetching me a drink and saying, "Don't worry, she'll be alright. It's you we're worried about."

I sobbed for a long time. "I'm sorry," I said. "I was crazy, I don't want to hit Beth, I'm so sorry."

The least upset was Beth. She came into the bedroom carrying, with fierce concentration, a plate with some bread and ham for my supper. She watched me with big eyes. "Nanny Nancy said you were poorly. That's why you hit me. So now you're better. So now you won't hit me."

"I'm sorry, darling. No, I won't ever hit you again. I'm better now." I sat up in bed and took the plate, putting it down on the cover so I could reach out and stroke Beth's hair.

"That's alright then. Daddy says you're to try to eat and have a bit more rest," she said, with the utter confidence of a child who knew everything had been made right by the grown ups.

My husband and parents and Marcelle treated me as if I was made of thin glass. As if for me to act so out of character was a sign of a mental illness or some other peculiar disease. 'Hysterics' came to mind. I'd always been an indulgent mother; too easy to forgive, Edward said; but they were happy go lucky children, not getting into much mischief. I didn't have to be stern. Pierre had apparently looked in briefly downstairs and asked how I was. I knew he had beaten Jeanne sometimes and maybe hitting a child was not, for him, such a great sin as it was for others.

I felt sick when I thought about what I'd done; I felt a bad, nasty, guilty, mad mother. Fit only for the gutter, fit to be kicked into it. No one needed to blame me; I did that very well by myself.

The next day Edward took the children out to play, tactfully avoiding the swings. Claire spent time with me, chatting about nothing much, until she said, in the middle of an idle conversation about ingredients for paté, "have you thought of talking to someone?"

"It won't happen again, Claire. I promise." No, I won't see anyone because then I would have to explain about the dreams, the vague fears, the occasional panic attack, the way I didn't know what I was doing yesterday or what set me off. Or a suspicion that rolled around in my mind that they were all related. "I'm going to find the children," I said, wiping surfaces down and hanging up tea towels, not looking at my sister.

She patted my shoulder, "another time perhaps. When you're ready to see a doctor." There wouldn't be another time. I was sure.

Over the next few days everyone gave me space to recuperate and watched from a distance, as if I'd been ill and was still weak. Or they thought I might do it again.

When I came back from a walk I didn't go straight in and pottered in the garden at the side of the house where Mum's roses were. The crimson flowers of her favourite, *Surpasse Tout,* were fading. I found some secateurs nearby and started to dead head them. *Surpasse Tout* - surpass all might have summed up my mother's comments five years ago. I still had to work on not brooding about her barbed words. It was hard trying to understand my mother. How could she say she wanted me to have an abortion and now take such delight in her grandchildren? She seemed so happy-brittle, all surface, her best face on and you could feel the effort it took to keep it there. Being near her, I thought she was fragile, as if a tap might cause a fracture that would show her misery inside. I'd never dared tell her about my dreams for fear of her reaction. My father didn't help either, with his 'look Nan' and his abrupt shifts in manner which ensured he had own way. I wanted to help, to mend whatever was wrong with Mum, yet another side of me said 'run away.'

The windows of the lounge were wide open. I could hear Edward and Philippe talking. I stood still, the better to hear. An hysteric, now an eavesdropper.

"Those swings," Edward said in his most tactful voice. "It must be awful for all of you after - well, you know. Isn't there anything that can be done?"

"It's Jeanne. Always Jeanne," Philippe said. "They're good for her. Perhaps *Maman* should do something about the swings and try to persuade Jeanne to live without them but she won't. She says they're needed. But they should not have set Rosemary off like that - they are only swings after all. Even though ... I don't understand. Perhaps it was something in her unconscious?"

"Unconscious - what a load of nonsense." Apparently Dad was there. I moved closer to the window, at the side so they wouldn't see me. "She's over Charles anyway. It can't be anything ... Or your influence." That was the voice he used when he blamed Mum for something; so she was in the room too. "Edward, Rosemary didn't know about him until afterwards - she wasn't around when it happened - and then we told her that her brother had gone to Heaven." Dad sounded as dismissive of my husband as of my mother. "We found a star for her to watch and said it was his very special star. She was fine about it."

Really, Dad? All I can remember is everyone ignoring me. And my wailing mother, absent from everything, curled up round her pain. I couldn't see, but I knew my father was lighting his pipe, looking away, closing the subject.

Dad again, in reply to something I didn't hear. "How will that help now? I can't believe that it's anything to do with ... "

I heard Mum's put-on brave voice, a rare sound. "Tom, maybe it's time. There might be ... connections. I think of all sorts of connections."

"Look, Nan. She just lost it for a minute, hit a child - Beth's alright now. That's nothing to do with anything else."

"They must know from us sooner or later. What about inheritance and everything like that. What happens when Beth and Harry have children?"

"Well, you ... now you're thinking, you didn't then." I imagined Dad pointing his pipe, his spare frame tense. "You never asked, did you? Never wanted to find out risks or whose fault it was. Yours, probably. All that trouble that summer ... look Nan, we've been through all this ... you let Marcelle ... "

I could hear movement and walked quickly away from the window. I breathed deeply at a rose, its scent a tranquiliser. My family talking about me; well, they would now I suppose. In a way I'd slapped them as well as Beth; I wasn't the perfect, happy mother and daughter I should be. There was something else: 'they must know from us.' What was that and what were these connections Mum was worrying about? I didn't like being an eavesdropper.

Edward and I put the twins to bed early. He'd worn them out. My forgiving children were busy recounting the hide and seek with Daddy in the woods, the walk to the village, the ice creams on the way back. Chocolate for Beth and strawberry for Harry. They'd forgotten their mother was a monster.

I helped Mum prepare dinner; Marcelle and Pierre were coming over. "Just the two of them," she said, speaking to her chopping board, not me. "Philippe and Lucette will have a meal at the big house with Jeanne." We peeled and sliced and sautéed in near silence. Mum's brave voice had left her and she spoke only about the food. I hoped she wasn't getting one of her odd episodes but she carried on turning out the little *terrines de lapin* Marcelle had taught her to make.

When the Aubins arrived Mum met them at the door, waved Pierre in and stopped Marcelle following him by blocking her way in the narrow passage. "Wait, Marcelle." I was in the kitchen, the door half open, listening again.

"It's wrong," Mum said. "I know I've agreed but I think we ought to stop this. You can't decide in a minute like that - just because Rosemary slapped Beth. That's nothing to do with it, do you hear - nothing! It's all too upsetting; I can't bear it. I want us all to go on as we are. It's all alright now, isn't it?" My mother's voice rose, pleading.

"Sod you!" Marcelle sounded shrill. "It's not about that - nor about your feelings for once - it's because it's time. What if we all died and Rosemary and Edward didn't ever know? Beth and Harry must know when they grow up. This must not go on, Nancy, for the sake of the children. She ought to know."

Marcelle slammed her way into the house and went straight out onto the patio, followed by Mum. I slipped through in their wake. Dad and Pierre and Edward were already there. Pierre got up to pour some wine but Dad put a hand on his arm and gently took the bottle from his shaking hand. "I'll do that, Pierre." These two were as thick as thieves lately; agreed about something, more than my mother and Marcelle were.

Claire came in and took a chair between Mum and Marcelle from where she could look directly at me. Beth and Harry had begged us to send *Tante* Claire up to tell them a story, and very likely to persuade her to give them some more nougat. "They're nearly asleep," she said.

"I'll go quickly and say goodnight." I got up and ran up the stairs; Edward followed me up to the bedroom. The twin beds had been pushed together and our fair haired children lay facing each other, eyes almost closed, identical teddies tucked in beside them. Edward and I kissed them and stood outside on the landing for a moment, holding hands.

"I don't know what's going on downstairs," I said, "but I'm so glad we've got those two. And ... " Tears stung. "I'm still very sorry - I still don't know what happened to me."

"Look," Edward said, putting his hands on my shoulders, "you were frightened for them; something about the swings worried you, it doesn't matter. You were very tired. Any mother could get cross with fear."

He didn't know about 'any' mothers, only his own, now a forgetful old lady, and me, but I basked briefly in his reassurance, in his anchoring of me, in the hug he gave me.

Out on the patio there wasn't the usual chatter. I felt I couldn't breathe, as if the oxygen had been sucked away. Only Claire looked serene, leaning towards Marcelle and saying something about dinner. Marcelle nodded and lit a cigarette. Mum was watching Marcelle like small prey wary of a predator. Dad sent up clouds of pipe smoke into the still air and Pierre leant back with his arms folded, scanning the faces.

Claire glanced up over to me, with her open faced look of confidence, the one that always said, 'don't worry little sister.'

Mum began it. "When Marcelle and I had our first daughters there were problems. You know, don't you Rosemary, my maiden name was Trowe ... " She sat up straight, about to give a speech, trying to be formal and in charge, but actually looking foolish. She'd started drinking early. "It used to mean truth a long time ago. And truth is what I'm going ... "

Dad took his pipe out of his mouth and pointed it at her, that old, angry gesture. "Either get on with it or shut up, Nan."

Marcelle took over. "I'll tell it, Nancy." She paused to stub out her cigarette and take a sip of wine. "Rosemary. My daughter is Claire and your mother's daughter is Jeanne. Jeanne is your older sister. We swapped because your mother had - difficulties ... " She took another drink. "Your mother had problems with a baby who had *le bec de lièvre* and who had to have such special care. I could do that better than she; it was better for Jeanne. Pierre and I let Nancy and Tom take care of Claire. We had had rows about Claire too. Pierre thought Claire wasn't his. The rows we had, it was all wrong for us for a time. After the war. The men - you wouldn't understand - they came back from the camps without hope or trust; they came back irrational. He left once, mad with jealousy for nothing. But that was soon over and we agreed - Pierre and I - to help with Jeanne.

So Claire become a Woods baby, even though ..." Marcelle stretched a hand out to Pierre without looking at him. He took it both his hands and turned his lop sided smile at her. "Then of course your parents travelled to Paris with you and Claire while I looked after Jeanne. There were other reasons, for both of us. The war's a weight we carry with us, it can't be put down; it bends our backs in different ways. For me, to make up for my family, for watching my brother die. For more than that though, for what else the Nazis did; they exterminated children like Jeanne. Caring for your mother's child was my small act of reparation. It is a story for another time, not now, not today. You will understand all these events have meanings that track back a long way into the past. Not to do with you directly, but I will tell you eventually." She stopped abruptly and closed her eyes.

 Mum took a deep breath and looked straight at me. "So my Jean became a French *Jeanne.*" She pulled her mouth down, as if there was a sour taste, even now disgusted with Jeanne - or herself. "I had the perfect Claire to play with." She put her hand to her mouth, wiping at the mistake. "No. To look after." She turned to Claire, regaining some dignity. "I am very sorry, my dear. Perhaps you should have known sooner, perhaps you should have had your mother after all."

But I'd heard Marcelle say, "she ought to know". Not 'they.' Did Claire know? That big letter to Marcelle years ago. The fuss in Aix over the birthmark.

Claire reached out for Mum's hand. She turned to glance at Marcelle who nodded at her. Go ahead. "I've known for a long time. Mum. Nancy. I still love you; you and Dad have brought me up, given me so much. And I love my French mother. Because of her I've wanted my part in Jeanne's life to be my contribution in France's reparation as well."

Her gaze fixed on me. "I thought that showing you the birthmark might give you some clue, Rosemary. But you didn't catch on. Then Marcelle and I agreed not to say anything until the right time. When you had babies of your own."

No wonder they were concerned about my children; even though they were perfect. A bit late to worry - a child like Jeanne would have been a shock. But Beth and Harry's children might inherit Jeanne's cleft palate and her other little difficulties. Now I knew why Mum had told me to get rid of the pregnancy. I could not begin to understand what these two women had gone through: the tearing of Marcelle's heart and the guilt of my mother as they watched their daughters, so different and in the wrong houses. That chain of events, begun with my father's manipulations, which led first from England to France, to his removal from the country to Paris, then back again, to such deceit. I looked in turn at Marcelle and Pierre, Mum and Dad, and then let my eyes rest on Claire, who was, and who wasn't, my sister. She should have told me; a worm of anger twisted in me at her lack of honesty, at something that felt close to betrayal. Although she had tried. Not hard enough. I would never have thought my sister kept this from me. Yet deep down it was ... unsurprising. I had this sense that some of this discomfort I carried had just been validated. One of the shadows disappeared in the light.

Edward reached out and squeezed my hand. There for me. Claire got up and came round the table to stand by me and pulled my head onto her body, standing while I leant into her, feeling the tears start. "I'm sorry" she said. "But you haven't lost me; I'm still your sister - we don't have to be related to be sisters. We grew up together; that's what matters." She crouched down beside my chair and put her hands round my face. "Look at me. We'll stretch the meaning of the word 'sister'; make it new. Make it work for us."

I whispered it, "but now I've got to love Jeanne as well?"

When I stopped crying I kept patting my top lip, feeling the perfect little groove, its pouty plumpness. I went up to the twins' bedroom and traced my fingers over Beth's lips: perfect and whole. My hand caught her sleeping breath. Harry was asleep on his stomach, his head turned towards Beth, his complete mouth closed. I looked at the Lego construction on the floor; it was a fat rectangle they called the Jam Sandwich Tower and they had demanded real jam and bread from Marcelle after they had made it. Quick little children, bright and eager. Not like their new found aunt, *Tante Jeanne,* my other sister.

I forced myself to get used to the idea of sister Jeanne. I had wanted to play with her, help her have fun, console her when Marthe died. But something - a soft barrier of reluctance, it's hard to describe - was always there between Jeanne and me and the idea of any sisterly closeness built up a higher barricade.

That next Christmas I tried to pay special attention to her but nothing I felt went deep. I acted, played to the gallery at the Mill House. My audience: Mum was pathetically pleased, Dad nodded at me. Marcelle watched with careful eyes as she arranged tables and organised food. Pierre looked on, taciturn. He seemed sad; he still corrected Jeanne, but with less interest in her. He'd lost weight again and appeared too calm: quiet, a little faded, pared down in a way I couldn't explain. As for Jeanne, I don't know what - if anything - they had told her and I didn't have the courage to ask Marcelle. Jeanne didn't use 'sister' but she was over me as never before. I played games with her and the twins; I choose the least competitive things to do, anxious to avoid bickering or any flaring of ill humour.

We left the day after New Year's day. As usual I had too much university work to do before term started and Edward wanted to get back to his writing. I was sorry to leave France and glad to get away at the same time. I had begun to dread Jeanne finding me each morning, tugging at me. " 'Allo, Rosemary. What shall we do today? Listen - my Funny English!" I was more aware of the old stitches turning her mouth, the way she chewed her food, her fat way of walking, her little eyes.

I was sad to leave as well; Mum was looking happy and taking photos of us with the camera Dad had given her for Christmas, catching the winter light sprinkling in. I didn't want to spoil things for her. If I had to play *soeurs heureuses* - then I'd do happy sisters - it might make up for times past.

Rosemary. France, 1987

THEN CAME THE years to wear black. Soon after that Christmas my grandfather died suddenly. Mum and Dad came over to England and everything went as well as expected for the funeral of an elderly man who had outlived most of his peers. A few friends and neighbours gathered, not many.

I was sad and concerned about Mum who wasn't, in fact, as bereft as I thought she might be "He's had a good innings," she said. "We'll have to look after Granny; she's not up to much any more."

It was Dad who telephoned about Pierre. Not Marcelle or Philippe or Mum. Dad. "He's not quite the ticket, Rosemary. Hasn't complained - you know what he's like. The doc said it's the end of the line - a bit more sudden than they thought. Would you and Edward come over? Marcelle says he wants to see people for the last time."

Thank God it was half term. I could get away and the twins could stay with my indulgent friend and colleague, Annabel. At ten years old they were able to understand more but the illness of *Oncle Pierre* was of less interest than the prospect of staying with Belle and Robert, their three children and their motley variety of dogs.

March is cold in the Loire, winds snap at you. I found Pierre in the big kitchen, wrapped up and roasting in front of the range. There was an oxygen bottle behind him, small, clear tubes reaching round to his nose. I tried not to glance at the catheter bag half hidden under a rug. He smiled his half smile and kissed me. He felt so boney I was cautious about hugging him too hard.

Dad was with him. "I'll leave you for a bit. Pierre, have a chat to Rosemary. I'll be back later, before dinner." He put a heavy hand on my shoulder as he went.

I took Dad's chair by Pierre's side; Marcelle fussed around making tea. She handed me a cup. "With milk, if you must. Why do you insist on it after all this time?" An old joke between us. "I'm glad you've come. I've got to go out to the hens. Sit with him a little while."

Pierre mislaid his English somewhere and spoke in rapid French. I shook my head. "*Parle tu lentement, s'il te plait!* Slow down, Pierre! Have pity on an English girl!"

In reply to my questions he said he didn't want to talk about his health. "It has to happen to all of us. Enough of that," he said. "But ... ah ... I've been reminiscing." He began to tell me about the farm before the war came, how Eva and Clément had run it. "They could keep going only if they didn't think about the last war. They had to forget it when it was finished, although impossible, in order to work and plan ahead. Then the next one came ... " He told me about the horses - *P'tit gris* and *Ma-Belle* - love and sadness breaking his voice, that the Germans took when the occupation started. "I went away, you know. I thought it was right at the time. I made an error. Those times, it's hard to make sense of them today. I want you to know why your parents came here." He closed his eyes between between sentences. "You mustn't let your father ... we all do what we think is the best thing, even though it's not and he did what he thought was right when he joined ... oh, the ideals ... it's brought him nothing but trouble ... he wrote all that stuff and got the timing wrong."

"Joined what, Pierre? Dad was proud of his flying years." A doubt crept in. "You do mean the RAF, don't you? What timing is this?"

The back door banged. Marcelle came in sideways with a bowl of eggs cradled in both hands. I got up to hold the door and glanced back at Pierre, whose chin had sunk on his chest. "Let him sleep," Marcelle said.

We ate dinner at the huge kitchen table; myself, Edward, Mum and Dad, Marcelle and Pierre, who grumpily insisted he could breath well enough to eat without the encumbrance of the oxygen. Philippe apologised for Lucette; his wife had to spend the evening with her own ailing mother. Jeanne ate somewhere else. Marcelle said she was upset, *papa* being so ill.

Pierre managed the soup and picked at some chicken. He refused any cheese or dessert although his glass was often refilled. When Marcelle took coffee into the lounge Pierre said he'd stay where he was and moved with uncertain, weaving steps to his chair by the range, waving any help away. Philippe got up quickly, arranged tubes and put the oxygen back on so deftly it wasn't noticed.

A little later Marcelle said, "Pierre wants to talk to you alone. Claire's going to phone, I'll call you when she does."

Pierre rambled about Pétain, Vichy, the camps. I knew some of it, but I let him carry on. My eyes strayed to a shelf at the side of the range where there was a dusty, black rimmed card. Pierre followed my gaze. "My sister, Catherine. My brave *résistante*. In her sleep, two months ago. My turn soon, they tell me. None of us last long after the camps; they kill your soul, deep down. Then with no soul your body starts to rot." He held his glass out.

"Your father's upset but don't tell Nancy. Not just Catherine ... you know why your father returned to France after the war?"

"No, Pierre. I don't know." I sat very still. Dad and Catherine? I didn't look at his face. "Is that why you and Dad had a fight years ago?"

"I heard he loved her early on, the first time he was here. But she couldn't stay. It's not that. It's what they told me afterwards about the second crash ... he'd betrayed the resisters. She was caught and tortured. I had it out with him that evening because she'd written. But then - what to do? You save yourself. After the war he couldn't go anywhere else but France, he was hounded in your country. Here, the resistance groups were mostly made-up of communists and celebrated - what irony! A party member was accepted here after the war - at least for a while." Pierre's sardonic laugh became a fading cackle.

"Pierre, I still don't know," I repeated. "We went to live in Paris, then we came back. It wasn't just for his job?"

"Wait a minute, young Rosemary. In the first place, in 1950, I invited him here. I lured him back to France, if you like. With his new wife. And it was easy. He was suspected of all sorts of things in England because he joined the communist party. It was different here then and there was plenty of work for a journalist.

"Back then I blamed him for Catherine being caught. The easiest and safest place to go for him was France when he still had a party card and I thought it would be revenge: I could make his life miserable here if he *had* to be here. It would make him stare at his past the whole time and hate himself. I wanted him to be eaten by that hate. Catherine wrote to say she would visit and your father left the day before. Marcelle made me think differently. For her side of it, you must ask Marcelle. Over the years I've forgiven. I made a mistake when I volunteered; he made a mistake after his second plane came down. We understand each other now; your father and I. He's not a bad man; he's made amends. And taking Jeanne on was reparation for what I did in the war. And you must ask Marcelle about her. Ask Marcelle why and how it was in the war for her. It wasn't so much ..."

The door to the lounge opened. "Claire's on the phone," Marcelle said. She looked over to Pierre who was breathing hard, holding his wine glass with two shaky hands and staring at a past only he could see, "I will tell you," she said, holding the door for me, making it obvious she had been listening. "When I'm ready."

Pierre wasn't much different when we had to leave for England, the children and work. I wished I could have stayed. He'd been there all my life and I wanted to be there at the end of his. And to comfort my parents. Dad was with Pierre a lot; after everything the two men had found some comfort in each other. Mum was different: she knew Pierre had been talking to me and her confusion showed with every tiny smile she gave me, as if she wanted and didn't want me to tell her. I said very little. I lied to protect her from any more distress. "It's just stuff about the war, Mum. Nothing you don't know." She accepted that, although I think she knew - really - there was so much more and Dad wasn't going to tell her.

Pierre held on beyond anyone's expectations. He seemed a little stronger in the summer when we returned for the vacation although he said very little and slept a lot in the long, hot days. I'd tried to ask him more about my parents those early years. "I'm too tired to talk now," he said. "Marcelle will tell you more. But take your time, Rosemary. Take your time to understand."

He died as an early winter set in that November. Marcelle called us. Pierre had been out in the yard. He'd insisted. To walk about a little, to see the poultry and the cattle. There was an unusual cold snap, sudden snow on the ground. The farm hand said afterwards, "I had to help *Monsieur* around ... *Monsieur* wanted to get over to the fence and see the cows. They were over the far side; I don't think he could really see them. I held him up so he could stand and look and I pointed over the field where they were. He felt so light. I wish I had been braver with him, not let him do it - but he insisted, he said he must do it."

"He was out there too long, just staring," Marcelle said. "Then he came in to sit by the range and have some *potage*. I went to take the bowl and he was slumped to one side. Now he's gone. Just as if he is fallen asleep. Now for all the time."

We got over to France late the day after. It was in the middle of a busy autumn term, a very bad, selfish time to take time out, to leave one's colleagues to cover seminars and marking, to put research papers on hold. A colleague, the head of the medieval department, had only two days off for his father's funeral and sorted out the necessary papers of death in his weekend time.

I took two weeks. I lied. It's a habit. I produced a florid account of family and distance and the difficulties of dealing with a death abroad; how much the widow could not do for herself. I don't remember the details of the facts and fictions I poured out before a hasty departure. Half my colleagues believed me, the backbiters in the other half didn't and probably hoped I'd resign and not come back.

It wasn't the widow who couldn't cope. Marcelle organised the funeral, the wake and everyone else almost completely by herself. I found her telling the new, young priest what to do. The poor man could only say, "*Oui, Madame,*" at regular intervals before scurrying away.

My parents were a different matter. When we arrived Dad was stoic. He hugged me without smiling. "There's nothing to do, everything's under control," he said. "Come and have a drink."

Mum was shocked into immobility. She watched Marcelle intently, a mouse hiding from a farm cat, as if fearful of having to do something of which she would be incapable. In the face of her friend's strength and tragedy she seemed diminished. When we arrived I found her huddled in the Mill House by the same range although Pierre's favourite chair had been changed. "It might be me one day," she whispered. She waved a hand towards Marcelle who was talking rapidly into the phone. "I couldn't be like this."

Marcelle was glued to the phone. " *Oui, merci ... c'est très gentil.* No - I'll let you know when it is ... no, I've Philippe and Lucette around ... Claire will come soon." It rang as soon as she put it down. "*'ello? Oui, Merci. Oui, Pierre c'etait un brave homme ... *"

My mother shook her head. "I don't know how to help her, Rosemary." From what I saw, Marcelle didn't need much help.

Mum had leant on Marcelle during all her time here; letting the Frenchwoman take over, take on my sister. I supposed that between Marcelle and my father she was prevented from growing anything like backbone or a will to stand up for herself. It wasn't her fault.

After we unpacked that first evening I tracked Dad down in his study. He was sitting at his desk, a new, longer one he'd recently bought. He never quite graduated into the technological age and it had a typewriter and a computer side by side. He could use either when he fancied, so he told me. I guessed Philippe helped him out with the desktop. The only light came from a yellowish side lamp and the air was fugged with smoke. He was staring at a blank screen and a half-empty whiskey bottle sat between the two machines.

I put my arm round his shoulders and kissed a stubbly cheek. "Oh, Dad. I'm so sorry." My arrogant, critical father, tears overflowing his glasses, was stoic no longer, melted down by Pierre's death.

His face folded up. "He was the only one who understood, you know."

Rosemary. London, January 1998

CALENDARS AND WATCHES lie. They tell great fibs about how time moves. The years turn faster and faster so you don't believe you're *now* when you should be *then*. My retirement had arrived at the end of the summer term last year and we were packing up to move to France for good. All thoughts of teaching and research sidled away unobtrusively; eighteenth century voices only occasional whispers as they left.

Edward had another book under way, a new stack of notebooks stood to attention on his desk. His short, spare novels of London life had been surprisingly successful and he was a contented author, if such a thing could exist, avoiding publicity and spending more time at home. He suggested writing about another city. "I might try Paris or Tours," he said. "Walk about, get the streets in my head; note all the local habits. You could do the museums and galleries."

I laughed. "Try it then, if you want. It'll get some weight off."

He threw a cushion at me. "Middle age spread's quite normal. What about some tea? And cake?"

There were two homes to arrange before our move across the Channel. The house in the Loire needed changes before it became permanent and we were letting our flat. I was clearing out enough clutter to stock every charity shop in the metropolis. The flat would be a safety net if we ever needed to return to England and left for the children when the time came.

We'd been wearing black again. In the October Edward's father had died suddenly, florid and pompous in the House of Commons' bar. He was much lauded for his good works by his colleagues who quickly shelved their partial memories and began to toady up to his successor. Edward's mother had followed her husband very quickly. She had disguised or ignored her cancer symptoms for so long there was nothing to be done except be grateful for the hospice care.

January was spent in cold, grimy London with brief spells in a winter countryside sorting out Edward's parents' estate, a process that dragged its feet and constantly interfered with our travel plans.

"I think Dad thought we were betraying the country by living over the Channel," Edward said as he stacked a pile of papers neatly and slid them into an envelope with the solicitor's address on it.

"Your father thought you were a traitor not living in Hertfordshire."

"One more week of this" Edward said, "and we're done. Then the ferry and straight home."

"I worry about Marcelle," I said. "I keep thinking she'll go on for ever but Claire and Philippe are bothered about her. That email hinted we shouldn't stay away too long." I pictured her as she was this last Christmas Day afternoon when we were there. Dressed in widow's black and sitting in the lounge looking out over the lawns, Pierre's photos on her side table close at hand.

Now Marcelle was the only one left. Edward's parents' deaths, so soon after each other, uncannily mirrored those of my Mum and Dad. One set after another. I took two weeks off for all them; Pierre would have approved. I remembered, 'take your time.'

Three summers' ago, at the end of a hot day, the *gendarmes* had called on Mum with their professional sadness and their respect and with only the bare details of the crash. Dad had driven off the road into a gorge and died instantly. She was spared knowing the alcohol content of his blood or the speed of the car. Nor did she ask. She had thanked them and walked over to tell Marcelle, the *gendarmes* in her wake, alert in case this elderly English woman broke down. Marcelle phoned us.

A few months' later Marcelle telephoned again. When the dark evenings came Mum became less sociable, spending more time on her own, not going over to the big house as often, more vague in her contacts with us. Marcelle's habits didn't change: her latest help had been sent over to spy on her and put extra food in the fridge. She found Mum peaceful and quite still as if she was taking an afternoon rest. The doctors said it was a heart attack, but I believe it was that fatal desolation loss brings when the person so closely bound to your existence dies; it isn't possible to survive on your own, however the bindings are made.

I hadn't been able to hold Mum or Dad in their final moments: it was only someone else's words that showed me their dying. Now I could never ask my questions of them.

All our parents. We were orphaned children in middle age. Edward was calm, the distance between he and his parents had been large; greater as the years went on. It was a longer journey for him to think back about Hertfordshire than it was for me to imagine my childhood in the *Loire*. In my head I still lived in the same space as all of them: Mum and Dad, Marcelle and Pierre. And Marthe, a sprite pulling faces at me. Claire, my sleek, career sister, not far away. Philippe and Lucette welcoming me at the big house, sharing their plans for the future.

I thought of Jeanne bobbing her head up and down in the hallway, *'Allo, Rosemary, play the Funny English game?* Was she English or French? Seeing her in my mind's eye with her round face and bisected mouth, I had an overwhelming sense of waste for my mother, of calamity, of her tiredness from the burden of what had happened. Of never being able to make anything better for this first daughter. Never being able to sincerely believe it wasn't her fault in bearing her. Had she felt relief or guilt about handing her over to Marcelle, giving Jeanne a better parent or reneging on a mother's duties?

It was Marcelle we had to worry about. I wanted to see her and there was a conversation I had to have before she died. Pierre telling me: ask Marcelle.

There was more stuff to pack than I realised; things we felt we couldn't do without in France, probably mistakenly. A removal firm had taken some furniture and clothes, nearly all the books and a box or three of odds and ends. In our car were winter clothes and the usual presents. Always difficult. Marcelle preferred Provençal lavender to English although she had developed a surprising liking for English Cheddar, the expensive, unpasteurised sort, of course. Philippe and Lucette were simple: pretty household items, they had a current passion for anything Scottish. Jeanne was easier still, providing I got her size right and was tactful about it.

I texted Beth and Harry to remind when we were going and to let them know how Marcelle was. We'd all spoken by phone but sometimes I still thought of them as children who might forget important dates and times.

My twins had gone to different universities - Elizabeth to Canterbury for history; Harry to Durham for Business Studies. Harry's recent girlfriend was a delight after the gothic, sullen sirens that had wafted through his first dating years. I'd thought she was a little plain for his tastes until she smiled and her whole face lifted and glowed. Harry never stopped grinning when he talked about her. They seemed settled. Sigh of relief.

Beth was post graduate teaching at Canterbury. Sensible boyfriend, safe like her father. Edward thoroughly approved of him, of course. I wondered if Marcus wasn't a little too dull, even though I couldn't imagine my daughter wanting anyone but another, rather obsessive, historian like herself.

Amazingly - to me anyway, not to Edward who always seemed to have expected such children as ours all along - they bubbled though life. They loved everybody in France. They laughed with Marcelle and avoided her more impertinent questions like experienced politicians; they got Pierre to produce his lop sided smile. They took Jeanne out and managed her little ways so that she came home giggling with them at private jokes all three had invented. She didn't pinch them and cried genuine tears when they left.

We left for France in early February, driving to Portsmouth under a loaded, leaden sky. The ferry rocked us roughly to sleep and we woke to Northern France obscured by rushes of sleet.

Edward was driving, scowling through the full speed wipers and slowing down in the onslaughts of snow primed with ice. I had been silent for most the journey. What I was had to say to him wouldn't obligingly form sentences, not even a few poor phrases. It had found a hiding place in my mind while we dashed round, packed, arranged and travelled. I hated the way it wormed itself back into my thoughts that morning. Towards Tours the sky became pearly grey and an insipid sun worked its way through the clouds. With the grudging light came all the detail of what I had to tell Edward. I'd been told talking it through with him would do me good. What I wanted was to take a vow of silence.

Edward straightened his back and flexed his hands on the steering wheel. "Are you alright, Rosemary? You've been very quiet."

"I'm fine." I knew I didn't sound it. "No, not ... I want to talk to you about something." There, make a start.

"What's the matter? Is it Marcelle? This is going to be a hard one, I think."

I put a hand on his leg, felt the solidity of him, hoping that this would sustain me the way it had always done. He'd looked after me when I was low, comforted me when I couldn't understand the dreams that had trailed me all my life; held me while I crawled into wakefulness away from them. Now I knew what they were about, the awful necessity of telling Edward haunted me like a day time ghost.

"Do you remember last summer, when I stayed at home and you went back to London for a few days?"

"That's right. You were ill when I got back, some awful 'flu. I remember. Is this to do with being poorly?" There was a touch of alarm in his voice; he always hated my being ill, scared for me and himself.

"I wasn't very ill. I'd caught a cold and then I just wanted to hide in bed for a while. I'd seen a doctor - not the usual one."

"Rosemary, what are you talking about?"

This wasn't the opening I'd wanted and I realised how little I'd actually told my husband. "Look," I said. "There's a service station signed at ten kilometres. Could we stop for coffee and talk a bit?" We hadn't said much to each other recently apart from about the move and letting the London flat. As if we were one of those middle aged couples who had little left to say to each other except 'where do you want these boxes put?' Or, 'supper's ready.' The big moments were talked out: Beth and Harry getting their degrees and moving away. Our parents' deaths, Pierre's further back in time. But not all: Marcelle was failing. We didn't talk about the problems with my other sister, as I'd to come to call Jeanne. How much responsibility I would have when Marcelle died? Philippe and Lucette ran the farm now and she lived with them; there was never any question of her not doing so. I wondered how much shared care they might want with Jeanne in the future. We would only live just over the lawns. My mouth went dry with the thought.

We sat under the service station glare that made the February sky outside look more like the November light that only gets darker.

"You'll feel better for something to eat," Edward said, frowning as I pushed a croissant around my plate and picked at greasy bits of it.

"I'm too tired - sorry. Not been sleeping well." Let's put it all off, I thought. Get back in the car and drive and forget. No chance; home is just where everything in my head is going to hurt and come alive like a virus I'd caught a long time ago and that has suddenly ceased to be dormant.

When I went to the ladies I saw a white face stare at me from the mirror; I had dark smudges under my eyes and my hair was lank. I put lipstick on; it looked like a slash of blood. I pursed my lips and blotted them with a tissue. My other sister couldn't do that.

Edward and I had the same idea. He called *Les Moulins* and spoke to Philippe. To get there a day later would be fine. We turned off and found a small hotel in a nondescript village that had given up its identity to the motorway's feeder road. In the courtyard a fountain was stopped until spring and a robin searched for food in the brown, weedy flower beds. We ate Normandy fish stew in a tiny, deserted restaurant and took our coffee with us to a corner of the lounge.

The bar tender came over with a dusty half bottle. "On the house," he said. "I leave one light on only. Please turn it off when you retire." We'd done this before; such a long time ago. Edward bribing *la patronne* to ignore her suspicions we weren't married.

Edward shared the wine out and put an arm round my shoulders. "Sweetheart, tell me - I can't help unless I know. What's going on?"

Rosemary. France, 1998

MONSIEUR DUCLOS SAT opposite in an identical leather arm chair and looked at me as if I was the most important person in the world. Between us was a low table with a carafe of water and glasses and a box of tissues, angled - of course - towards me. I had already told him about my family, my apparently incomprehensible dreams with Mum screaming and my episodes of melancholy. Now for the rest of it.

It started when one of the cats went missing. Edward had just driven off to catch the ferry and I walked over the lawn to visit Marcelle and see if any shopping was needed. Nicole, the most recent help, asked if I'd seen Lizzie, a fat calico cat, who normally didn't stir far from home. She hadn't been around looking for food since early morning. An unusual absence: a cat of her size has a good appetite. Nicole handed me a box of dry cat food to rattle. She had to help *Madam* Aubin now, so, if I didn't mind, would I be good enough to give Lizzie a call?

I walked back across the lawn and took the path that led around the vegetable patch. I didn't think the tubby, lazy cat would go as far as the woods at the back but I heard a high pitched mewing from the edge of the woodland. I found poor Lizzie suspended at shoulder height in a tree with a branch and one foreleg caught through her collar. She wasn't quite strangling as her back paws rested on a lower branch, although the collar was very tight. I tried to free her but she was too frantic to stop struggling and bared sharp teeth at me in a hiss of fear and pain. "Don't go away," I said nonsensically and ran back to the house for some scissors.

As I came back to the wood Lizzie's cries had changed. I heard a muted sound like a hen being inexpertly strangled. Jeanne was there, twisting Lizzie's collar around her foreleg, neck and the branch. Lizzie was no match for Jeanne's big, pudgy hands and the cat had almost stopped wriggling.

I tried to pull Jeanne away, grabbing my sister in anger. "Stop that! Jeanne! No!" But she shook me off with a sneer that showed her scarred lip livid and made her little eyes crunch up in her face. Everyone knew Jeanne could be cruel; everyone tried to ignore it. But her tricks were usually obvious and there was always someone to divert her. Not now.

"Let her go, Jeanne!" I shouted. "Go and play on your swings."

"No. Don't like Lizzie. Want to choke."

Something clicked inside me. Something I'd heard as a child, something I'd been forbidden to say. I took a deep breath and shouted as loud as I could. "Let her go, split lip! Split lip! Split lip! Split lip!" I went on repeating it, yelling the breath out of me.

Jeanne took her hand out of the collar and pushed the poor cat hard away from her. She put her face close to mine. "Hate you too." She shoved me so that I fell back and staggered to keep my feet. I caught a whiff of the gum disease she was plagued with. She ran off, lumbering down the path to the lawn and her swings.

I cut Lizzie free and she tore away from me. I walked slowly back to the big house, feeling as if my legs were made of thin glass and might shatter. I took deep breaths to stop myself from crying. Relief at having freed Lizzie shaped into thoughts about Jeanne. That was my sister, that big, vicious lump who wanted to hurt, wanted to choke the life out of small creatures. That girl-woman, whom nobody would deal with.

I met Nicole outside the house getting laundry in. "I've found Lizzie." I made my voice level. "She caught her collar up in a branch and I've cut her free. I had to cut her collar off too. I think she'll be back soon." I handed Nicole the scissors which she took with a hand from underneath the huge pile of washing she was carrying.

"Thank you, *Madame* Bellingham. *Madam* Aubin will be pleased."

I wondered how pleased Marcelle would be if she knew how her favourite cat was nearly killed. And who nearly choked it to death. I cried when I got home. I held my hands out and to my surprise they were steady. The shaking was deep inside. The perfume of Mum's roses drifted across to me on the warm velvet of the day but I was shivering. I wrapped a blanket around me and poured a glass of wine, seeing again Jeanne's face, a scarred carnival mask, close to mine. I could still hear Lizzie's cries diminish as she choked under those fat, twisting fingers. And I heard: split lip. split lip. Who else had been told off for calling her that?

I didn't sleep that night. I tossed and turned; got up and made tea; waited for the dawn to come with a comforting sun. Which was no comfort. When the light became brighter and the open curtains let in streaks of warm gold I slept. Then I was in a cinema, held to my chair against my will in a dream grip. I was watching a documentary of my life roll past. It wouldn't stop: clip after clip, a strangled cat, the soundtrack of Mum's screams and Charles like a large, dead animal flopped on the ground.

I woke exhausted and the memories began to come back.

❧

How many sessions across that summer did I have in Monsieur Duclos' leather armchair? I can't remember. I don't want to look back and count them. For a few months I lived for that weekly hour, where I could relive in safety what I'd seen and heard as a child and make sense of the fears and dreams that had shadowed me all my life. Guilt was the tough one to crack. It was a many headed monster that sat on my chest, stopping breath. Guilt that I hadn't done anything then, even though I was only a child who didn't know what had to be done. When Edward came back for the rest of the holidays I'd lied about where I was going once a week. I reinforced careful fictions. I couldn't face him, as if bringing everything into the open would endanger me in some way. Threaten us. And I would have to cope with his tenderness and sympathy when there was barely anything left of me inside to respond. All I could bear was the psychologist's careful, forensic examination of my memories and feelings. The process sucked so much energy out of me I barely staggered home. I told Edward the dance classes were wonderful and may I have a drink please?

❧

It's summer and the lawns are dusty. I sit in the thorny hedge that runs along one side, providing some small shade. It's where I like to be with my dolls and watch the families come and go. We peer out of a spy hole I have cut with stolen, forbidden scissors. Spots of blood ooze on the back of my hand. I lick them and like the salty taste. I tell the dolls what and who I see. I call my collection of dolls the 'hedge people' and I have Cherie, my very best doll, next to me. I'm reminding her of their names and we're all looking over to the swings where Charles is playing.

I see him clamber up and lie with his tummy resting across the wooden seat of a swing. He rocks back and forth, staring at the ground, his face near the earth. I wonder what he can see. Grass, beetles, patches of earth? Nothing much. It's not the right way to swing I think with nine year old disapproval. I suppose I will have to go and help him. But in a minute because I haven't finished talking to Cherie. I might show him the hedge people if he's good. I don't mind playing with him; I can make him laugh and he's fun. Sometimes he gets a bit boring and then Mum will have him back or Claire might come along and find a game we all play.

We've been told to invite Jeanne to play with us if she's around. We have to be nice to her. She can be fun too but at other times she spoils our games. Then she's very moody and she makes a mess of things. I think it's because she wants to - she runs away laughing! Claire and I are not supposed to say anything. We know that this would get us into trouble, it would be telling on her and Mum doesn't like that. We have to forgive her because it's not her fault.

Charles doesn't know this, he's only four. He gets very cross with Jeanne. If she takes a toy off him and tries to break it or go off with it, he says, "I don't like your face!" Or he shouts, "split lip!" She's upset then and Charles is naughty because he knows that happens. "You're wrong, it's all sewn up," she says. She puts her dirty fingers in her mouth to feel around and check it really is stitched up. She might run off or she might try to pinch us, but we can wriggle away, we're quicker than she is.

I'm watching Jeanne come across the lawn from her house. She walks with a roll like she's on one of the boats that go down the middle of the big river. Mum said there was something wrong with her that makes her walk like that so we have to be kind to her. We asked Jeanne's Mum and she told us that when she was born she had a gap in her top lip that had to be stitched up by the doctors - like doing needlework - so there was a scar there and it makes her talk funny. And we were never, ever, to stare at her face or say anything about it. I never say anything, but I think unkind things when she does her nasty and naughty tricks

Of course, Charles does. If Claire and I feel a bit wicked we don't stop him staring and calling her names. We have a pact not to tell.

She's walking over to the swings now. With my fingers I feel my own top lip with its two soft bumps. My little ridges are like the way the sea leaves the soft sand when the tide drags out. It can't be nice for Jeanne to have that bit in two halves with the hard, crooked join up the middle.

Charles is still front down on his swing and Jeanne sits on the seat next to him. I can see her talking to him but I can't hear what she says. I don't want them to see me so I slither back into the hedge. Perhaps I'm camouflaged like the chameleons I've been reading about. I'd like to be able to change colour to be the same as wherever I was. So if I stood by Marcelle's tomatoes I'd turn red.

Charles gets off his swing and lifts himself back the right way round. Jeanne stands up and starts to push him. Jeanne stops pushing Charles and climbs the rope ladder at the end of the swings. She reaches the top, peers beneath her, comes down a few rungs and jumps the last few feet. She goes back up and does it again. Charles copies her, hauling himself with a frown on his face, giggling when he jumps. I can see he gets better at it each time he goes up the ladder, he jumps down faster. I think I might go and join in.

Jeanne's very fast when she wants to be. She's climbed to the top of the ladder and is balancing on the top rung, leaning against the frame of the swings. Charles is below her, pushing out his body to make his small leap. Jeanne, ever so quick, slips a piece of knotted rope round his neck. She twists it tight with the wooden rung and Charles cries out - a little cat miaow. He struggles and he's swinging out and banging back onto the metal frame of the swings while Jeanne holds the rope with both hands and strains her body upwards.

I crawl along the hedge to get nearer, on my knees and one hand because I have Cherie in the other. Now I can see Charles' face; it's all puffy and blue and his tongue is sticking out. He's wet himself and he's floppy like a rag doll. Jeanne's still at the top of the swings holding the rope tight around Charles. She untwists the rope and pushes. He drops to the ground. He looks like a big mouse our cat might bring in with its neck broken. Jeanne jumps down and runs off, waving her arms and wobbling.

I can't move. I try to get up and my legs won't work. I turn Cherie away so she can't see what's happened to Charles and I turn my back to the lawn and curl up over my doll to look after her, holding her very tight. I wait but I don't know what for. I hear Mum calling, "Charles! Charles, where are you?" Mum shouts, then screams, a great, long, shrieking sound which stops me thinking of anything but the awful noise. It makes me feel ill so I sort of push my way back into the hedge to get away from it. But I can't.

❧

We sat in the lounge for over an hour. The fire was cold.

Edward put his arm round me. "Thank you for telling me."

"I'm sorry. I should have said something earlier, or seen someone long before this. But I didn't remember all of it until last summer - I didn't find out all about it. I couldn't have blurted it out before. All I've heard in my head all my life is *ca n'est pas sa faute*. It's not her fault. But it is."

He looked at me with the intense stare he that always went straight to my heart. "Don't feel guilty. Did the psychologist tell you not to?"

"Of course; that's what they have to say. I know he's right. I just can't feel it." I looked past Edward into the gloom of the hotel lounge. It was chill and the small lamp in the corner flickered as if the electricity might fail. "Even so ... if I'd said something, told Mum, told Marcelle ... I couldn't get near them; I was on the outside and there was Charles's body between me and all the grown ups. They just said he'd gone to heaven and there was a star for him in the sky. They didn't say anything else. It was as if there was a solid wall between me and them and I was frightened. Claire helped, took me away and found things for us to do. I can't remember what we did but I knew I couldn't tell her about it either.

"I couldn't - it felt like - if I told Mum - it would have been as if I broke some awful taboo. When you're that age you know you can't say, but not why. It just won't come out. Like your throat's blocked. Something you sense: that if you tell, it would make it all worse. It's better not to remember anything at all. What do you say? I saw Jeanne murder Charles? You can't say that when you're nine."

Rosemary. France, 1998

MARCELLE WAS FAILING when we reached *Les Moulins*. Two nurses came twice a day to attend her and a new woman, Camille, was there as well. She combined chores and some nursing and helped with Jeanne, making sure she had meals and clean clothes, amusing her when she got bored.

Claire was staying, huddled in her winter sweaters against a winter that wasn't giving up yet. I came across her and Camille in conference in the big kitchen. They were sitting by the range drinking coffee and didn't hear me come in.

I heard Claire say, "You have to keep her away from *Madame* Aubin. Distract her. Wrap her up well and send her over to the swings if you can. Marcelle - *Madame* Aubin - mustn't be disturbed by her."

I hadn't seen much of Jeanne since arriving and gathered, in the way you collect something from the atmosphere in a house, that Marcelle did not want to see Jeanne.

Claire turned towards me. "There's fresh coffee and the little butter biscuits. Help yourself." She glanced at Camille, a sign that they had finished.

Camille left, nodding. "*D'accord.*"

I sat down in her vacant chair. "Jeanne?"

"Marcelle won't have her anywhere near her. It's the first time she's ever been like that with her. It's the best thing to do - let *Maman* have some peace from that cranky creature."

I remembered Marcelle banging her stick at Christmas. "Put her away when I die."

I needed to tell Claire about my sessions with the psychologist and what had come back to me; the memories that had come out of the shadows. I'd waited with the pain of it since last summer and now it must be told.

"Claire, I must talk to you, I want to tell you I've remembered ... "

Claire was drifting, thinking of something else, not heeding me. "She gave me this." She held out Marcelle's blue, enamel coffee pot. "The one she's used forever, even when we wanted the nice, new electric makers. She always said it made the best coffee and I must use it now. She's given the nurses things as well, some china I think."

"Sorry. I was going to say - it's difficult - I talked to someone last summer. It's about Jeanne; I've had memories ... " The words stuck. "I'll tell you later."

My sister's eyes were still brimming; she took my hand in both hers. "Hold tight, Rose. Listen to me." She took a deep breath. "It's alright, I know. Marcelle told me about Charles and Jeanne. She's always known. She thought when Jeanne was born she could help her, more than your Mum could. Nancy wasn't in a good place back then, and Dad wasn't any use. Marcelle waded in, like she does. And then four years later nothing could bring Charles back. Marcelle wanted to spare Mum from knowing her daughter murdered her son. Mum wouldn't have coped; Jeanne would have been locked away in a terrible place. It's one of the reasons she didn't make too much fuss when they took me and left Jeanne with her. Pierre wanted that too. There are other things; Marcelle says she wants to talk to you, to explain."

Marcelle didn't hear me come in and sit beside her. Her eyes were closed and she was propped up against a mound of pillows, tiny in an ocean of white linen. She was muttering some names: '*Papa* ... Henri.' Talking to those gone before her. More clearly: "We did the right thing. Let me show you how to do it, Nan - like this." Then, "Pierre ... you didn't care about my mother ... I couldn't help Henri ... have to stay away from them ... my mother's sins on us ... all the *Boche* ... sorry ... can't tell Nancy, sorry ... I could have stopped it ... *qui est coupable?*"

Where does the guilt lie? I sat as quiet as I could, as still as I had sat in the hedge all those years ago.

Marcelle was fainter, barely whispering. "Sorry ... Marthe ... keep her away ... best girl." I slipped out of the room, not wanting to see Marcelle's face, her tissue paper skin falling in on parchment-white cheeks.

I took a tray up to her later expecting the same ramblings but she was awake. Her eyes were bright and she looked me up and down, checked me out as usual, as if she wasn't a frail, elderly woman and wasn't dying.

"I want to tell you, Rosemary, about myself. How I came to the farm. You and Edward will carry on living here and you should have the history of the place and the people. Especially about your sister. Claire knows, Philippe and Lucette know. Somehow you were never told very much, almost like an only child who had to be protected. I'm sorry, it just worked out that way, how you all were as children." She raised an eyebrow. "Your mother was never one for talking was she?"

I shook my head and moved her supper a little nearer so she could reach the soup.

"Pierre wanted your father here to punish him for Catherine; I think he told you. They both changed, maybe your father said sorry, I don't know. But they were reconciled, good friends even, before they died.

"Your mother and I - it was different for us - it wasn't right for Nancy to be here, so young, in a strange place, but we women follow our husbands. I wanted to help her. When we had our babies, Claire and Jeanne, and Jeanne was as she was, I saw Nancy struggle.

"I felt when I first came here as a teenager I was carrying a great burden, a heavy sin I had to atone for. The church teaches us, *n'est-ce pas*? It was like a bag of stones I'd picked up, like the ones you clear in the fields before ploughing, and I had to carry it on my back every day."

She took some soup, carefully and slowly. "*Voici, une histoire pour toi.* A story for you, Rosemary. Before the war St Jacques was a sleepy place. Shops were handed down through families and there were a few outlying farms like this one. My parents ran a little café and bistro in the centre and the Aubins supplied us. Pierre came down from the farm with Eva, his mother, with vegetables, eggs and poultry; he came on his own when he got older. We didn't know much about the war coming; the older people would read the newspapers and sigh, shaking their heads. Some said France was now so well-defended another war couldn't happen again.

"My father was called up in 1939 and the strangest sight to my eyes was his Army uniform. I was used to seeing him very smart, serving customers in the bar and having a good time with them. Now he was all in this tan uniform and he had trouble winding his stupid putees round his calves. 'There's nothing to cry about, Marcie,' he said, hugging me. 'It won't last. The Germans can't get through.' He came home a few times, sighing with pleasure over my mother's cooking. 'Boredom's the problem,' he said, 'not the Germans.' He dragged his beret down at an angle and pulled funny faces at me. *'C'est une drôle de guerre. C'est amusant'* A strange war, it's funny. It wasn't just my mother's cooking he enjoyed; I think then they made another baby.

"The Germans did what they weren't supposed to do: they drove their tanks through the Ardennes, never mind the other defences everyone was so proud of. On 14th June they were in Paris. My father never came home again.

"Suddenly the village was full of people running away from Paris. Rumours everywhere: all was lost, *les torses nus* were coming - Germans stripped to the waist in the summer heat, terrifying, invincible. All the north wanted to get across the Loire away from the occupation and into the *zone libre*; those from the cities thought the countryside was safe, that there was enough food here to go round and heading south was best. They had no idea where in the south, just to run was enough. All was chaos: very old people who had been on the road for days came here and died. Children were desperate, separated from their parents and screaming. A horse reached the end of its strength and died in the traces. It upset pots and pans and mattresses and blocked the road. Someone fetched the butcher.

"There was nowhere to put them all. The fields were brown and stinking because there were no toilets. There was not enough food for everyone. And my mother began to make money."

Marcelle paused, pushed her soup bowl away and drank a little water; she pulled her particular cross face I knew so well. "I would like a glass of wine, Rosemary. The doctor disapproves - this new man. Says it won't mix with my medicines." She looked at me expectantly.

Pierre's cellar had not quite given up all its treasures. Marcelle put on her smug, satisfied look when I produced the bottle I had beside me, its cork already pulled. "*Château Latour,* 1982. My god, Pierre - I didn't know about this one!"

I wondered if she might flag, leave her story for later, but she continued, eyes bright. She took a sip of wine and settled herself into the pillows. "When I saw how dusty and thirsty these poor people were I grabbed a jug of water and ran out to them. They were so grateful! A woman asked if there was anywhere they could buy bread. 'We're sure to have plenty,' I said.

"My mother came out. 'Go inside and keep the others with you!' She took the jug and cups and pushed me. I stopped my brother and sister from going out and watched her from the window. She was talking to the people gathered in front of the bistro and holding her hand out. That's the wrong way round, I thought, she should be giving them something.

"I had never thought of my mother as venal, but I was young and couldn't understand. I didn't know for a long time my father was dead. My mother had three children and another on the way. The bistro and bar had done well enough but we weren't rich. I suppose my mother did what she thought she had to do to keep us all, although I didn't like it. She sold everything we had in the store cupboards and sent me to the Aubins to ask for fresh produce. They knew what was going on and I had to brave the hard, angry stares of Eva as I ran home from the farm with my head down, ashamed. I was very friendly with Pierre by then but he'd disappeared at some point, volunteering for the STO, seduced by Pétain's ideas. Catherine had left at the very beginning, full of teenage zeal: she had to be - she must be - *une resistante*. There was nothing else in her mind.

"I had all the housework to do and my brother and sister to look after. My mother was too busy buying and selling to do anything with us. And heavily pregnant as well.

"The refugees eventually went away; back to Paris and the North. I didn't notice much because of what went on indoors. I found my sister Claudine screaming; she'd found *Maman* in labour, bloody and grunting; I remember thinking about the cows on the *Aubin's* farm.

"She employed a woman from La Roche to attend her. I heard one neighbour say, 'How can she afford that, then?' And, 'ideas above her station, she's only a café owner.' The baby was a sickly boy called Henri. I had to look after him a lot, *Maman* wasn't much bothered.

"The village was quiet for a while but in November, 1942 the *zone libre* ended, all of France was occupied and the Germans came here. They hadn't far to come anyway, we're only a few kilometres away from where the line was. I was cleaning in the bar when my mother heard the news. 'Get upstairs and start on the bedrooms,' she shouted and busied herself in the kitchen.

"I was sweeping in the big bedroom, and trying to get Claudine to dust and to keep Henri quiet all at the same time when I heard my mother talking with a man who spoke slow, accented French. I heard my mother say, 'I must charge for the best bedroom. You will find it very well appointed. I could accommodate two officers.' She sounded so arrogant. 'And there is, of course, the restaurant.' Our little bistro wasn't grand enough for a restaurant. I listened from the stairs and heard a shrill yelp. I peered down and saw my mother with her hand to her face where big slap marks were blooming scarlet.

'For disrespect,' the German officer said.

"They took the best two bedrooms, mother had my bedroom and I squeezed in with my older brother André, and Claudine and Henri. It was awful and hot and too close. The four of us were always coming down with colds and bad temper; we became more like enemies than brothers and sisters.

"The Germans took over the bar and bistro in the evenings together with other harsh sounding officers and mother spent all her time scurrying round to find food and drink for them. I didn't know what they did in the day - ran the war, I supposed.

"I never slept; there was Henri to attend to and when he was asleep I laid awake, hating what I heard from the other bedrooms. My mother's giggles, farmyard noises from the men. I watched my mother going into the best bedroom, her dress too low and too tight over her hips, leaving a waft of cheap scent on the landing.

"Little Henri kept me going; I loved him and I knew he loved me even though he was so tiny - the only one who did in that terrible household. It felt like I was abandoned by everyone except this baby boy.

"He didn't grow up for any better times. He took a fever. I watched hectic spots arrive on a white face. I sat with him for hours, sponging him down, trying to get him to drink. I sent Claudine with a message for the doctor. I put in it that we were able to pay well. He refused to come. I blamed myself; the note wasn't written properly. Later, I knew it was because of my mother.

"Henri died in my arms. His temperature made him fit, then his hot body stopped breathing.

"I found my mother in the best bedroom. Thank God she was alone! There were dirty ashtrays, empty bottles and the stench of men's sweat. She struggled out of twisted sheets to come and look at him. *'Eh bien,'* she sighed, turning her mouth down. Ah well.

"At Henri's funeral the priest's face was distorted with distaste for our family. No one else came to listen to Father Raynaud rush through the rituals. He was as plump as a goose from German food. I'd seen German officers coming out of his run-down stone house next to the church. My mother wasn't the only collaborator in the village but when the war ended no one shaved Father Reynaud's head.

"After Henri's death I went to work at the Aubin's farm. Eva had asked me to help with some chores and my mother said, 'go, we need the money.' I didn't think so - she was making enough on her back - but I fled here anyway. I was spat at in the village if I went out and Eva and Clément Aubin were kind; on the farm no one called my mother a whore. I'd abandoned André and Claudine but they were helping *Maman* and it was as if all three were collecting hate as well as Germans around themselves in that house. I could no longer stand it."

Marcelle finished her wine and smiled at me. "I helped with the airmen as well, you know. I remember your father. *Charmant!*" She still could manage a mischievous glance.

I refilled her glass and she thanked me with a nod. "Do you want to stop? Are you tired? I asked.

"No. I want to continue. When we were liberated, as it was called, *Maman* was dragged out into the street and pinned down. She screamed and cried until a scrawny, spotty girl, who I knew had entertained a German or two herself, kicked my mother in the ribs. That shut her up. They stripped her and shaved her head. *Collaboratrice horizontale* was shouted over and over.

"What happened to me, Rosemary, was that I caught her disgrace like a disease. I knew I couldn't stop my mother doing what she did, or save little Henri, but nevertheless I was infected. Pierre was the only man who would have me, who didn't blame me. After all, he had too much to blame himself for, leaving his family for stupid ideas even before the STO became compulsory.

"I wanted to recover some self respect. My mother left me none. I know in my head that it's not my place to atone for another but my heart still carries the weight of the shame. So I helped this poor English woman with *her* child.

"But it wasn't just to make amends. It was my own resistance to *les boches*. I was eaten up with anger. Too late, of course. You know the Germans destroyed defective children? Jeanne had to live because of that. *Malgré tout* - you understand? Despite everything. She had to live."

Marcelle paused, each breath became a tired struggle. I took the empty wine glass from skeletal fingers. "Thank you," I said. "Thank you for telling me."

"Rosemary, there's one more thing. Pierre was sorry. He made his amends. But there is something very great for me to be sorry about." She was speaking reluctantly; as if she pushed the words out against her will. "Sorry. Yes. It is this stubborn resistance of mine. This getting back at the *boche*. I have been wrong; I have made a grave error. I have allowed another sin to stay with us. *Elle doit ont été laissée dans un courant d'air.*"

It took me a second to fathom the French. She should have been left out in a draught.

When everything has been said that had to be said there is a special, light sort of silence. A patch of time when two people are content to sit quiet and still. I held my hand palm up and Marcelle rested her hand on top, so gently that there was no weight, a touch of skin only.

The nurse knocked and opened the door enough to see in without intruding. "*Bonsoir*. I will make *Madame* Aubin *confortable* for the night if I may," she said.

I stood up, smoothed down the quilt where I had been sitting and bent to kiss Marcelle. "*D'accord.*"

Claire was waiting outside. "How is she?"

"She's very tired. I've been listening to her past."

Claire shook her head. Ghosts walked through that house for both of us. "I've heard some of it. I've looked a lot of things up, as well; about the extermination of anyone with a defect. Enough to understand why she couldn't let Jeanne go."

These days the lines on Claire's face showed more, writing regret on her skin; that she could not have persuaded Marcelle to do something other than keep Jeanne's secrets, other than keep Jeanne. "Renée tried to tell Nancy years ago. You won't remember her, I can't either, but Mum said once she there was an awful old woman who was a best friend of Marcelle and whispered terrible things to her. Claire imitated Mum's high, offended voice, 'I can't think of repeating it.' "

"Where's Jeanne?" I asked.

"In bed. She's been told Marcelle will see her later, but that won't happen. Philippe found some out of date sedative they'd stopped using ages ago. It's really strong. He put some in her coffee because she was getting agitated. She's getting more difficult now Marcelle's not around to be with her and she's not allowed in the bedroom."

"Who's going to tell her when … ?"

Claire looked at me for a moment. "We'll all do it together," she said. She looked a little calmer. "Jean-Paul's arrived. He's taken time off to come up"

I was relieved. Claire's husband was kind and sensitive, good for her. We'd both married men who didn't throw moods and criticism about in the way Dad used to do.

"He and Edward are trying out some wine. They found a cache at the back of the cellar where the bottle for Marcelle came from. God knows how long it's been there." She shook her head. "Why not? Pierre would want them to enjoy …" The tears weren't far away again. "I'll sit with her when the nurse is finished. Philippe will be with me as well. You go down stairs for a break, you've got enough to think over. I'll fetch you in a while."

The men were in the lounge with solemn faces and their wine barely touched. I curled up on the sofa and pulled a rug over me. I texted Elizabeth and Harry again, keeping them in the picture, reading their messages: 'be strong, Mum,' 'love you.'

I dozed and woke when Claire stood at the door of the lounge.

"It's best to come now," Claire said. "The nurse is back and she thinks ... "

Marcelle stayed with us while we kissed her goodbye. Her eyes were closed and she was smiling to herself, her lips moving slightly. I might have heard her say 'Pierre.'

Grief reaches everyone differently. It can rush up and slam into you, winding you. Or it can creep slyly up without your notice; then you find it's lodged so tight it can't be shifted. I should have been used to it; known the pain would eventually go into remission. My parents and Marthe and Pierre had taught me this with their dying but I hadn't remembered the lessons.

I held onto Edward when I could and tried to be practical at the same time, moving slowly about as if under water with weeds clogging my ankles. Childlike, I wanted my Mum and Dad but all I had left were the delicate phone calls in the past, breaking bad news.

Claire sobbed without ceasing for hours, only stopping when she hiccupped with exhaustion. Jean-Paul silently provided tissues; put his arms round her. Philippe was dry eyed but absent from us, staring blankly and not hearing anything. Lucette, tearful in small spasms, stayed close by him, watching.

Marcelle's funeral was sombre but the new priest had made an effort to get to know her in the last few years; his words kept her spirit alive. An early spring was promised that day; there was sunshine for her going.

At home I busied myself with chores until ten o'clock. The letter from Jeanne lay on the kitchen table. I couldn't imagine anything of Marcelle's Jeanne would have for me. She'd never given me anything except long stares reserved for me alone after I'd rescued the cat from her. I wanted to talk to Marcelle, who would know what to do. Who knew what Jeanne was.

After finding out she was my sister I had tried to imagine how we would have been if she were normal. I wanted her to be different: to be as bright as we all were, to have a career or an interesting job; to have children and give me nieces and nephews. To be a devoted aunt to my twins. To be part of our family and dote on my parents. Not this violent child-woman we all had to care about.

Vignettes from the past turned up unannounced. Marthe was pulling at my sleeve saying, "Come on, we'll run down to the river and no one will notice!" I saw her laughing and then remembered the mess of mushrooms on the lawn, white and yellow.

Claire saying, 'you're still my sister.'

Pierre finding Marthe and I stealing from the larder and winking at us and walking away. Not chastising us as he did Jeanne, who had to be disciplined for her own good. So we were told.

Philippe: 'I can't send her away, she's family now. She needs to be looked after.' Barricading Jeanne against the world.

Edward: 'poor thing, she can't help how she is.'

I'd kept my misgivings to myself for a long time. I'd been too scared to share them and when I did see clearly, with a nine year-old's sight, what had happened I found others had known all along. My memories felt like a child's hoarded treasure that turned out to be nothing much at all.

My mother, most of all, pretending everything was fine when she was ruined by the shame of a baby and the death of another. Fading inside, away from the light. My mother screaming. Screwing up a photo. Dad saying, 'look Nan, just stop it!'

Marcelle, who had always known and couldn't find a way out that would help because the weight of her guilt and her own family's shame stopped her. 'Put her away when I die.'

I walked over to the big house as the wind got up, gusting at my back. Crows struggled to fight the air to go about their business. The hedge where I had hidden as a child was no longer there. I'd taken a saw to it in temper and told everybody I wanted to plant something new. I didn't do it properly and there were ugly, bare stalks coming up.

Jeanne was waiting for me and led me through to the big lounge. She'd put on more weight in the summer since Marcelle's death and she breathed heavily though her open mouth. Her nose must be blocked up again, I thought, with the same habit of worrying about her that everyone always had. She went to the desk in the corner, where

Marcelle used to sit with her paperwork. It was tidy and polished; just her inkwell and pens left on it. These days Philippe's farm office was stuffed with computers in a converted outbuilding.

Jeanne opened a drawer and took out a knife with an inlaid mother of pearl handle; it was the paper knife Marcelle always had to neatly slit open envelopes which she stored in a straight pile for scrap and lists.

"This is where *Maman* sat," Jeanne said, putting herself heavily down on the chair. "I like to sit here now." She had tears in her eyes. "Maman looked after me. Now I have to look after myself."

To my surprise I felt sorry for her. "Philippe and Lucette will always be here to look after you, Jeanne."

"I know." She turned the little shiny knife over and over. "This is for you, Rosemary. *Maman* used it all the time. It's very pretty. Do you like it?"

"That's lovely, Jeanne. Yes. Yes, I do like it. May I take it?" I held out my hand.

Jeanne didn't move. It was cold in the lounge and I glanced out of the window, wondering where Philippe and Lucette were. I couldn't see the swings from here but I knew they would have their particular rhythm in the wind; just for a second I wondered why my mother was screaming.

The knife was blunt and it hurt as it carved a deep red line in my skin as Jeanne dragged it across my palm.

"No, Jeanne! That's very bad! Stop!" I held my right hand up in my left. Fat drops of blood dripped down to my wrist as I moved away, walking backwards towards the door.

"Put that knife down, Jeanne! I'm going home now," I cried. Terrified she'd come after me, I slammed the lounge door behind me. I dashed through the kitchen and into the yard.

"*Bonjour, Philippe!*" I called in a squeaky voice, trying to slow down. One of her difficult turns, I told myself. I'll fetch Philippe or Lucette to calm her. Camille was around somewhere but I hadn't heard her.

Jeanne might catch sight of them and give up her game. That's all it was to her; all everything had ever been. I'll get away, I thought, and it'll blow over. I didn't convince myself, not with the burden of what I knew. I heard her call behind me, "Rosemary!"

The barn doors were open and Philippe's Audi wasn't there. Nor was Lucette's small Citroen. Jeanne came lumbering up behind me with her hand outstretched, the little knife bright and nasty in the morning light.

I ran, wrapping a tissue around my bloody hand as I went. Jeanne came after me, pointing the knife towards me with her right hand, her left arm held out to her side for balance. The yard had a gate on one side that led to the path around the big vegetable bed. The last of the tomatoes and *haricots verts* were on one side and the cows on the other. Years ago an earlier generation of cows had inspected Edward with their gentle eyes and lolling tongues; now the herd was over on the far side, incurious and unaware.

The path came out to the side of the lawns and then my house would be in front of me. I could see the swings to my right on the slight rise in the big lawn. Jeanne might give up her fun with me to go over to them. She wasn't keeping up very well, I could hear her panting and muttering to herself as she barged after me.

I stopped, turned and pointed. "Go and play on the swings, Jeanne! Please. Go over to the swings! Go over there and have a rest."

It worked. She stopped and looked across the lawn. She frowned as she decided what to do. A fitful wind pushed the swings as if someone was already on them. I started walking backwards, very slowly. "Go on, Jeanne. It's a lovely day - go and play on the swings."

I was a better game than the swings and she came at me with a rush, the knife held as straight as ever. I spun round and ran again, jumping over a coiled hosepipe that was used for the vegetables, left there until we had more rain.

I kept running for some moments after I heard the thump, then I realised couldn't hear Jeanne, only my own breathing.

I took a long, deep breath and turned round, willing Jeanne not to be right behind me with the pretty knife. She was still, stretched out on the dusty path with her face turned to one side. Her hands were palms down in front of her, as if she might push herself up. Blood seeped from underneath her head. I ought to worry about the blood, I thought. Always worry about Jeanne.

The knife lay a metre away. I picked it up, put it in my pocket and dared to go closer. I didn't want to touch her. I held my left hand at the side of her face. I couldn't feel any breath but I wasn't sure. She gave a tiny gasp and I jumped back. I was panting and sweating. At arms' length I shook her shoulder gently but there was no further response. She looked uncomfortably asleep. Or knocked out. She might come round.

The next hour passed quickly at home. I needed a distraction to keep my mind blank; I turned a cupboard out. I went back, braver this time, and checked for a pulse. There was none and no more fresh blood. The ghosts in my head fell asleep. I waited another hour.

I picked up the telephone. "Help, please. I have just found … "

The ambulance came within minutes and the *gendarmes* very soon afterwards at the paramedic's request. They were solicitous. Madame must rest, not get upset, have a little brandy. No, please don't go out there … an accident. Madame, she must have tripped on the hose pipe. It's a great shock to find … Madame Aubin's daughter? Yes. You hadn't seen her this morning? No. We are so very sorry … there's nothing to be done, the ambulance will take her away as soon as possible. Yes, we will contact your husband for you. You must remain calm.

BV - #0024 - 111121 - C0 - 216/140/14 - PB - 9781913425524 - Matt Lamination